THE DOCTOR
SHE LEFT BEHIND

BY
SCARLET WILSON

TAMING
HER NAVY DOC

BY
AMY RUTTAN

Scarlet Wilson wrote her first story aged eight and has never stopped. Her family have fond memories of *Shirley and the Magic Purse*, with its army of mice all with names beginning with the letter 'M'. An avid reader, Scarlet started with every Enid Blyton book, moved on to the *Chalet School* series and many years later found Mills & Boon®.

She trained and worked as a nurse and health visitor, and currently works in public health. For her, finding Mills & Boon® Medical Romance™ was a match made in heaven. She is delighted to find herself among the authors she has read for many years.

Scarlet lives on the West Coast of Scotland with her fiancé and their two sons.

Born and raised on the outskirts of Toronto, Ontario, **Amy Ruttan** fled the big city to settle down with the country boy of her dreams. When she's not furiously typing away at her computer she's mom to three wonderful children, who have given her another job as a taxi driver.

A voracious reader, she was given her first romance novel by her grandmother, who shared her penchant for a hot romance. From that moment Amy was hooked by the magical worlds, handsome heroes and sigh-worthy romances contained in the pages, and she knew what she wanted to be when she grew up.

Life got in the way, but after the birth of her second child she decided to pursue her dream of becoming a romance author.

Amy loves to hear from readers. It makes her day, in fact. You can find out more about Amy at her website: amyruttan.com

THE DOCTOR
SHE LEFT BEHIND

BY

SCARLET WILSON

First published in Great Britain 2015
by Mills & Boon, an imprint of Harlequin (UK) Limited,
Eton House, 18-24 Paradise Road, Richmond, Surrey, TW9 1SR

© 2015 Scarlet Wilson

ISBN: 978-0-263-24718-3

Dear Reader,

What could be worse than being stranded on an island with your ex?

The short answer is—not much! But that's what happens to Rachel Johnson and Nathan Banks.

They parted company eight years before, and there's a lot for them to get through before they can finally reach their happy-ever-after.

I had great fun writing this book. Rachel and Nathan have the pleasure of being the medical crew on a fictional TV show. Both of them are doing a favour for a mutual friend who hasn't let either of them know the other is going to be there. Sparks certainly fly!

I love to hear from readers. You can find me at scarlet-wilson.com, on Facebook, and on Twitter as @scarlet_wilson

Hope you enjoy!

Scarlet

For Cathy McAuliffe, Catherine Bain and Shirley Bain
with lots of love for the women
who manage to put up with all these Bain boys!

Books by Scarlet Wilson

Mills & Boon® Medical Romance™

Rebels with a Cause
The Maverick Doctor and Miss Prim
About That Night…

The Boy Who Made Them Love Again
West Wing to Maternity Wing!
A Bond Between Strangers
Her Christmas Eve Diamond
An Inescapable Temptation
Her Firefighter Under the Mistletoe
200 Harley Street: Girl from the Red Carpet
A Mother's Secret
Tempted by Her Boss
Christmas with the Maverick Millionaire

**Visit the author profile page at
millsandboon.co.uk for more titles**

**Praise for
Scarlet Wilson**

'*Her Christmas Eve Diamond* is a fun and interesting read.
If you like a sweet romance with just a touch of the holiday
season you'll like this one.'

—*HarlequinJunkie*

'*West Wing to Maternity Wing!* is a tender, poignant and highly
affecting romance that is sure to bring a tear to your eye.
With her gift for creating wonderful characters, her ability to
handle delicately and compassionately sensitive issues and
her talent for writing believable, emotional and spellbinding
romance, the talented Scarlet Wilson continues to prove to
be a force to be reckoned with in the world of contemporary
romantic fiction!'

—*CataRomance*

CHAPTER ONE

'YOU REALLY THINK this is a good idea?' Nathan Banks shook his head. Nothing about this sounded like a good idea to him.

But Lewis nodded. 'I think it's a great idea. I need a doctor. You need a job.'

'But I already have a job.' He lifted his hands. 'At least I think I do. Is my contract not being renewed?'

His stomach turned over a little. Last night had been a particularly bad night in A & E. His medical skills were never in question but his temper had definitely been short. It hadn't been helped by hearing a car back-fire on the walk home and automatically dropping to the ground as if it were gunfire. His last mission for Doctors Without Borders had been in a war zone. Dropping to the floor when you heard gunfire had become normal for him. But doing it in the streets of Melbourne? Not his proudest moment. Particularly when a kid on the way to school had asked him what was wrong.

Lewis smiled. The way he always did when he was being particularly persuasive. Nathan had learned to spot it over the years. 'The last few days in A & E have been tough. You came straight out of Doctors Without Borders after five years and started working here. You've never really had a holiday. Think of this as your lucky day.'

Nathan lifted the buff-coloured folders. 'But this isn't a holiday. This is a form of torture. My idea of a holiday is walking in the hills of Scotland somewhere, or surfing on Bondi Beach. Being stranded on an island with nine B-list celebrities? I'm the least celeb-orientated person on the planet. I couldn't care less about these people.'

Lewis nodded. 'Exactly. That's what makes you perfect. You can be objective. All you need to do is supervise the fake TV challenges and monitor these folk's medical conditions for the three weeks they're on the island. The rest of the time you'll get to sit around with your feet up.' He bent over next to Nathan and put one hand on his shoulder, waving the other around as if he were directing a movie. 'Think of it—the beautiful Whitsunday islands, the surrounding Coral Sea, luxury accommodation and perfect weather with only a few hours' work a day. What on earth could go wrong?'

Nathan flipped open the first folder. Everything about this seemed like a bad idea. It was just a pity that the viewing public seemed to think it was a great one. *Celebrity Island* had some of the best viewing figures on the planet. 'But some of these people shouldn't be going to a celebrity island, let alone doing any challenges. They have serious medical conditions.'

Lewis waved his hand. 'And they've all had million-dollar medicals for the insurance company. The TV company needs someone with A & E experience who can think on their feet.'

'I hardly think epidemic, natural disaster and armed conflict experience is what a TV crew needs.'

Lewis threw another folder towards him. 'Here. Read up on snake bites, spiders and venom. The camp will be checked every night but you can't be too careful.'

The expression on Lewis's face changed. The hard sell wasn't working and it was obvious he was getting desperate.

'Please, Nathan. I agreed to this contract before I knew Cara was pregnant. I need to find someone to replace me on the island. The last thing I want is to end up sued for breach of contract. You're the one person I trust enough to ask.'

Nathan took a long, slow breath. Working for a TV company was the last thing he wanted to do. But Lewis was right. He was close to burnout. And in some ways he was lucky his friend had recognised it. How bad could three weeks on an island in the Coral Sea be? The celebs might have to sleep by a campfire but the production crew were supposed to have luxury accommodation. He shook his head. 'Why didn't you just tell me this was about Cara's pregnancy?'

Lewis looked away for a second. 'There have been a few issues. A few complications—a few hiccups as we've got closer to the end. We didn't really want to tell anyone.' He slid something over the desk towards him. 'Here, the final sweetener. Look at the pay cheque.'

Nathan's eyes boggled. 'How much?' He shook his head again. 'It doesn't matter what the pay cheque is, if you'd told me this was about Cara I would have said yes right away.' He lifted his hands. 'I would have volunteered and done it for nothing. Sometimes you've got to be straight with people, Lewis.'

Lewis blinked, as if he was contemplating saying something else. Then he gave his head a little shake. 'Thank you, Nathan.' He walked around and touched Nathan's shoulder. 'I need a medic I can trust. You'll have back-up. Another doctor is flying out from Canberra to join the TV crew too. Last year I was there I worked twelve hours—tops—over three weeks. Trust me. This will be the easiest job you've ever had.'

Nathan nodded slowly. It still didn't appeal. He had a low tolerance to all things celebrity. But three weeks of easy paid work in a luxury location? He'd have to be a fool to say no. Plus, Lewis had helped him when he'd landed in Australia straight out of Doctors Without Borders and with no job. Of course he'd help. 'What happens when I get back?'

Lewis met his gaze. 'You're a great medic. We're lucky to have you. I'll give you another six-month contract for A & E—if you want it, of course.'

He hesitated only for a second. Lewis was one of his oldest friends and he knew they'd waited four years for Cara to fall pregnant. There was no way he could let him down. Even if it was the last place on this earth he wanted to go.

He picked up the pen. 'Tell Cara I'll be thinking about her. Okay, where do I sign?'

Rachel Johnson took a few final moments lying on the sun lounger at the pool. She couldn't believe for a second she was getting paid for this.

She'd been here two days and hadn't had to do a minute of work. Apparently her job started as soon as she hit the island. Which was fine by her. From what she'd seen of the nine celebrities taking part in *Celebrity Island,* she suspected they ranged from mildly whiny to difficult and impossible. Her old university friend Lewis Blake had persuaded her to take part and the fee was astronomical. But that wasn't why she was here.

She was here because her Hippocratic oath seemed to have her over a barrel. Her ex—an Australian soap star—was taking part. And she was one of the few that knew his real medical history. It seemed that one of his bargaining chips had been to ask for a doctor he could trust. And even though there was nothing between them, part of her felt obliged to help.

'Are you ready, Dr Johnson? The seaplane has just landed.'

Rachel jumped up from the comfortable lounger and grabbed her rucksack packed with her clothes. Two days staying in the luxury five-star resort had been bliss. All the medical supplies she would need had already been shipped. Apparently the other medic was already on the island. And since there was no way off the island for the next three weeks she hoped it was someone she could work with. Between the two of them, they would be on call twenty-four hours a day for three weeks. Lewis had assured her that apart from monitoring the challenges there really wasn't anything to do. But, as much as she loved him, Lewis had always been economical with the truth.

Rachel climbed into the seaplane that was bobbing on the blue ocean. She'd never been in one of these before and the ride was more than a little bumpy. But the view over the island worth it.

The pilot circled the island, letting her see the full geography. 'This is the beach where some of the celebrities will be dropped off. The beach on the other side is for the crew. It has umbrellas, sun loungers and a bar—so don't worry, you'll be well looked after.' As he crossed the middle of the island the view changed to a thick jungle. 'Camp is in the middle,' he said. 'Don't tell anyone but they actually have a rain canopy they can pull overhead if we get one of the seasonal downpours. We didn't have it the first year and the whole camp got swept away in a torrent of water.'

Rachel shifted uncomfortably in her seat. That sounded a little rougher than she'd expected. 'Where will I be staying?'

He pointed to some grey rectangular buildings in the distance. 'The three big grey buildings are the technical huts and production gallery. You'll be staying in a portable cabin. The medical centre is right next to you.' He let out a laugh that sounded more like a pantomime witch's cackle. 'Just next to the swamp and the rope bridge. The celebrities love those.' He gave Rachel a nod. 'I won't tell you how many of them have fallen off that rope bridge.'

For a second her throat felt dry. Lewis's version of the truth was already starting to unravel. A portable cabin and a hotel were not the same thing. Her dreams of a luxury bed and state-of-the-art facilities had just vanished in the splutter of a seaplane's engines. There might be an ocean right next to her but there was no swimming pool, no facilities and definitely no room service. This was sounding less and less like three weeks in the sun and more and more like she would be wringing Lewis's neck the next time she saw him.

The seaplane slowed and bumped to a landing on the water, moving over to a wooden quay. A burly man in a grey T-shirt tinged with sweat grabbed the line so she could open the door and jump down.

'Doc Johnson?'

She nodded.

He rolled his eyes. 'I'm Ron. Welcome to paradise.'

The wooden quay gave a little sway as she landed on it.

They walked quickly along the beach and up a path towards the grey portable cabins. 'Kind of out of place for paradise?' she said.

Ron laughed. 'Is that how they got you out here? Told the same story to the other doc too. But he's been fine. Said he's used to sleeping in camp beds anyhow and it doesn't make any difference to him.'

A horrible shiver crept down Rachel's spine. She'd spent five years at university in London with Lewis and a group of other friends. Then another couple of years working in the surrounding London hospitals. Lewis knew everything about her. He knew everything about the guy she'd dated for five years back then. Lewis was the common denominator here. He wouldn't have done anything stupid, would he?

Ron showed her up to the three cabins sitting on an incline. 'The rest of the crew stay along the beach a little. You and the other doc are in here. Medical centre is right next to you. And the one next to that is the most popular cabin on the beach.'

'Showers?' she said hopefully.

'Nope. Catering,' he answered with a broad smile.

'Okay. Thanks, Ron.' She pushed open the door to the cabin and sent a silent prayer upwards.

The cabin was empty. There was a sitting area in the middle with a sofa. A bathroom with a shower of sorts, and two rooms at either end. It wasn't quite army camp beds. They were a little better than that. But the rooms were sparse, with only a small chest of drawers and a few hooks on the wall with clothes hangers on them.

Rachel dumped her rucksack and washed her face and hands, taking a few minutes to change her T-shirt and apply some more mosquito spray and sunscreen.

Her stomach was doing little flip-flops. It was pathetic really. Ron had only made one remark about a camp bed. It was nothing. It could apply to millions of guys the world over. But she had a bad feeling about this.

Lewis had been especially persuasive on the phone. He'd given her the whole 'my wife is pregnant' and 'one of the celebrities is being difficult' routine. When she'd heard who the celebrity was she hadn't been surprised. She'd met Darius under unusual circumstances. Both of them had been vulnerable. And he'd loved the thought that by dating a doctor he had an insider's view of treatments.

But dating Darius Cornell—Australia's resident soap opera hunk—had been an experience. They'd dated for just over a year. Just enough to get both of them through. She'd been relieved when the media attention had died down.

Her stomach flipped over one more time as she walked outside and reached for the door handle of the medical centre. It was strange to be here at his request. But Darius could be handled.

Her biggest fear was that the person behind this door probably couldn't.

He was dreaming. More likely he was having a nightmare. He pushed his hat a little further back on his head and blinked again.

No. She was still there.

Rachel Johnson. Brown hair tied in a ponytail, slightly suntanned skin and angry brown eyes set off by her pink T-shirt.

'Just when I thought this couldn't get any worse.' He pulled his feet off the desk.

Her lips tightened and her gaze narrowed. 'I'm going to kill Lewis Blake. I'm going to kill him with my bare hands. There's no way I'm getting stuck on this island with you for three weeks.' She folded her arms across her chest.

He pointed out at the sky. 'Too late, Rach. You just

missed your ride home.' The seaplane was heading off in the distance.

Her forehead creased into a deep frown. 'No way. There must be a boat. Another island nearby. How do they get supplies?'

Nathan shrugged. 'Not sure. I've only been here a day. And don't worry. I'm just as happy to see you. Particularly when I've just looked through the medical notes and saw your lovely ex is one of the celebs. No wonder you're here.'

He couldn't help it. When they'd split up years ago Rachel had come to Australia and a few months later been photographed by the press with her new boy-friend—an Australian soap star. It had been hard enough to get over the split, but seeing his ex all over the press when he'd been left behind to take care of his younger brother had just rubbed salt in the wounds. *She'd* gone to Australia. The place they'd planned to go to together.

'What exactly are you doing here, Nathan? You seem the last person who'd want a job like this.'

He raised his eyebrows. 'And what's that supposed to mean?'

She shrugged. 'I'd heard you were working for Doctors Without Borders. *Celebrity Island* seems a bit of a stretch of the imagination.'

He tried to ignore the little surge of pleasure that sparked; she'd been interested enough to find out where he worked. He'd never wanted to ask any of their mutual friends where Rachel was. Everyone knew that she'd gone to Australia without him and they were much too tactful to bring up her name.

He folded his arms across his chest. 'I think you know exactly why I'm here. At a guess I'd say he hoodwinked me just as much as he hoodwinked you.' He gave his hands a little rub together. 'But don't worry. I've got three weeks to think of what I'll do to him when I get back.'

She frowned again. 'How did he get in touch?'

Nathan's gaze met hers. 'I've been working with him.'

'In A & E?'

Nathan shrugged. 'Seemed the most logical place to work after five missions with Doctors Without Borders. He offered me the job as soon as my feet hit Australian soil.'

She gave a little nod. He could almost hear her brain ticking. He'd been the logical one and she'd been the emotional one. He'd thought they'd counterbalanced each other and worked well together. He'd been wrong.

'And don't think I've not noticed.'

Her cheeks were flooded with colour. 'Noticed what?' she snapped.

'That there's information missing from his medical file. What does your boyfriend have to hide?'

'Stop calling him that. He's not my boyfriend. Hasn't been for more than seven years. It might have escaped your notice but he's actually engaged to someone else. There's absolutely nothing between us.' She was getting angrier and angrier as she spoke. The colour was rushing up her face to the tips of her ears. He'd forgotten how mad she could get about things. Particularly when something mattered to her.

He lifted up the nearest folder. It took both hands. 'Look at this one.'

She frowned and placed her hands on her hips. 'Who does that belong to?'

'Diamond Dazzle. Model. Grand old age of twenty-two and look at the size of her medical records. I know every blood test, every X-ray and every piece of plastic surgery and Botox she's ever had. This one?' He held up Darius's records. Paper-thin. 'I know that Darius had an appendectomy at age eight. That's it.'

She folded her arms across her chest. 'And that's all you need to know. I know the rest.'

'No physician works like that, Rach.'

'You work like that every day, Nathan. You rarely know the history of the people who turn up in A & E, and I imagine on your missions you must have had patients from everywhere. They didn't come with medical files.'

He stood up. She was annoying every part of him now. It didn't matter that the angrier and more stubborn she got—the more her jaw was set—the more sensations sparked around his body. Rachel had always had this effect on him. He'd just expected it would have disappeared over time and with a whole host of bad memories. The rush of blood around his system was definitely unwelcome. 'So, you're going to look after one patient and I'll look after eight? Is that how we're going to work things?'

She shook her head fiercely, her eyes flashing. Rachel had always hated it when someone suggested she didn't pull her weight. After all these years he still knew what buttons to press.

'No, Nathan. I'll look after *all* the patients—just like you will—if required.'

But Nathan wouldn't be beaten. Not after all these years. He folded his own arms across his chest and matched Rachel's stance. He couldn't help but smile. It was like a stand-off. 'Well, I don't think I can do that if I don't have all the facts about the patient.'

The colour of her face practically matched her T-shirt now and he could see tiny beads of sweat on her brow. It was unquestionably hot on the island. But he was quite sure that wasn't why Rachel Johnson was sweating.

She shifted her feet. It was unusual to see her in khaki shorts, thick socks and heavy boots. She'd obviously been warned about the island paths. Rachel had spent her time as a student and junior doctor dressed smartly. Always in dresses and heels. This was a whole new look for her. Maybe her time in Australia had changed her outlook on life?

'Of course you can, Nathan. Stop being difficult. Three weeks. I can tell you'll be scoring off the days on the calendar just like I will.'

She turned to walk away. And it surprised him just how much he actually didn't want her to. If you'd asked him if he wanted to come face to face with Rachel Johnson again he'd have said, *Not in this lifetime*. But reality was sometimes stranger than fiction.

She stopped at the door. 'How's Charlie?'

The question caught him off guard and his answer was an automatic response. 'Charlie's fine. Not that you would care.'

She sighed. 'That's not fair, Nathan, and you know it.'

He shrugged. 'Why? You didn't want to hang around when I had to look after my little brother for a couple of years. Why bother now?'

She shook her head. He could see her biting her lip. She probably couldn't find the words for why she'd run out on them both. 'I always loved Charlie. He was great. Did he finish university?' A thought must have flickered across her mind. 'How was he when you were away?'

'Charlie was fine. He finished his engineering degree and got a job before I left for my last mission. He's married now with two young children.'

She gave a little nod of her head. 'Glad to hear it. Tell him I'm asking for him.'

She walked out of the door, letting it slam behind her. Nathan picked up the bottle of water on the table and downed it in one, wishing it was a beer. No matter how he tried to avoid it, his eyes had settled on her backside and legs as she'd walked out of the door. Eight years on and Rachel Johnson was as hot as ever.

And eight years later she still drove him crazy.

I always loved Charlie. The words echoed in his mind. 'Just as well you loved one of us,' he muttered.

She'd thought the cabin was hot but outside was even hotter and the high humidity was making the sweat trickle down her back already, probably turning her hair into a frizz bomb.

She stopped for a second to catch her breath, leaning against the metal bodywork and hoping to feel a little of the coolness on her body.

Trapped on an island with two exes. You couldn't make this up.

A little wave of nausea rolled over her. Nathan Banks. Eight years had done nothing to diminish the impact of seeing him again. Her hands were trembling and every hair on her arms stood on end. She'd never expected to come face-to-face with him again.

His blond hair was a little shorter. His build a bit more muscular. But his eyes were still the neon green they'd always been. They could stop any girl in her tracks—just like they'd done to her.

They were supposed to be continents apart. What on earth was he doing in Australia? She knew he'd spent five years working for Doctors Without Borders. He was still friends with a lot of the people they'd trained with.

And even though she'd pretended not to, she'd spent the last five years searching mutual social media sites with her heart in her mouth, hoping she wouldn't ever hear bad news about him. That was the trouble with working in humanitarian missions—sometimes they took you into places with armed conflict.

Trouble was, five minutes in Nathan's company could make her *mad*. No one else in her life had ever managed to spark that kind of reaction from her. But there was just something about Nathan and her alone in a room together. Sparks always flew. Sometimes good. Sometimes bad.

It was clear he still hadn't forgiven her for leaving. She couldn't blame him. But if she'd told him why she was really leaving he would have put his life—and Charlie's—on hold for her. She hadn't wanted that— she couldn't do that to them. They'd just lost their parents; they'd needed to focus on each other.

And if she told him now why she'd left, she would be betraying Darius's trust. Caught between the devil and the deep blue sea.

She stared out at the perfect blue Coral Sea. It was no wonder they'd picked one of the Whitsunday islands for this show. At any other time, with any other person, this would be perfect.

Too bad Nathan Banks was here to spoil it for her.

CHAPTER TWO

'EXACTLY HOW LONG will this take?' The director was scowling at them both.

Nathan shrugged. He couldn't care less about the man's bad attitude. 'It'll take as long as it takes. We need to see every participant and have a quick chat about their medical history—then we'll be able to tell you if anyone is unsuitable for the challenge tomorrow.'

The director stomped out of the door, closing it with an exasperated bang.

Nathan smiled at Rachel. 'Now, where were we?'

Rachel lifted the printed list. 'Okay, we have nine celebrities and one backup that we'll need to assess if he arrives.' She frowned. 'This doesn't seem right. Aren't they all supposed to be filmed jumping from a plane and rowing or snorkelling their way here? What are they doing already on the island?'

Nathan shrugged. 'The magic of television. They arrived yesterday when I did. They plan to do the filming later on today, pretending they've just set foot on the island. But they haven't seen the camp yet. They spent last night in one of the cabins and you want to have heard the list of complaints.'

She shook her head as she looked over the list. 'More fool me. I had no idea they faked their arrival. Want to take a bet on how quickly one will bail?'

He held out his fist. Old habits died hard. He and Rachel used to do this all the time. She blinked as if she were having a little flash of memory, then held out her fist, bumping it against his. 'Six days.'

He shook his head. 'Oh, way too ambitious. Four days.'

She frowned. 'Really? But they're doing it for charity. Surely someone wouldn't give up that easy?'

He raised his eyebrows. 'You really think these people are doing it all just for charity?'

'Of course.' She looked confused and Nathan sighed and picked up the list.

'Let's see. Darius Cornell—actor—let's leave him for now. Diamond Dazzle—model—she's looking for a lingerie contract. Frank Cairns—sportsman—he's looking for a presenter's job somewhere. Molly Bates—comedienne—she needs the publicity for her upcoming tour. Tallie Turner—actress—she just needs a job. Pauline Wilding—politician—always likes to be in the papers. Fox—boy band pop star—he's hoping some teenagers remember his crazy name. Billy X—rapper—with his past history he's probably about to be arrested for something, and Rainbow Blossom—reality TV star. She probably doesn't want to fade from the spotlight. Are any of these people actually celebrities? Do any of them have a real name?'

He saw Rachel's lips press together and waited for her to immediately go on the offensive for her apparent ex. But she surprised him. She didn't.

'I didn't realise you were such a cynic.'

'I guess we really didn't know each other at all, did we?' he shot back.

The words hung in the air between them. He sounded bitter. And he was. But even he was surprised by how quickly the words had come out. They'd never had this conversation before. She'd just told him she was leaving and hotfooted it out of the hospital as if she were being chased by a bunch of killer zombies.

Five years of missions for Doctors Without Borders had loosened his tongue. He'd dealt with armed conflict, natural disasters and epidemics. He was less willing to placate and tolerate. Life was too short—he knew that now. He and his brother had lost their parents to an accident eight years ago, and he'd lost too many patients all over the world.

She flopped down into the chair next to him, letting her floral scent drift under his nose. That was new. Rachel didn't smell like that before. She'd always worn something lighter. This was stronger, more sultry, more like something a woman eight years on would wear. Why would he expect anything to stay the same?

'Actually, you're right,' she muttered, going back to the original conversation and completely ignoring his barb. 'Darius is probably the most well-known of them all. Five of them I don't recognise and three I've never even heard of.'

It was almost a relief that finally they could agree on something.

'How do you want to do this?' She pointed to the pile of notes. 'Do you want to go over each patient individually or do you just want to split them up?'

Splitting the pile would be easier and quicker. But Nathan wasn't about to let her off so easy. He needed to have another doctor he could rely on. Rachel had been a good doctor eight years ago—but he'd no idea how she was now. 'Let's do them together. That way, if either of us is on call we're familiar with all the patients. There's only nine—this won't take too long.'

He picked up the nearest set of notes and started flicking. 'Diamond Dazzle—real name Mandy Brooks. She's had liposuction, two breast enlargements, one skin biopsy, one irregular smear test and lots of Botox. She apparently had her lips done a week ago—so we'll need to keep an eye on her for any signs of infection.'

Rachel shook her head. 'Why would an already beautiful twenty-two-year-old think she needs all this?'

Nathan put the file back on the desk. 'Beats me.' He folded his arms across his chest. 'Do you think this makes her ineligible for the challenge? Having spiders or rats crawl over her body—and probably face too—will make her more vulnerable to infection.'

'I think just being in the jungle alone makes her at higher risk. Who would do that? Know that they're coming somewhere like this and go for a procedure less than a week before?'

Nathan smiled. He knew exactly where she was coming from but he also knew the answer. 'Someone who wants to be on TV.'

Rachel shook her head. Some of her hair was coming loose and the curls were starting to stray around her face. It was odd. She hadn't aged as much as he had. There were a few tiny lines around her eyes and her body had filled out a little. But nothing else. She was every bit as beautiful as he remembered.

His face and skin had been weathered by five years of on and off postings in countries around the world. The last had been the worst. The sand felt as if it would never wash off and the darkening of his skin—coupled with lots of lines—made him more weathered. It didn't help that he felt about a hundred years older.

'Shall we call her in?' He had to focus on work. That was what they were here to do. Lewis hadn't lied about everything. On the surface, this could be three weeks of paid vacation time. Supervising the challenges would only take a couple of hours each night. He could live with that.

Rachel stood up and walked to the door. 'I'll get her. They're down on the beach with the director. Apparently they're going to make it look like they had to row part way here.'

Nathan just rolled his eyes.

It didn't take long to chat to each celebrity and review their medical files. A few were taking medications that they'd still require in the camp. A few others had intermittent usage of medications for angina, migraines or asthma that Rachel and Nathan agreed they could still take into camp. None of that stuff would be shown on camera.

Eventually it was time to speak to Darius. As soon as the guy walked into the room Nathan bristled. He just didn't like him—would never like him. For some reason, the pictures of Darius and Rachel together were imprinted on his brain.

Rachel smiled nervously. 'Darius, this is Nathan, the other doctor on duty. We are having a chat with everyone about their medical file and requirements in the camp.'

Darius had that soap actor look. Clean tanned skin and straight white teeth. He looked as if on occasion he might work out at the gym and he also looked as if he needed to gain a little weight.

Nathan held up his file as Rachel shifted from foot to foot. 'There's not much in here, Darius. If I'm going to be the doctor looking after you I need to know a little more about your medical history.'

Darius's eyes shifted over to Rachel. He was a confident guy who was obviously used to things going his way. 'There's no need. Rachel knows my medical history. That's why she's here.'

Nathan leaned across the desk. 'But Rachel might not always be available. She's not on call twenty-four hours a day for the next three weeks, you know. And she'll have other patients to treat too. The rest of your campmates and the crew need doctor services too.'

Darius gave a fake smile as he glanced at Rachel. 'I'm sure she'll cope.'

Nathan's hand balled into a fist as he kept his voice deadly calm. 'Any allergies I should know about? Are you in good health right now? Do you require any medications or special diet requirements?'

Darius took a few seconds to reply, almost as if he was rehearsing his answer. 'No allergies. I'm in perfect health and I'm not taking any medication right now.'

Measured. That was the word that Nathan would use. Rachel, in comparison, looked like a cat on a hot tin roof. What on earth had happened between these two?

There was something in the air. But it wasn't like the spark Nathan had felt between him and her when Rachel had first walked in here. It was something different. Something easier—at least it seemed easier to Darius. He seemed cool and confident around Rachel. Assured.

Darius stood up and put a hand on Rachel's shoulder. 'Thanks for being here, Rach.' He glanced at Nathan. 'I hope it doesn't cause you too many problems.'

He disappeared out of the door to where the director was assembling the production crew.

Nathan folded his arms. 'Well, that was informative. What does he have on you, Rach?'

Her expression of relief changed quickly. It was amazing how quickly he could put her back up. 'What do you mean? Nothing. He has nothing on me. Why would you even think that? I've already told you I'll be looking after Darius. There's nothing you need to know.' She was getting angrier by the second and he knew he was right.

He moved around the desk, leaning back against it, only inches away from where she stood. Her perfume filled the air around him. 'Really? So what did he mean by "I'm not taking any medication *right now*"? When was he taking meds and what for?'

He could see the conflict flitting across her eyes. The rational part of her brain knew exactly why he was asking. His suspicion hadn't been misplaced. There was something to tell; that was the whole reason Rachel was here. But what was it? Three weeks of this would drive him crazy.

She stared him straight in the eye. 'This is ridiculous. I don't want to be here. You don't want to be here. Why doesn't one of us just leave?'

She was cutting straight to the chase but he hadn't missed the fact she'd just circumvented his question.

This was the closest he'd been to Rachel in eight long years. Her pink lips were pressed in a hard line and her hands were staunchly on her hips. He tried not to look down. He tried not to notice the way her breasts were straining against the thin pink T-shirt. He tried not to notice the little lines around her brown eyes. Or the faint tan on her unblemished skin.

But everything was there. Everything was right in front of him. He breathed in and her scent was like an assault on his senses. He bristled, the tiny hairs on his skin upright and the beat of his heart increasing in his chest. This was crazy. He wasn't interested in this woman. He wouldn't *let* himself be interested in this woman. She'd walked away. More accurately, she'd flown away when he and Charlie had needed her most.

Australia hadn't just been her dream. It had been *their* dream. They'd both planned on going there after they'd worked as senior house doctors for a year. It was easier for Rachel. Her mother was Australian and Rachel had dual nationality. But the application to work had been in both of their names and nothing had hurt more than when Rachel had just upped and left without him.

The words were on the tip of his tongue. *You leave.* But he couldn't bring himself to say them. And it drove him crazy. It should be easy. She deserved it. So why couldn't he say it?

He turned his back and sat back down. He had to get away from her smell, her stance, the look in her eyes. He could do without all these memories.

'I can't leave. I'm working with Lewis. Believe it or not, I'm doing this as a favour to him. Cara's near the end of her pregnancy and he needs to be there. When I go back he'll give me another six-month contract at the hospital.'

She frowned, wrinkling her nose. Rachel had always looked cute when she was frowning. 'He's blackmailing you into being here?' It sounded worse when she said it out loud.

He couldn't help the rueful smile on his face. 'Not really. He gave me "the look". You know—the one he always gives you when he needs his own way? Anyway, he really didn't want to be away from Cara and apparently I needed a holiday. A break. Some time off.'

Now she looked worried. 'He thought you needed some time off? Is something wrong? Did something happen?'

You. But he'd never say that word out loud. He hadn't realised how big an effect all this was having on him. And he didn't even want to acknowledge it. He'd spent the last eight years blanking Rachel out of his life. Forgetting about her. Locking her away in a box, along with all the unresolved feelings he had about her. It wasn't quite so easy to do that when she was standing in front of him.

He took the easy route. 'I spent five years working for Doctors Without Borders. I've been halfway around the world. I didn't really have a holiday when I finished my last tour. Just came to Australia, looked up Lewis and started working for him on a temporary contract.'

She hesitated, something flitting across her eyes. 'You never talked about going to Doctors Without Borders. What made you go?'

He couldn't bite back his natural response. 'We didn't talk about lots of things.'

She flinched, almost as if she'd been stung.

He took a deep breath. 'An old friend came back after working for them. When he told me about the work he'd been doing—the epidemics, the natural disasters and in areas of armed conflict—I was interested. Who wouldn't be? Lots of these people have absolutely no access to healthcare. Doctors Without Borders is their only hope. I felt as if I had to go. Charlie had finished university and got a job. The timing worked out. I was only going to do one mission in Africa for nine months. But one year turned into two, then three and eventually five.'

He paused. She was watching him carefully, almost holding her breath. 'It was good experience.' It seemed the best way to sum things up. Rachel didn't need to know what he'd seen or what he'd dealt with. She had a good enough imagination. He'd already told her more than he'd intended to.

But curiosity about her was getting the better of him. 'What's your speciality?'

For a second she seemed thrown. She bit her lip and fixed her eyes on a spot on the wall, her hand tugging nervously at her ear.

With Rach, it had always been a telltale sign. And his instant recognition came like a thunderbolt. He'd thought he'd known this woman so well. But he hadn't really known her at all. That was probably what stung the most.

'I took a little time off when I came to Australia.' Her eyes looked up to the left. 'Then I worked as a general medical physician for a while, dealing with a mix of diabetic, cardiac, respiratory and oncology patients.' Her feet shifted on the floor.

Her gaze meshed with his and something shot through him. A wave of recognition. She tugged at her ear. *She's going to change the subject.*

After all these years he still knew her little nuances. 'I thought you might have gone into surgery. That's what you were always interested in.'

She was right. He had talked about going into surgery. And he'd certainly had his fair share of surgical experience around the world. But even though he'd just acknowledged that he still knew her little nuances, he was annoyed that she thought she still knew things about him.

She'd walked away. She'd lost the right to know anything about him. She'd lost the right to have any insight into his life.

His voice was blunt. 'A surgical internship would have taken up too many hours. At least with A & E I had regular shifts without also being on call.'

The implication was clear. Looking after his brother had changed his career pathway. He didn't like to think about it. He didn't like to acknowledge it—especially not to someone who had turned and walked away. Maybe if Rachel had stayed he could still have chosen surgery as his path? It would have been easier to share the load between two people.

But Rachel didn't seem to be picking up his annoyance. 'You must have got a wide range of experience with Doctors Without Borders. Did you do some surgery?'

'Of course I did. It's all hands on deck out there, even though you're in the middle of the desert.' His eyes drifted off to the grey wall. If he closed his eyes right now he could almost hear the whump-whump of the incoming medevac helicopters. He could feel the sensation of the tiny hairs on his arms and at the back of his neck standing on end in nervous anticipation of the unknown.

Sometimes civilians—men, women and children—sometimes army, navy or air force personnel. You never knew what you were going to see when you pulled back the door on the medevac.

The medical services were some of the best in the world, but at times Nathan's surgical skills had been challenged.

The tick-tick of the clock on the wall brought him back into focus. A little shiver ran down his spine.

A warm hand touched his arm and he jolted. 'Nathan? Are you okay?'

A frown creased her brow. The concerned expression on her face made him angry. How dare she feel sorry for him?

He snatched his arm away. 'Of course I'm fine.' He crossed his arms over his chest and walked around to the files again. 'I'm going to write up some notes. Make a few recommendations to the director. Why don't you go over to the beach or something?'

It was dismissive. Maybe even a little derogatory. But he just wanted her out of here. Away from him.

For a second Rachel looked hurt, then her jaw tightened and the indignant look came back in her eyes. The Rachel he'd known would have stood her ground and torn him down a few pegs.

But this Rachel was different. This Rachel had changed. She nodded, almost sarcastically. 'Sure. That's exactly what I'll do.' She picked up one of the pagers from the desk, clipping it to her waist without even acknowledging the act. She walked away without a glance. 'They better make cocktails at that bar…'

The door closed behind her with a thud and he waited a few seconds before he collapsed back into the seat. One minute he was mad with her, the next he was being swamped with a whole host of memories.

One thing was for sure. This island wasn't big enough for the both of them.

CHAPTER THREE

RACHEL WAS FURIOUS. She couldn't wait to put some distance between her and Nathan.

She rubbed the palm of her hand against her shorts. It was almost burning. The contact with his skin, the gentle feel of the hairs on his arms underneath her hand was something she hadn't been ready for.

It was hard enough being around him again. She felt catapulted into a situation she was unprepared for. In her distant daydreams, she'd been sure that if she'd ever met Nathan again she would have been ready. Mentally. And physically.

She'd be wearing her best clothes. Something smart. Something professional. Her hair would have been washed and her make-up freshly applied. She would have practised how to casually say hello. All her responses would be easy, nonchalant. Or at least rehearsed over and over again so they would seem that way.

She would have a five-minute conversation with him, wishing him well for the future, and then walk off into the distance with a little swing of her hips.

She would be composed, controlled. He would never guess that her heart was breaking all over again. He would have no idea at all.

But most of all there would be absolutely no touching. *No touching at all.* Because, in her head, that was the thing that would always break her.

And she'd been right.

Her hand started to shake. Rubbing it against her thigh was no use. No use at all.

Her footsteps quickened on the descending path. The beach was only a matter of minutes away. A few of the crew members were already on the beach, sitting on the chairs. But the truth was she couldn't stay here for long. In an hour's time the celebrities would be split into two teams and dropped into the middle of the ocean.

Their first challenge would be to row to the island. The winning team would be rewarded with better sleeping facilities and more edible food. The others would spend a night sleeping on the jungle floor. Just the thought of it made her shudder. The rangers had already pulled a few spiders as big as her hands from the 'camp' and a few snakes she had no intention of identifying. The book that Lewis had given her on poisonous creatures had photographs of them and then notes on antidotes, treatments and antivenoms. It wasn't exactly fun bedtime reading.

She climbed up onto one of the bar stools, which gave a little wobble. It seemed to be designed for people of an Amazonian stature. She looked down to the sandy matting beneath her.

'What'll it be?' asked the guy behind the bar. He didn't look like a traditional bartender. He looked like a guy running between about five different jobs. Most of the crew seemed to be doing more than one thing.

'Remind me not to get too drunk. I don't fancy falling off this bar stool. It's a long way down.'

The bartender smiled. 'It's okay. I know a handsome doc that will be able to patch you up.'

She shook her head. 'Absolutely not.' She held out her hand. 'Rachel Johnson. The other doc. And, believe me, he's the last person who'd be patching me up.'

'Len Kennedy. You don't like Nathan? I'm surprised.' He set a glass in front of her. 'Don't tell me. Diet soda or fruit juice?'

She nodded ruefully. 'You guessed it; I'll be on duty soon. A diet cola will be fine.' She watched as he poured and tossed in some ice, a slice of orange and a couple of straws.

He watched while she took a sip. 'Nathan seems like a good guy. What's the problem?' The bartender's voice was steady with a curious edge. But it felt as if he'd just drawn a line in the sand as to where his loyalties lay. Great. She couldn't even come to the bar for a drink.

She gave her shoulders a shrug and took a sip through her straw. 'Some might say it's ancient history.'

Her eyes met the guy in front of her. He was handsome, but a little rough around the edges. A scar snaked from his wrist to his elbow, he had a closely shorn head, a few days' worth of stubble and eyes that had seen things they shouldn't. She wondered what his story was.

He gave her a knowing kind of smile. 'Then maybe that's the best place to leave it. Sometimes history should be just that—history.'

She'd been wrong. He didn't seem like a crazy crew member. He was a typical bartender. The kind that seemed to be able to read your mind and tell you exactly what you didn't want to hear.

She looked out at the perfect ocean. This place might not have the luxury facilities she'd been promised. But it was an incredibly beautiful setting. The kind of place where you should relax and chill out. The kind of place that probably had the most gorgeous sunsets in the world. She gave a sigh. 'Sometimes history is too hard to let go of.'

Len put another glass on the bar and filled it with lemonade. He held it up to hers. She hesitated, then held up her glass and chinked it against his. He smiled. 'Maybe you should look at this a new way. Maybe it was fate that you both ended up here at the same time.'

Fate. More like an interfering friend. She arched her back, her hand instantly going to the skin there, tracing a line along her own scar. She hadn't thought for a second Nathan would be here. Her backpack had two bikinis that she'd never wear in front of him; they'd have to spend the next three weeks languishing at the bottom of her bag. She didn't want him asking any questions. She didn't want to explain her scar. It went hand in hand with her relationship with Darius. Things he didn't need to know about.

She didn't really want to consider fate. It didn't seem like her friend.

She smiled at Len. 'So what are your duties around here? I haven't had a chance to look around much yet.'

'Apparently I tend the bar, refill the drinks, supply ice and help the crew with setting up some of the tasks.' He took another sip of his drink. 'I've got experience in rock climbing. They said it would be useful for one of their tasks.'

Rachel's eyes widened. 'You might have experience rock climbing but I'm betting none of the celebrities have. How safe is it to make them do something like that?'

Len shook his head. 'I've no idea. I'm just the extra pair of hands. I'm assuming they'll have a safety briefing before they start. At least I hope they will.'

Rachel gave a sigh and looked out over the perfect

blue Coral Sea. This place really could be an island paradise. She rested her head on her hands. 'What on earth have I got myself into?'

Len laughed. He raised his glass again and gave her a worldly-wise gaze. 'Probably a whole load of trouble.'

She lifted her glass again and clinked it against his. She had a sinking feeling he could be right.

CHAPTER FOUR

RACHEL WATCHED AS the celebrities rowed towards the island. At least that was what she thought they were trying to do.

'There's going to need to be some serious editing,' said the quiet voice behind her. 'This is really quite boring.'

She didn't turn. She didn't need to. She could actually feel his presence right behind her.

He was right. The journey to the island didn't seem like much of a journey. They'd been put into two boats and asked to row ashore as if they'd done it from the mainland. The truth was they were only a few hundred yards away. The boat with the sportsman Frank Cairns was already miles in front of the other. On a hot day his patience was obviously at an all-time low and he'd decided to do most of the rowing himself. His fellow celebs arrived onshore with big smiles on their faces.

The second boat arrived filled with long, grumpy faces and instant moans. 'My agent said I wouldn't have to do anything like this,' moaned Dazzle.

'Your agent lied,' muttered Pauline Wilding, the politician. 'Haven't you learned anything yet?'

The male and female TV presenters appeared, trying to placate the celebrities and keep the atmosphere light.

Rachel scanned her eyes over them all. One of the older women was limping already. The trek through the forest to the campsite wouldn't help.

Darius appeared comfortable. The row didn't seem to have bothered him in the slightest. It made her feel a little easier. Everywhere she looked she could see potential problems. Scratches and bites that could become infected. Lack of proper nutrition. Contaminants from the horrible toilet the celebrities would need to use. If Darius had asked her if this was a good idea—she would have told him to run a million miles away.

If any patient who'd just finished another dose of chemotherapy had asked if they should come here she would give a resounding no. A relaxing holiday in the Whitsunday islands on a luxury resort was one thing. Being dumped in a jungle to sleep for the next three weeks was another thing entirely.

She'd been lucky. She'd only had to take a year out of her medical career. A long, hard year involving surgery to remove her cancerous kidney; chemotherapy, radiotherapy and annual check-ups for five years.

Darius hadn't been so lucky. They'd met in the cancer centre, with her fighting renal cancer and him fighting non-Hodgkin's lymphoma. He'd relapsed twice since, each time becoming a little sicker than the last.

What the world didn't know was that Darius really hadn't been her lover. He'd been her friend. Her confidant in a place she'd just moved to without any real friends.

Nathan had no idea why she'd left. He'd just lost his parents and realised he needed to be his brother's guardian for the next two years. She hadn't mentioned any of the symptoms she'd had—the blood in her urine, the sick feeling and loss of appetite. They'd both been so busy in their first year as junior doctors that she'd barely had time to think much about her symptoms. A simple urine test dipstick on the ward had made her realise she needed to get some professional advice. But then Nathan's parents had been killed and they were both left stunned.

She'd held him while he'd sobbed and tried to arrange a joint funeral and sort out all the family finances. He'd just lost two people he loved. She'd nearly forgotten about her investigatory renal ultrasound. When her diagnosis had come she couldn't possibly tell him. She couldn't put him and Charlie through that. They needed time to recover. Time to find themselves. Charlie needed healthy people around him. Nathan needed to concentrate on getting his life back and learning how to be a parent to his brother.

Neither of them needed the uncertainty of someone with a cancer diagnosis. So she'd done the only thing that seemed right. She'd phoned her mother in Australia and made contact with the local cancer unit over there. Her notes transferred and her treatment planned, she'd bought her plane ticket and packed her case.

Australia had always been on the cards for Nathan and Rachel. They'd applied together. They'd meant to go together. But the death of Nathan's parents meant all those plans had to be shelved.

It was too risky to stay in England and be treated. Someone, somewhere, would have come across her and word would have got back to Nathan. She didn't want that. She loved him with her whole heart. He, and Charlie, had been through enough. She knew the risks of renal cell carcinoma. Not everyone survived. She couldn't take the risk of putting Nathan and Charlie through that.

And she knew Nathan better than he knew himself. At the time of his parents' death he'd tried so hard to be composed, to keep on top of things. This would have been the final push. Nathan would have stood by her— of that she had absolutely no doubt. No matter how hard she tried to push him away, he would have been by her side every step of the way.

In a way, she hadn't felt strong enough to be brave for herself and for Nathan too. She had to be selfish. She had to put herself first.

So that was what she'd done. She'd bought her ticket and gone to the ward where Nathan was working to let him know she was leaving.

It was the hardest thing she'd ever done. She'd been flippant, matter-of-fact. A job opportunity had arisen in Australia that was too good to give up. She didn't want to cause a scene so she hadn't warned him.

He'd be fine. Charlie would be fine. They'd been together too long. They both needed some space apart. She'd wished him and Charlie well for the future.

Her legs had been shaking as she'd made that final walk down the corridor, knowing that every single word that had come from her mouth had been a lie.

Horrible heartless lies that had hurt the person she loved.

No wonder Nathan couldn't bear to be around her.

No wonder at all.

Nathan was watching the celebrities crossing the swinging bridge made of rope and planks of wood suspended sixty feet above the jungle canopy. Any minute now…

Right on cue, one of them vomited over the bridge, clinging on for all she was worth. He couldn't stifle the laugh. He shouldn't really find it funny. But it was ridiculous. None of them had expressed a fear of heights.

It took nearly an hour for all nine celebrities to cross the bridge. It reminded him of the hysteria he'd witnessed as a student doctor at a school immunisation session when one teenage girl after another had a panic attack in the waiting room. The celebrities' legs seemed to have turned to jelly and even some of the guys made a meal of it.

Darius wasn't one of them. Neither was the sportsman. Both walked over the bridge as if they were crossing the street. Darius was beginning to pique Nathan's curiosity. What had Rachel seen in the guy? And why was he so stoic? He didn't seem fazed by the jungle— or the potential challenges. It was as if he had so much more to worry about.

There was a yell behind him and he spun around. A few other shouts followed and his legs moved automatically, crashing a path through the jungle towards the noise.

It only took him a few seconds to reach a scene of chaos. Some of the crew had obviously been transporting equipment and a whole pile of barrels that had previously been in a tower were spilled all over the ground.

'What's wrong? Is someone hurt?'

'It's Jack,' yelled one of the burlier men as he grabbed hold of one of the barrels and tried to move it aside. 'He's caught underneath.'

Nathan didn't hesitate. First priority—get to the patient. There was no way to see or assess how Jack was right now, so he used his muscle power to grab an end of one of the barrels to try and throw them out of the way. The weight of each of the barrels was extreme. 'What on earth is in these?' he grunted.

'Sand.'

'What? Why on earth do we have barrels filled with sand?'

The muscles in his arms were starting to burn as he kept pace with the others grabbing barrels and moving them away from the site.

'For one of the challenges,' shouted the crew guy.

There was a flash of pink near to him, then a figure shot past him and wriggled in between some of the barrels. 'Stop!' came a yell.

He moved forward, crouching down. 'Rachel, what on earth are you doing?'

He could only see the soles of her boots as she continued to wiggle forward, her slim body and hips pushing sideways through the barrels. None of the rest of the crew could have fitted.

Her voice seemed to echo quietly back to him, reverberating off the curved sides of the barrels. 'I've got him. He's unconscious. Give me a second.'

The site director appeared next to Nathan, talking incessantly in his ear. *Health and Safety...not safe...insurance...liability...*

'Shut up,' said Nathan sharply, tuning the man out. 'Rachel. How are you doing in there?'

There was a creak above him and several of the crew ran forward with their hands above their heads. 'Watch out, Doc. Some of these are going to go.'

Of course. They'd been so close they couldn't see the bigger picture. They'd been so quick to think about getting to Jack they hadn't considered the swaying semicollapsed tower.

Rachel gave a little squeak. 'He's breathing. But he's unconscious,' she shouted. 'Definite sign of a head injury with a head lac, and a possible fractured ulna and radius.'

'Any other injuries?'

'Give me a sec. I can't see his legs but I can feel his pelvis and abdomen.' Nathan held his breath. His brain was trying to calculate how long it would take to mede-vac someone out of here. A few seconds later she shouted again. 'His pelvis seems intact and his abdomen is soft. But there's a few barrels right above us that look ready to come crashing down. Do you have anything we can use to keep us safe?'

Nathan started shouting to the crew. 'We need some-thing to put over Jack and the doc. What do we have?'

A few members of the crew pointed to some piles of wood. But there was no chance of squeezing those in amongst the barrels. Nathan's brain was working franti-cally. Yesterday, he'd read a list of the challenges that the celebrities would do over the next few weeks. It sparked something in his brain. 'Wait a minute. What about the inflatables for the water challenge later—anyone know where those are?'

He hadn't even seen them but, from what he could remember about the challenge, they might help.

Ron's eyes lit up. 'Yes! They'll be perfect!' He turned on his heel and ran towards one of the equipment stor-age cabins.

Nathan's black medical bag thumped down beside him. He didn't even know who'd brought it. He just stuck his hand inside and pulled out a stethoscope. He ran for-ward and threw the stethoscope inside. 'Rach, can you sound his chest?'

There was a muffled response. Ron and the others were still running around. The feeling of camaraderie struck him. When something happened, all hands were on deck. He didn't know most of these people. He could count on one hand how many names he knew. But it didn't matter; everyone was working towards one purpose and that he could understand. It had been the way of his life for five years in Doctors Without Borders.

Ron stopped next to him, clearly out of breath—he'd need to remember to check him over later. 'We've got them—almost like giant sausages. They're thin enough when they're deflated to wiggle them through next to the doc.'

'How do you inflate them?' His brain was starting to see where this could go.

'With a pressure machine.'

'How quickly can they go up?'

'Within ten seconds.'

He ran his fingers through his hair. 'When that inflates will it push all those barrels outwards?' How on earth could he keep Rachel and Jack safe?

He turned to the technician next to him. His logical brain was trying to calculate how to do this. 'Put one on either side. They stay in the middle. That way, all the barrels will fall outwards.' At least he hoped and prayed they would. He glanced at the anxious face next to him. 'What do you think?'

Ron gave a small nod. 'I think you're a genius, Doc. Let's get to work, guys.'

They moved quickly, trying to get things in position.

Nathan took a deep breath and moved forward. 'Rach?'

Her voice echoed towards him. She sounded stressed. Climbing in amongst the barrels was probably starting to feel like a bad idea. 'It's harder than I thought. Chest clear and inflating on one side, but I can't get access to the other—he's lying on that side.' There was a definite waver in her voice. What he really wanted to do was crawl in beside her. But unless that space got about two foot wider there was no physical possibility of that—not without putting the already teetering pile at further risk.

He signalled to Ron. 'How soon will you be ready?'

Ron's face was red and sweating. He gestured towards the other guys. It might look like chaos around them but everyone seemed to know exactly what they were doing. They all had a purpose. 'Two minutes.'

Nathan crouched down, pushing himself as close to the entrance as he could. 'Good. Rach, listen to me. We need to get you and Jack out of there. The barrels aren't safe; they could fall at any minute. But we think we've got something that could help.'

'What is it?'

'Ron and the guys are going to manoeuvre some inflatables in beside you. They're rolled up like sausages and should squeeze through the gap. One will be in front of you and Jack, and the other behind. I'll give you a signal and we'll flick the switch to inflate them. It's quick. It only takes ten seconds, and once they inflate they should push all the surrounding barrels outwards. You need to keep your head down. Are you okay with that?'

'Is there any other option?' Her voice sounded shaky.

Nathan bit his lip. He was trying to make it sound as if this was perfectly planned when they both knew it wasn't. 'This is the quickest and safest option. You'll be out of there soon.' He switched back to doctor mode. 'How's the patient?'

He tried to shut out all the outside noise and just focus on her. How was she feeling in there? Any minute now the whole pile could come crashing down on top of her. He didn't even want to give that head space. He *couldn't* give that head space. Because it might actually make his hands shake. It didn't matter that he hadn't seen her in years. It didn't matter he had all this pent-up frustration and rage wrapped up in memories of her. This was Rachel.

He didn't want her to come to any harm. No matter what else went on in this world. He couldn't push aside his protective impulses towards her. He didn't dare to think about anything happening to her.

He'd just managed to see her for the first time in eight years. And, no matter how he felt about anything, he wasn't ready for that to be over.

Her bravado was obviously starting to crash. 'He's still unconscious. We'll be able to assess him better when we get out.'

Ron tapped him on the shoulder, standing in position with the bright yellow, tightly coiled inflatables in the crew's hands.

'Rach, hold on. Ron's ready. Get yourself in position.'

He couldn't imagine what it must be like in there with the heavy barrels stacked all around. It took a good ten minutes for Ron and the rest of the crew to slowly edge the giant sausage-like inflatables into position and connect them to the air pressure machines.

It was the first time in his life Nathan had ever cursed his muscular frame. He should be the one in there. Not her.

He spoke in a low voice. 'Are you sure the rest of the barrels will fall outwards? None are going to land on them?'

Ron met his gaze; there was a flicker of doubt in his eyes. 'I'm as sure as you are.'

Nathan glanced towards the crew member standing with his hand on the air pressure machine. 'Get back,' he yelled to the rest of the crew members, who scattered like leaves on a blustery day.

Nathan couldn't help himself. He rushed forward as he signalled to the crew guy. 'Now, Rach,' he shouted. 'Get your head down!'

Strong arms pulled him backwards just as the switches on the machine were thrown. It was only ten seconds. But it felt like so much longer.

The giant sausages started to inflate, pushing everything around them outwards. The barrels teetering at the top started to rumble and fall, cascading like a champagne tower. Nathan couldn't breathe. It was almost as if everything was happening in slow motion.

One blue barrel after another thudded heavily to the ground, some landing on their side and rolling forwards, gathering momentum as the crew dived out of their path. From beneath the pile the thick yellow PVC was emerging, continuing to throw the blue barrels outwards as the air gathered inside.

Relief. He didn't even want to consider what might have happened. As the last barrel rolled past, Nathan sprinted towards the yellow PVC, crossing the ground quickly. He could hear the thuds behind him and knew that the rest of the crew were on his heels but it didn't stop him bounding over the thick inflatable.

Rachel was still crouched behind it; her body over the top of Jack's, protecting him from any falling debris. Her head was leaning over his, with her hands over the top of her head. The other yellow inflatable had protected them from behind, creating the shelter that Nathan had hoped it would.

Nathan landed beside her with a thud, dropping to his knees and gently touching her arms. 'Rachel? Are you okay?' He couldn't stop the concern lacing his voice.

Her arms were trembling and she lifted her head slowly, licking her dry lips. Her eyes flicked from side to side. 'It's done?'

The wave of relief in her eyes was obvious. He had to hold back. He had to really hold back. It would be so easy just to wrap his arms around her and give her a quick hug of comfort and reassurance. But this was Rachel. This was *Rachel*.

He'd already experienced the briefest contact with her skin and he'd no intention of doing it again. No matter how relieved he was to see she was okay.

His black bag thumped down next to him again—the black bag he should have been carrying in his hand. Something shot through him. His first thought should have been for the patient but it hadn't been. His first thought had been Rachel.

She was still looking at him. Staring at him with those big brown eyes. As if she were still in shock after what had just happened.

He had to focus. One of them had to do their job.

He grabbed the stethoscope from her hands and bent over to sound Jack's chest. Now that the barrels were out of the way he could get access quite easily. It only took a few minutes to hear the air entry in each lung. He pulled a pen torch from his back pocket and checked both of Jack's pupils. Both reacted, although one was slightly sluggish. He grimaced. 'We really need to get some neuro obs started on this guy.'

His voice seemed to snap Rachel to attention. She jumped to her feet and held out her hands towards the crew members who were handing a stretcher towards them. It only took a few seconds to load Jack onto the stretcher, with plenty of willing hands to help them carry him back to the medical centre.

If this accident had happened in the city Nathan would have a full A & E department at his disposal, with a whole host of other doctors. Here, on this island there was only him and Rachel. She'd always been a good, competent doctor. He hoped that nothing had changed.

He didn't even glance behind the stretcher as he walked alongside the patient. His brain was spinning furiously, trying to remember where all the emergency equipment was in the medical centre.

Medical centre. It could barely even be called that. It had the basics, but was better designed for general consultations than emergency medicine. He'd expected to treat a few bites and stomach aches. Not a full scale head injury.

The crew members carried Jack inside and helped Nathan slide him across onto one of the trolleys. He did the basics and hooked Jack up to the cardiac monitor and BP cuff; at least they had one of those.

Rachel seemed to have gathered herself and was pulling Jack's notes from the filing cabinet. 'No significant medical history,' she shouted as Nathan pulled an oxygen mask over Jack's face and quickly inserted an IV cannula.

'Do we have any Glasgow Coma Scales?' It was unlikely. The Glasgow Coma Scale was used the world over to monitor unconscious patients. Rachel pulled open a few admin drawers and shook her head, passing him a recording sheet for pulse and BP, then taking a blank sheet of paper and making some quick scribbles.

She walked over and handed it to him as she slid the pen torch from his back pocket as though she did it every day, lifting Jack's eyelids and checking his pupils.

Nathan glanced at the paper. It was Rachel's attempt at an impromptu Glasgow Coma Scale. It had captured the basics—eye response, verbal response and motor response. Both of their heads snapped up as the monitor started alarming.

He ran his fingers down Jack's obviously broken arm. The colour of his fingertips was changing. They were beginning to look a little dusky, meaning that the blood supply was compromised. He swapped the oxygen saturation probe over to the other hand and watched as it came back up to ninety-eight per cent.

He looked up and his gaze meshed with Rachel's. He didn't even need to speak; she could see the same things he could.

'Nathan, do you have keys to the medicine fridge?' He nodded and tossed them in her direction. For a doctor who didn't routinely work in emergency medicine, she'd certainly remembered the basics. He finished his assessment of Jack, recording all the responses while she drew up some basic pain medication.

Even though Jack wasn't awake they were going to have to straighten and splint his broken arm to try and re-establish the blood supply. No doctor could assume an unconscious patient couldn't feel pain. It didn't matter that Jack hadn't responded to the painful stimuli that Nathan had tried as part of the assessment. His breathing wasn't compromised so they had to administer some general pain relief before they started.

His arm fracture was obvious, with the bones displaced. Thankfully, they hadn't broken the skin so the risk of infection would be small.

Rachel spun the ampoule she'd just drawn into the syringe around towards Nathan so he could double-check the medicine and the dose. He gave a little nod of his head while she administered it.

He couldn't help but give a little smile as she positioned herself at Jack's shoulder. 'Do you remember how to do this?'

She shook her head. 'Of course not. Why do you think I'm in the anchor position? The responsibility for the displaced bones and blood supply is yours.'

Of course she was right. It would have been years since she'd been involved in repositioning bones. He'd done it three times in the last month.

It only took a few minutes to reposition the bones and put a splint underneath the arm. The most promising thing was the grunt that came from Jack.

'Can you patch that head wound?' he asked. 'I'm going to arrange to medevac Jack back to the mainland.'

Rachel opened the nearest cupboard and found some antiseptic to clean the wound, some paper stitches and a non-adhesive dressing. She worked quickly while he made the call. She waited until he replaced the receiver and gave him a nervous smile. 'I haven't sutured in a while so I've left it for the professionals.'

He nodded. It was good she wasn't trying to do things she wasn't confident with. She'd just been thrown in at the deep end and coped better than he'd expected. If the shoe was on the other foot and he'd found himself in the middle of a medical unit, how well would he do?

He might be able to diagnose and treat chest infections, some basic cardiac conditions and diagnose a new diabetic but would he really know how to treat any blood disorders or oncology conditions off the top of his head? Absolutely not.

Nathan picked up the phone and dialled through to the emergency number. Thank goodness he'd checked all these yesterday when he arrived. It didn't matter that Lewis had told him nothing would happen. Working for Doctors Without Borders had taught him to be prepared.

The call was answered straight away and arrangements made for the dispatch of the medevac. 'It's coming from Proserpine Airport. We're in luck; they were already there.'

Her sigh of relief was audible and he joined her back at the trolley. Jack still hadn't regained consciousness. Nathan took a few more minutes to redo the neuro obs and stimuli.

'Do you know where the medevac will land?'

He gave a nod of his head. 'Can you go outside and find Ron? We'll need some help transporting Jack down to the beach. They've probably cleared the landing spot already.'

She disappeared quickly and he sucked in a breath. This was a whole new experience for him. They'd trained together at university and spent their first year working as junior doctors in the same general hospital. But they'd never actually done a shift together. She'd done her six months medical rotation first while he'd done his surgical placement. They'd swapped over six months later.

He'd already known he wanted to specialise in surgery at that point, whereas Rachel had expressed a preference for medicine. They'd applied to the same hospital in Melbourne and been accepted to work there. But he'd been unable to take up his job and had a frantic scramble to find another in England. He'd always assumed that Rachel had just carried on without him. Now he wasn't so sure.

Ron's sweaty face appeared at the door. He'd really need to check him over at some point. ''Copter should be here in a few minutes. Once it's down, there are four guys outside to help you carry the stretcher.' His brow creased as he glanced at Jack. 'How is he?'

Nathan gave a little nod. 'We've patched him up as best we could but he's still unconscious. Hopefully, he'll wake up soon.'

Ron disappeared and ten minutes later the thwump-thwump of the helicopter could be heard overhead. A wave of familiarity swept over him. For a few seconds he was back in the sand, war all around, his stomach twisting at the thought of what throwing back the mede-vac door would reveal. But then Rachel rushed back in and the moment vanished. He finished another blood pressure reading and pupil check, then disconnected the monitor.

He pulled the blanket over Jack's face to protect him from the downdraught and any flying sand but it actu-ally wasn't quite as bad as he'd expected. Helicopters didn't faze him at all. He'd spent the best part of five years travelling in them and pulling patients from them. But Rachel looked terrified.

She ducked as they approached the helicopter even though the spinning blades were high above her head. Several of the crew members did the same. The para-medic flung open the door and jumped down.

The handover only took a few seconds. 'Jack Baker, twenty-four. A few tons of sand-filled barrels landed on him. Suspected broken ulna and radius, blood sup-ply looked compromised so it's been realigned. Uncon-scious since the accident. GCS six with recent response to pain. His right pupil has been sluggish. No problems with airway. Breath sounds equal and abdomen soft.' He handed over the charts he'd made, along with a pre-scription chart and Jack's notes. 'He's had five of dia-morphine.'

The paramedic nodded as he anchored the stretcher inside and started connecting Jack to his equipment. His eyes met Nathan's. 'Our control centre will give you a call and keep you updated.'

Nathan pulled the door closed and backed off towards the trees next to the beach. The water rippled as the blades quickened and the helicopter lifted off. After a few minutes the members of the crew started to disperse, mumbling under their breath as they headed back towards the accident site. It would take hours to clean up. It would take even longer to write the report for the insurers.

Nathan started to roll up his khaki shirtsleeves. Report writing could wait. He'd rather be involved in the clean-up and get a better idea of the general set-up. Health and Safety might not be his direct responsibility but, as one of the doctors on the island, he didn't want to have to deal with something like that again.

Something caught his eye in the foliage next to the beach—a little flash of pink. It wasn't the tropical flowers that he'd spotted earlier; they'd been yellow, orange and red. This wasn't fauna. This was man-made.

Rachel was sitting on the edge of the beach, just as it merged with the dark green foliage. Her pink cotton T-shirt stood out. She hadn't even noticed him, her knees pulled up to her chest and her eyes fixed on the sky above.

He bit his lip. He couldn't leave her there like that. She wasn't used to trauma. She wasn't used to accidents. This was totally out of left field for her.

Part of him wanted to walk in the other direction. The Nathan of eight years ago wanted to leave her sitting there alone. But the Doctors Without Borders medic wouldn't let him. In his five years he'd never once left a colleague alone after a traumatic incident. He wasn't about to start now.

His legs moved before his brain started to function. They were on automatic pilot. He didn't even think. He just plopped down on the sand next to her and put his arm around her shoulders.

'Okay?'

She didn't speak, but she didn't pull away either—not like earlier. Her breathing was shaky and her shoulders gave the slightest quiver beneath his arm. He moved closer, pulling her to him and speaking quietly. 'You did good, Rach. Emergency medicine doesn't come easily to some folks. You acted as though it was second nature.'

'I just acted on instinct.' Her voice wavered.

'Did that include when you dived amongst those barrels that could have pounded you to pieces?' He still couldn't believe she'd done that. He still couldn't believe he hadn't been quick enough to stop her.

Her head sagged onto his shoulder. She stared out at the sea. 'I don't know why I did that.'

He smiled. 'Probably because you're headstrong, stubborn and don't listen to anyone around you.'

She gave a little laugh. 'I guess some things don't change at all.'

He felt himself tense a little. Part of him didn't want to offer comfort to her. Part of him didn't want to reassure and support her. He could feel his body reacting to hers. The familiarity of her underneath his arm, leaning against him as if they still fitted together—even after all this time.

His breath was caught somewhere in his throat. He wanted to tell her that everything changed. Things changed in the blink of an eye and the world you thought you had just slipped through your fingers.

But he couldn't let the words out.

He'd been down this road himself—acting on instinct

in places where it could get you into trouble. But he'd been lucky. He'd always been surrounded by supportive colleagues. Doctors Without Borders was like that.

He didn't even want to touch on his natural instinct to the car backfiring in Melbourne that ended with him crouched in a ball on the street. Working in war zones did that to you. And it was hard to shake it off.

And, because of that, he took a deep breath and stayed where he was. Sometimes—even for a few minutes—a colleague just needed some support. He'd had colleagues who'd supported him. Now, it was his job to return the favour. No matter what else was going on in his head.

Right now it was just them. Just the two of them for the first time in eight years, sitting together on a beach.

He pushed everything else away. Three weeks on an island with Rachel?

There would be plenty of time for repercussions. But, for now, he would just wait.

CHAPTER FIVE

THE SHOWER WAS distinctly dodgy, spouting an uneven trickle of water. With thick hair like Rachel's, rinsing the shampoo out was a challenge. She pulled on a plain pink button-down shirt and another pair of khaki shorts and her hiking boots again. The smell of breakfast was wafting around. Ron had been right; the catering cabin was definitely the most popular place on the island.

Part of her felt bad for the celebrities who had spent their first night in camp, half of them lying on the equivalent of yoga mats on the jungle floor. If it had been her she would have stuck her head in the sleeping bag, pulled the tie at the top and not come out again until morning. But, then again, she wasn't here to entertain the audience.

Last night in the cabin had been hard enough. Knowing that across the simple sitting area and through the thin walls Nathan was lying in another bed made her skin tingle.

She'd spent years trying not to think about Nathan. Guilt always ensued when she thought about him. For the first year she'd had to concentrate on her own treatment and recovery. The support from Darius had actually helped; he'd been a welcome distraction. He liked to be the centre of attention in his own little world—

even if he was keeping it secret. Sometimes it had felt as if Rachel was his only confidante and that could be a bit overwhelming—especially when she had her own recovery to consider.

Last night had been pretty sleepless. She tried to rationalise. She was on the Whitsundays—beautiful islands in the Coral Sea with a whole host of wildlife around her. The nightlife sounds were always going to be a little different. But that wasn't what had kept her awake.

If she closed her eyes really tightly she could almost imagine that she could hear Nathan breathing in the other room. It brought back a whole host of memories she just wasn't ready for. Her hand on his skin, watching the rise and fall of his chest and feeling the murmur of his heart beneath her palm. The soft noises he made while he slept. The fact that in their five years together, he'd never ever turned his back when they'd slept together. His arms had always been around her.

The feelings of comfort and security swept over her—things she'd missed beyond measure these last few years. And that didn't even begin to touch on the passion. The warmth. The love.

Getting up and heading for the shower to try and scrub off the feeling of his arm around her shoulders had been all she could do. Nothing could change what had happened between them. Nothing could change the look in his eyes when he'd first seen her.

She'd felt the buzz yesterday. She'd heard the concern in his voice when she dived in amongst those barrels. She still wasn't quite sure why she'd done that. It seemed like a good idea at the time—she was the only person small enough to get through the gap and to the patient.

But once she'd been in there she was scared. Hearing

Nathan's voice was not only reassuring but it also bathed her in comfort, knowing that he was concerned about her. She shouldn't read anything into it. She shouldn't. She knew him. Or at least she used to know him. Nathan would have been concerned for any colleague.

Had five years working for Doctors Without Borders changed him? Had her walking away from him changed him? She hoped not. She hoped his good heart was still there. Even if he only showed it to her in a moment of crisis.

She followed the smell of eggs and bacon. Most of the crew were already eating at the variety of tables. Nathan was in the corner, having a heated discussion with one of the directors.

Rachel filled her plate with toast, bacon, eggs and coffee, then walked over, putting her tray on the table. 'Anything I should know about, guys?'

The angry words instantly dissipated as both sets of eyes looked at her in surprise. The hidden similarities between a television crew and a hospital was amazing. Rachel had spent too many years working amongst people with big egos to be thrown by anything she came across.

'Is this a medical matter or a technical matter?' she asked as she sat down and spread butter on her toast.

Nathan blinked. He still seemed surprised at her frankness. 'It's a mixture of both. Bill just presented me with a revised list of the challenges. I think some of the changes could impact on the health and safety of the contestants. He's telling me that's not our concern.'

'Really?' Rachel raised her eyebrows and bit into her toast. She chewed for a few seconds while she regarded Bill carefully. On this island, he obviously thought his word was law. To the rest of the production crew it probably was. But he hadn't met Rachel or Nathan before. No matter how at odds they were with each other, he was about to find out just how formidable they could be as a combined force.

She gave Bill her best stare. 'So, just out of interest, what would the insurance company say if both your doctors bailed?'

A slow smile started to spread over Nathan's face. He knew exactly what she was doing.

'What do you mean?' snapped Bill.

She shrugged and started cutting up her bacon and eggs. 'I'm just asking a question, Bill. I'm pretty sure you can't have this production without your medical team in place. After yesterday, I think you'll find Nathan and I aren't prepared to negotiate on anything.' She popped a piece of bacon in her mouth. 'You either listen to us or you don't.'

She was so matter-of-fact about it. Probably because she wasn't prepared to negotiate. Employees, including herself, had been put at risk yesterday. They'd already identified a few celebrities who couldn't take part in certain challenges. She didn't even know the schedule for today. But, no matter how many years had passed, if Nathan knew enough to get angry about it, that was good enough for her.

Bill stood up abruptly, knocking the table and sloshing some of her coffee over the side of the cup. 'Fine. I'll change it back to the original plan.'

Nathan watched Bill as he stormed across the large cabin and slammed the door behind him. None of the crew even batted an eyelid. This obviously wasn't news to them.

Rachel mopped up her coffee with a napkin. Now it was just the two of them her earlier bravado was vanishing. She was thinking about his arm on her shoulders last night and the way he'd just sat and held her until she'd composed herself. When she'd finally taken a deep breath and felt calm, he'd just given a little nod and stood up and strolled off into the sunset.

She'd no idea where he'd gone. But it had given her a chance to go back to the shared cabin, have a quick wash and change and hide in her room. She'd lain there for hours until she'd eventually heard the click of the door.

But she was a fool. He hadn't come to speak to her. And she should be grateful. Her initial reaction to him earlier had been pure and utter shock. She'd more or less said she couldn't work with him, which wasn't true. He'd just been the last person she'd expected to see.

Nathan's breakfast plate was empty, as was his coffee cup, and he picked them up. 'I've heard that filming last night varied from boring to very boring. I think they were trying to spice things up today at one of the challenges and I'm not sure I trust Bill not to still try. Are you happy to come along to the filming?'

She nodded as she glanced at the now congealed egg on her plate. Her appetite had definitely left her.

He stood up. 'I've also put up a notice saying we'll have a surgery every morning for an hour for the crew. Anyone with any difficulties. I take it you don't have a problem with that?'

She gulped. She was an experienced medical physician. Why did the thought of general practice fill her with fear? 'That should be fine.' No way did she want to express any concerns around Nathan. He'd already seen her wobble last night. That was already once too many.

'Good,' he said. 'We start in ten minutes.'

He walked out ahead of her as she scrambled to pick up her tray and she felt a flash of annoyance. Ratbag.

This was something they actually should have sat down and discussed together. He wasn't senior to her. They were both here as doctors. She could almost bet if she were any other person he would have discussed this with her first.

A few of the crew were waiting when she arrived. Thankfully, there was nothing too difficult to diagnose. A few chesty crackles, another inhaler for someone and an emergency supply of blood pressure tablets for someone who'd misplaced their own.

An hour later, Ron arrived in a Jeep to pick up her and Nathan and take them to the first challenge on the other side of the island.

'Challenge has been changed,' were Ron's first words.

'What a surprise,' said Nathan. 'What to?'

'The underground scramble.' Ron kept driving while Rachel exchanged a glance with Nathan. The underground scramble was not a challenge she'd want to do. She searched her brain. Several of the celebrities suffered from claustrophobia and would have to be exempt from scrambling through the dark underground tunnels filled with a variety of creatures.

'What about Diamond?' she asked. 'I think there's too big a risk of infection.'

'I agree. I'll tell the producer she's ineligible.'

'Shouldn't that have been decided before the public voted?'

Ron looked over his shoulder. 'Don't worry about it. Vote's already decided that Darius will be doing the challenge. Diamond's safe.'

Nathan's eyes fixed hard on her as her stomach flipped over. A man who'd just undergone a bout of chemotherapy shouldn't be dragging himself through dirty, water-filled tunnels with a variety of biting creatures and insects. But she already knew what he'd say.

'I'll need to speak to Darius before he starts,' she murmured.

Ron laughed. 'Don't think you'll have a chance. They'll announce live on TV it's him and do the challenge immediately afterwards. You won't have time to talk.'

'But I need time. He'll get a safety briefing, won't he? I'll make time then.'

Nathan's gaze narrowed. 'What's wrong? Doesn't he like the dark? If he can't do a challenge shouldn't I know about it?'

She pushed back her retort. Nathan was right. It was already a bugbear that Darius was her ex. The fact that his medical details hadn't been released to Nathan was obviously annoying him. It wasn't her fault. It wasn't her choice.

But she was being paid to do a job. And she wouldn't be doing a good job if she didn't warn Darius of the risks to his health—whether he listened or not.

'He can do the challenge—and I'm sure he will. I just need to discuss some underlying issues with him.'

Nathan folded his arms across his chest and fixed his gaze back on the road ahead. The jungle foliage was beginning to thin as they reached the hollowed out tunnels at the other side of the island.

All of the celebrities were perched on a bench, talking to the hosts. Rachel jumped from the Jeep and made her way quickly to the entrance of the caves. 'How deep are they and what's in them?' she asked one of the nearby crew.

He guided her over to the side, where some TV screens were set up, showing the cameras with infra-red filters that were positioned in the man-made tunnels. She grimaced at the sight of scampering creatures. 'Anything that bites and could break the skin?'

One of the rangers nodded. 'Just about everything.'

Rachel squeezed her eyes closed and pushed her way past the hosts, grabbing hold of Darius's arm. She was making an executive decision. This whole thing was fake anyway. She was pretty sure the only thing that was real was the viewers' votes.

'What's wrong, Rachel?' Darius's brow creased as he glanced to make sure no one could overhear them.

'I don't think you should do this challenge,' she said quickly. 'There's a strong possibility of getting cuts, bites or scrapes. Any break to the skin is a risk of infection and your immunity will already be low right now. There's no telling what the infection risks are from the unknown creatures or the dirty water.'

Darius shot her his famous soap star smile as he realised what her words meant. 'Lighten up, Rach. I've won the public vote? Fantastic.' He shook his head. 'I'm not worried about the tunnels. Why should you be?' He glanced over her shoulder. She could already tell that Nathan had closed in and was listening to their conversation. 'You can check me over for broken skin when I come out.' Darius gave her a wink and walked back to the bench with the other celebrities.

The producer hurried over to her, hissing in her ear. 'What are you doing? You'll spoil everything. This is supposed to be a surprise.'

She spun around. 'My job. That's what I'm doing. And what are you worried about—didn't you know Darius is one of the most famous soap stars in Australia? I'm sure he can act surprised.'

She stomped away back to the television screens.

Darius was more concerned about his screen time and popularity than his health. It was maddening.

Nathan appeared at her side. 'Are you going to tell me what's going on?'

She gritted her teeth. 'I can't.'

He turned without another word and walked away.

After shooting her a few glares, the TV hosts smiled right on cue for their live broadcast. Darius was suitably surprised when he found out he'd been voted for the challenge. He smiled all through the televised safety briefing, then dived head first into the tunnels. Some of them were a tight fit. There was no way the sportsman could have forced his way through these tunnels. If Darius had been at his normal weight he probably wouldn't have fitted either. He must have lost a little weight during chemotherapy. In the end he completed the challenge in a few minutes and emerged wet and muddy with his rewards in his hands. There was a large gash on one leg and a few nips on the other from some baby alligators.

She waited impatiently for the filming to finish. 'In the Jeep,' she said as the cameras stopped.

Darius flinched and rubbed at the open wound. 'I think we're supposed to go back directly to camp.'

Nathan appeared at his back. 'Do what the good lady says. You won't like her when she's angry.'

There it was. That little hint to Darius that he actually knew her a whole lot better than Darius did. She could see the instant recognition on Darius's face as they eyed each other suspiciously. It was ridiculous— like pistols at dawn. She was irritated enough already and this wasn't helping.

Ron appeared, sweating as always, and smiling. 'Back to the medical centre then, folks?'

All three climbed wordlessly into the Jeep. The journey back seemed so much longer. Ron talked merrily as if he hadn't noticed the atmosphere in the car, dropping them all at the path leading down to the medical centre.

Rachel strode ahead, flinging open the door and pulling things from cupboards. She gestured towards the examination trolley. 'Climb up there.'

She was so angry with them both right now she couldn't even look at them. Darius for being so stupid and Nathan for being so stubborn. Part of her knew that Nathan was right. Any other doctor would want to know the patient's history too.

But any other doctor wouldn't get under her skin and grate like Nathan could.

He was like a permanent itch. Part of her still felt guilty around him. Part of her felt angry. Irrational? Yes, of course. She was the one who had walked away. She had left him and Charlie and put herself first.

Even if she could turn back the clock she wouldn't change that—no matter how much it had hurt them both. Her outcome could have been so different. She was one of the lucky ones; she knew that. She'd had her treatment and reached the five-year magic survival milestone. That was good; that was positive.

But this whole place had just thrown her into turmoil. She'd distanced herself from Darius these last few years. He needed to find others to rely on. Coming here had been a mistake.

As for the sizzle in the air whenever she and Nathan were in the same room? She really couldn't have predicted it. If anyone had asked her, she would have sworn it would never exist again. But it did exist. Every time she looked at him her skin tingled. Every time he stood close enough, all the little hairs on her body stood on end, almost willing him to come into contact. She couldn't control her body's responses. And it was driving her nuts.

She washed her hands and opened the sterile dressing pack. Nathan had angled a lamp over Darius's leg, even though he hadn't touched it. He seemed to sense it was wise to stay out of her way.

She slipped on her gloves and leaned over to get a good look at the wound. It was around four inches long and ragged, with a few tiny pieces of debris. She took a deep breath and irrigated with saline, removing the debris with tweezers. 'It's not deep enough to stitch. I'll close it with paper stitches. But it does give a route of entry for infection. Who knows what was in that mud or those tunnels? You're going to need this dressed and observed every day.'

Darius sighed. 'That seems like overkill. This place is miles away from the campsite. I don't want to have to come here every day. The rest of the celebrities will think I'm getting special treatment—either that or they'll think something is wrong.'

Nathan cleared his throat loudly. 'Actually, Darius, Rachel's right. And it isn't overkill. Since Rachel has highlighted you're susceptible to infection, I think it would be wise to put you on antibiotics. It's pretty much a given you're going to get some kind of infection in that wound.'

Rachel was surprised to hear Nathan back her so quickly. She finished cleaning the wound and applied some antiseptic cream and a dressing.

'It might be easier all round if either I or Rachel come up to the campsite every day to dress the wound. We can bring supplies with us and it should only take a few minutes. That way, it's pretty obvious why you're being seen. It's not special treatment. It's wound care.'

Darius nodded. He seemed oblivious to the fact she was mad at him. But of course the world revolved around Darius. At least his world did. What made her more curious was the way Nathan was actually giving him some leeway. She hadn't expected it. Hadn't expected it at all.

'That sounds great. Thanks for that.' He slid his legs from the examination couch while she got rid of the waste and Nathan dispensed some antibiotics. He held them out for Darius. 'You do realise I'll tell the producer you can't be eligible for tomorrow's challenge?'

'What?' He had Darius's instant attention. 'But it sounds like one of the best ones!'

'You can't go swimming and diving with a potentially infected leg. No way.'

Nathan was still holding onto the antibiotics. All credit to him. He knew exactly how to deal with Darius.

'But it'll look as if I'm using it as an excuse not to take part.'

Nathan shrugged. 'The producer and director have to abide by our recommendations. Feel free to say on camera that the docs have refused to let you take part. Feel free to let the world know you've got a potentially life-threatening infection in your leg.'

Rachel could almost see the headlines running through Darius's head. He gave a little nod. 'Thanks for this.' He took the antibiotics and a bottle of water from Nathan. 'I'll see you both tomorrow.'

He exited the medical centre and disappeared down the path to where Ron was waiting to drive him back to camp.

Rachel folded her arms and leaned against the wall. She could tell Nathan knew she was watching him. He started opening the filing cabinet and flicking through notes.

'That was very kind of you. What's going on?'

He glanced upwards. 'I have no idea what you mean.'

'Yeah, right. We both know you don't like Darius. Why are you being so obliging?'

Nathan sat down behind the desk. 'How much weight has he lost recently?'

She blinked. It wasn't the response she'd expected.

She shook her head. 'I'm not sure. He lost weight a few months ago. I just presumed he hasn't put it back on again yet. He is looking a little gaunt, but I'm sure once his time in camp has passed he'll be fine. All the celebrities lose some weight in camp.'

Nathan looked thoughtful. 'I don't care that you're not telling me his medical history. I just don't like the look of him.' His mouth curled upwards for a second. There was a definite glint in his eye. 'In more ways than one.' He looked serious again. 'I think there could be something else going on with Darius Cornell.'

She took a deep breath. She was having a professional conversation with Nathan Banks. It was just so weird. She'd been so wrapped up in Darius's history of non-Hodgkin's and keeping it confidential she hadn't really thought about anything else. Sometimes you needed someone else to help you look at the big picture.

She bit the inside of her lip and gave a little sigh of recognition. 'This way we get to keep a direct eye on him every day?'

Nathan smiled. 'You got it.'

So this was what working with Nathan Banks could be like. She'd waited over eight years to find out. She'd never really expected it to happen. Even though they'd attended the same university, they'd never actually worked on a ward together. Once they'd qualified, choosing different specialities meant that it was unlikely to ever happen. This had been totally unexpected.

She watched as he flicked through a few files. His hair was so short she had an urge to run her palm over his head and feel the little bristle beneath her skin. He must have got used to wearing it in the buzz-cut style while he was working away.

The first thing she'd noticed was the little lines around his eyes. He'd aged. But, like most men, he'd done it in a good way. He'd lost the fresh face of youth and replaced it with something much more lived in and a whole lot more worldly-wise.

Nathan had always managed to take her breath away. Before, it had been with his good nature, laughter and sex appeal. Now, it was something entirely different. The man in front of her made her suck her breath between her teeth and just hold it there. He had so much presence. His bulkier frame filled the room. But it was whatever was hidden behind his eyes that made her unable to release the breath screaming in her lungs.

It could be a whole variety of things. The loss of his parents. His time over the world for Doctors Without Borders. Did Nathan have a medical history she didn't know about? Why had he changed his career pathway? It could even be the fact that his brother had now settled down with a family before him. But she doubted that very much.

She wanted to peel back the layers. She wanted a diary of the missing years. But she wanted it all about Nathan, without revealing anything of herself.

Pathetic, really.

But she just wasn't ready to go there.

His head lifted and their gazes meshed. 'Is there anyone else you're worried about?' he asked.

Her brain scrambled. *You. Me.* She bit back the obvious replies.

'Ron,' she said quickly. 'I don't know if he just has a sweating disorder but I'd like to check him over.'

Nathan nodded. 'Me too. We'll get him in soon.'

He stood up and walked over to the door. 'I'm going to go for a run along the beach before we need to supervise the diving challenge.'

Rachel bit her lip. An empty beach and the open ocean sounded like a great idea. Somewhere to clear her head. Somewhere to get her thoughts together. But if Nathan was going to be there it was too crowded already.

She stood up. 'I'm going to go and talk to the production crew about the diving challenge. I'll talk to you later.'

As she stepped outside the medical centre she took a few gulps of air. This island seemed to be getting smaller by the second...

CHAPTER SIX

RACHEL STRETCHED OUT on the sun lounger and wiggled her toes, the only part of her currently in the sun. The last few days had been odd. After the hiccup on the first day and Darius's minor injuries on the challenge, things had pretty much been how Lewis had promised. A few hours' work every day followed by hours and hours to kill. That would be fine if they were staying at a luxury resort, or in the middle of a city. Instead, they were on an island with a distinct lack of facilities and where the only entertainment was the Z-list celebrities. The days seemed longer than ever.

The challenges had been going well. Frank, the sportsman, had aced the diving challenge around the coral reef without managing to do himself any damage. The next challenge had been to scale a thirty-foot tree to reach a fake bird's-nest. Billy X, the rapper, had proved surprisingly agile but Darius had obviously been annoyed that he'd not been voted for by the public.

His wound was gradually healing and the antibiotics seemed to have warded off any sign of infection. He still wasn't looking any better though and Rachel had started to wonder if they should be monitoring his weight. The celebrities had to prepare and cook their own food over a campfire and, even though there weren't excessive amounts of food, there was still enough to keep them sustained. Maybe Nathan was right—maybe there was something else to worry about?

She shifted uncomfortably on the sun lounger. If Darius's non-Hodgkin's relapsed he would be in big trouble. He had already relapsed twice. Each treatment plan had been more intense than the one before. She knew firsthand exactly what these treatment plans involved. He wouldn't be able to keep his illness a secret much longer.

She heard muffled voices up in the trees around her. The crew were gossiping again. She smiled. They were a great bunch but sometimes it was like being trapped on an island with a bunch of teenage girls.

Thankfully, no one seemed to have picked up on the tension between her and Nathan. Or, if they had, she hadn't heard anyone mention it.

Ron caught her eye as he walked slowly towards the medical centre. Rachel had asked him to come in twice in as many days and she was glad he'd finally showed up. Nathan was on duty and would check him over.

As he reached out his hand towards the door he winced. His face was bright red. He almost looked as though he could burst.

She hesitated for a few seconds. Nathan was an experienced A & E doctor. He could handle this—she knew he could. If she went in now, he might be resentful of her interference.

But the expression on Ron's face couldn't let her sit there much longer. She sat up and dug her toes into the sand for a second as she reached underneath the lounger for her sandals. She wasn't getting much of a tan anyway. She was too worried that if she took her sundress off and just wore her bikini people might ask questions about her scar.

She wasn't normally self-conscious and if Nathan hadn't been on the island she would have worn her bikini without a second thought. But suddenly she was wishing she had a schoolgirl-style swimsuit in her backpack— one that covered all parts of her back and front. It might not be stylish but would stop any awkward questions.

She shook the sand from her feet and pushed them into her sandals. Ron. That was who she needed to concentrate on now. It was time to stop fretting about the future and put her professional head back into place.

Nathan was feeling restless. The last few nights he hadn't been able to sleep. Lying in a cabin with only two thin walls separating him and Rachel was driving him crazy. Every time he heard the shower running he imagined her soaping her smooth skin under the spluttering water. He imagined the water running in rivulets down her straight spine, in long lines down to her painted pink toes.

The pink toes had been haunting him. It was practically the only part of her skin that could freely be seen. Unlike the rest of the crew on the island, Rachel had kept herself well covered up. T-shirts and long shorts coupled with socks and hiking boots were the flavour of the day. Even in the evening she wore long pants and long-sleeved T-shirts. The only part visible were her toes.

All his memories of nights with Rachel had revolved around short satin nightdresses and shoestring straps. There certainly hadn't been a lack of skin.

And it certainly wasn't helping his male libido. His imagination was currently working overtime. He needed to find himself a distraction, a hobby. But finding something else to do on this island was proving harder than he'd thought.

He'd put a call through to Len to see what his plans

were for later. Maybe a hike around the island would help him think about other things.

Nathan was just replacing his phone when the door opened. Ron walked in, panting heavily, with a strange expression on his face and his signature sweat marks on his grey T-shirt.

He really didn't look great. His face was highly coloured with beads of sweat on his brow. Nathan stood up quickly and helped him over to the examination trolley, lifting his legs up onto it and helping him to rest back.

He could hear Ron rasping for breath so he switched on the monitoring equipment, connected it and pulled an oxygen mask over Ron's face.

'How long have you been feeling unwell?'

'Just…today,' Ron wheezed.

The blood pressure cuff started to inflate. 'Ron, are you having any chest pain?'

Ron frowned. 'Not really. Well…maybe a little.'

Great. He'd suspected Ron wasn't feeling great but he hadn't responded to any of Nathan's invitations to be checked over. Right now, he had heart attack written all over him.

Nathan looked at the reading on the monitor and opened the drug cabinet, taking out an aspirin. First line treatment for an MI. Actually—the only treatment they had on this island. Not ideal. Still, it was better to be safe than sorry. 'Here, take this.' He handed Ron the tablet and a glass of water.

'Not really pain…' Ron continued. 'Just indigestion.'

'Indigestion? How often?'

Ron thumped the glass of water back down; even taking a sip had been an effort. 'Every day,' he gasped.

Nathan raised his eyebrows. 'Ever had problems with your blood pressure?'

Ron gave a nod.

'Does your indigestion come on when you're working?'

Another nod.

'Does it ever go down your arm?'

Ron's high colour started to pale. The oxygen was finally getting into his system and his heart rate was starting to steady.

'How bad is your indigestion today?'

'B…bad.'

'Feels like something is pressing on your chest?'

Nathan stood at the side of the examination trolley. He watched the monitor closely. It gave a clear tracing of Ron's heart rate. The PQRS waves were all visible. No ST elevation. 'The good news is you're not having a heart attack. The bad news is you've probably got angina—and had it for quite a while. I'm going to give you a spray under your tongue to see if that eases the tightness across your chest.'

It only took a second to administer the spray and another few minutes for it to take effect. Nathan frowned. In a way it was a relief that angina was Ron's problem but on an island this would be difficult. Uncontrolled angina could easily lead to a heart attack. Ron really needed to be reviewed by a cardiologist. Chances were, an angiogram would reveal blocked arteries that would need to be stented and cleared. He could just imagine how Ron would take the news. But keeping him here would be dangerous. They didn't have the equipment that would be needed if Ron did have a heart attack. Apart from aspirin, they didn't have any clot-busting drugs.

'Ron, I think you probably know this isn't indigestion you've been having. It looks like angina. You need a twelve-lead ECG, a cardiac echo and an angiogram—none of which we can do here.'

Ron waved his hand. 'I can get all that when we get back to the mainland. I'll be fine until then.'

Nathan sat down next to the examination trolley. 'It's too big a risk. Tell the truth, Ron; you're having angina every time you exert yourself.' He nodded at the monitor. 'Your blood pressure is too high and you're constantly out of breath. Your heart is working too hard because the blood vessels aren't clear. You need to see a cardiologist.'

Ron shook his head. 'Forget it. I'll be fine.'

'No, you won't.' Nathan turned at the voice. Rachel was standing at the doorway, wearing her trademark pink. This time it wasn't a T-shirt and long shorts. This time it was a pink summer dress. She must have been down on the beach. His eyes went immediately to her painted toenails, visible in her flat jewelled sandals.

She walked over next to the trolley and put her hand in Ron's. He met her gaze immediately. Rachel had the people-person touch. In A & E you rarely got a chance to form any kind of a relationship with your patients. Medical physicians were different. They frequently saw their patients year on year.

'Ron, it's time to look after yourself. This really can't wait. Tell me honestly—how long have you been having these symptoms?'

Ron hesitated. His breathing had gradually improved. 'A few months.'

'Have you seen anyone about this?'

He shook his head. 'I've just kept taking my blood pressure tablets.' He gave a rueful smile. 'I did think it was indigestion.' He pulled a pack of a well-known brand of antacids from his pocket. 'I've been going through half a packet of these a day.'

Nathan could tell that Rachel was hiding a wince behind her smile. 'If your symptoms have been getting worse then it's definitely time for some investigations. We don't need to call a medevac to get you off the island, but we can arrange for you to go back by seaplane. We can arrange that for tomorrow. In the meantime I'll give you a spray and some instructions on how to use it. I don't want you going back to work. I want you to rest.'

Nathan watched carefully. For some reason Ron seemed to relate better to Rachel's instructions than his. She had a gift for talking to patients. Her tone was firm but friendly. He liked it.

His time working for Doctors Without Borders had been fraught. There had hardly been any time for conversations like this. As soon as he finished patching one patient—he was on to the next. There was barely time to think, let alone speak.

He sucked in a breath for a second. Something else had just struck him. He'd spent five years working with people, but not getting close—never staying in one place long enough to form true relationships. That thought started to chip away at his brain as he watched Rachel empathise and relate to Ron.

Rachel squeezed Ron's hand. 'Stay here for the next few hours, then I'll take you down to the canteen for dinner. We can have a further talk about things then.'

It was almost as if a giant weight had been lifted from Ron's shoulders. He sighed and rested back on the examination trolley, letting his eyes close. 'Dinner with a beautiful woman,' he muttered. 'I'd be a fool to say no.'

Rachel shot Nathan a smile—a smile that sent a little jolt all the way down his body. Maybe it was her humanity that was drawing him in. Even though he knew better, he'd spent the last few years labelling Rachel as heartless in his head. It had been easier to do that—because he'd never been able to get his head around the way she'd walked away and left him and Charlie.

He'd known her for seven years. The first few years of university they hadn't dated—just casually flirted. The five years after that, they'd been inseparable. Rachel had never seemed heartless to him. That just wasn't her. That wasn't how she worked. No one could spend five years with someone and not know them. It just wasn't possible to put on a good enough act to hide all your flaws and character traits for that long. He did know her. Or at least he *had* known her.

So why had she done something so out of character? What on earth had happened?

Their eyes locked. Chocolate-brown, framed with dark lashes, her eyes had always been one of his favourite parts of her. Her tan was deepening slightly after a few days on the island. Her dark hair was pulled up at either side of her face and tied in a rumpled kind of knot, the rest sitting on her shoulders. And the pink sundress covered everything, just giving enough of a hint of the soft curves that lay underneath. *Pretty as a picture.* Those were the words he'd always used for Rachel in his head. And no matter how angry he'd been with her—still was with her—some things were just buried too deep. The underlying frustration and resentment was still there.

No one had hurt him like Rachel had. What she'd done was unforgivable. But now he was in her company again he kept having little flashes of the good stuff. The way she tilted back her head and laughed when she was joking with some of the crew. The way she frequently reached out and touched someone when she was talking to them. The way that every now and then she drifted off, thinking about something else. All sparked waves of memories for Nathan. Memories of good times…memories of better times. Five years of shared memories.

Why had she walked away?

She wiggled her toes, the sand from the beach obviously caught between them. He dragged his eyes away from her painted toes and stood up. 'I'll stay with Ron for the next few hours. Come back and take over at dinner time.'

She gave a nod and glanced around the cabin. 'I promised Tallie I'd get her some petroleum jelly for her dry skin. She's trying to ward off an eczema flare-up. Do you know where it is?'

He looked up from Ron's notes and pushed the stool towards her. 'There's not enough storage in here. I think it's at the top of the cupboard over there.'

'Great, thanks.' She dragged the stool over to the counter and climbed on top to open the cupboards. Nathan glanced at Ron. Thankfully, his eyes were still closed and he wasn't watching Nathan fix on Rachel's bare legs and backside as she rummaged through the cupboard. The corners of his mouth turned upwards. Most of the prescribed medicines were easily accessible but the more routine things had to be packed away wherever there was space.

After a few minutes she finally found what she was looking for. 'Here it is.' She bent down and placed the container on the counter at her feet, ready to jump back down. But her rummaging had dislodged a few of the precariously stacked items in the cupboard and, as she looked back up, a few packages of bandages tumbled from the cupboard, bouncing all around her. It was pure instinct. As the items started to fall, Rachel lifted her hands, crouched down and curled into a ball.

The movement made her dress ride up, and not just a little. She was wearing a bikini under her dress—pink, of course. He'd already noticed the straps tied around her neck. But this time he got a flash of something else. The bright pink bikini bottoms covered some, but not all, parts of her. She was quick to grab at her dress and pull it back down, colour flooding into her cheeks.

She spun around as he got to his feet to come over and help. She lifted her hands quickly. 'Oops. Bit of a disaster.' She couldn't meet his gaze as she jumped down from the stool and made a grab for the wrapped bandages that had landed all around her. He bent to help, their hands brushing.

He saw her gulp as for a split second he caught her gaze. 'Just as well you've seen it all before,' she said quickly.

He didn't reply. He couldn't. He was still crouching down as she grabbed some of the bandages and set them on the counter. 'I'll let you get the rest. I'll take this to Tallie and be back in a few hours.'

She rushed towards the door, still talking nervously as she made a quick exit. Nathan still hadn't moved. He sucked in a deep breath as he reached for the last few bandages.

He couldn't be sure—he just couldn't be sure. But he'd seen more than enough battle scars in his time. He'd definitely seen something. But what it was he just couldn't fathom.

He'd seen Rachel's bare body a thousand times. He knew every contour of her body, every blemish, every mark. What he didn't know was the flash of a surgical scar just above her right hip. He'd no idea how far it went; she'd pulled her dress back down much too quickly. And it had only been the tiniest flash. Maybe he was wrong. Maybe he was reading too much into something.

He closed his eyes for a second, trying to visualise what he'd just seen. It wasn't ragged; it was clean. It couldn't be from an accident. It had to be deliberate. It had to be surgical.

Rachel had always been in perfect health. She still looked in perfect health today. So where on earth had the scar come from and what was it?

CHAPTER SEVEN

NATHAN SAT ON the sidelines while Rachel had dinner with Ron. It was clear she was onto the health promotion part. She was pointing at his plate and obviously talking about food choices. Next she swapped his soda for a diet one. Then she persuaded him to have some salad with his steak.

Ron wasn't eating much but the flushed colour of his cheeks had faded. Next, Rachel held his GTN spray for angina in her hands and talked him through how and when to use it.

'Earth to Planet Nathan. Are you home?'

Len was grinning at him from the other side of the table.

'What is it?'

Len gestured with his fork. 'You haven't taken your eyes off her for the last ten minutes. I keep expecting you to make an excuse to go on over there.'

'What? No way.' He speared a bit of his steak.

Len raised his eyebrows. 'I know.'

'Know what?'

'That you two have history.'

He almost dropped his fork. 'What do you mean?' He shot a quick wayward glance in her direction again. He'd love to say that Len was far too observant for his own good. But Len was one of the crew members he had a rapport with. He hoped Len would be on his side.

Rachel reached across the table and put her hand over Ron's, obviously offering some words of comfort.

Just as well he knew there was absolutely nothing in it, otherwise he was pretty sure his stomach would be twisting right now.

Len had started eating again. 'I knew it when I talked to her down at the bar. She mentioned you then.'

'She did?' All of a sudden Len had his instant attention. 'What did she say?'

Len laughed. 'Oh, nothing good. I take it you didn't leave things on the best of terms?'

Nathan started toying with his food. His gaze drifted back to Rachel. Her dark hair had fallen in waves over her shoulders and she'd put a pink wrap around her shoulders.

Rachel liked pink. She always had—at least seventy per cent of her wardrobe was pink. But what she probably didn't realise was just how good she looked in the colour; it didn't matter what the shade was. It seemed to make her lightly tanned skin glow and her dark hair and eyes shine.

He hesitated. It was obvious Len was waiting for an answer. 'We've not been on the best of terms for eight years.' The words kind of stuck in his throat. 'Before that, we were good together...' he paused '...really good.'

As he said the words out loud he realised how much they hurt. How little he understood about what had happened in his own life. Charlie was settled now. He'd grown up before his time and was married with a family. If his parents hadn't died that was pretty much where he'd expected him and Rachel to end up. Married with a family, probably here in Australia.

But he'd lost all that. He'd lost not just the woman, but also his dreams and aspirations. The life he'd been supposed to live. The career pathway he'd had all plotted out in his head without even knowing if he could be a decent surgeon. He'd barely had the chance to hold a surgical scalpel.

The resentment had flowed through his blood for years. He'd resented her for walking away and leaving him. He'd resented her for carrying on with her career. He'd resented the fact she'd had a life whilst he felt as if he'd been stuck in limbo.

His training in London hadn't fulfilled him; it hadn't captured his passion and enthusiasm and he'd wondered if he would ever get that back.

Joining Doctors Without Borders was his way out. It was his way of trying to live again. Trying to feel useful. He'd saved lives. He knew he had. And knowing that had helped in a way. He might not have been able to save his parents, but he had been able to save others. And for five years he had. In lots of different ways. He still felt a little numb. Some days that had been the only way to survive out there, to just block out certain things so you could continue to function. But the camaraderie with the other staff had been amazing. He'd felt valued—an essential part of the team. He'd worked hard to make others feel that way too and do the absolute best job that he could.

And he'd made friends—good friends that he would have for life.

But the truth was that everyone burned out over there. He had too.

And once you'd burned out it was time to leave. The bosses at Doctors Without Borders often recognised it before the staff did.

Australia had always been the aspiration. Now, it was a reality. But it wasn't working out quite how he had thought. Lewis was a good colleague. And the hospital he'd been working in was fine. But, the truth was, when he woke up in the morning his job wasn't the first thing on his mind.

He'd changed. Life had changed. And as he glanced across the canteen he wondered how life had changed for Rachel too.

Len cleared his throat, then took a drink of his beer. He was off duty tonight. Officially, Nathan was off duty too. But even a couple of beers didn't appeal.

'Well, maybe it's time.'

Nathan frowned. 'Time to do what?'

'Time to find out if eight years' worth of bad feeling is worth it.' He winked at Nathan. 'I've got a nice bottle of chilled Barramundi behind the bar.' He nodded towards the wall that had the shooting schedule on it. 'There's nothing scheduled for tonight. Nothing will happen, apart from the celebrities fighting over whose turn it is to empty the dunny. Why don't you take a seat down at the beach with the fine lady and have a chat? I hear the sunsets around here are to die for.'

'Not a chance.' The words were out of his mouth immediately. He hadn't even given it a moment's consideration in his head.

Because it was more than a little tempting.

Len stood up. 'Well, if you change your mind I'll leave the bottle in some ice at the bar. Up to you, buddy. I'll see you tomorrow at the cliffs. Let's see how fast you can climb.'

Rachel and Ron had stood up and were clearing their trays. Len picked up his and walked over to the kitchen doors, exchanging a few words with them on the way.

Nathan stared down at his steak. The food here had been surprisingly good. He'd heard from the crew that television jobs were often judged on the catering and, if *Celebrity Island* was anything to go by, people would be fighting to get a job here. But his appetite had left him.

The seed that had planted in his brain earlier was beginning to bloom and grow. The more he was around Rachel, the more he realised just how much he'd done to try and avoid being in the same position again—the position where Rachel walking away had hurt more than any physical pain he'd experienced.

He'd spent eight years never really forming true relationships. He still had a good relationship with his brother, Charlie, and a few good friends from university. But other than that? The experience of losing his parents and Rachel so soon after seemed to have affected him more than he'd realised. Trusting someone with his heart again just seemed like a step too far. It was much easier to totally absorb himself in work and other issues. Trouble was, this island didn't have enough work to keep him fully occupied, leaving him with far too much thinking time.

He cleared his tray and murmured a few words of greeting to some of the other crew members. He didn't feel like socialising tonight, but on an island as small as this—with some parts out of bounds for filming—it could be difficult to find some space. The atmosphere in the cabin was becoming claustrophobic. And he was sure it was all him. Rachel seemed relaxed and at ease. She'd obviously got over the whole thing years ago. It wasn't giving her sleepless nights.

He kicked off his trainers and wandered down to the beach. The path was only lit with a few dull lights and the insects were buzzing furiously around him. The waves around this island were a disappointment. Nathan had counted on spending a few hours in the surf every day but it wasn't to be. As a result, he hadn't spent much time on the beach.

He saw her as soon as his feet touched the cool sand. Saw the pink wrap around her, rippling in the night-time breeze.

Len had obviously whispered in her ear. A silver wine cooler was on the sand next to the sun lounger she was sitting on, a glass of wine already in her hand.

He should leave her in peace. She was probably trying to escape, just like he was.

Or he could join her. He could ask her about Ron. It was a pathetic excuse. Even he knew that. But from a fellow medic it was a reasonable question. He stuck his hands deep into his shorts pockets as he moved across the sand towards her.

She was silhouetted against the warm setting sun, which sent a peachy glow across her skin. The condensation was visible on her wine glass as she took a sip.

'Don't spoil this, Nathan.'

Her words almost stopped him in his tracks. He paused for a second, his toes curling against the sand. He knew exactly what she meant. But somehow he still didn't want to go there with her.

'Don't worry. Wine's not really my thing. I prefer a beer.' He missed out the obvious remark. *Remember?*

It was flippant, completely circumventing the whole issue. She didn't turn at his voice, just kept her gaze fixed on the horizon and let out a sigh.

She sipped at her wine. 'I'm tired, Nathan. I'm tired of all this.'

It seemed as if the barriers were finally down. Rachel

was saying what had been on her mind since she'd first set foot in the medical cabin and caught sight of him.

If she'd said those words a few days ago his temper would have flared. How dare she be the one to be tired of the atmosphere between them when it was just as much her fault as his?

But the last few days had made his head spin. He couldn't work out how he really felt about her.

He'd felt it all. Searing jealousy when Darius had appeared. A whole host of sensations when his skin had come into contact with hers. Confusion and rage for the first few days. Flares of passion. His gaze couldn't help but linger on her when he thought she wouldn't notice. Certain glances, nuances, would make his heartbeat quicken and send his blood racing around his body. All sensations he wanted to deny, to ignore.

He hadn't expected to see Rachel again. And he certainly hadn't expected to feel like this around her. Feeling was the problem. It was interfering with everything and because they were virtually stranded on an island together, that seemed to amplify it all.

He stepped forward—it felt like crossing a line—and bumped down on the sun lounger beside her. Her barriers were down. Maybe it was time for some home truths.

She shuffled over a little to make room for him. He reached over and took the glass from her hand, taking a sip of the chilled wine and handing it back. His eyes were focused entirely on the orange setting sun. It seemed easier. Like sitting in a movie theatre together.

The sharp wine hit the back of his throat.

'I didn't expect to see you again, Rach.' He let the words hang in the air between them.

When she finally spoke she didn't sound quite so exasperated. 'I didn't expect to see you again either.'

She turned her head towards him. Her voice had changed; it wasn't so strong. There was the tiniest waver. 'I don't know how to be around you. I don't know how to act. I don't know what's normal for us any more. I don't think things can ever feel normal for us again.'

She was right. She was saying everything that was running through his head. They'd gone from normal to nothing. One day she'd been there—the next she had gone. With a fifteen-minute fraught and tearful conversation tacked on the end.

This situation was alien to them both.

After spending a couple of years at university together with flirtation and attraction, he'd finally acted on instinct and asked her out. They'd been together for five years—through finals, through placements as medical students and then out into the world together as junior doctors, and then senior house officers.

Their relationship had been good. There had been passion and mutual respect in equal measures with only the occasional cross word. She'd been his best friend. Losing her had devastated him at a time when he'd needed her most.

In a way it was a relief that she was struggling with this too. He'd always thought he'd been instantly replaced by Darius Cornell. He'd never understood how she could just walk away from their relationship without a backward glance. And it made him doubt himself— doubt his own ability to read people. He'd questioned that he'd ever known her at all.

She turned her body towards his. 'Would it help if I said sorry? I'm sorry that I left?'

'It would help if you told me why you left.' It came out without any censorship. Without any thought. After eight years, he had to say the thing that was truly on his mind. He needed an explanation. He *deserved* an explanation.

She paused, obviously searching her brain for the right words. 'I had to go.' The words were measured— deliberate. 'It was the right thing for me. It was the right thing for you. It was the right thing for Charlie.'

The mention of his brother made his temper flare. 'Don't you dare tell me that was the right thing for my brother. You weren't there. You didn't see. You *chose* to not see. In a world of madness you were the one thing to give him a sense of normality. You never even told him you were going. Have you any idea how hurt he was? He'd just lost his mum and dad. He didn't need to lose someone else who'd been a permanent fixture in his life for five years.'

A tear rolled down her cheek. She reached over and touched his arm, the cold fingers from the wine glass causing him to flinch. 'I know that. Don't you think I know that? And I'm sorry. It broke my heart; it really did. But I had to. I just had to.' She was shaking her head, oh, so slowly. As if she'd had no choice. But that was rubbish. There was always a choice.

It was words. It was just words. There was no explanation. No rational reason to explain what she'd done. But it was just the two of them sitting alone on this sun lounger on the beach in the glow of the setting sun. And she was confusing him all over again. How could she still do that after eight years?

He could see the sincerity in her eyes. He could hear the emotion in her voice. She wasn't lying to him; she meant every word—even if she wouldn't explain them.

Frustration was simmering in his chest. All he wanted was an explanation. A reason. Something he could make sense of in his head. 'Why, Rach? Why can't you tell me now? It's been eight years. Surely whatever mattered then is in the past?'

Her lips were quivering, her fingertips still on his arm. He could feel the tension in the air between them, hanging like the fireflies above their heads. But there was more than that. There was the buzz, the electricity that still sparked between them.

All he wanted to do was reach up and catch the tear that was rolling down her cheek and wipe it away.

But she moved first. Something flitted across her eyes and she leaned forward, crossing the gap between them. Her perfume surrounded his senses, invading every part of him. He stopped breathing as her lips touched his. It was gentle, coaxing. Her fingertips moved from his arm to the side of his cheek.

His first reaction was to pull back. He'd thought about this from the first second he'd seen her. But he hadn't actually imagined it would happen. He hadn't even let his mind go that far.

But his body had other ideas. His hand tangled through her long hair, settling at the back of her head and pulling her closer to him.

He couldn't think straight. But he could kiss.

And Rachel was kissing him right back.

Her fingers brushed against his tightly shorn hair, sending tingles down his spine as the kiss intensified.

Eight long years he'd waited to do this again. Eight long years to feel her familiar lips against his. They fitted, just the way they always had. Memories of kissing Rachel swamped him.

In their student accommodation...in one of the on-call rooms in the hospital...at one of the hospital balls... and on the street one night in the pouring rain when they just couldn't wait to get home.

All of those memories raced around his head. This was too tempting. *She* was too tempting. Her hair was softer than cashmere, the skin around her neck and shoulders smoother than silk.

His hands slid down her back, feeling the contours of her spine and the curve of her hips. He paused. This was where he thought he'd glimpsed a scar. But now his brain felt as if it were playing tricks on him.

Every pore in his body wanted to move closer, to lie backwards on the sun lounger and pull her body against his. To feel the warm curves underneath her sundress press against the hard angles of his body. But the beach was too exposed. Any minute now some of the crew could appear. Anything that happened between him and Rachel was private—not for public consumption.

Then he felt it—the tear brush against his cheek. Was it the one that was already there? Or was she still crying?

He sucked in a breath. She gently pulled her lips from his, not breaking contact, leaving her forehead resting against his while she gave a few little gasps.

He had so many unanswered questions. So many things he wanted to say.

But she lifted her finger and placed it against his lips before he had a chance to speak. She gave the tiniest shake of her head. As if she was still trying to stay in the moment. Not trying to face up to the past, the present or the future.

His hand lifted and stroked her cheek. It was wet with tears. 'Rach?' he murmured.

She pulled back, her cheeks glistening. 'I'm sorry,' she whispered. 'I really am. But I just can't talk about it. I can't give us that time back. I just can't.' Her voice cracked and she stumbled to her feet, making a grab for her wrap. 'I'm sorry. This was a mistake. I need to go.'

She was off in a flash, running towards the path away from the beach and back to the cabins. Nathan didn't move. His heart was thudding against his chest. The caveman instinct in him wanted to run after her. But he could hardly get his head around what had just happened. Why had she kissed him?

He'd wanted to kiss her…but Rachel? Making the first move? It left him stunned.

Then his legs moved before he had a chance to think any more.

No. No, he wouldn't let her do this. He wouldn't let her disappear out of his life without explaining what had just happened. He pounded across the sand after her, catching up easily and grabbing her hand, spinning her around until she was back in his arms. His heart was thudding and his breathing rapid.

'No, Rach. Don't do this. This is it. This is the chance to clear the air between us. You have to tell me. Don't you think after all this time I deserve to know?'

Her face was wet with tears now. He hated that. He hated to think he had anything to do with that.

But he couldn't let this go. He just couldn't. It was time for the truth.

His voice was rich with emotion. 'Tell me.'

It was the thing that she'd always dreaded. The thing she'd never thought she would have to explain.

A thousand variations of the truth spun around in her head. Everything about it swamped her. The words she didn't want to say out loud just came to her lips. It was almost involuntary, but she'd been holding it in so long it just had to come out.

'I had renal cancer,' she whispered. Her voice could barely be heard above the quiet waves. The final rays of the sun had vanished now. The beach was in complete darkness, with only the occasional twinkling star.

Every part of Nathan's body stiffened. He turned towards her. He couldn't hide the horror written across his face. 'What? When? Why didn't you tell me? Why didn't anyone tell me?' He stiffened. It was as if something in his brain had just clicked. 'That's what the scar is on your back? You had your kidney removed?'

Her heart squeezed. It was obvious he was totally and utterly stunned.

The tears spilled down her cheeks and she nodded. 'No one knew. I didn't tell anyone.' Her voice broke.

His arms moved from her shoulders. This time he put both his hands on the tops of her arms. He shook his head. 'But why, Rachel? Why would you go through something like that alone? Why wouldn't you tell me?'

Anger flared inside her. Years of pent-up frustration at having to do what she'd thought was right. 'How could I? You and Charlie had just lost your parents. You were barely holding it together. I almost didn't go for the tests. I knew something wasn't quite right, but I'd pushed all that to one side while I'd helped you plan the funeral.'

'You ignored your symptoms because of me? Because of Charlie?' He looked horrified. He kept shaking his head. 'But when did you find out? When did you get the results?'

Her voice was shaking. 'Just before I left. I arranged to get my treatment in Australia.'

'That's why you left? That's why you left me?' He was furious now. The ire in his voice was only vaguely clouded by disbelief.

She shook his hands off her arms. 'Yes, that's why I left. Why did you think I left? Because I didn't love you any more?' She was shouting now; she couldn't help it.

'Why? Why would I do that? Do you know what the statistics are for renal cancer? Do you know how it's graded? You think I should have stayed? I should have stayed and put you and Charlie under even more pressure, even more stress? You were broken, Nathan—you both were. Can you imagine getting through your parents' funeral and spending the next year trying to support a girlfriend who might die? What would that have done to you? What would that have done to Charlie? Why on earth would I do that to two people that I loved?'

She was almost spitting the words out now, all the years of pent-up frustration firing through her veins. All the anger. All the bitterness of being on her own and not being supported by the people that she'd loved. She'd had her mother, but their relationship had been different. She hadn't lived with her for more than seven years—since she'd gone to the UK and started university. It wasn't the same as having the people she'd grown to love beside her. It wasn't just Nathan and Charlie she'd walked away from—she'd also left her father. He'd tried to understand, he really had, but it had changed their relationship too.

Nathan stood up and paced the beach with his hands on his hips, his head constantly shaking. 'I can't believe it. I can't believe that's why you left. You didn't trust me? You didn't trust me enough to tell me about the cancer? You didn't think I would support you through it? You didn't think I could handle it?'

He was angry but she felt even angrier. If she could stamp her feet on the soft sand that was exactly what she'd be doing.

'That's just it. I *knew* you would support me through it. And I knew Charlie would too. But in a year's time you might have ended up organising another funeral.

I couldn't do that to you. I couldn't put you both in that position.'

'That wasn't your choice to make!' he spat out. 'We were together. We were a partnership. I thought we meant something to each other. I loved you, Rachel.'

'And I loved you. That's why I left!'

Their faces were inches apart. He was furious at her, and she was equally furious with him. How dare he think she'd just upped and walked away without a second thought? She hadn't even realised that she'd been angry with him too. Angry that he didn't come after her. Angry that he didn't jump on a plane to Australia to find her.

Of course she knew that hadn't been a possibility. She knew that he'd had Charlie to look after, but it still made her feel as if he hadn't loved her enough.

Not as much as she loved him.

Wow. The thought muddled around in her brain. She wasn't thinking about the past. She was thinking about the present. No matter what had happened between them, she still loved Nathan Banks. She'd never stopped. Her legs wobbled a little.

'I can't believe you didn't trust me, Rachel. I can't believe you didn't trust me enough to let me be by your side when you were sick.' The anger had left his voice. Now, it was just disbelief. It was obvious he'd been blindsided by this. He looked as if she'd torn his heart out and left it thrown on the beach.

'I've always trusted you, Nathan,' she said quietly. She couldn't look at him right now, with the tears falling down her cheeks. 'I thought I was doing what was best for both of us. If things had gone the other way we wouldn't be standing here having this conversation. You've no idea how many of the people I met at that treatment centre aren't here any more. I was lucky. I beat the odds. I just couldn't guarantee that. I didn't want you to have to bury someone else that you loved.'

He stepped forward, his finger brushing a tear from her cheek. 'I didn't need guarantees from you, Rachel. I just needed you.' His voice cracked and she shook her head.

'I'm sorry, Nathan. I'm sorry I didn't stay and help with Charlie. I'm sorry you had to change your speciality. But even if I had stayed, I couldn't have helped. I was too sick, too weak to have been of any use. There was no way I wanted to be a burden to you. You wouldn't have been able to stand the strain of working long hours, looking after Charlie and looking after me. No one would.'

'You can't say that! You don't know. You didn't give us the chance to find out.' Pure frustration was written all over his face.

She pressed her hand to her heart and closed her eyes. These were selfish words but she had to say them. There was no other way. She had to try and make him understand just a little. 'But what about me, Nathan? I had to concentrate on getting better. I had to concentrate on getting well. I couldn't afford to worry about you and Charlie too. I barely had enough energy to open my eyes in the morning let alone think about anyone else. I wouldn't have been a help. I would have been a hindrance, a drain.' She shook her head again. 'You didn't need that.'

Nathan didn't hesitate for a second. He stepped forward and gripped her arm. 'You had no right. No right to make that decision for me. You had no right to make that decision for Charlie. You were our family. You were all we had left.'

His words took the air right out of her. In every scenario she'd imagined over the last few years she'd always believed that what she'd done had been for the best. But the force of his reaction was wiping her out. She'd always felt guilty but she'd never really considered this. He'd been grief-stricken—already feeling abandoned by his family. But hearing his words now made her feel sick.

Yes, her actions had been selfish. But she'd thought she'd done it out of love. Now, she was beginning to wonder if playing the martyr had been the most selfish thing that she could have done.

Her legs wobbled underneath her and she collapsed back down onto the blanket, putting her head in her hands. Everything was going so wrong.

Minutes ago she'd been in Nathan's arms—the place she truly wanted to be. Minutes ago he'd been kissing her and now, with one sweep of his fingertips and the touch of a scar, there was just a world of recriminations. Exactly what she'd dreaded.

She'd expected Nathan to storm off and not talk to her any more. But he hadn't.

He stepped forward and took her hands in his. Pain was etched on his face. 'I'm sorry. I'm sorry you had renal cancer. I'm sorry you thought you had to go to the other side of the world alone to be treated. But you should have never done that, Rachel. You should have never walked away—no matter how well-intentioned you thought it was. This was about trust. This was about you and me. You didn't trust me enough to stay.' He dropped her hands. 'I just don't think I can get past this.'

He stepped back and she felt a wave of panic come over her. 'I did love you, Nathan. Really, I did.' Her voice dropped as she realised how painful it must be to hear those words.

He spun back around and glared at her. 'Really? Well,

you replaced me as soon as you got to Australia. With Darius.' He almost spat the words at her.

It was pure frustration and she knew it. 'You decided you trusted him enough to help you through your surgery and treatment. Someone you barely even knew. So don't give me that, Rachel. Don't lie to me. I've had just about as much as I can take.'

He turned on his heel and strode across the beach, never once looking back.

She crumpled to the ground and started to sob. The night was ruined. Everything about this was wrong. She'd always been sure about her decision—so sure that she'd done the right thing. Now, her brain was spinning. Her thoughts were jumbled. For the first time in her life she wondered if she might have been wrong.

It was pathetic. She was pathetic. But all she'd wanted to do was kiss him. So she had. No rational thought behind it. She'd acted purely on selfish instinct.

It was just too hard. It was too hard to be this close to him again and not touch him. In the past when she'd been with Nathan she'd spent most of her time in his arms. He'd completed her. He'd given her confidence when she'd doubted her abilities and strength when she'd struggled with the long hours of being a junior doctor.

She'd loved being with him. She'd loved being part of his family. Her own mother and father had split years before, her father staying in England and her mother settling in Australia. And although they loved her and she loved them, it had been a disjointed kind of upbringing.

When Nathan and Charlie's parents had died it had broken her. She'd wanted to be strong for them both. And she'd managed it right up until she'd found out about her diagnosis.

It had been the final straw.

And all of this was flooding back. For too long she'd kept it in a box—far out of reach, somewhere it couldn't affect her emotions. She couldn't concentrate on what her leaving had done to Nathan and Charlie. She'd been so focused on getting well and getting through her treatment that she hadn't allowed herself space to think about any of this. When her treatment was over, she'd focused on her career, trying to get things back on track after taking a year out.

But she'd never got over the guilt attached to leaving Nathan. She'd never got over the fact she didn't have the guts to say goodbye to Charlie; one tear from him would have been the end of her and she would never have made it onto that plane.

She was lucky. She'd had a good outcome and for that she was so grateful. But it hadn't been guaranteed. The prospect of deteriorating and forcing Nathan and Charlie to be by her side had been unthinkable.

And, even though she had a barrel-load of regrets, if she had her time over she would still get on that plane. She would still walk away to face the cancer on her own.

Except she hadn't really been on her own. She'd had her mum in Australia and then, even though it wasn't what people thought, she'd had Darius too.

It could barely be called a romance. There might have been a few kisses exchanged but it had been entirely different from the relationship she'd had with Nathan. There had never been the passion, the deep underlying attraction. It had almost been like a mutual support society. At times he had been a shoulder to cry on. And during her surgery and renal cancer treatment that was exactly what she'd needed.

Nathan hated her. It didn't matter that he'd kissed her back. Every time he looked at her she could see it in his eyes. If only she could have just five minutes when he looked at her like he'd used to. Just five minutes.

But the world was full of people with 'if only's. It was too late to be one of those. She wasn't here to re-examine her faulty love life. She'd never managed to sustain a decent relationship since the break-up with Nathan. At first she'd had no time or energy for it. No one quite seemed to live up to the man she'd left behind.

But this Nathan was different. He wasn't the same person she'd loved. She could see the changes behind his eyes. In the weathered lines on his face—textured in the eight years she hadn't known him. Who had he loved in that time?

What had she just done? If she'd thought this island was claustrophobic before, she'd just made the situation ten times worse.

She'd been so careful. After her initial exchange of words with Nathan she'd tried to be so cool about things. She understood his resentment. Nathan must hate her.

But it couldn't stop all the feelings he was reviving in her—all the memories. She'd dealt with her renal cancer the best way she felt she could. But it didn't stop her regretting her actions every time she looked at him.

Part of her was resentful too. How would life have turned out if the renal cancer hadn't happened? Would they have come to Australia together and settled here? Would they both have stuck at their chosen specialities? She already knew that Nathan had changed his plans— would that have happened if they'd still been together?

Something coiled inside her. Her life could have been so different.

His life could have been so different.

Their lives could have been so different.

CHAPTER EIGHT

NATHAN WAS PACING. He hated waiting.

The crew were all standing around watching him. Did they know about last night—or was he just being paranoid? Sometimes this island was just far too small.

Rachel. He hadn't had a chance to speak to her since last night and he wasn't quite sure what he wanted to say.

He could still feel the sensation of her lips on his. He could still feel the tremble in his body when she'd run the palm of her hand over his bristled hair. He could still remember the dampness on her cheek…

There was a murmur around him as he saw her approach. His eyes automatically went to the ground. He wanted to have a conversation with Rachel—but not like this. Not when cameras and twenty members of the crew were around them.

He gave a nod to Len, one of the safety instructors for this challenge, and stepped into his harness, pulling on his gloves and fastening his helmet.

Focus. That was what he needed to do right now. The time for conversations was later.

To say the atmosphere was awkward would be putting it mildly.

Neither of them could look at each other. Rachel

hadn't emerged from her room this morning until she'd heard Nathan get up and use the shower and then the cabin front door banging shut.

When the director had told her that she and Nathan were responsible for checking out the safety of the challenge together this morning she'd thought of a hundred and one excuses.

But this was work. Rachel Johnson had her professional pride. And a stubborn streak a mile wide. Part of her felt responsible. *She'd* kissed him last night. She'd been the one to set the wheels in motion. Not Nathan.

Trust. The word was burning in her brain, and it had done for most of the night. The look of hurt in his eyes had been gut-churning.

Up here, on the top edge of the cliff, with the sea winds swirling around her, trust was certainly an issue.

'There is absolutely no way I'm going down there.'

The director sighed. 'You both have to inspect all challenge sites. You can't do that from here.'

Nathan still hadn't made eye contact with her. It was apparent he'd already had this conversation because he was standing with a harness around him, gloves on his hands, receiving special instructions from Len, one of the crew members who would be overseeing their descent.

A boat bobbed on the water at the bottom of the cliff face. It was a *long* way down.

'I can do this myself, Rach, if you'd prefer.'

Nathan's low voice carried on the wind towards her. It sparked fury in her stomach. There was no way she was letting him think she was scared. She wouldn't give him the satisfaction.

She ignored him completely and stalked over to where Len was holding out the harness for her to step into. His safety briefing was thorough. She would be held safely in place; all she had to do was feed the line slowly through the carabiner. She clipped her helmet into place, then swapped her boots for the rock climbing shoes supplied by Len to ensure her grip on the rock face and pulled the gloves on to protect her hands. Lewis had never mentioned *this* in the hard sell of *Celebrity Island*.

It wasn't that she was particularly afraid of heights. She just didn't really want to step off a cliff edge into oblivion and dangle from a piece of rope.

From the corner of her eye she saw Nathan get himself into position and step backwards, easing his way down the cliff face like Spider-Man. Typical.

She turned and faced the cliff edge.

'Not that way,' joked Len as he turned her around so her back was facing the sea.

She gulped. She knew everything she was supposed to be doing. But leaning back, letting the rope take the strain of her weight and stepping into nowhere wasn't really appealing.

Len stood in front of her, talking steadily and smoothly, but the words all seemed to run into one. She'd stopped listening. Right now, she was concentrating on her breathing. Trying to stop the hysterical beat of her heart. How on earth would the celebrities manage this without having a whole bunch of heart attacks?

Len put both hands on her shoulders, edging her back. He stopped for a second and spoke again. She was pretty sure that she must resemble a ghost.

Everyone in the crew was looking at her. Watching to see what her next move would be. It was embarrassing. And it gave her the kick up the backside that she needed.

She leaned back, keeping her eyes firmly on Len as he nodded encouragingly. Her heart was in her mouth.

As she took the step backwards it felt like stepping into mid-air. She was almost over the edge when she felt a hand on her backside. She was already midway. It was too late to stop.

There was only one person who could have their hand there.

Things were in motion now. Her rubber-soled shoes connected with the white cliff as she leaned back and let the rope take her whole weight. After a second, the hand moved. Nathan was right next to her.

'Are you sure about this?'

She glared at him. 'Oh, I've never been more sure.'

The edges of Nathan's mouth turned upwards. If she hadn't been holding onto the rope for dear life she could have cheerfully punched him.

'Do we know which celebs have been picked for the challenge?'

He nodded. 'It's Diamond Dazzle and Fox, the pop star. I guess a boys against girls kind of thing.'

Rachel groaned. 'Did they really get voted for the challenge?'

Nathan shrugged. 'Who knows?'

She took a moment to look around. The view from here across the Coral Sea was nothing short of spectacular. It would be even better if she didn't have a helmet stuck on her head. It gave her a real bird's eye view of the other islands dotted around them. In any other life, this might actually be a place where she could spend some holiday time. Provided, of course, that there was something resembling a hotel with proper beds.

Her descent was slow. Len's instructions had been spot-on and easy to follow.

She frowned. 'What happens with the celebs? Does someone come down alongside them?'

Nathan nodded. 'No way are they being left to come down on their own. Len will be with them every step of the way. One of us will have to be there too. I'm assuming you'll be okay if I do that? If there are any problems I'm right on hand to fix them. You'll be in the boat in case there are any problems at the bottom.'

It was so odd. Hanging from a cliff, having a conversation with someone you'd kissed the night before. Neither of you saying what you should be saying.

She nodded. 'Fine with me.' She didn't even care that the boat was being buffeted by the waves below them. She'd much rather be in the boat than on the cliff.

'Great.' Nathan bounced down the cliff a bit—just bent his knees and jumped back, letting his rope out easily. Anyone would think he'd done this professionally in a past life.

Rachel wouldn't be bouncing anywhere. She eked out her rope slowly, taking tentative corresponding steps down the cliff face. Up above she could see nothing— just her rope. It was currently looking like a strand of thread. Could that really keep holding her?

Nathan, in the meantime, was driving her crazy. He'd bounced, and now he bounded. There were different coloured flags at various points on the cliff face. The celebrities were supposed to race down the cliff later and collect as many as they could. He was moving sideways and checking the little ledges they were positioned on, making sure it was easy to reach each one.

She'd only passed two. Both seemed to mock her on her careful descent. Thank goodness she wasn't doing this against the clock. She would fail miserably.

He bounced next to her and she could hear his heavy breathing. 'If you'd told me a few weeks ago I'd be abseiling down a cliff in the Whitsundays I wouldn't have believed you.'

His movement and voice distracted her, startled her. Her hands faltered as she eased the rope through, her feet coming up against the crumbling part of the cliff face. As the rocks loosened beneath her feet she lost her concentration. For a second she was falling into oblivion.

But it was only for a spilt second before the rope locked into place and she was left dangling in mid-air, scrambling to find her feet again.

She saw something out of the corner of her eye. It was Nathan. He'd moved sideways across the rock face and he was above her in an instant, leaning all the way back, holding his hand out to hers.

'Rach, take my hand!' He looked nervous.

As she dangled from the rope, things moved all around her, disorientating her and making her lose her sense of focus. The only one consistent thing she could see was Nathan's hand.

Her own gripped hard onto her harness. One foot connected roughly with the cliff, only for the rocks to crumble again. Panic was starting to grip her.

'Rachel, take my hand!' he shouted again. She could hear something in his voice. It was echoing the panicked reactions of her own body.

His hand brushed against her hair. He was trying to make a grab for her.

She was spinning now on the rope, her own body weight causing the momentum. If she didn't stop she'd be sick.

After last night, no part of her wanted to touch Nathan Banks again. Not when she knew the reaction it caused to her system. Not when she knew the havoc it caused.

Trust. The word echoed through her head. He'd

accused her of not trusting him enough. At the time, she'd thought the opposite was true. She'd trusted him too much to stay. Too much—because she knew what he would give up for her.

'Rachel!' Now he sounded angry.

Her body acted instantly; it was pure instinct. She thrust out her hand.

There were a few seconds of scramble. Skin touching but not quite grabbing, then his hand closed over hers and he pulled her straight, yanking her towards his body.

It took another few seconds for her head to stop spinning. To gain some equilibrium again.

'Rach, are you okay?' He had her anchored against his hip, his warm breath hitting the side of her cheek.

The rubber soles of her shoes planted against the cliff. Now she'd straightened, the strain of her rope held her harness firmly in place. Her hands moved, going automatically to the carabiner.

Her breath was starting to come a little easier, but her heart was still thudding in her chest. She wasn't quite sure if that was due to the shock of what had just happened or the feel of Nathan's body next to hers.

She glanced down between her legs. It wasn't quite such a long way down now. For the first time, she thought she might actually make it.

'Rachel, are you okay?'

She still hadn't answered. She took a deep breath, securing her hands on the rope and moving sideways to steady herself on the rocks.

Nathan fixed her with his gaze. There was so much they should be saying to each other right now.

But it was almost as if they were still shell-shocked from the night before. And this was hardly the time, or the place.

She nodded. 'I'm fine.' A few seconds later she added, 'Thank you.'

He hadn't moved. He just stayed next to her. His eyes were serious.

'What do you think?'

Her heart thudded again. 'About what?' The sea wind was whipping around them, her hair blowing across her face and her shirt plastered against her body.

'About the challenge?'

The challenge. Of course. Ever the professional, Nathan was thinking about the job.

He wasn't thinking about last night. At least—she didn't think so.

She sucked in her breath. 'I think it was my own fault I slipped. I lost concentration. Part of the cliff is crumbling. But I have to assume that all cliffs are like that.'

This challenge is crazy was what she wanted to say. But she didn't want to seem weak, to seem scared. Especially not in front of Nathan.

He gave a little nod. 'Okay, then. Are you ready to continue down to the boat?'

She looked at the boat bobbing beneath them. The sea seemed quite calm. It almost seemed reachable.

She gave a nod. Nathan knees were bent and he was bouncing on his rope again, ready to make the final part of the journey. She just wished she was.

'Let's go then.'

She watched as he started down, controlling his descent with confidence. She glanced at the rope in her hands. *Slow and steady wins the race.* A distant memory of her father's voice echoed in her head.

I'm not sure I want to win any race against Nathan.

He looked up. 'Come on,' he shouted.

The harness was starting to pinch around her waist

and hips. The tension on her rope was almost as much as the tension between them.

Would it ever be resolved?

'You're going to do the challenge in that?' Rachel couldn't hide the disdain in her voice. Diamond Dazzle was wearing the tiniest white sequin bikini known to man. Hanging from a cliff with cameras underneath? Definitely not family viewing.

But Diamond was too busy climbing into the harness. 'Do I have to wear this?' she whined, wincing as they fastened the clips.

Rachel sighed. 'I'm off down to the quay. I'll see you at the bottom.' But Diamond wasn't listening. She was too busy admiring her reflection in a mirror that one of the production crew had handed her. The celebrities weren't supposed to bring beauty products onto the island with them. But Diamond had a whole beauty counter—and made no secret about it.

Yesterday, she'd spent most of the day 'washing' herself in an equally tiny orange bikini. Rachel could only imagine she'd made most of the red-top front pages this morning. There really wasn't much to do in camp. She only hoped Diamond listened to the safety briefing at the top.

It took ten minutes for the boat to reach the bottom of the cliff face. From here, it looked a long way up— and a long way down.

She was glad Nathan had volunteered to stay at the top. The last thing she wanted to do was abseil again. Being in the boat was bad enough; the currents were a lot stronger than they looked out here.

One of the crew nudged her as Len appeared over

the top of the cliff face. The challenges were normally filmed later in the day, but as this one was on the cliff it was essential it was completed in daylight.

Fox quickly followed. It seemed the pop star was a natural. He appeared comfortable in his holding position at the top of the cliff, gloves and helmet with camera attached in place, waiting to start.

Diamond was a whole other story. After twenty minutes Rachel picked up the radio. 'Nathan?' It crackled loudly. 'Anything I should know about?'

'Give me a sec,' was the sharp reply.

She rolled her eyes at the nearest crew member. 'I guess we wait then.'

After another few minutes, Diamond's perfectly tanned legs and barely clad bottom appeared over the edge of the cliff. 'Look away, guys,' muttered one of the crew members.

It was clear Diamond was making a meal of it. Rachel had no idea what the camera was capturing but she was sure that by tonight, she would be able to watch every second. She did have the tiniest bit of sympathy. Standing at the top of that cliff had terrified her. How was Diamond feeling?

After a few seconds Nathan's voice came over the radio. This time it was low. He let out a sigh. 'To be honest, I'm not happy.'

'What's wrong? Did she have a panic attack?'

'That's just it. She was making a fuss, but it all seemed put-on. She did complain of some abdominal pain earlier but she said that she was due her period and she always has some abdominal pain. I gave her some analgesia.'

Rachel kept her eyes on Diamond's descent. It was very stuttered. Had hers looked like this? Len was right alongside her, obviously giving her instructions and talking her down. In the meantime, Fox had waited gallantly until Diamond was in position and then taken off at a rate of knots, bouncing down the cliff face, gathering flags as he went. The other boat had already moved position ready to pick him up once he reached the water.

It happened so quickly. The tiniest flash of white. Arms waving. Legs flapping, a slight body tumbling, still inside the harness, and a helmet coming into contact with the cliff face.

Len was over to her instantly, talking into his radio. 'Diamond—talk to me. Guys, I might need some assistance. Give me a second.'

'What happened?' Nathan's voice cut across the radio.

'She lost control of the descent, her hands slipped and the autoblock came into play. She lost her foothold on the cliff.'

Rachel was looking up from the bottom, conscious of the fact Nathan couldn't see what she could. She knew exactly how Diamond felt. At least Rachel hadn't hit her head on the cliff.

'Is she conscious, Len?'

Even as she said the words she could hear Diamond's hysterical voice coming through Len's mike. 'I'm dying out here! I feel sick. I'm dizzy. Oh, my stomach, this harness is killing me.'

Len's voice was steady. 'Diamond, stay calm. You're absolutely fine. I'm right beside you. You're quite safe. Your harness will hold you in position. Take some deep breaths.'

'I'm not fine. I'm dangling from a cliff!'

Rachel grimaced. This was going to be a nightmare.

'Len? Do you need some assistance down there?'

She could picture Nathan stepping into his harness already.

Len made a quick assessment. 'I think it would be better if you and I helped Diamond back down the cliff face to the boat.'

Within a few seconds she saw Nathan come over the edge of the cliff and descend easily to Diamond and Len's position. It was clear this challenge was over. Poor Fox. He wouldn't even get his five minutes of glory. Tonight's television would be all about Diamond.

She waited patiently while Diamond continued to have a panic attack dangling in mid-air and flapping her arms and legs between Len and Nathan.

It was difficult to tell if it was all real or all fake. She hated being cynical, she really did.

After a few minutes Nathan spoke. 'There's no head injury, just a few small grazes on her legs and arms. We'll just take things slowly.'

She let out a long breath. They'd already had drama on the first day and then again with Ron. They really didn't need anything else.

The descent was slow. Rachel could hear the whole thing through the radio she had pressed against her ears. Nathan had the patience of a saint. He'd always been like that in doctor mode—calm, rational, reasonable. Even if he wasn't too sure what he was dealing with. How was he feeling about doing this twice in one day?

After a while the crew started to get restless. 'Can someone give me a hand with this?' The cameraman's arms were obviously burning under the strain of constantly trying to focus on the figures on the cliff face while being buffeted around in a boat. Several of the other crew members moved to assist with a lot of general grumbling.

After a painstaking half hour, Nathan, Len and Diamond finally reached the bottom of the cliff and were assisted into the boat. Diamond glanced around her and sank to the bottom of the boat curled in a ball. For a second Rachel wondered if she'd spotted the camera behind her.

Len looked exasperated and he leaned over to release her harness.

'Don't touch me!' she screamed.

Rachel flinched and dropped to her knees. 'Let me loosen your harness.' She didn't wait for agreement, just moved swiftly and unclipped it. Len and Nathan were having a quick discussion.

If Diamond hadn't had Botox it was quite possible her face would be scrunched in a deep frown. Rachel ran her eyes over Diamond's skin. There were no abrasions or redness on her abdomen. It couldn't be the harness that was causing her problems.

She shot Nathan a glance. 'Diamond, would you like to sit up?'

Diamond groaned and clutched her arms around her stomach. 'No. I can't. This is agony.'

The boat was rocking fiercely on the waves as they made their way back to the quay. She placed a hand over Diamond's and saw her flinch. 'When we get onshore I'll take you up to the medical centre and we'll have a look at you.' Her eyes flickered over to Joe, the cameraman. 'And there will be *no* cameras.'

She wasn't quite sure if she said it for her own reassurance or for Diamond's. In any case, she wanted a chance to take a closer look.

The boat pulled in and one of the crew jumped out and ran to get a stretcher. Nathan was biting his lip. She knew he was still suspicious—wondering whether Diamond's pain was genuine or not.

She watched as he walked over and murmured in the cameraman's ear, putting his hand over the front of the camera. The guy nodded and pulled it down from his shoulder.

It only took a few minutes to get Diamond onto the stretcher and up to the medical cabin. It was probably the biggest strength of the production crew—they never hesitated to assist.

Rachel helped Diamond over onto the examination trolley and waited until everyone had left the room and Nathan had closed the door.

She switched on the angle lamp. It gave a much better view of Diamond's colour, which was distinctly pale. She quickly fastened a BP cuff around her arm and pressed the button to start the reading, then walked to the sink to wash her hands.

Nathan gave her a little nod. He was obviously happy to let her take the lead on this, which was a little strange—given that he was the emergency doctor.

She waited a few seconds for the reading. It was a little below average but not worryingly so. 'Diamond, I'm going to put my hands on your stomach. Is that okay?'

The model's eyes widened. 'Do you have to?'

She nodded. 'Nathan told me earlier today you complained of period pain. Is that normal for you?'

Diamond nodded. 'I always get it. Just cramps—and that's what it was like this morning. But this is much worse. The painkillers haven't touched it.'

'Any other symptoms? Have you been going to the toilet frequently?'

Diamond wrinkled her nose. 'Maybe.'

'What about your bowels? Are they moving normally?'

'*Eeoow.* Don't ask about things like that.'

Rachel smiled. 'I have to. It's part of being a doctor.'

Diamond winced again. 'No problems then.'

She flinched as Rachel gently laid her hands on her stomach.

'Can you tell me where the worst of the pain is? In your front or around your back?' She pressed very gently. Diamond seemed to wince at every movement, then she pulled her knees up quickly.

'*Yaoow!* It's definitely worse on that side.'

Rachel lifted her hands. 'Have you been eating? Feeling sick, nauseous?'

'I've felt sick most of the day. But I haven't actually been sick.'

Rachel bit her lip. Diamond's pain was on the opposite side from her appendix. 'Do you think you could give me a urine sample? I'd like to dipstick it for any sign of infection.'

Diamond groaned. 'You want me to get up?'

Rachel nodded. 'We don't exactly have a lot of equipment here. I'll help you to the bathroom. It's only a few steps.'

She gently swung Diamond's legs to the edge of the trolley and helped her limp over to the bathroom, handing her a collection bottle.

Rachel and Nathan waited outside the door. He glanced at her, mouthing the words, 'What do you think? UTI or ectopic?'

She lifted her shoulders. 'Could be either.'

After a few minutes Diamond opened the door and handed her specimen container over with shaky hands.

'Your colour's not too good. Let me help you back over.' Nathan didn't wait. He picked her up in his arms and carried her over to the trolley.

Rachel took the specimen over to the countertop and dipsticked it with a multistick for blood and protein, and dropped some onto a pregnancy test. It would take at least a minute until it showed.

She took a few steps nearer Diamond. 'I know that you said your period is due, but can you tell me how long it is since your last one?'

Diamond screwed up her face, her arms still across her belly. 'I'm not that regular. Probably around six weeks. I always get cramp—but not usually as bad as this. I feel as if it could come any minute.'

Nathan wound the BP cuff back around her arm. 'I'm just going to check this again.' He pressed the button. 'This will get quite tight.'

Rachel glanced over towards the tests on the bench. A positive pregnancy test and some blood in her urine. She swallowed. 'Diamond, is there any chance you could be pregnant?'

Diamond's eyes opened quickly. It was almost as if she were trying to rationalise the possibility.

Rachel reached for her hand. 'I don't think the pain you're experiencing is normal period pain. I think it's something else.'

Nathan moved closer. 'Diamond, we don't have all the facilities here that we need.' His voice was sympathetic. 'Your urine shows a positive pregnancy test, but it also had some blood in it—even though you might not have noticed. Your blood pressure is on the low side and with the pain you have in your side—it could be that you're having an ectopic pregnancy.'

Diamond looked stunned. She started shaking her head. 'I can't be pregnant. I can't be.'

Rachel squeezed her hand. 'Have you had unprotected sex in the last six weeks?'

Her pale cheeks flushed. 'Well…yes.'

'Have you had any bleeding at all?'

She glanced between Rachel and Nathan. 'I had a tiny bit of spotting yesterday. I just thought my period was starting.'

Nathan nodded. 'Do you know much about ectopic pregnancy, Diamond?'

She shook her head quickly. 'Nothing.' There was something about Diamond's wide-eyed reaction that made him slow down.

He glanced towards Rachel. He was surprising her—which was ridiculous, as Nathan had always been a compassionate doctor. The truth was they'd both had doubts about Diamond's symptoms.

He spoke slowly. It was obvious he was trying to make things as clear as possible, whilst he knew he was dealing with a highly sensitive issue.

'In an ectopic pregnancy the embryo doesn't implant and grow in the womb as it should. It gets stuck somewhere along the fallopian tube and the embryo starts to grow there. That would be why you're having pain. There isn't room for the embryo to grow.'

She looked scared. 'So what happens now?'

He spoke carefully. 'In an ideal world, we'd do an ultrasound to confirm our diagnosis. But we don't have ultrasound equipment here, so we just need to go on your symptoms and the fact you've had a positive pregnancy test. We class this as an emergency. Your fallopian tube can rupture and cause internal bleeding. Because of that, we'll arrange a medevac to take you off the island and to a hospital on the mainland where it's likely you'll need to go for surgery.'

'I need to leave the show?'

It wasn't the response Rachel was expecting to hear. But Diamond just looked stunned.

'You definitely need to leave the show.'

She nodded. 'Okay. Can someone phone my agent?'

Rachel and Nathan exchanged glances. Diamond seemed to have switched into professional mode.

Rachel walked over and took her hand. 'No problem. Nathan will get someone to do that.' He gave a quick nod. Rachel walked over to the medicine cabinet and quickly drew up some analgesia. 'I'm going to give you something for the pain meantime'

Rachel leaned forward and kept talking as she administered the injection, 'This is an emergency, Diamond. I don't want to scare you, but if your fallopian tube ruptures it will cause more pain and the bleeding can be serious. You need to be in a place that can deal with that kind of emergency.' She held out her hands and looked around. 'And that's certainly not here.'

Nathan nodded in agreement. 'We don't have any medication that we can give you here to try and stop the embryo growing. You have to go to a specialist hospital.'

Diamond winced as she tried to sit up. Her eyes widened and she fixed them on Rachel. 'I'm pregnant? I'm really pregnant?' The look of disbelief on her face was obvious. It seemed things were just starting to sink in.

Rachel walked back over to Diamond and started the BP monitor again. Diamond looked completely shocked.

'I'm pregnant?' she asked again.

Rachel chose her words carefully. If a pregnancy was ectopic there was no hope for the growing embryo. Diamond's reactions earlier had been odd—almost as if she wasn't taking in what they'd been saying to her. Maybe the truth was just hitting her now.

Nathan appeared at the other side of the trolley. It was as if he sensed how she might react.

Something squeezed inside Rachel. This was a horrible experience for any woman. She'd never been in this position. Chances were, after the treatment she'd received for her renal cancer, she might never be in the position to be pregnant.

Although they'd been junior doctors, she and Nathan had never been afraid to talk about the future. They'd been so sure that their future would be together. They'd talked about eventually getting married and having children together, Nathan as a surgeon and Rachel probably working as a GP at that point. Looking back, it had been a strange conversation for two young, ambitious, career-orientated people to have. But both had loved the idea of having a family together. As doctors, they both knew they would need support with their children. Nathan had been adamant that he, as well as Rachel, should only work four days a week. That way, both would have a day at home with the kids, with Nathan's parents or Rachel's dad helping on the other days.

She flinched. More hopes and dreams that had disappeared in the blink of an eye. Destroyed by a car crash and a cancer diagnosis.

Had she really taken on board how big an impact these things had had on both their lives?

She lifted her head. Nathan's gaze interlocked with hers, his green eyes holding her steady. She swallowed. There was pain etched on his face. It was almost as if all the same thoughts were going through his head. Did he remember the conversations they used to have about family?

Rachel took a deep breath and turned her attention back to her patient. 'You had a positive pregnancy test and the symptoms you're showing suggest you have an ectopic pregnancy. Nathan explained earlier that the embryo is growing in your fallopian tube instead of in your womb. That's why you're in so much pain.' She squeezed Diamond's hand. 'I'm really sorry, Diamond. But what this means is that this pregnancy isn't viable. This pregnancy could never result in a baby for you.'

She hated saying those words out loud because she already knew the impact it would have on their patient.

Diamond shook her head as a tear slid down her cheek. 'But I always thought I couldn't get pregnant.'

'Why did you think that?' Nathan's voice cut in before Rachel had a chance to reply.

'They told me my tubes were scarred. They told me if I ever wanted to get pregnant I'd probably need to use IVF.' She was shaking her head in disbelief.

Scarred tubes—exactly the kind of place an embryo could implant. It made the diagnosis of ectopic pregnancy even more likely.

Nathan checked her BP reading. Low, but steady. 'You saw an ob-gyn?'

Diamond's face flushed a little. 'I had an infection a few years ago. She did some follow-up tests.'

He'd read her medical notes; this hadn't been in them. She clearly wanted to keep it secret.

He nodded sympathetically. 'It makes the chances of this being an ectopic pregnancy even more likely, but we can't tell you for sure. They'll need to scan you once you reach the mainland. How is your pain? Is it any better since Rachel gave you the injection?'

Diamond gave a little nod just as there was a knock at the door. 'Five minutes, docs,' came the shout.

Rachel still wasn't entirely sure about Diamond. 'How do you feel about transferring in the medevac?'

There was no getting away from it. The medevac could be terrifying. The noise and buffeting from the air currents could make it a bumpy trip. Rachel wasn't certain that she'd like to be the one going.

Diamond nodded slowly. 'I really can't come back?' Her voice was quiet, almost whispered.

'Absolutely not.' Nathan didn't hesitate. 'You need to be in a place where you can be taken care of and get the support that you need. The island isn't the place for that.'

Her eyes were downcast and Rachel wondered if the true nature of what had happened was now sinking in. 'Is there someone you'd like me to phone for you?' She wasn't sure if Diamond had a partner or a boyfriend. She didn't really keep track of celebrity relationships. Being in the spotlight herself for a few months had been bad enough. Whether the pregnancy had been planned or not, losing a baby could be a big shock to any couple.

Diamond shook her head. The tears were flowing freely now. 'I think that's a phone call I need to make myself.' Her voice was shaking now and Rachel could feel tears springing to her own eyes.

Nathan walked over and put his arm around Diamond's shoulders. 'I'm really sorry, Diamond. I'm really sorry about your baby and I'm really sorry it happened here.' He glanced at Rachel. 'We're going to give you something else for the flight. It can be a little bumpy and I want to make sure your pain is under control and you're as relaxed as possible.'

He walked over and unlocked the medicine cupboard, taking out another vial and turning it for Rachel to double-check. She nodded as she dialled the number and spoke urgently into the phone, giving the medevac all the details they would need.

Nathan administered the medicine quickly.

Rachel nodded as she left the cabin. 'I'll get the crew to prepare for the medevac and I'll let the producer know what is happening.'

Thank goodness they were out of earshot because Phil, one of the producers, nearly blew a gasket when she told him she'd arranged a medevac for Diamond.

'What? You've got to be joking. We need her for the viewing figures. This will affect our ratings.'

'And if she doesn't get appropriate treatment this could affect her life,' she said sharply. She was getting tired of this—tired of how some people didn't seem to care about the actual individuals—just the figures.

In fact, she was getting tired of everything. Tired of being trapped on an island with Nathan. Tired of the way they tiptoed around each other constantly. Tired of her conflicting emotions around him. And the fact that on an island like this there was no privacy, no escape.

Next time she saw Lewis Blake she was going to kill him with her bare hands. It didn't matter what the salary was here—he'd got more than his money's worth.

By the time she'd finished with Phil, she received a message to say the medevac had arrived. The crew, as always, were only too happy to assist.

As they headed down to the beach the downdraught from the helicopter swooshed around them and Diamond started to shake. Nathan kept his arm around her the whole time. It only took five minutes to do the handover and get her loaded on board. The paramedic winked at them both. It was the same guy who'd picked up Jack. 'This is getting to be a habit. Here's hoping I don't hear from you two again.'

Nathan pulled the door closed and retreated to the trees, watching the helicopter take off before heading back to the cabin. They could hear Phil somewhere in the complex, shouting at the top of his voice.

Nathan gave Rachel an ironic smile. 'So much for working twelve hours in three weeks.'

Her eyebrows lifted. 'Lewis used that line on you too?'

'Oh, yes.'

Their smiles locked for a few seconds. She felt the buzz. It was hanging in the air between them. Familiar. Sparking lots of warm, passionate memories.

Something washed over her. More than regret. More than sadness. The awareness of what might have been. The loss of the life they could have had together.

She couldn't help it. It brought instant tears to her eyes. Nathan had been her soulmate, the person she'd thought she would grow old with.

And in two fell swoops everything had changed.

A driver's momentary distraction on a country road, and the view of cancer cells under the microscope.

Where would they have been in the life they should have lived? Married? Probably. With children? She certainly hoped so. It didn't matter that this parallel universe didn't exist. It didn't matter that this was all a figment of her imagination.

At times, during her treatment, it had been the only thing that had kept her going. Imagining that Nathan had built a new life for himself, met someone else and moved on had been just too much for her. It didn't matter that she'd told herself that was what she wanted for him. A long lifetime of happiness.

Her own heart told her differently.

'Rachel?' His voice was quiet and he stepped closer to her. 'Are you okay?'

He must have noticed the tears glistening in her eyes. It would be so easy to make an excuse—to say it was the sand thrown up by the helicopter blades, to say it was the sea breeze in her eyes. But she didn't want to. She didn't want to tell lies. She was so tired of it all. Keeping her guard up continually around Nathan was wearing her down.

She fixed on his neon green eyes. She'd always loved looking into Nathan's eyes. She'd spent the last week virtually avoiding them, skirting past them whenever she could for fear of the memories they might stir up.

'No,' was all she replied.

He blinked and waited a few seconds, his gaze never wavering from hers. 'Me neither.' His words were low. So low she wondered if she'd even heard them.

He reached over and touched her arm. She froze, her breath stuck in her throat.

'Rachel, do you want to have dinner tonight—just you and me?'

She nodded.

He didn't smile. 'We both have a few things to do. And we can't talk in the canteen. I'll meet you back here at seven and arrange some food for us.'

The filming for the day was already done. By seven the sun would almost be setting and the beach should be quieter.

'Sounds fine. I'll see you then.' She turned and walked away, her heart thudding in her chest.

Dinner.

It sounded so simple. But it wouldn't just be dinner. They both knew that. It would be so much more. It was time to put the past to rest.

CHAPTER NINE

NATHAN LOOKED DOWN at the hamper one of the chefs had given him. It should be perfect. It was packed with all the kind of foods that he enjoyed—and the ones that he remembered Rachel liked.

Stuffed in next to the food were two bottles of wine and a couple of glasses nabbed from behind the bar.

Would he even be able to eat anything? His stomach turned over. There was no doubt the attraction between him and Rachel was still there. The attraction had never been in doubt. It was the history that was the problem.

He couldn't act on his instincts around her. Every time he looked at her he felt his self-protection barriers fall into place. Guys didn't admit to being hurt. Guys didn't admit to being broken-hearted.

But he'd felt both when Rachel had left.

Eight years on, he hadn't moved past that and it was crippling him. He hadn't really formed a proper relationship since then. Initially he'd been too busy watching out for Charlie, then he'd been too busy working.

For the last five years he'd been trying to save the world. He hadn't been able to save his parents—they'd been left trapped in their twisted car for the best part of an hour before anyone had found them. By then, both of them had been unconscious. His mother had never made it to the hospital. His father had barely survived the journey and had died before Nathan was notified about the accident. At least with Doctors Without Borders he knew his work counted. He knew he could look back on the lives he'd saved—the difference he'd made. And in a tiny way it had helped patch his heart back together.

But recognition was dawning slowly—he'd spent so much time trying to save other people and not enough time trying to save himself.

Seeing Rachel had brought everything to the forefront again. There were things—feelings—that he couldn't deny. At some point in his life he was going to have to move on. He'd just never expected that moving on with Rachel might even be a remote possibility. He still wasn't entirely sure it was. But tonight it was time to find out.

All he felt right this minute was hideous guilt. Rachel had told him she'd had renal cancer. And, instead of asking her all the questions he should have, he'd been so overcome with anger that he'd forgotten all the important stuff. He'd forgotten to ask her all the medical questions that had been spinning around in his brain ever since. Her treatment—and the outcome. The future. What kind of guy was he? What kind of friend was he?

He hated this. He hated all of this.

He walked down to the beach. There were a few people around, chatting and talking at the bar.

He didn't want to join in. He was already too wound up. Chances were, they'd meet and be fighting within five minutes. But fighting wasn't what he wanted to do with Rachel.

His fingers were itching to touch her. He wanted to run them through her shiny hair; he wanted to stroke them across her perfect skin. He wanted to touch the place where she had that scar. He wanted to kiss it.

He wanted to let her know that the renal cancer didn't change how he felt about her. Wouldn't *ever* change how he felt about her. More than anything, he wanted her lips to surrender to his. It was bad enough his dreams at night were haunted by her. He'd started to daydream about her too.

He couldn't go on like this. He couldn't function. Things just had to come to a head. Who knew where it would lead?

But the electricity in the air between them could light up this whole island. It was time to find out if she agreed.

Rachel stared in the mirror. She'd showered and her hair was washed and dried. She'd put on some bronzer, mascara and lipstick. She should be ready. She *could* be ready. If only she could decide what to wear.

Maybe it was delaying tactics. Maybe it was because her stomach was churning and she wondered if the nerves could make her sick. Or maybe it was because, deep down, she wanted to look perfect for Nathan.

Her rucksack was upended on the bed. Three pink sundresses, four pink shirts and three T-shirts all seemed to mock her. Nothing was right. Nothing *felt* right. And she wasn't sure why it was so important.

She rummaged around the bottom of the rucksack to see if she'd missed anything. Her hand slithered over some material and she pulled it out. A pink sequin bikini. She'd thrown it back inside as soon as she'd realised Nathan was here—her scar would have raised too many questions she didn't want to answer.

But now Nathan knew. Now, there was nothing to hide.

Except how he felt about what she'd done. Except the whole reality of her non-relationship with Darius. It was time to come clean about that. It was time to clear the air between them. Could that even be done?

Her stomach twisted. She was going to a beach. The night air was still warm. There were lots of reasons why her bikini was the perfect outfit.

Her black sheer kaftan with silver embroidery was hanging on the other side of the room. She walked over and grabbed it.

More than anything, she wanted Nathan to stop looking at her the way he did. With recriminations. With an undercurrent of anger. She wanted Nathan to look at her the way he'd used to. With love. With passion—even devotion. Just the way she'd looked at him too.

She'd almost seen it the other night before she'd ruined everything by telling him about the renal cancer. Maybe that was all he wanted to do tonight—ask her more questions about the cancer. Maybe she was getting herself all worked up over an attraction that wasn't even there.

She glanced at her watch—it was after seven. Nathan would be wondering where she was. She pulled on the bikini and kaftan before she changed her mind and slipped her feet into some sandals. There was no need for anything else. There was no time to think about anything else.

Her initial quick steps slowed as she reached the beach. She was nervous. After eight years, the thought of spending time alone with Nathan made her stomach flip over. In good ways and in bad.

Part of her couldn't wait for this to start and part of her couldn't wait for this to be over. She wanted to be with Nathan. She wanted to spend time in his company. She wanted to get past the bitterness, past the recriminations. She wanted to find out how Nathan really was.

How he'd spent the last eight years and, most importantly, if anyone had touched his heart. She wanted to acknowledge the buzz between them, the attraction. She wanted to know if she could trust her instincts and that, no matter what had happened between them, he wanted to act on them as much as she did.

Nothing in her head was certain right now.

She walked down the path. To her right, several members of the crew were at the bar, laughing and joking together. To her left were the sun loungers. All were empty except one. Nathan was sitting staring at the ocean with a basket at his feet.

The corners of his lips turned upwards as she walked towards him. He was so handsome when he smiled. It made her skin tingle and her heart melt—it was a pity he didn't do it more often. He didn't even hide the fact he was looking at her bare legs. He was dressed casually too, in shorts and a T-shirt. If he was surprised at her lack of clothes he didn't mention it. He just continued with the appreciative looks. It made her whole body shiver with anticipation.

He stood up as she approached and lifted the basket. Her stomach flip-flopped. She was even more nervous than she'd expected.

He gave a little nod. 'Let's get away from everyone. There's another beach just around the corner, set in a cove of its own.'

Let's get away from everyone. He had no idea what those words were doing to her heart rate and her adrenalin levels.

'Really? I had no idea.' She was trying so hard to appear casual but her smile had spread from ear to ear. Why hide it?

He grinned and raised his eyebrows. 'Neither did I.

Len told me when he caught me raiding the bar.' He picked up a blanket from the lounger and took a few steps down the beach.

'What did you get from the bar?'

'Some wine. Rosé.' His footsteps hesitated. 'It's still your favourite, isn't it?'

Even her insides were smiling now. He'd remembered. He'd remembered her favourite drink.

'Yes. It's still my favourite,' she said quietly.

'Good.'

There was a gentle breeze as they walked along the beach together. The orange sunset reflected across the undulating waves and the muted burnished rays across the water gave a remarkable sense of calm. As they walked, behind them, in amongst the trees, the insect life was rustling and chirping.

But the beach was quiet, the only noise the rippling waves on the sand.

As the voices behind them drifted further and further away Rachel felt herself relax a little. The lights from the bar area faded and as they rounded the bay towards the other beach the only light was the orange setting sun.

Nathan shook out the blanket and set it down on the sand. She hesitated as he opened the basket and took out the wine and some glasses. 'Aren't you going to sit?' he asked as he unscrewed the bottle.

How close should she sit? The blanket wasn't too big and as she lowered herself down her bare legs brushed against his.

It was like an electric jolt and his head lifted sharply, their gazes meshing. He handed her a glass without saying a word. Something fired inside her. All of a sudden this felt immediate. She didn't want to wait. She didn't want to think about this any longer. Words could get in the way of what she really wanted to do. She glanced over her shoulder. They were definitely alone and undisturbed.

When she reached for the glass she was slow, deliberate. Her fingers brushed over his.

His gaze was fixed on hers. It was almost as if he couldn't tear it away. Almost as if this was the moment they had been waiting for.

'How are you, Rachel?' he asked. She felt as if something had blown away in the gentle breeze. It was almost as if they hadn't seen each other before this. There was no guilt or recrimination. This was a new start.

It was time for complete honesty. 'Pretty rubbish,' she whispered.

This was it. This was where the doors were finally opened. This was the point of no return.

Nathan reached his hand over and touched hers. She didn't flinch. She didn't pull it away. 'Let me start,' he said slowly. 'I have to apologise.'

'What for?'

He took a deep breath. 'I didn't even ask you.' He fixed his eyes on the horizon. He couldn't even look at her right now. He was still angry with himself for not asking the questions he should have.

'Ask me what?'

He ran his hand over his short hair. 'What stage cancer you had—what treatment you had. You never even told me how you discovered it.' He shook his head. 'I should have asked—I'm sorry. When you told me that night I was shocked. I just needed a bit of space to get my head around it.'

She bit her lip. He could tell she didn't really know where to start.

'I was tired.' It seemed the simplest explanation and, as a medic, he knew it was probably the truest. 'My symptoms were mild. Fatigue, a bit of weight loss, just generally feeling unwell. I couldn't sleep very well—and that was even before your parents' accident. So I couldn't put it down to that. I had a few unexplained temperatures. Then, one day, I dipsticked my urine in the ward. Once I realised I had blood in it and not a simple infection I started to piece everything together.' She shook her head. 'I didn't like what I found. But my appointment for investigation came just a few weeks after the funeral. We'd had too much else to deal with—too much else to think about and I almost never went.'

His stomach turned over. Was he ready for this? Was he ready to hear that she'd been so worried about him she hadn't been thinking about herself? 'What stage were you at?'

She took a sip of wine. 'I had stage three. The tumour was bigger than seven centimetres and had spread through the outer covering of the kidney to the adrenal gland. I needed a total nephrectomy and some radiotherapy and chemotherapy.'

He nodded his head slowly while his insides cringed, twisting and turning at the thought of cancer invading the body of someone he loved. He knew exactly how serious her cancer had been and how invasive the treatment would have been. Every doctor knew about the staging of cancers.

He put his head in his hands. What if she'd ignored it? What if she'd been so busy with him and Charlie that her renal cancer had got even worse? The thought made him feel sick to his stomach.

He waited a few seconds then spoke, his voice steady.

'Would you have told me? If my parents hadn't died—would you have told me then?'

He heard her suck in a breath. She took a few seconds to answer the question. 'Of course I would, Nathan.'

He squeezed his eyes shut. He was trying not to be frustrated but the truth was he wanted to scream and shout. He shook his head. After a few seconds some strangulated words came from his throat. 'Everything—everything changed. When my parents died, everything I'd planned just changed in an instant.'

He turned to face her, still shaking his head. He couldn't contain anything that was inside any more. Eight years' worth of grief and frustration came bubbling to the surface. 'You. You left. You wouldn't have if my parents had been alive. You would have told me you were ill. I could have supported you. If they'd still been there I wouldn't have changed my speciality—I wouldn't have needed to; Charlie would have been fine. I could still have been a surgeon.' His fists were clenched and his jaw tight. 'I mean, what's the point?' It was as if now the words had started he just couldn't stop. 'What's the point of being a doctor if you can't save the people that you love? One second—one second on one road on one night—changed everything about my life. I lost you. I lost my career. I lost them.'

He'd never felt so angry. Eight years ago he'd never been prone to temper flares or angry outbursts. Even when his parents had died he'd been quiet, obviously upset, but subdued. She shrank back a little.

He stood up and started pacing. 'They were trapped in their car for an hour. If they'd had medical assistance they might have lived. Where were we that night? We were at the cinema. What if I'd been with them in the car? What if I could have helped?'

She stood up and stepped in front of him. 'What if you'd been killed too? I hate to say it, Nathan, but the car was crumpled. If you'd been in the back you wouldn't have stood a chance. Charlie would have lost you all.' Her anxious voice quietened. 'I would have lost you all.'

He responded immediately, his bright green eyes locking with hers, the anger dissipating from his voice. This time it was quiet. 'But you lost us all anyway, Rachel. Or we lost you.'

The two of them stood in silence and looked at each other. She could see every weathered line on his face. She understood now. She understood his complete frustration. That was why he'd stayed with Doctors Without Borders. Nathan was all about saving people. He hadn't been able to save the people he'd loved the most—so he tried to make up for it by saving others. And she felt as if she'd compounded it all by walking away when she was ill.

And he was still handsome. He would still turn any woman's head. But he was worn out. He'd reached the end of his emotional tether.

Something curled inside her. What if she hadn't left? What if she'd told him about her renal cancer and stayed with him? How would Nathan have reacted if he hadn't been able to save her either?

She'd spent most of last night tossing and turning, wondering if she'd done the wrong thing. Maybe she should have told Nathan? Maybe she should have stayed to help out with Charlie? It was so easy to have regrets now. She'd lived. She was a cancer survivor and had come out the other side. Because she had the gift of life again, she could easily spend the rest of her time asking *What if?*

But eight years ago she hadn't known that. She hadn't been able to take that chance. Would her treatment in the UK have been as successful as her treatment in Australia? She would never know that.

Even though she'd only been there for a little while, she'd hoped she'd helped Nathan and Charlie deal with their parents' death. Now, she was beginning to realise just how wrong she'd been. None of it was over for Nathan. He'd spent the last eight years consumed by guilt because he hadn't been able to save the people he loved.

He'd spent the last eight years trying to save everyone else.

A horrible feeling crept over her. Just how broken would Nathan have been if he couldn't have saved her either? She shifted uncomfortably and swallowed. She reached for his hand, giving it a little squeeze. She was full of regrets—full of emotion she couldn't even begin to fathom. 'We lost each other,' she said sadly.

Her breath came out in a little shudder. She needed to step away from Nathan again. It didn't matter that he looked muscular and strong. Now, she was realising that, with her strong and smart Nathan, appearances were deceptive.

A wave of fear came over her. In the back of her mind she'd had the tiniest flicker of hope. Hope that something could rekindle between them. Hope that she could feel a little of the magic she'd felt before with Nathan. It could be so perfect if she could just capture that again.

But her insides were turning over. She felt sick. All of a sudden she could see how damaged and worn down the guy she loved had become. With every tiny line and crease on his face she could see his pain, see how much he'd tried to patch himself back together. And in a way she'd contributed to all this.

Five years. She'd passed the golden five-year point for being cancer-free. But somehow it would always hang over her head. There would always be the possibility, however remote, that it could come back. What if she formed a relationship with Nathan again and had a recurrence?

It had always been in the back of her mind. But she'd tried to be so positive, tried to be so focused on recovery that she hadn't allowed any room in her mind for those kind of thoughts.

But as she stood in front of Nathan now she felt herself unravelling. She wasn't just going to have to walk away from Nathan once; she was going to have to do it twice.

What if, for one minute, he was the person she loved— the way that she had always loved Nathan? The way that he might still love her?

She couldn't do it. She hadn't been able to do it before. And she couldn't do it now.

She couldn't take the tiniest chance that her cancer might return and she could destroy the man she loved.

Before, she hadn't been afraid. She'd been on her own. Any future relationship that might develop would be based on the foundation that she was a cancer survivor.

Now, standing in front of Nathan, she was terrified.

She wanted to love him. She wanted to hold him. She wanted his big strong arms wrapped around her with the feel of his skin next to hers. She wanted to run the palms of her hands over his short hair. She wanted to feel his breath on her neck, the beating of his heart against her own.

But the realisation of how he'd suffered over the last few years was too hard. He'd spent the last five years trying to save the world. It couldn't be done. It could never be done. But it seemed, for Nathan, that was the only thing that healed him. His only redemption.

She reached out and touched his face, letting her fingertips come into contact with his cheek. 'I had no idea,' she whispered. 'I had no idea that's how you felt.' She spoke softly. 'Your parents had a horrible, hideous accident. There was nothing you could have done, Nathan. There was nothing anyone could have done.' Her fingers moved gently down his cheek. 'I'm so sorry I couldn't stay to help you work through this.' Her voice was shaking now. 'But look at the work you've done. Look at the lives you've saved, Nathan.' She gave her head a shake as tears sprang to her eyes. 'It's a horrible thing to say, but if your parents hadn't died—if I hadn't had the cancer diagnosis—things would have been different. We both know that. But who would have saved those lives, Nathan? Who would have made a difference to the kids you've helped through Doctors Without Borders?' As the tears slid down her cheeks she let herself smile. 'Maybe you've saved the next Louis Pasteur or Edward Jenner? Maybe, if you hadn't been there, they wouldn't have been saved?'

She pulled her hand back. It was too tempting. It was too tempting just to step forward and wrap her arms around his neck. To turn her lips towards his.

But she couldn't. She couldn't dare risk that.

He was shaking his head, his green eyes fixed on her. As she breathed he licked his lips and his pupils dilated a little.

She took a tiny step back. 'I have no idea about fate, Nathan. But I have to believe that things happen for a reason. Otherwise, I would be lost in the fact that too many good people are taken much too soon. I have to believe that you went to the places you were supposed to, and saved the people that you should.'

He looked so confused. It was almost as if a little scattering of lights had switched on behind his eyes. He was finally starting to realise how he'd been living. 'But what about you? What about us? What did we do that meant we had to be apart?'

She could almost feel a fist inside her chest grip her heart and squeeze it tight. 'I don't know,' she whispered. Her feet edged back further.

She could so easily slip. She could so easily tell him how she'd never stopped loving him and wanted to try again. She could so easily tell him that she'd thought about him every day for the last eight years.

But now the cancer seemed like a black cloud above her. If Nathan loved and lost her again, what would that do to him?

It was best to keep things platonic. No matter what her brain and body said about that. She could almost feel the little portcullis slide down in her brain—cutting off her emotions from the rest of her. It took her to a safe place and stopped her from thinking about the things that could break her heart.

She straightened her back and wiped a tear from her cheek.

'What happened when you got to Australia?' he asked. 'What happened with you and Darius?'

Her head dropped. He hadn't put the pieces together yet. He would at some point. But she'd passed the point of keeping secrets from Nathan.

She could trust him. She knew that now beyond a shadow of a doubt. This wasn't about her and Darius. This had never been about her and Darius.

'Ask me how I met him,' she said steadily.

Nathan moved. He set his glass down on the sand and held his hand out towards her. She put her palm in his, letting herself revel in the delicious sensations tingling up towards her shoulder. Her glass was still in her hand as she stepped forward, pressing the whole of her body up against his and wrapping her arm holding the glass around the back of his neck. His hands settled on her hips. The tension in the air between them was palpable.

It was as if they'd waited eight years to have this conversation. It was as if they'd waited eight years to finally be in this place, at this time.

'Rach, how did you meet him?' There was the tiniest tremor in his voice.

The tears flowed. 'I met Darius at the cancer treatment centre,' she whispered.

He froze, his fingers tightening around her waist. For a few seconds their eyes were just locked together in the darkening light. She could see everything on his face. The realisation. The acknowledgement. The recognition.

She could read everything he was thinking—the secrets, the paper-thin medical file.

'Is Darius well? Should he even be here?'

It was the doctor in him. He'd gone from seeing Darius as a rival to seeing him as a patient.

'He had non-Hodgkin's lymphoma. He's relapsed twice over the last few years. As far as I know, he's well right now.'

She could sense him start to relax a little. She licked her lips. 'Darius was never really my boyfriend. We leaned on each other while we were undergoing treatment. I was his sounding board. I knew how to keep a secret. I've never betrayed his trust. That's why he wanted me here. That's the only reason he wanted me here.'

He nodded and reached up, brushing the tears from

one cheek, then the other. He didn't ask her any questions. He seemed to instantly respect her explanation.

His anger towards Darius seemed to disappear in the sea winds. It was easy now he knew why she'd been keeping secrets from him. Now, it seemed his only focus was on her.

'Rachel?' he whispered. His fingers ran up her arm to her shoulder and he cradled her cheek in the palm of his hand. 'What next?'

Her blood was warming every part of her skin. This was exactly what she remembered. Exactly what she'd dreamed of. She remembered every part of him. His muscles had changed slightly; they were a bit more defined and a bit more angular. But her body still melded against his the way it always had done. They fitted together. That was how it was with a soulmate. That was the way it was supposed to be.

No one had ever felt as perfect next to her.

She let out a little sob as his hands brushed over her skin. She'd waited for this moment for eight years. She'd spent days and nights dreaming about this.

Dreaming about the moment she would be in Nathan's arms again and she could act on instinct.

He knew now. He knew everything. And although he'd initially been angry, now he had the full picture it seemed he felt exactly the same way she did. They might have been separated by continents, years, accidents and disease but their spark had never died. Their attraction had never died.

His hands were busy, reacquainting themselves with her body. It was like butterflies dancing on her skin. 'This could get wet,' he whispered as her hand slipped and a splash of wine landed on his shoulder. She laughed

and stepped back, unwinding her arm and finishing what
was left of the wine.

The sea was dark, with a few burnished orange beams
from the setting sun scattering across it. This time of
night it would be cold. But her skin was so heated she
didn't care.

All she felt right now was relief. Relief that she could
finally reconnect with the man she'd always wanted.

'Fancy getting completely wet?' she taunted. She set
the wine glass down on the sand and held out her hand
towards him as his eyes widened.

He didn't hesitate; he put his hand in hers and pulled
her towards the water. Nathan wasn't shy. His T-shirt
was pulled over his head in seconds and his shorts
dropped on the beach. Rachel didn't need to do that.
Her bikini was in place and she left the sheer kaftan
covering her hips.

The water chilled her thighs as they strode out into
the dark sea. Once they'd reached waist height Nathan
turned around and grabbed her. She didn't wait for a
second. Talking wasn't what she wanted to do right
now.

The chilled water hadn't stilled the thudding of her
heartbeat. As Nathan's hands pulled her closer the
buoyancy of the water let her wrap her legs around
his waist.

His lips came into contact with hers. It was what she'd
been waiting for. Since they'd kissed yesterday. Since
she'd walked away eight years ago.

And the promise of his lips hadn't changed. He didn't
just kiss her. He devoured her. It was everything she
remembered. It was everything that had haunted her
dreams for the last eight years.

Nathan's lips had been made for hers. And she remembered exactly why they'd been so good together. Her hands curled around his head, brushing his buzz cut, feeling the bristles under her palm. His hands ran through her hair; one hand anchored her head in place whilst his lips worked his way around her neck and shoulders and his other hand was held against her bottom.

The waves continued to buffet them, pulling them one way, then the other. Every current pulled them even closer together, his hard muscles against her softer curves.

Now his hands moved lower, swiftly grabbing the bottom of her kaftan and pulling it over her head. It disappeared into the waves.

His hands were back on her bare skin, cradling her and pulling her tighter towards him. The chilled water did nothing to hide his response to her.

She leaned back a little and ran her palms up the planes of his chest. His years in Doctors Without Borders had left him leaner, more muscular. It was understandable. The places where he'd served would have required long hours and hard labour. Nathan wouldn't have shirked any of that.

Something pinged. The snap on her bikini top sprang apart and the cold water rushed underneath the pink Lycra. It billowed between them and was swallowed by the sea as his fingers brushed against her nipple.

Even in the dark she could see his green eyes on hers. Her teeth grazed the nape of his neck as she kissed even harder. He started walking, striding back towards the beach with her legs still wound around his waist. 'Let's take this back to land,' he said.

This time his hands fitted firmly around her waist, anchoring her in place. This time the pads of his fingers came in contract with the curved scar on her back. This time she had no cover. The bikini top and kaftan were lost amongst the waves. He inhaled sharply.

It was a jarring reminder of the gulf between them.

He fixed her with a stare she hadn't seen before—one of wariness—as he set her down. Then he didn't speak. He just moved her gently to one side, pushing her onto one hip.

She was holding her breath as he gently traced his finger down the curve of her scar. Her chest was hurting, struggling under the strain of little oxygen. Her stomach churned. She had no idea what he would do, what he would say.

But, as she let the breath whoosh out from her chest, he took it away all over again. He bent and gently brushed his lips against her scar.

His voice was husky. 'You should have told me, Rach. You should always have told me.'

His voice was cracking. She could see his emotions written on his face. It was breaking her heart all over again.

She hadn't stayed around the last time to witness this. Last time around she'd witnessed his shock, disbelief and then a little bit of anger. She knew exactly what she'd done to him. She just hadn't waited around for the fallout.

This time it was right in front of her. The hurt, the confusion, the sadness. This was why she hadn't stayed. She couldn't have stood this. She just wasn't strong enough for this.

Her voice was cracking. 'I always think I messed up. But I did the best thing in the circumstances. Even though I regret it every single day.'

Suddenly she felt swamped. Swamped by what had just happened between them, and confused by it even more.

She'd been so caught up in the fantasy of this. For a few moments, the beautiful setting and the man in front of her had just swept her away. But his lips connecting with her scar brought her back to the harsh reality of life and the decisions that she'd made.

She'd wished for this for the last eight years. But now it was right in front of her she couldn't let herself go. She couldn't lose herself in the moment with Nathan because of the multitude of fears she still had. The rational parts of her brain were telling her to move on. She was past the five-year cancer-free mark.

Now was the time to think about a new relationship and maybe even see if she could revive her dream of having a family.

But some part of her heart just couldn't let her take that final step.

The hurt on his face had been a painful reminder of what she'd already put him through. She didn't want to take the chance of hurting Nathan more than she already had.

Everything had happened too soon for her. Her brain really hadn't had time to process how she felt about all this. She needed some time. She needed some space.

Above all, right now, she felt as if she needed to get away. Needed to get away from the man she still loved with her whole heart.

She jumped up and made a grab for his T-shirt that was lying on the sand. 'I'm sorry, Nathan. I can't. I just can't.'

Confusion racked his face. 'What? What are you talking about?'

She waved her hand. 'This. It's all just too much, too soon. I need some time to think about things.' Her feet were already moving across the sand. Back towards the cabin. Back towards safety.

'Rachel, wait!' He jumped to his feet as if to come after her but she put up her hand.

'No, Nathan. If you care about me at all, you'll give me some space. We haven't seen each other in eight years. *Eight years, Nathan.* There's so much unfinished business between us. I can't straighten out how I feel about everything.'

She was still walking.

'Do you love me, Rachel?'

His voice cut through the sea wind and stopped her cold.

She turned again, but the words were stuck in her throat. Of course she loved him—she'd never stopped. She just wasn't ready to say that yet. She could never guarantee that she'd be healthy. She could never guarantee her cancer wouldn't come back. Was she brave enough to expose him to that? Was she brave enough to expose *them* to that? It was all about trust again. Could she trust their potential relationship to see them through anything? She just wasn't sure.

'Because I love you, Rachel. I'll always love you. I've spent so much time being bitter. I've spent so much time being angry about my parents dying. I've never stepped back to see how much it impacted on my life—on Charlie's life.' He gave a little laugh. 'It turns out my little brother is more of a man than I ever thought. He's got past it—he's moved on. He's found love. He's got a family. And I envy him every single day.' He emphasised those words as he stepped towards her.

But he didn't reach out and touch her. He kept his

hands by his sides. 'You've had cancer, Rachel. It's time for you to move on too. It's time for both of us to move on.' He took a deep breath. 'But I'll give you time. I'll give you space. You need to get to the same place as me. The one where you can say that you're ready to love me again.'

He let the words hang in the air between them.

The sky was dark. She was too far away to see the expression on his face. All she could feel was an invisible weight pressing down on her chest.

Her head was so jammed full of thoughts that she just needed to get away. So, before he could say anything else, she turned on her heel and ran.

Ran as fast as she could along the beach and back to the cabin, slamming the door behind her and heading straight to her bed.

She had to make a decision. She had to try and find a way to think straight.

Because right now she just couldn't.

CHAPTER TEN

'How many times has he refilled that water bottle?'

Nathan was watching the monitor that was fixed on the camp. Camp life was boring. There was no getting away from it. The director had spent most of the day trying to stage a fight between two of the celebrities.

And Nathan had spent the last two days trying to avoid Rachel.

Part of him thought that giving into the undeniable chemistry between them might have diminished the tension between them. He couldn't have been more wrong.

There was nothing like being stranded on an island with your ex for increasing tension to epic proportions—particularly after what had just happened between them.

Part of him felt sick. Rachel—*his Rachel*—had suffered from renal cancer.

His brain couldn't get past the part that she hadn't told him.

But now... *Now* he had a reason why she'd left. And the lack of trust was hard to stomach. But with a bit more thinking time and a bit more reason he could almost understand why she'd thought she was doing the right thing.

He still believed she had been wrong. The thought of Rachel having cancer might burn a hole inside him, but now the fact that she *hadn't* walked away because she didn't love him—as crazy as it sounded—that part was almost a relief.

That part had preyed on his mind constantly. He'd always wondered why she'd done it. Now there was a reason. She said she'd loved him too much. She said she'd walked away *because* she loved him. He still couldn't quite get his head around that.

The other night had been an epiphany for him. He'd stood on the beach and known that, no matter how he felt or how angry he'd been, he would always love her. Always. He'd always want her in his life.

The feelings were so overwhelming that he'd understood when she'd said she needed time. Now he'd found Rachel again, he didn't want her to slip through his fingers. Not again.

Parts of his heart still squirmed, his self-defence mechanism wanting to kick into place and stop him from being vulnerable. How on earth would he feel if Rachel walked away from him again? It was almost unthinkable.

But it could happen. And if he considered it too much he would simply turn and walk away himself. Eight years was a long time. They'd both changed so much. Niggling doubts were creeping in because Rachel hadn't been able to look him in the eye and say for sure what she wanted. He was taking a huge risk.

He'd survived her walking away once—but what about twice?

He took a deep breath and focused on the screen in front of him. He was here to do a job. Other parts of his life would have to wait. He asked the question again. 'How many times has he refilled that water bottle?'

The technician looked up from the monitor and

frowned, breaking him from his thoughts. 'Three—maybe four times? He spends most of his day in the dunny too.' He paused. 'Or sleeping.'

Nathan ran his fingers over his buzz cut. The dunny—the Australian equivalent of a toilet. He'd even used the word himself the other day. Darius was drinking too much and peeing frequently. Something was wrong. He was in doctor mode now. He had to stop focusing on Rachel. His gut instinct told him that something wasn't right here. It didn't help that now he knew Darius's medical history he was even more worried. There was no getting away from the fact the guy just didn't *look* well.

He hated to admit it, but Darius was generally a good-looking guy—well-built, with dark hair, tanned skin and a movie star smile. He was kind of surprised the guy had stayed in a soap opera in Australia and not tried to hit Hollywood.

He watched as Darius tugged at his shorts, pulling them up. His weight loss had been evident the first time Nathan had seen him. Now, it was even more marked. And if the clothes he'd brought with him were falling off—it was time to act.

Nathan walked over to the director's chair. 'Darius Cornell. Get him out of there. I want to check him over.'

The director looked up. 'What are you talking about? Darius is fine. He hasn't complained about anything.' He looked at the rest of the people in the cabin. 'Has he?'

The ones that were listening shook their heads. The director held up his hands. 'See?'

Nathan leaned on the desk and pointed at the screen. 'Does that guy look well to you?'

The director glanced back at the screen and hesitated. 'He has been going to the dunny a lot. Maybe he has one of those parasitic bugs? Maybe he's picked up something in the jungle?' Unconsciously, the director started to scratch his skin.

Nathan put his hand on the man's shoulder. 'Leave the diagnosing to me. Can you send someone to get him out of there for a quick check over?' He looked around. There was no getting away from it—he couldn't avoid her for ever. 'And could someone find Dr Johnson and ask her to report to the medical cabin?'

He didn't wait for an answer, just walked back to the medical centre and tried to keep everything in his head in check.

Rachel and Darius in a room together. For the first time since he'd got here he couldn't care less. Now he knew Darius's history, he was worried about him—really worried. If the guy was having a third recurrence of his non-Hodgkin's it couldn't possibly be good.

It only took a few minutes for Darius to arrive and he was less than happy to see Nathan. 'What are you doing here? I thought I made it clear I'd only deal with Rachel.'

Nathan held up Darius's empty medical file. 'Rachel will be along soon. I'm worried about you, Darius. You don't look well. You can't possibly feel well. How much weight do you think you've lost?'

Darius scowled at him as he sat down in a chair and started scratching at his skin.

But Nathan wasn't going to let this go. He wasn't about to betray what Rachel had revealed to him but he had to get to the bottom of what was wrong. 'Darius, let's not play games. What I need to know right now is what your symptoms are. I'm worried about you.'

Darius blinked—as if a whole host of thoughts had just flooded his brain—and Nathan heard a sharp intake of breath behind him. Rachel.

'What's going on?' She walked straight in. 'Darius? Is something wrong?'

Darius, who normally spent his time trying to charm everyone around him, was unusually bad-tempered. 'Don't ask me—ask him. It was him that pulled me out of the jungle.'

'With good reason,' cut in Nathan.

'What have you told him, Rach?' Darius looked mad.

Nathan's eyes fell on the water canister that Darius still held in his hands. He hadn't even put it down when he'd been called to the medical cabin. He obviously had a raging thirst. The question was—why?

Nathan took a deep breath and leaned against the desk. He tried not to fixate on Rachel in her unusual get-up of pink sundress, thick socks and hiking boots. He'd no idea where she'd been. But he could almost feel her brown eyes burrowing into the side of his head.

She paused at the doorway, taking in the situation in front of her. In the unflinching bright lights of the medical centre it was obvious that Darius was unwell. She walked towards him. 'I haven't told Nathan any-thing—but I'm just about to.' Her eyes met Nathan's, a silent thank you for not exposing what she'd already revealed. 'He's the doctor on duty and he needs the full facts. Darius and I met when we both had cancer treat-ment. I had renal cancer and Darius had non-Hodgkin's lymphoma. He's relapsed twice since.'

Darius glared at Rachel and gritted his teeth. But he didn't speak.

Nathan tried again. 'Darius, tell me honestly—how are you feeling? Because, to be frank—you look like crap.'

Rachel's eyebrows shot upwards and Darius almost

growled at him. He stood back up and pushed himself into Nathan's face. 'Who do you think you're talking to?'

And with that simple act Nathan's suspicions were confirmed. Darius's breath smelled of pear drops—something Nathan hadn't tasted since he was a child. It was a classic sign of diabetes and that, combined with all the other signs, probably meant that he was in ketoacidosis. Onset could be really rapid. He put his hand gently on Darius's arm and steered him back towards the chair, walking over to the cupboard and pulling out a glucometer. Rachel's eyes widened for a second and he could almost see the jigsaw pieces falling into place for her.

'Darius, I need to do a little test on you. It's just a finger prick; I'll squeeze out a little blood and we'll know what we need to know in ten seconds.'

'No.' Darius's aggression wasn't lessening but it wasn't him; it was his condition.

Nathan sat down opposite while Rachel moved over and kneeled in front of Darius. She put her hand on Darius's water canister. 'How much have you been drinking?'

He automatically took a swig from the bottle. 'I'm just thirsty.'

She nodded. 'And have you been going to the toilet a lot?'

'Well, I would. I'm drinking a lot.' He was snappy.

She reached over and took the glucometer from Nathan's hands. 'You've lost weight, Darius. More than we would have expected in the jungle. I think you might be suffering from diabetes. Let me do this little test.'

She was quick. He barely had a chance to reply before she'd done the little finger prick. The machine counted down rapidly and she grimaced and turned it to face Nathan.

She put her arm behind Darius and stood him up, leading him over to the examination trolley. 'We're going to set up a drip. Your body is dehydrated. Do you know what diabetes is?'

He scowled. 'Of course I do. My mum had it, remember?'

Nathan could see the flicker across Rachel's face. She remembered now. And diabetes could be hereditary. He should be feeling a little more relaxed. They had a diagnosis for Darius. Nathan looked through the drawers and pulled out a cannula and an IV giving set. It only took a few seconds to find a drip stand and a bag of saline. Rachel was an experienced medical physician. She must have looked after plenty of newly diagnosed diabetics. The condition was becoming more prevalent across the world. He'd certainly diagnosed it often in his time with Doctors Without Borders.

He walked around the other side of Darius and quickly inserted the cannula while Rachel was still talking.

'This is serious, Darius. We don't have a lot of facilities here. I'd like to transfer you to a hospital. That's the best place for you to be right now. We need to get some insulin into you and stabilise your condition. Once you're stabilised you'll feel a lot better. It only takes a couple of days.'

'I'm not going to hospital.' The words were sharp.

He saw her take a deep breath. Being unreasonable was right in there with the rest of the symptoms for diabetes, along with weight loss, drinking too much, peeing frequently and the acidotic breath.

He pulled out his stethoscope and tried to place it on Darius's chest but he batted his hand away. Nathan didn't even blink. He just calmly put his fingers on Darius's wrist, checking his pulse rate.

Rachel fixed her eyes on his. He spoke clearly. 'Only slightly tachycardic. Let's check his blood pressure.' He was trying to determine just how near to crisis Darius was.

'Do we have any insulin?'

Nathan nodded. 'There are a few varieties in the drug fridge. But we don't have an insulin pump.'

She gave a little nod and walked quickly to the fridge, unlocking the door and examining the contents. She looked over at Darius. 'You should be in hospital. You need your bloods taken and a few other assessments. You should be on a continuous pump and your blood sugar constantly monitored until we get you stabilised.'

She was saying everything she was supposed to be saying. But Nathan had the strangest feeling this wasn't going to go the way it should. Darius seemed strangely determined.

Darius was looking at her. 'If I go to a regular hospital they'll want to know my medical history. Can't you just give me insulin here and look after me? You do this stuff all the time.'

She shook her head. 'I do this stuff all the time in a general hospital with staff to assist me. I don't have the equipment I need. I can't even do a blood panel on you right now. I would class this as a medical emergency. I think we should call the medevac again.'

Nathan could see the mild panic in her eyes. Part of him understood and part of him didn't. Yes, this was a diabetic crisis. But, as an experienced physician, Rachel could administer the approximate dose of insulin and monitor Darius herself. With the IV in situ to correct his dehydration, it wasn't an ideal situation but it could be managed. There was no question Darius would have to be referred to a diabetic specialist but, in the immediate future, this could be controlled. He'd stabilised lots of newly diagnosed diabetics with far less equipment than they had here. Nowadays, for most patients, they tried to avoid admission to hospital unless they were at crisis point and instead had them attend a day care centre.

Nathan took a deep breath. Things were still raw between them both. And padding round about Rachel's ex wouldn't help. But he was rational enough to know that Darius was a patient. He had a right to make requests about his treatment.

It was time to get down to basics. He turned to face Darius. 'Why is it you don't want to go to a hospital? Is it because of your medical history—or because of the show?'

'The show,' Darius said without hesitation. 'It's in the contract that if I leave early—medical condition or not—I won't get my full salary. I promised Lynn she'd get her dream wedding. If I don't stay, I won't be able to do that.' He still sounded angry. He was still agitated. The condition was impacting every part of his body.

Nathan glanced at Rachel. She'd told him Darius was engaged to someone else but this was the first time he'd heard Darius mention his fiancée.

Rachel was still frowning. 'We need a set of scales.' She was moving out of panic mode and into doctor mode.

Nathan found the scales and brought them around to the side of the trolley where the drip was. He helped Darius stand up for a few seconds and took a note. He gestured towards the medical file. 'Do we have his weight when he first arrived?'

She flicked through a few pages. 'We have one— from the insurance medical.' She looked at the records.

'It was done just over a month ago. According to the scales now he's lost ten pounds.'

Nathan nodded and touched Darius's arm. 'Do you know what kind of diabetes your mother had?'

'She had it from childhood and was always on insulin. That's Type One, isn't it?'

He nodded. 'From your symptoms, it's likely that's what you have too.' He glanced at Rachel. 'Agree?'

She nodded as she dialled up the dosage on an insulin pen. 'We'll need a GAD test for confirmation but that's the way we'll treat it right now. We need to get your blood glucose levels down.'

Darius leaned back against the pillow on the trolley. 'I want to speak to the director. I want to go back into camp. But—' he closed his eyes for a second '—can I sleep for a bit first?'

Rachel gave a little tap at his abdomen. 'Pull up your shirt. I'm going to give you the first shot of insulin. Then I'm going to take some bloods and see if we can find a way to get them onshore. We need to keep doing the finger prick tests. Feel free to try and sleep through them.'

She gave him the insulin, then spent two minutes taking blood from inside his elbow. Nathan picked up the phone and spoke for a few minutes to one of the crew. He gave her a nod. 'The supply boat is due in an hour. They'll make special arrangements for the bloods.' He took the vials and stuck them in a transport container.

He hesitated and looked over as she scribbled some notes. Darius already looked as if he was sleeping. 'I'll grab us some coffee and we can have a chat about how best to handle this outside.'

Rachel's stomach was in knots. Everything that could go wrong had gone wrong. She couldn't believe it when she'd got the call about Darius and now she was kicking herself that she hadn't investigated sooner.

When she'd walked in, she'd thought he'd had a relapse. Seeing him in the bright lights of the medical cabin rather than the shaded canopy of the jungle had been a shock to the system. His skin pallor was terrible, the dehydration obvious and the weight loss evident on his face.

But knowing that it was diabetes and not a recurrence of his non-Hodgkin's lymphoma was a relief.

Diabetes she could manage. Nathan was right. She was an experienced physician—as was he. As long as she had insulin and glucose monitoring equipment they could stabilise him in a few days. His long-term care would have to be monitored by a diabetes specialist but there was no reason she couldn't manage his immediate care.

She'd just gone into shock when she'd first realised something was wrong. It had taken her a few minutes to calm down and be rational. She gave a little smile. Darius did have his good points. It was sweet that he wanted to see out his contract in order to give Lynn her dream wedding. He wasn't as self-obsessed as some might think. And the nice part was that she knew if Lynn heard that he'd done this she'd be furious in case he'd put himself at risk. They really were a devoted couple.

Nathan walked up and handed her a mug. The coffee aroma swept around her, along with something else. Hazelnut. Somewhere on this island Nathan had found her favourite drink—a hazelnut latte. He didn't even wait for her to speak. 'We have a patient to look after.'

She was surprised—surprised that he hadn't even mentioned what had happened a few nights ago. He'd said he'd give her space, and he had. She just wasn't sure that she'd entirely believed him that night. But Nathan had been true to his word. She'd never seen him alone since.

And now it felt as if he'd been avoiding her. Her stomach curled. She was sure he must regret saying those words to her. Telling her that he still loved her—that he'd always loved her. She hadn't reciprocated, even though she'd wanted to. It must have felt like a slap to the face. What would happen when he found out what her plans were? She didn't even want to go there.

She lifted her head. 'Yes. Darius…'

His shoulders set and there was a flicker along his jawline. 'How do you want to handle this?'

Work. She could talk about work. She could talk about a diabetes plan for Darius. 'I'll stay with him for the next few hours, monitoring his blood sugar. If he needs more insulin I'll talk him through doing an injection. I've no idea what his consultant's plan will be for him, but he's got to start somewhere. Might as well be here.'

Nathan nodded and placed his hands on his hips. At least he was being professional—at least he was being courteous. Then his green eyes looked right at her and she felt a jolt right through her system. 'What do you want me to do?'

What do you want me to do? She could answer that question and give him a dozen different variables that were nothing to do with diabetes.

But she was trying not to think about Nathan Banks, the man. She was trying only to think of Nathan Banks, the fellow health professional.

She tried to clear her head and be rational. 'I'd appreciate it if you could speak to the director and work out a plan so Darius can go back into camp for a few hours every day. Just for the camera. The director will need to tell the other campmates what's happened. And he'll need to agree to one of us being there.'

Nathan gave a sharp nod. 'I can do that. What about you? Do you want me to take over at some point? We'll still need to supervise the other challenges.'

She hesitated. She already knew that Darius wouldn't like it. But she had to be realistic. She could probably wake every few hours and monitor Darius's blood sugar, but she couldn't keep doing that for ever. It made more sense to spread the load.

'I want to try and get him back to normal as much as we can. How about we assess him later and, if he's up to it, he could walk to the canteen with you for dinner?'

He tried his best to hide the tiny grimace that she could see flicker across his face. 'Fine. I'll speak to the director and be back around six.'

He turned on his heel and walked away as she leaned against the doorjamb. She still had the coffee cup clenched in one hand and it crumpled beneath her fingers, sending the remainder of the coffee spilling down her pink dress.

She wanted to cry again. She wanted to go into her room, get into her bed, curl up in a ball and just cry.

Everything just felt like too much. Just being on this island felt like too much. The fact that Darius was sick. The fact that, after all these years, she could see the damage that had been done to Nathan—the man she still loved.

That tore at her heart most of all. Her barriers were breaking, her walls were crumbling. At work, if things got tough, you could always retreat to the sanctity of your own home. But there was nowhere to retreat to on this island.

There would always be someone there—a crew member or a camera to make you realise how little space there was. And now, with all the emotions—and the secrets she was trying to keep—there wasn't even room for her own thoughts.

All of a sudden she couldn't wait to get away from this place. It might be an island paradise for some, but for her it had turned into something entirely different.

How many more days could she try to avoid the man she had to work with? How many more days would she have to push aside everything she felt for him? This place was rapidly becoming unbearable.

For a tiny second she even considered phoning Lewis and telling him he had to get his butt out here so she could leave.

But she couldn't do that. His wife would be anxious enough waiting for her baby without her husband disappearing at short notice.

There was a cough behind her and she spun around. Darius was rubbing his eyes and sitting up a little.

'How are you feeling?' She dumped the crumpled cup in the bin and walked over to him.

His brow creased and he pointed at her stained dress. 'How long have I been asleep and what have you been doing?'

She shook her head. 'Nothing. Nothing at all. Now, let's get your blood sugar tested again and see if we can start to make you feel better.' She adjusted the flow rate on the drip and reached for the glucometer.

Doctor business. She could do this. She'd always been good at her job and at least if she was thinking about Darius she wasn't thinking about anyone else.

She quickly pricked his finger and waited ten seconds to see the result. She pasted a smile on her face.

'It's coming down slowly. What say I get some insulin and teach you how to do the next injection?'

She straightened her back. She had to start thinking about herself. 'Then we need to have a chat. I've made a decision I need to tell you about.'

CHAPTER ELEVEN

IT WAS MORE than a little awkward. Nathan didn't want to be there any more than Darius wanted him to be.

But they'd walked slowly down to the canteen together and were now sitting across from each other while Darius stirred his soup round and round.

There was no getting away from the fact the guy looked bad. His face was gaunt and there were big dark circles under his eyes. If he had any idea how he looked he'd probably be shouting for a mirror and make-up.

But Nathan could tell that Darius was just too tired. It was all part and parcel of the diagnosis of diabetes. The extreme fatigue would lift in a few days and his muscles would start to rebuild. Within a month he should look normal again. He still had an excessive thirst—he'd drunk three glasses of water since they'd sat down—but his appetite had obviously left him.

Nathan took a deep breath and let his professional head stay in place. 'You going to eat that? You've just taken another shot. You don't want to end up the other way and let your blood sugar go too low.'

Darius let out something equivalent to a growl and finally lifted the spoon to his lips. His eyes were fixed firmly on Nathan. There was clearly a mixture of resentment and curiosity in them. It seemed these feelings worked both ways.

'So, you're the famous Nathan Banks,' he finally said.

Nathan felt an uncomfortable prickle down his spine. He tried his best to be calm. 'I don't know what you mean.'

Darius lifted his eyelids just a touch. 'It took me a while to realise exactly who you were. You were her favourite topic of conversation.'

He was? The thought of Rachel and her then new boyfriend discussing him didn't sit well.

'I would have thought I was the last thing you'd want to talk about.'

Darius sat back and folded his arms across his chest. It was apparent he wanted to direct this conversation. 'You're not as good-looking as I thought you'd be.'

Nathan didn't know whether to laugh or punch him. This clearly wasn't a doctor-patient conversation any more.

He set his fork down. It was clear they wouldn't be eating any time soon. 'Really.' It wasn't a question; it was a statement of fact.

Darius shook his head. 'No. I saw a picture of you once. Rachel kept it in her bag.' He gave a little half-smile. 'Time obviously hasn't been kind to you.'

Nathan shook his head. On any other day of the week, in any other set of circumstances he'd probably knock Darius out cold. But this guy was clearly trying to play him. And he had no idea why. The thought that Rachel had kept a picture of him in her bag was sending strange pulses through his body. But this wasn't the time to get all nostalgic.

He countered. 'Botox has clearly been kind to you.'

He couldn't help it. Even though he hated to admit it,

Darius was normally a good-looking guy, with tanned skin and perfectly straight white teeth. Nathan was quite sure that with his weather-beaten skin and lines around his eyes he'd come up short in comparison.

He just couldn't help the fact that everything about this guy annoyed him. His hair, his skin, his teeth— even the way he ate. If Darius Cornell had been your average soap star Nathan wouldn't have cared less. But Darius Cornell was the soap star who had dated Rachel and that made his insides feel as if they were curling up and dying inside and gave him a completely irrational hatred of the guy.

He was trying so hard to put Darius in the 'patient' box in his head. That would help him try to keep everything professional. But then he'd go and say something about Rachel and all rational thoughts went out of the window.

He knew. He knew why they'd been friends. He just hadn't managed to push all the ideas that had fixated in his head over the years out of the way yet.

Because in his mind Rachel Johnson was still his.

In his mind, Rachel would always be his.

The other night he'd acted on instinct; he'd put his heart before his head and just told her that he still loved her. So many things she'd said had set off little pulses of recognition in his brain.

He *had* spent the last five years trying to save the world. Even if he hadn't realised it at the time. No one could do that. No one. All his pent-up frustration about his mum and dad had been channelled into his job. In that respect, it was time for change. It was time to re-evaluate and decide where he wanted to be. There was a tiny idea flickering in the back of his mind.

But, in other respects, things were exactly the same. Eight years on, nothing had changed.

Eight years on, he still loved Rachel Johnson.

Darius was still studying him as the feeling started to fully form in his brain.

'I always wondered what you were like,' Darius said. His tone was verging on disparaging.

'Why should you care what I was like? I was in England. You were the one in Australia—with her.'

For a few seconds Darius's gaze was still locked on his. It must be the actor in him. The overwhelming confidence. But Nathan wouldn't break the stare. It was almost like marking his line in the sand.

He didn't want anyone else to have any claim on Rachel.

Darius sucked in a deep breath. 'But Rachel was never really with me,' he muttered quietly. 'You were the one she was always thinking of.' His shoulders sagged as if all the wind had gone out of his sails. Maybe he was tired? Maybe he needed to find him something else to eat?

Darius looked up from under his heavy lids, his expression a little glazed. 'Rachel... She was never mine. You were always the person in her head.' He gave a little laugh. 'It does wonders for the confidence. And you're about to lose her all over again.'

The words made his head shoot up and focus. 'What did you say?'

What on earth did Darius mean? He wanted to give the guy a shake, but as he looked at Darius he realised that right now there was only room for doctor mode. His eyes were glassy. He reached into his back pocket and pulled out the glucometer, not even waiting for

Darius's permission. 'You haven't eaten enough. What do you want?'

'Toast.' A one-word answer from someone who obviously wasn't feeling great. Nathan strode across the canteen and walked straight into the kitchen, bypassing the baffled chef. He grabbed a few slices of bread, putting them in the toaster and opening the fridge for some butter and jam.

The chef lifted his eyebrows. 'Help yourself.'

Nathan patted him on the shoulder. 'Sorry, Stan. Darius isn't feeling too well. Just want to get some food into him.'

Stan nodded. 'No worries.' He carried on with his dinner preparations.

After a minute the toast popped and Nathan spread the butter and jam, pouring a glass of milk too. He walked back across the canteen, ignoring the curious stares around him, putting the plate and glass in front of Darius.

He needed this guy to feel well again—he needed to ask him what he'd meant about Rachel.

Darius didn't even look up—he just automatically started eating. After five minutes the glazed expression left him and he sat back in the chair, looking at the empty plate in front of him. His gaze narrowed and he folded his arms across his chest and glanced over his shoulder to check if anyone else was listening. When he was satisfied that the rest of the crew were more interested in their food than listening to anyone else's conversation, he turned back around.

'Do you feel better?'

Darius gave a brief nod. His look was still a little belligerent. But Nathan wasn't prepared to wait a second longer.

He leaned across the table. 'What did you mean about Rachel?'

Darius scowled. 'I was a bit foggy there. I might have said something I didn't mean to.'

'Lots of diabetics say odd things when their blood sugar goes a bit low. But you said something about Rachel. You said I was about to lose her all over again. What did you mean?'

Darius shook his head. 'It's private. Anyway, we should only be discussing doctor stuff.'

Nathan fixed his gaze on Darius and sucked in a deep breath, trying to keep professional. 'We should really discuss how you felt when your blood sugar went down. You need to be able to recognise the signs.' He turned the glucometer around. 'Normal blood sugar is between four and seven. But you've been running much higher in the last few weeks. Your blood sugar was ten. That's obviously the point you start to feel unwell. All that will change, but we need to keep notes.'

There was complete silence for a few seconds.

After a minute Darius stood up and picked up the glucometer. 'I'm feeling a bit better now. I think I'd prefer to discuss the diabetes stuff with Rachel.' He glared at Nathan. 'While I've still got the chance, that is.'

Nathan stood up too. 'You're not going anywhere until you tell me what you mean.'

Darius snapped at him, 'It's all your fault. She's supposed to stay on the island the whole time I'm here. But she's not. She's leaving. She's getting on the next supply boat that arrives the day after tomorrow. And she's doing that to get away from you!'

He turned on his heel and stalked out of the canteen as the bottom fell out of Nathan's world.

No. She couldn't. She couldn't leave him again.

Not Rachel. Not when he finally felt as if there was a real chance of a future together.

He just couldn't let it happen.

CHAPTER TWELVE

THE TV PRODUCER and director had finally listened to reason. Nathan had been surprisingly persuasive. If she hadn't known better, she might have thought that he and Darius were friends.

They'd reached a compromise. Darius was hydrated enough to be off his IV fluids. They'd had his blood results sent back and spoken to a diabetic specialist about a treatment regime. Rachel would start his treatment, then, as soon as filming was finished, Darius would fly back to the mainland for a proper consultation.

He'd been quietly amenable. The background information he already knew about diabetes had been helpful. But treatments and plans had changed a lot since his mother had been diagnosed and Rachel was keen to make sure he got the best information.

The trickiest part had been the other celebrities. The phrase 'special treatment' had been readily bandied about. Nathan had ended up in the middle of the camp telling them straight how crucial it was for Darius to be monitored during these first few days. He would only be back in camp for a few hours each day for filming. The rest of the time he'd be monitored and recuperating in the crew area. Tallie Turner, the actress, had been the most disgruntled. The thought of someone else sleeping on anything other than a lumpy camp bed, away from the spiders and bugs, was obviously too much for her.

The rest of the celebrities had spent most of the day talking about it. Frank Cairns, the sportsman, was proving the public's obvious favourite. He didn't get involved in griping, rarely tolerated tantrums and had a real, self-deprecating sense of humour. Most of the votes in the last few days had been for him. Billy X, the rapper, was the second most popular. He'd done well in the challenges and had started a heavy flirtation with Rainbow Blossom, the reality TV star. Rachel was quite sure it was a calculated move for popularity but she wouldn't dream of saying so. There was only one more day to go. Tomorrow she would be on the supply boat and away from Nathan completely. She still couldn't figure out if that was what she really wanted.

She'd stayed at the medical centre last night with Darius but they'd both agreed that Darius should be allowed to bunk in with some of the crew tonight. One of them would go and wake him to check his blood sugar a few times in the middle of the night, but getting him back to normal as soon as possible was important. If he'd been diagnosed in the city he would maybe have had a one or two nights' stay in hospital if he was close to crisis to stabilise him, then he'd spend the next couple of days with a few hours at day care. All his other follow-ups would be done as an outpatient.

It was time to get things back to normal.

Normal? What was that? Because she didn't know.

Was it normal to wake up every morning and feel sick? Was it normal not to be able to sleep at night because of all the thoughts tumbling around in your brain? Was it normal not to be able to think straight and have a conversation with your colleague?

Normal didn't seem to exist for Rachel Johnson any more. Not since Nathan Banks had reappeared in her life.

Footsteps sounded on the path outside the cabin and her body tensed. She could even recognise his steps now. It was going from bad to worse. Her bed was currently covered with the contents of her wardrobe as she tried to cram them back into her rucksack. What would he say when he noticed? She still hadn't told him she planned to leave.

As she lifted up yet another carefully folded T-shirt she stopped to take a breath. Why had it taken her so long to pack? If she was really desperate to leave the island she should have just shoved everything into her rucksack. Instead, she'd been carefully folding everything, rolling up dresses and skirts. It was almost as if her head had made one decision and her heart another.

Was running away really the answer?

As the footsteps grew closer she squeezed her eyes closed for a second. *This* was what she needed to do. *This* was the conversation she needed to have—no matter how hard. She couldn't walk away from him again without talking to him first.

It wasn't fair to her. It wasn't fair to him.

Eight years ago she'd run away.

Eight years later, it was time to face things head-on.

'Hey, Rach?'

His happy tone took her by surprise. They'd spent the last day tiptoeing around each other and barely making eye contact.

She turned around. He had a bottle in his hand and two champagne glasses. She stood up, forgetting that she was only wearing her short pink satin nightdress. Nathan strode across the cabin and put the bottle on the table.

He didn't mention the clothes spread everywhere. 'Look what Lewis sent us. It just arrived on the supply boat.'

Her eyes widened as she spun the bottle around. Pink champagne from the man she planned to kill. It was kind of ironic. Then her brain clicked into gear.

'They've had the baby?'

Nathan was beaming. 'They've had the baby—a happy, healthy eight-pound girl.' He reached over and gave her a spontaneous hug. 'You know he'd been really worried, don't you? Every other female in his wife's family had developed pre-eclampsia while they were pregnant. I think Lewis spent the whole pregnancy holding his breath.'

He was still holding her and she was trying to pretend her body wasn't responding to his touch as his male pheromones flooded around her. The stubble on his chin grazed her shoulder and every tiny hair on her body stood on end. She'd always loved Nathan with stubble.

'No,' she whispered. 'I didn't know that.'

He was holding her gaze, his good mood still evident. This was the Nathan she remembered. This was the Nathan who'd kept her buoyed and supported through six years of hard study and work. This was the guy who made her laugh. This was the guy who she had always trusted, the person she trusted with her heart. Why couldn't she have him back? It was almost as if the little shadows behind his eyes had fallen away. He seemed more relaxed. He seemed at ease with the world around him. And whilst the tension emanating from him had diminished, the pheromones were sparking like fireworks.

He hadn't let her go. And she didn't really want him to.

Maybe for five minutes she could pretend that she'd never had cancer? She could pretend that she'd never left and he'd spent the last five years trying to save the world. Maybe for the next five minutes they could try being happy with each other. She wanted that so badly.

'What's the baby's name?' she asked.

His nose wrinkled. 'Gilberta.'

She pulled back a little. 'What?'

He shrugged. 'Apparently it's a family name.' He glanced over at the champagne on the table. 'What do you say, Rach? Wanna drink some champagne with me?'

His arms released her as he reached over to grab the bottle and she felt the air go out of her with a little whoosh. Nathan didn't notice. He was too busy popping the cork and pouring the bubbling liquid into glasses.

No. She couldn't do this. She couldn't keep living this life. If you'd asked her a few weeks ago about Nathan Banks, her heart would have given a little twist in her chest and she'd have said kind of sadly that he was an old friend. Then she would have spent the rest of the day miserable, wondering where he was and if he was happy.

She'd never met anyone else like Nathan Banks. She'd never met anyone who'd pushed her, inspired her, challenged her and loved her like Nathan Banks.

Her life had seemed so settled. Her career plan had been in place. She had a nice place to stay and good work colleagues. But it wasn't enough. It would never be enough.

She'd met lots of nice guys. But no one she wanted to grow old with. No one she could still picture holding her hand when they were both grey-haired and wrinkled. That was how she'd always felt about Nathan. As if they were a perfect fit. As if they could last for ever. No one else would do.

Meeting Nathan again had made her realise just how much she was missing out. She craved him. Mentally, physically, spiritually. Being in the same room as him and not being able to have him was painful.

Why did she have to have cancer? Why did those horrible little cells have to replicate and cause damage in her body?

She winced. This was making her become a terrible person. The kind of person who wished cancer on someone else. She didn't want to be like that. She couldn't let herself be like that.

'Rachel?' Nathan was standing in front of her, holding the glass out towards her. His brow was creased as if he could see that something was wrong. The bubbles in the champagne tickled her nose. 'Are we going to toast the baby?' he asked, a little more warily.

She met his gaze full-on. Everything had just fallen into place for her. She couldn't be this person any more. 'No.'

He started and pulled the glass back, setting them both down on the table.

She braced herself to be hit by the wave of questions. Questions she had no idea how she would even begin to answer. But Nathan didn't ask any questions. He stepped forward and put his hands on her hips. She could feel the warmth of his fingers through the thin satin of her nightdress. His body was up against hers.

She was going to leave. She wanted to get away. So why did Nathan's body feel like an anchor against hers?

'Enough.' His voice was husky. 'Enough of this, Rachel. Eight years is too long. Eight years is far too long.' He reached up and gently stroked her cheek. 'I've missed you. I've felt lost without you. I need you to be with me. I need you to trust me again and know that I'll be here for you. I'm sorry you faced cancer alone.' He closed his eyes for a second. 'I'm sorry that for a whole host of mixed-up reasons you ended up on one side of the planet whilst I was on the other.' He gave his head a shake. 'I didn't know and I didn't understand.' His eyes fixed on hers. 'I now know about Darius. I don't know everything, and I don't need to know. But I do know why you have that tie to him. I feel as if I've spent the last eight years waiting for this moment—I just didn't know it. I need to move on. *We* need to move on. We don't get those eight years back again. I need to let things go, and so do you.' He slid his fingers through her hair. 'Otherwise,' he said throatily, 'we'll never get this. We'll spend the rest of our lives just drifting—not really living.' He pressed his head against hers. 'There's no way I'm letting you get on that boat without me. Not again, Rachel. Don't walk away from me again.'

He knew. He knew she planned to leave. But he hadn't come to shout at her. He'd held back. He'd given her some space. Had she really wanted to leave?

Her breath was stuck in her throat as she tried to strangle her sobs. She lifted her hands and placed them on his chest as she moved forward, letting her head rest on his shoulder. She could feel the beat of his heart beneath her palm. It was so familiar. It felt *so* right.

When they'd used to lie in bed together that was always how she would fall asleep—with her hand on his heart. It gave her comfort and reassurance and feeling it now was sending a wave of pulses throughout her body.

She couldn't lift her head. She couldn't look at him as she spoke. 'I love you,' she whispered. 'I've always loved you and I'll never stop.' Her hand moved upwards, along his jaw line with the day-old stubble she loved so much. She took a deep breath and lifted her head. 'I don't know why we ended up here together. Maybe it was some kind of twisted fate. I've been so confused these last few days, and there's only one thing I know for certain. I can't be the one to break you. I might have passed the five-year cancer-free mark. But it's not a guarantee. It's always there—always hanging over my head. I don't want to be sick around you, Nathan. I don't want you to have to nurse me. I don't want you to have to look after me.' She pressed her hand against her chest. 'And it's not because *I* would be sick. It's because of what it would do to *you*. I couldn't bear to see you like that. I couldn't watch you suffer.'

'And that's a reason? That's a reason not to have a chance to live our life together? That's a reason to run away again? Haven't you learned anything, Rach?' There was an edge to his voice, but he wasn't angry. He was incredulous.

'So you're going to spend the rest of your life hiding away? From life?' He threw up his hands. 'What if you never get cancer again, Rachel? What if the worst-case scenario just doesn't happen? Are you going to be sitting on your rocking chair wondering why you let life slip through your fingers?'

He stepped forward, his face right in front of hers. 'What if I get sick? What if *I* develop cancer? Would you walk away from me? Should I walk away from you because I don't want to see you upset? Don't you see how ridiculous that sounds?'

He put his hands on her shoulders. 'People take this leap every day, Rachel. When people commit to each other there's no guarantee of a happy ever after. You have to just take what life throws at you, and hope that you're strong enough to see each other through it.'

He put his hand on his chest. 'I believe we are, Rach. I believe we can be. I believe we should get our happy ever after. We've waited eight years for it. I don't want to wait a second longer.'

She was shaking. Her whole body was shaking now as the enormity of his words set in. This was what it felt like. This was what it felt like to have someone declare they would face anything for you. This was what she would have given anything to hear eight years ago—but she hadn't given him the chance.

He ran his hands down her arms. 'Don't walk away from this, Rach. Don't walk away again. That's the one thing that I can't take. Anything else I can face. Anything else I can face—with you by my side.'

She lifted her head as the tears streamed down her cheeks. He was smiling at her and she drank in every part of him. The weathered little lines around his eyes and mouth, the dark line of his stubble and the sincerity in his bright green eyes. She could spend an eternity looking at his face.

Her breathing was stuttering but her heartbeat felt steady. 'You've no idea how much I want this. I'm just so afraid.' Her voice was shaking. It felt like stepping off the side of a cliff into an abyss. There could be so much out there if you were willing to take the leap.

But Nathan had enough confidence for both of them. His smile widened and he held out his hand towards her. 'You don't have to be afraid, Rach. We're in this together. Every step of the way.'

His hand closed around hers. Warm, solid and reassuring. It sent a wave of heat up her arm.

'But what about everything else? Where will we stay? What about jobs? What will we do?'

He pulled her hard and fast against him. 'Let's take it one step at a time. The rest we'll figure out together.' One hand snaked through her hair and the other followed the curve of her satin nightdress. He whispered in her ear, his voice low, throaty and packed with emotion. 'What say we start at the very beginning and get a little reacquainted?'

His bright green eyes were sparkling. It was like stepping back in time. And that look in his eyes sent the same quiver of anticipation down her spine that it always had.

Her lips danced across the skin on his shoulders, ending at the sensitive nape of his neck. Some things didn't change. 'I would very much like to get reacquainted with you, Dr Banks.'

He stepped back towards his bedroom and held out his hand towards her. It was the first time she'd felt certainty in eight long years. She reached out and grabbed it and let him lead her to her happy ever after—no matter what it contained.

EPILOGUE

One year later

RACHEL WAS PACING. Her nerves were jangling and her heart was thudding in her chest, the swoosh of her cream wedding gown the only noise in the quiet bathroom.

Nathan reached over and grabbed her hand, pulling her towards him. He smiled as he settled one hand on her lace-covered waist and lifted the other to touch one of the little brown curls of her carefully coiffed hair.

'Anyone would think you were nervous,' he said, clearly feeling no nerves.

'Of course I'm nervous. I feel sick.' She looked back towards the sink. 'What time is it?'

He shook his head. 'Be patient, Rachel. We have all the time in the world for this.' He gestured his head towards the door. 'Our guests will think I'm in here trying to talk my bride out of her cold feet.'

Rachel sucked in a deep breath. 'Oh, no.' Her hand flew up to the sweetheart neckline of her dress. 'That is what they'll think, isn't it?' She broke from his grasp for a few seconds as she paced again, then stepped over and placed her hands on his chest, her sincere brown eyes fixing on his. 'You know I'd never get cold feet about marrying you. This is the surest I've ever been about anything in my entire life.'

He leaned forward and dropped a soft kiss on her pink lips. 'I know that,' he said. He looked over her shoulder. 'If the celebrant catches me kissing the bride before we say "I do" we might be in trouble.'

She nodded nervously. 'Is it time yet? Is it time?'

He glanced at his watch again, then took her hand in his. 'You know, I don't want you to be disappointed if it's not what you hoped. I'm marrying the woman that I love. I want our day to be about you and me and the fact we're committing to a life together.'

'I know that, I know that. But I just can't help thinking that there has to be another reason for my late period. It can't just be the stress of the wedding.'

He laughed. 'I don't think a wedding car driver has ever had to stop for a pregnancy test before. You nearly gave him a heart attack.'

She squeezed her eyes shut for a second. 'You look— I can't.'

Her head was spinning. They'd planned their wedding in the space of a few months. In less than two weeks they would be back in the UK, both in new jobs nearer to Charlie, Nathan's brother. She was to start training as a GP, and Nathan to start his training as a surgeon. He was already cracking jokes about being the oldest surgeon in town.

She'd always worried that her cancer treatment would have affected her fertility. Nathan had known that when he'd asked her to marry him. *Families can be made up in many ways.* Those had been his words. He was more concerned about not missing out on another eight years with the woman he loved.

Nathan took a step forward and glanced at the white stick.

She clenched her fists. She couldn't bear the waiting. 'One line or two?'

His eyes widened and his face broke into a smile as he grabbed her and lifted her up, spinning her around in the cramped bathroom at the courthouse. 'Two.'

'What?' She couldn't believe it. Not today.

He was still spinning her and she put her hands around his neck as he gently lowered her to the floor. 'So, are you ready? Are you ready to make me the happiest man on the planet, Mrs Banks?'

She rested her head on his shoulder as things started to sink in. 'Mrs Banks. Oh, wow. This day can't get any better, can it?'

There was a twinkle in his green eyes. 'Oh, I think it can.' He picked up her bouquet of pink roses that had been abandoned next to the sink and handed them to her. 'Let's settle our guests' nerves. They'll think we're not coming back out.'

There was a knock on the door and Charlie stuck his head in. 'Are you two okay? Freddie has already dropped the rings off that cushion twice. If he does it again you can find them.'

Charlie's little girl, Matilda, was their pink-gowned flower girl and Freddie, his little boy, was their pageboy.

Nathan gave Rachel a wink. 'Sorry, Charlie, it seems we've got some news.' He intertwined his fingers with hers. 'It seems that two are about to become three.'

It took a few seconds for the news to click, then Charlie's eyes widened. 'What?' He crossed the bathroom in two strides, enveloping Rachel in a bear hug. 'Fabulous.

I can't wait to meet my new niece or nephew.' He stepped back. 'Wait—is this a secret; can we tell anyone?'

They glanced at each other, Rachel's hand automatically going to her stomach. 'We need to wait, don't we? We need to get it confirmed?'

Nathan picked up the pregnancy test. 'We've already done that. Let's tell the world, Rachel. Let's tell them just how good life's about to get.' He winked. 'We'll just get married first.'

She nodded and took a deep breath.

Charlie led her over to the door. 'Now, let's get this show on the road. I've still to make you my sister-in-law.' He gave her a kiss on the cheek as he disappeared outside.

Nathan turned to face her. 'Your dad will be having a heart attack out there. Are you ready?'

She nodded. 'I've never been more ready.' She smoothed down the front of her dress and took a quick check in the mirror to straighten her veil. She'd embraced the whole pink theme for her wedding. Her cream satin and lace dress had a deep pink sash in the middle, matching her bouquet and the few scattered roses in her hair. Nathan had obligingly worn a pink shirt and tie and had the same coloured rose in his lapel. All for her.

Nathan walked out first and she joined her nervous-looking father. He'd been so happy when he'd found out she and Nathan were moving back to London. It had been an easy decision to make. They'd stayed and worked in Australia for another ten months before talking about plans for the future. Both of them agreed they'd like to be closer to Charlie, and she'd been over the moon when Nathan had proposed to her at Darius's wedding a few months before. They'd decided both things at once—to find jobs back in England and plan their wedding.

Her dad held out his arm. 'Everything okay?'

She gave him her widest smile. 'Everything's perfect, Dad, and it's going to get even more so.'

His brow furrowed curiously as he glanced towards the doors of the courthouse just as they were opened by the staff. Nathan and Charlie went in first.

She smiled and her stomach gave a little flip-flop. Eight years ago she'd thought her life was about to end—now, it was just beginning.

As the sun streamed through the windows Rachel walked in on her father's arm to join the man that she loved.

Her husband. Her baby's father.

Her fate.

* * * * *

TAMING
HER NAVY DOC

BY
AMY RUTTAN

First published in Great Britain 2015
by Mills & Boon, an imprint of Harlequin (UK) Limited,
Eton House, 18-24 Paradise Road, Richmond, Surrey, TW9 1SR

© 2015 Amy Ruttan

ISBN: 978-0-263-24718-3

Harlequin (UK) Limited's policy is to use papers that are natural, renewable and recyclable products and made from wood grown in sustainable forests. The logging and manufacturing processes conform to the legal environmental regulations of the country of origin.

Printed and bound in Spain
by CPI, Barcelona

Dear Reader,

Thank you for picking up a copy of *Taming Her Navy Doc*.

I have a huge admiration for the men and women who serve in the armed forces. I recently met a naval officer who said that, 'To give the ultimate sacrifice to your country is why men and women *serve* their country.'

His words touched me so deeply. My family has a military history, dating back to when Canada was not a country but a colony of Great Britain. My admiration for those who serve runs deep.

Thorne made the ultimate sacrifice for his country. He loved being a SEAL, and in one tragic circumstance that was all taken away from him—by the woman who has now come to the naval base he's stationed at. He's conflicted by the promise he made to his dying brother and his desire for Commander Erica Griffin. He's not sure he deserves happiness.

I hope you enjoy reading Thorne and Erica's story as much as I enjoyed writing it.

I love hearing from readers, so please drop by my website, amyruttan.com, or give me a shout on Twitter @ruttanamy

With warmest wishes

Amy Ruttan

Dedication

This book is dedicated to all of
those men and women who give the ultimate sacrifice.
Thank you.

Books by Amy Ruttan

Mills & Boon® Medical Romance™

Safe in His Hands
Melting the Ice Queen's Heart
Pregnant with the Soldier's Son
Dare She Date Again?
It Happened in Vegas

**Visit the author profile page at
millsandboon.co.uk for more titles**

Praise for
Amy Ruttan

'I highly recommend this for all fans of romance reads
with amazing, absolutely breathtaking scenes, to-die-
for dialogue, and everything else that is needed to make
this a beyond awesome and WOW read!'

—*GoodRead*s on
Melting the Ice Queen's Heart

'A sensational romance, filled with astounding medical drama. Author Amy Ruttan made us visualise the
story with her flawless storytelling. The emotional and
sensory details are exquisitely done and the sensuality
in the love scene just sizzles. Highly recommended for
all lovers of medical romance.'

—*Contemporary Romance Reviews* on
Safe in His Heart

PROLOGUE

IT WAS PITCH-BLACK and she couldn't figure out why the lights were off at first. Erica moved quickly, trying to shake the last remnants of sleep from her brain. Not that she'd got much sleep. She'd come off a twenty-four-hour shift and had got maybe two, possibly three, hours of sleep. She wasn't sure when the banging on her berth door roused her, telling her they needed her on deck.

What struck her as odd was why had the hospital ship gone into silent running.

She'd been woken up and told nothing. Only that some injured officers were inbound. She hadn't even been told the nature of their injuries. When she came out on deck, there was only a handful of staff and a chopper primed and waiting.

Covert operation.

That was what her gut told her and the tension shared by those waiting said the same thing.

Top secret.

Then it all made sense. She'd been trained and gone through many simulations of such a situation, but in her two years on the USNV *Hope* she'd never encountered one.

Adrenaline now fueled her body. She had no idea what was coming in, or what to expect, but she knew she had to be on her A-game.

Not that she ever wasn't on her A-game. Her two
years on the *Hope* had been her best yet and she'd risen
in the ranks finally to get to this moment, being trusted
with a covert operation. She had no doubt that was what
it was because it must be important if their mission to aid
a volcanic eruption disaster zone in Indonesia was being
stalled. As she glanced around at the staff standing at
attention and waiting, she saw it was all senior officers
on deck, except for a couple of on-duty petty officers.

"How many minutes did they say they were out, Petty
Officer?" Erica had to shout over the sound of waves.
It was unusually choppy on the Arabian Sea, but it was
probably due to the fact that the ship was on silent running. Only the stabilizers on the sides kept USNV *Hope*
from tipping over. She couldn't see Captain Dayton anywhere, but then she suspected her commanding officer
was at the helm. Silent running in the middle of the In-
dian Ocean at night was no easy feat.

"Pardon me, Commander?" the petty officer asked.

"I asked, how many minutes out?"

"Five at the most, Commander. We're just waiting
for the signal."

And as if on cue a flare went off the port side and,
in the brief explosion of light, Erica could make out the
faint outline of a submarine. The chopper lifted from
the helipad and headed out in the direction of the flare.

"Two minutes out!" someone shouted. "Silent running, people, and need-to-know basis."

Erica's heart raced.

This was why she'd got into the Navy. This was why
she wanted to serve her country. She had fought for this
moment, even when she had been tormented at Annapolis about not having what it took.

Dad would've been proud.

And a lump formed in her throat as she thought of her father. Her dad, a forgotten hero. She was serving, and giving it her all helping wounded warriors, and being on the USNV *Hope* gave her that. She had earned the right to be here.

The taunts that she'd slept her way to the top, telling her she couldn't make it, hadn't deterred her. The nay-saying had strengthened her more. Even when her dad suffered with his PTSD and his wounds silently, he would still wear his uniform with pride, his head held high. He was her hero. Now she was a highly decorated commander and surgeon and it gave her pride. So she held her head up high.

The better she did, the more she achieved the shame of her one mistake being washed away. At least, that was what she liked to think, even if others thought she'd end up with PTSD like her father: unable to handle the pressures, her memory disgraced. Well, they had another think coming. She was stronger than they thought she was.

The chopper was returning, a stretcher dangling as it hovered. Erica raced forward, crouching low to keep her balance so the wind from the chopper's blades wouldn't knock her on her backside.

With help the stretcher unhooked and was lifted onto a gurney. Once they had the patient stabilized they wheeled the gurney off the deck and into triage.

It was then, in the light, she could see the officer was severely injured and, as she glanced down at him, he opened his eyes and gazed at her. His eyes were the most brilliant blue she'd ever seen.

"We're here to get you help," she said, trying to reassure him as they wheeled him into a trauma pod. He seemed to understand what she was saying, but his gaze was locked on her, his breath labored, panting through obvious pain.

There was a file, instead of a commanding officer, and she opened it; there was no name, no rank of the patient.

Nothing. Only that he'd had gunshot wounds to the leg three days ago and now an extensive infection.

Where had they been that they couldn't get medical attention right away? That several gunshot wounds could lead to such an infection?

Dirty water. Maybe they were camped out in the sewers.

"What's your name?" she asked as she shone a light into his eyes, checking his pupillary reaction. Gauging the ABCs was the first protocol in trauma assessment.

"Classified," he said through gritted teeth. "Leg."

Erica nodded. "We'll take care of it."

As another medic hooked up a central line, Erica moved to his left leg and, as she peeled away the crude dressings, he let out a string of curses. As she looked at the mangled leg, she knew this man's days serving were over.

"We'll have to amputate; prep an OR," Erica said to a nurse.

"Yes, Commander." The nurse ran out of the trauma pod.

"What?" the man demanded. "What did you say?"

"I'm very sorry." She leaned over to meet his gaze. "Your leg is full of necrotic tissue and the infection is spreading. We have to amputate."

"Don't amputate."

"I'm sorry, but I have no choice."

"Don't you take my leg. Don't you dare amputate." The threat was clear, it was meant to scare her, but she wasn't so easily swayed. Being an officer in the Navy, a predominantly male organization, had taught her quickly that she wasn't going to let any man have power over her. No man would intimidate her. Something she'd almost forgotten at her first post in Rhode Island.

"Don't ever let a man intimidate you, Erica. Chances are they're more scared of you and your abilities."

She'd forgotten those words her father had told her. *Never again.*

"I'm sorry." She motioned to the anesthesiologist to sedate him and, as she did, he reached out and grabbed her arm, squeezing her tight. His eyes had a wild light.

"Don't you touch me! I won't let you."

"Stand down!" she yelled back at him.

"Don't take my leg." This time he was begging; the grip on her arm eased, but he didn't let go. "Don't take it. Let me serve my…" His words trailed off as the sedative took effect, his eyes rolling before he was unconscious.

His passionate plea tugged at her heart. She understood him, this stranger. She'd amputated limbs before and never thought twice. She had compassion, but this was something more. In the small fragment she'd shared with the unnamed SEAL, she had understood his fear and his vulnerability. It touched her deeply and she didn't want to have to take his leg and end his career.

If there'd been another way, she'd have done it. There wasn't.

The damage had been done.

If he'd gotten to her sooner, the infection would have been minor, the gunshot properly cared for.

It was the hazard of covert operations.

And her patient, whoever he was, was paying the price.

"Let's get him intubated and into the OR Stat." The

words were hard for her to say, but she shook her sympathy for him from her mind and focused on the task at hand.

At least he'd have his life.

"Petty Officer, where is my patient's commanding officer?" Erica asked as she came out of the scrub room.

"Over there, Commander. He's waiting for your report." The petty officer pointed over her shoulder and Erica saw a group of uniformed men waiting.

"Thank you," Erica said as she walked toward them. *Navy SEALs.*

She knew exactly what they were, though they had no insignia to identify themselves. They were obviously highly trained because when she was in surgery she'd been able to see that someone had some basic surgical skills as they'd tried to repair the damage caused by the bullets. Also, the bullets had been removed beforehand.

If it hadn't been for the bacteria which had gotten in the wound, the repair would've sufficed.

At her approach, they saluted her and she returned it.

"How's my man?" The commanding officer asked as he stepped forward.

"He made it through surgery, but the damage caused by the infection was too extensive. The muscle tissue was necrotic and I had to amputate the left leg below the knee."

The man cursed under his breath and the others bowed their heads. "What caused the infection? Couldn't it be cleared up with antibiotics?"

"It was a vicious form of bacteria," Erica offered. "I don't know much about your mission."

"It's classified," the commanding officer said.

Erica nodded. "Well, you obviously have a good medic. The repair was crude, but stable."

"He was our medic," someone mumbled from the back, but was silenced when the commanding officer shot him a look which would make any young officer go running for the hills.

"If it hadn't been for the bacteria getting in there… Depending on whatever your situation was, it could've been caused by many factors," Erica said, trying to take the heat off the SEAL who'd stepped out of line.

"Like?" the commanding officer asked, impatience in his voice.

"Dirty water?" Erica ventured a guess, but when she got no response from the SEALs she shook her head. "I'm sorry, unless I know the details of your mission I can't help you determine the exact cause of how your man picked up the bacteria."

The commanding officer nodded. "Understood. How soon can we move him?"

"He's in ICU. He has a high temperature and will require a long course of antibiotics as well as monitoring of his surgical wound."

"Unacceptable," the commanding officer snapped. "He needs to be moved. He can't stay here."

Erica crossed her arms. "You move him and he develops a post-op fever, he could die."

"I'm sorry, Commander. We have a mission to fulfill."

"Not with my patient, you don't."

"I'm sorry, Commander. We're under strict orders. I can give him eight hours before our transport comes." The commanding officer nodded and moved back to his group of men as they filed out of the surgical bay.

Erica shook her head.

She understood the protocols. It was a covert operation, but she didn't agree with all the regulations.

Their medic was useless. He needed medical care for quite some time and as a physician she wanted to see it through.

When that young SEAL had blurted out that the man she'd operated on was their medic, her admiration for her patient grew. He'd operated on himself, most likely without anesthetic, and probably after he'd removed the bullets from the other man they'd brought on board after him. That man didn't have the same extent of infection but, from what she'd gleaned from a scrub nurse, the gunshot wound had been a through-and-through. It hadn't even nicked an artery.

The man was being watched for a post-op fever and signs of the bacterial infection but would make a full recovery.

Her patient on the other hand had months of rehabilitation and, yes, pain.

I wish I knew his name.

It was a strange thought which crept into her head, but it was there all the same, and she wished she knew who he really was, where he was from. Was he married? And, if he was, wouldn't his wife want to know what she was in for as well?

Her patient was a mystery to her and she didn't really like mysteries.

She headed into the ICU. He was extubated, but still sedated and now cleaned up. There were several cuts and scratches on his face, but they hadn't been infiltrated by the bacteria.

Erica sighed; she hated ending the career of a fellow serviceman. She grabbed a chair and sat down by his bedside.

She had eight hours to monitor him, unless she appealed to someone higher up about keeping him here for his own good. At least until he was more stable to withstand a medical transport to the nearest base.

USNV *Hope* was a floating hospital. It was not as big as USNV *Mercy*, but just as capable of taking care of his needs while he recovered. And it wasn't only the physical wounds Erica was worried about, but also the emotional ones he'd have when he recovered.

She knew about that. There were scars she still carried.

Her patient had begged for his leg because he wanted to serve. It was admirable. Hopefully, he'd get the help he needed. The help her father hadn't had.

She reached out and squeezed his hand. "I'm sorry," she whispered.

He squeezed back and moaned. "Liam?"

Erica didn't know who Liam was but she stood so he could see her. "You're okay."

His eyes opened—those brilliant blue eyes. "What happened?"

"You had a bacterial infection. Your leg couldn't be saved."

He frowned, visibly upset, and tried to get up, but Erica held him down.

"Let me go!" He cursed a few choice words. "I told you not to take it. You lied to me. You lied to me, Liam! Why the heck did you do that? I'm not worth it. Damn it, let me out of here."

Erica reached over and hit a buzzer as she threw as much of her weight on him as possible, trying to keep him calm as a nurse ran over with a sedative.

It was then he began to cry softly and her heart wrenched.

"I'm so sorry."

"It was your life, Liam. My life… I have nothing else. You left me. We promised to stay together. I need my leg to do that."

Erica didn't know who Liam was, but she got off of him as he stopped fighting back. "I'm sorry." She took his hand once more. "I'm so very sorry."

He nodded as the drugs began to take effect. "You're so beautiful."

The words caught her off guard. "I'm sorry?"

"Beautiful. Like an angel." And then he said no more as he drifted off to sleep.

Erica sighed again and left his bedside. She had to keep this man here. He couldn't go off with his unit.

He needed to recuperate, to get used to the idea that his leg was gone and understand why. He was a medic; he'd understand when he was lucid and she could explain medically why she'd taken his leg.

Pain made people think irrationally. She was sure that was why her father had gone AWOL during a covert mission, endangering everyone. That was why he had come home broken and that was why he'd eventually taken his own life.

"Watch out, she's going to go AWOL like her father!"

The taunts and jeers made her stomach twist.

Block them out. Block them out.

"You need to get some sleep, Commander Griffin. You've been up for over thirty hours," Nurse Regina said as she wrote the dosage in the patient's chart. "Seriously, you look terrible."

Erica rolled her eyes at her friend and bunk mate before yawning. "Yeah, I think you're right. Do you know where Captain Dayton is?"

"He's in surgery now the ship isn't on silent running," Regina remarked. "Is it urgent?"

"Yeah, when he's out could you send him to my berth? I need to discuss this patient's file with him."

"Of course, Commander Griffin."

Erica nodded and headed off to find her bunk.

She was going to fight that man's unit to keep him on the hospital ship so he could get the help he needed.

There was no way any covert operation was going to get around her orders. Not this time. Not when this man's life was on the line.

He deserved all the help she could give him.

The man had lost a leg in service to his country. It would take both physical and mental healing.

He'd paid his price and Erica was damn well going to make sure he was taken care of.

CHAPTER ONE

Five years later, Okinawa Prefecture, Japan

"CAPTAIN WILDER WILL see you now, Commander Griffin."

Erica stood and straightened her dress uniform. She'd only landed in Okinawa five hours ago on a Navy transport and she was still suffering from jet lag. She'd flown from San Diego after getting her reassignment from the USNV *Hope* to a naval base hospital.

Another step in her career she was looking forward to, and the fact that it was in Japan had her extremely excited.

It was another amazing opportunity and one she planned to make the most of. Hopefully soon she'd get a promotion in rank but, given her track record, it seemed like she had to fight for every promotion or commendation she deserved.

It's worth it. Each fight just proves you can do it. You're strong.

Captain Dayton taking a disgraced young medical officer under his wing and letting her serve for seven years on the *Hope* was helping her put the past to rest.

Helping her forget her foolish mistake, her one dumb moment of weakness.

Erica followed the secretary into the office.

Dr. Thorne Wilder was the commanding officer of the general surgery wing of the naval hospital. They wouldn't see as much action as they'd see in a field hospital, or on a medical ship, but she'd be caring for the needs of everyone on base.

Appendectomies, gall bladder removals, colectomies—whatever needed to be done, Erica was going to rise to the challenge.

Dr. Wilder had requested her specifically when she'd put in for reassignment to a Naval hospital. She'd expected some downtime in San Diego while she waited, but that hadn't happened and she didn't mind in the least. She'd spent almost a year after her disgrace at Rhode Island in San Diego, waiting to be reassigned, and then she'd been assigned to the *Hope*. Perhaps her past was indeed just that now.

Past.

It also meant she didn't have to find temporary lodging or, in the worst-case scenario, stay with her mother in Arizona where Erica would constantly be lectured about being in the Navy. Her mother didn't exactly agree with Erica's career choice.

"You're in too much danger! The Navy killed your father."

No, the Navy hadn't killed her father. Undiagnosed PTSD had killed her father eventually, even if his physicians had had a bit of a hand in it by clearing him to serve in a covert mission.

Her mother wanted to know why she hadn't gone in to psychiatry, helped wounded warriors as a civilian. Though that had been her intention, working in an OR gave her a sense of satisfaction. Being a surgeon let her be on the front line, to see action if needs be, just like her father. It was why she'd become a medic, to save men and women like her father, both in the field and in recuperation.

"Commander Erica Griffin reporting for duty, sir." She stood at attention and saluted.

Dr. Wilder had his back to her; he was staring out the window, his hands clasped behind his back. It was a bit of an uneven stance, but there was something about him: something tugging at the corner of her mind; something she couldn't quite put her finger on. It was like when you had a thought on the tip of your tongue but, before the words could form, you lost it, though the mysterious thought remained in your head, forgotten but not wholly.

"At ease, Commander." He turned around slowly, his body stiff, and she tried not to let out the gasp of surprise threatening to erupt from her.

Brilliant blue eyes gazed at her.

Eyes she'd seen countless times in her mind. They were hauntingly beautiful.

"You're so beautiful... Beautiful. Like an angel."

No man had ever said that to her before. Of course, he'd been drugged and out of his mind with shock, but still no one had said that to her. Not even Captain Seaton, her first commanding officer when she'd been a lowly and stupid lieutenant fresh out of Annapolis. Captain Seaton had wooed her, seduced her and then almost destroyed her career by claiming she was mentally unstable and obsessed with him after she'd ended the relationship.

She was far from unstable. She had a quick temper, but over time she'd learned to keep that in check. Her job and her status in the Navy intimidated men, usually.

So his words, his face, had stuck with her. As had the stigma and that was why she'd never date another officer. She wouldn't let another person destroy her career.

Dating, if she had time, was always with a civilian. Though she didn't know why at this moment she was thinking about dating.

"Like an angel..."

As Erica stared into Captain Wilder's blue eyes, a warmth spread through her. She'd always wondered what had happened to him. Since he'd been moved against her wishes, she'd assumed he hadn't made it.

She'd apparently been wrong. Which was good.

Five years ago when she'd woken up, she realized she'd slept for eight hours. So she'd run to find Captain Dayton, only to be told that, yes, her request had been heard, but had been denied by those higher up the chain of command. When she'd gone to check on her patient, he was gone.

All traces of him were gone.

It was like the covert operation had never happened.

Those men had never been on board.

Even her patient's chart had gone; wiped clean like he'd never existed. She'd been furious, but there was nothing she could do. She was powerless, but she always wondered what had happened to that unnamed medic.

The man who had begged her not to take his leg.

The man who'd cried in her arms as the realization had overcome him.

Now, here he was. In Okinawa of all places, and he was a commanding officer.

Her commanding officer.

Dr. Thorne Wilder.

Captain Wilder.

She'd never pictured him to be a Thorne, but then again Thorne was such an unusual name and she wasn't sure many people would look at someone and say, "Hey, that guy looks like a Thorne." His head had been clean shaven when he'd been her patient, but his dark hair had grown out. It suited him.

The scars weren't as visible because he wasn't as thin, his cheeks weren't hollow, like they'd been when she'd treated him and his skin was no longer pale and jaundiced from blood loss and bacterial infection. She hadn't realized how tall he actually was—of course when she'd seen him he'd been on a stretcher. She was five foot ten and he was at least three inches taller than her, with broad shoulders.

He looked robust. Healthy and absolutely handsome.

She couldn't remember the last time she'd seen such an attractive man. Not that she'd had much time to date or even look at a member of the opposite sex.

Get a grip on yourself.

He cocked his head to the side, a confused expression on his face. "Commander Griffin, are you quite all right?"

He didn't remember her.

Which saddened her, but also made her feel relieved just the same. Erica didn't want him blaming her for taking his leg or accusing her of something which would erase all the work she'd done over the years to bring honor back to her name and shake the venomous words of Captain Seaton.

It was the pain medication. The fever. It's hardly surprising that he doesn't remember you.

"I'm fine… Sorry, Captain Wilder. I haven't had a chance to readjust since arriving in Okinawa. I'm still operating on San Diego time."

He smiled and nodded. "Of course, my apologies for making you report here so soon after you landed at the base. Won't you have a seat?" He motioned to a chair on the opposite side of his desk.

Erica removed her hat and tucked it under her arm before sitting down. She was relieved to sit because her knees had started to knock together, either from fatigue or shock, she wasn't quite sure which. Either way, she was grateful.

Thorne sat down on the other side of the desk and opened her personnel file. "I have to say, Commander, I was quite impressed with your service record. You were the third in your class at Annapolis."

"Yes," she responded. She didn't like to talk about Annapolis—because it led to questions about her first posting under Captain Seaton. She didn't like to relive her time there, so when commanding officers talked about her achievements she kept her answers short and to the point.

There was no need to delve in any further. Everything was in her personnel file. Even when she'd been turned down for a commendation because she was "mentally unfit".

Don't think about it.

"And you served on the USNV *Hope* for the last seven years?"

"Yes."

He nodded. "Well, we run a pretty tight ship here in Okinawa. We serve not only members of the armed forces and their families but also residents of Ginowan."

"I look forward to serving, Captain."

Thorne leaned back in his chair, his gaze piercing her as if he could read her mind. It was unnerving. It was like he could see right through to her very core and she wasn't sure how she felt about that.

Everyone she'd let in so far had hurt her.

Even her own mother, with her pointed barbs about

Erica's career choice and how serving in the Navy had killed her father. Her mother had never supported her.

"The Navy ruined our life, Erica. Why do you want to go to Annapolis?" Erica hadn't been able to tell her mother that it was because of her father. Her mother didn't think much about him, but to Erica he was a hero and she'd wanted to follow in his footsteps.

"I'm proud to serve my country, Erica. It's the ultimate sacrifice. I'm honored to do it. Never forget I felt this way, even if you hear different."

So every remark about the armed forces ruining their life hurt. It was like a slap in the face each time and she'd gone numb with her mother, and then Captain Seaton, who had used her. She shut down emotionally to people. It was for the best.

At least, she thought she had, until a certain Navy SEAL had crossed her path five years before. He'd been the only one to stir any kind of real emotion in her in a long time.

"I have no doubt you'll do well here, Commander. Have you been shown to your quarters on base?"

"Yes."

"Are they adequate?"

"Of course, Captain."

He nodded. "Good. Well, get some sleep. Try to adjust to Okinawa time. Jet lag can be horrible. I'll expect you to report for duty tomorrow at zero four hundred hours."

Erica stood as he did and saluted him. "Thank you, Captain."

"You're dismissed, Commander."

She nodded and placed her hat back on her head before turning and heading out of the office as fast as she could.

Once she was a safe distance away she took a moment

to pause and take a deep breath. She'd never expected to run into him again.

Given the state he'd been in when she'd last seen him, she'd had her doubts that he would survive, but he had and he was still serving.

Even though he was no longer a Navy SEAL, at least he hadn't been honorably discharged. It had been one of his pleas when she'd told him about his leg.

"This is your life, Liam. My life... I have nothing else. I need my leg to do that."

The memory caused a shiver to run down her spine. It was so clear, like it had happened yesterday, and she couldn't help but wonder again who Liam was. Whoever he was, it affected Captain Wilder.

It doesn't matter. You're here to do your job.

Erica sighed and then composed herself.

She was here to be a surgeon for the Navy.

That was all.

Nothing more. Dr. Thorne Wilder's personal life was of no concern to her, just like her personal life, or lack thereof, was no one else's concern.

Still, at least she knew what had happened to her stranger.

At least he was alive and that gave her closure to something that had been bothering her for five years. At last she could put that experience to rest and she could move on with her life.

After Erica left, Thorne got up and wandered back over to his window. From his vantage point he could see the walkway from his office and maybe catch a glimpse of Erica before her ride came to take her back to her quarters on base.

She'd been surprised to see him, though she'd tried

not to show it. She hid her emotions well, kept them in check like any good officer.

Erica remembered him, but how much else did she remember?

Bits and pieces of his time on the USNV *Hope* were foggy to him, but there were two things he remembered about his short time on the ship and those two things were losing his leg and seeing her face.

He remembered her face clearly. It had been so calm in the tempestuous strands of memory of that time. He remembered pain.

Oh, yes. He'd never forget the pain. He still felt it from time to time. "Phantom limb" pain. It drove him berserk, but he had ways of dealing with it.

At night, though, when he closed his eyes and that moment came back to him in his nightmares, her face was the balm to soothe him.

A nameless, angelic face tied with a painful moment. It was cruel. To remember her meant he had to relive that moment over and over again.

And then, as fate would have it, a stack of personnel files had been piled on his desk about a month ago and he'd been told to find another general surgeon to come to Okinawa. Her file had been on the top as the most qualified.

It was then he'd had a name for his angel.

Erica.

As he thought about her name, she came into view, walking quickly toward an SUV which was pulling up. He thought he adequately remembered her beauty, but his painful haze of jangled memories didn't do her justice.

Her hair wasn't white-blond, it was more honey colored. Her skin was pale and her lips red. Her eyes were dark, like dark chocolate. She was tall and even taller in her heels. He was certain she could almost look him in the eye.

She walked with purpose, her head held high. He liked that about her. Mick, his old commanding officer in the Navy SEALs Special Ops, had told him a month after his amputation that the surgeon who'd removed his leg wouldn't back down. Even when Mick had tried to scare her off.

He'd been told how his surgeon had fought for him to get the best medical care he needed. How she'd sat at his bedside. She'd seen him at his most vulnerable. Something he didn't like people to see.

Vulnerability, emotion, was for the weak.

He'd been trained to be tough.

He'd been in Special Ops for years, even though he'd started his career just as a naval medic like Erica.

And then on a failed mission in the Middle East they'd become cornered. He'd thrown himself in front of a barrage of bullets to save Tyler from being killed. Bullets had ripped through his left calf, but he'd managed to stop the bleeding, repair the damage and move on.

Only they'd been surrounded and they'd had to resort to the old sewer system running under the city to make their escape and meet their transport.

The infested and dirty water was where he'd probably caught the bacteria which had cost him his leg, but it was his leg or his life.

For a long time after the fact, he'd wanted to die because he couldn't be a Navy SEAL any longer. He'd almost died. Just like his twin brother, Liam, had on a different mission. He remembered the look of anguish on Liam's wife's face when he'd had to tell her that her husband was gone. It was why Thorne wouldn't date.

Seeing the pain in Megan's eyes, the grief which ate at her and her two kids… It was something Thorne never wanted to put anyone through. It was best Thorne severed all ties. He wasn't going to stop serving and it was better if he didn't leave behind a family.

And it was his fault Liam was dead and that Megan was a widow. One stupid wrong move, that was what Thorne had done, and Liam had pushed him out of the way.

Liam had paid with his life and Thorne would forever make penance for that mistake.

Thorne had enlisted in the Special Ops and was accepted as a SEAL. It had been Liam's passion and Thorne planned to fulfill it for him.

And then he'd lost his leg saving another.

He didn't regret it.

Though he was ashamed he was no longer in the Special Ops. When he'd taken that bullet for Tyler he'd been able to see Liam's face, disappointed over another foolish move.

Thorne had returned to serve as a medic ashamed and numb to life.

He wasn't the same man anymore, and it wasn't just the absence of his leg which made him different.

At least he still had surgery. When the assignment to command the general surgery clinic in Okinawa had come up, Thorne had jumped at it—and when he'd seen that Erica, a highly recommended and decorated surgeon in the Navy, was requesting reassignment to Okinawa Prefecture, Thorne had wanted the chance to know more about the woman who'd taken his leg and saved his life.

Had she?

His mother didn't like the fact he'd gone back to serving after he lost his leg.

"I lost your brother and almost lost you. Take the discharge and come home!"

Except Thorne couldn't. Serving in the Navy was his life. He might not be an active SEAL any longer, but he was still a surgeon. He was useful.

He was needed. If he couldn't be a SEAL and serve that way, in honor of his brother he could do this.

Thorne scrubbed his hand over his face. His leg was bothering him and soon he'd head back to his quarters on the base and take off his prosthetic. Maybe soak his stump in the ocean to ease the pain. He couldn't swim, but he could wade.

Water soothed Thorne and aided him with his phantom limb syndrome. Seeing Erica face-to-face had made his leg twinge. As if it knew and remembered she'd been the one to do the surgery and was reacting to her.

Perhaps bringing her here was a bad idea.

She knew and had seen too much of his softer side. He'd been exposed to her, lying naked on her surgical table, and Thorne was having a hard time trying to process that.

Perhaps he should've kept her away.

A flash behind him made him turn and he could see dark clouds rolling in from the east. It was typhoon season in Okinawa, but this was just a regular storm. The tall palm trees along the beach in the distance began to sway as the waves crashed against the white sand.

A dip was definitely out of the question now.

The storm rolling in outside reflected how he felt on the inside and he couldn't help but wonder if he was losing his mind by bringing her here.

When had he become so morbid and self-obsessed?

He couldn't reassign her without any just cause. It

would damage her reputation and he wouldn't do that to Erica.

No, instead he'd force her to ask for a reassignment on her own terms.

Though he didn't want to do it, he was going to make Erica's life here in Okinawa hard so that she'd put in for the first transfer to San Diego and he could forget about her.

Once and for all.

CHAPTER TWO

"YOU'VE BEEN HERE a week and you've been getting some seriously crummy shifts."

Erica glanced up from her charting at Bunny Hamasaki, a nurse and translator for the hospital. A lot of the residents of Ginowan knew English, but some of the older residents didn't. Bunny was middle-aged, born and bred on Okinawa. Her father was a Marine and her mother a daughter of a fisherman.

She'd been born at the old hospital down the road and seemed to know everyone and everything about everyone.

"I could say the same for you," Erica remarked.

Bunny snorted. "I'm used to these shifts. This time of night is when I'm needed the most. Plus I can avoid my husband's snoring and bad breath, working the night shift."

Erica chuckled and turned back to her charting.

Bunny reminded her of her scrub nurse, bunk mate and best friend Regina. Truth be told, she was a wee bit homesick for the *Hope* and for her friends.

This is what you wanted. You'll make captain faster this way.

And that was what really mattered—proving herself.

"I don't think I'm getting crummy shifts."

Bunny snorted again. "Commander, with all due respect, you're getting played with."

Bunny moved away from the nursing station to check on a patient and, as Erica glanced around the recovery room, she had to agree.

Since her arrival a week ago all she'd been getting was night shifts.

Which seriously sucked, because by the time she'd clocked out she was too exhausted to explore, socialize or make friends in Okinawa. Then again, she was here to work, not to make friends. After her shift, she'd return to her housing on base and collapse.

Maybe she'd unpack. Though she didn't usually do that until she'd been on-site for at least a month.

No. She'd probably just crash and sleep the day away. Except for the first day she'd arrived and met with Dr. Wilder, she hadn't seen Okinawa in the daylight.

He's putting you through your paces.

That was something she was familiar with.

Even though she was a high-ranking officer, she was positive the other surgeons were having fun initiating her, seeing how their commanding officer was doing it.

"Stupid ritual," she mumbled to herself.

"What was that, Commander?"

Erica snapped the chart closed and stood to attention when she realized Dr. Wilder was standing behind her. "Nothing, sir."

Thorne cocked an eyebrow, a smile of bemusement on his face. "You're not up for formal inspection, Commander. At ease."

Erica opened her chart again and flipped to the page she'd left off at, trying to ignore the fact that Dr. Wilder was standing in front of her. She could feel his gaze on her.

"I heard the whole conversation with Bunny," he mentioned casually.

"Oh, yes?" Erica didn't look up.

"I'm scheduling you for the night shift deliberately. You do realize that?"

"I know, Captain Wilder."

"You know?" There was a hint of confusion in his voice.

Erica sighed; she was never going to finish this chart at this rate. She set down her pen and glanced up at him. "Yes. Of course you are. I'm not a stranger to this treatment."

"I bet you're not." He leaned against the counter. "You think it's a stupid ritual?"

"I do." She wasn't going to sugarcoat anything. She never did.

His eyes widened, surprised. "Why?"

"It's bullying."

"You think I'm bullying you?" he asked.

"Of course. I'm new."

"And it doesn't bother you?"

"The ritual bothers me. I think it's not needed, but it's not going to dissuade me from my job."

There was a brief flash of disappointment. Like he'd been trying to get her to snap or something. She was made of stronger mettle than that and he'd have to do a damn lot more to sway her. She was here to stay for the long haul, or at least until she made captain—and then the possibilities would be endless.

"Well, then, you won't mind working the night shift again next week."

So much for unpacking.

"Of course not." She shrugged. "Is that all you wanted to talk about, my shift work?"

His gaze narrowed. "You're very flippant to your commanding officer."

She wanted to retort something about him being on her operating table five years ago, but she bit her tongue. The last time she'd lost her cool, when she'd forgotten about the delicate and precise hierarchy, she'd lost her commendation. Of course, that had been a totally different situation with a former lover. Captain Wilder wasn't her lover. He was just a former patient and now her commanding officer.

She was to this macho behavior. Erica could take whatever he had to throw at her. As long as he didn't bring up what happened during her first post, but she seriously doubted he knew all the details about it because he would've mentioned it by now.

Everyone always did.

"Sorry, sir." Though she wasn't. Not in the least.

"It won't last forever." He was smirking again.

"Can I be frank, Captain Wilder?"

He shrugged. "By all means."

"Perhaps we should go somewhere privately to discuss this."

"I don't think so."

"Fine, suit yourself." The recovery area was usually quiet, but it was even more so now, and it felt like everyone was fixated on her and Captain Wilder. "If this is your way to try and make me crack, you won't succeed."

Thorne crossed his arms. "Really? You think this is a means to drive you away?"

"I do and you won't succeed. If there's one thing you'll learn from my file, Captain, it is that I don't give up. I won't give up. So I'll take whatever you have for me, Captain, and I won't complain. So, if you're looking to see me break, you won't. If night shifts are what you want to give me, so be it. I've done countless night shifts before. It's fine. If your plan is to ostracize me, well, then, you won't succeed unless I'm the only one working and there are no patients. I'm tougher than I appear, Captain Wilder."

Thorne was impressed. He didn't want to be, but he was. She barely saw the light of day, yet she came in and did everything without a complaint. When he'd heard her mumble something about stupidity, he'd been planning to swoop in and make his kill. Push her to the breaking point.

Only she'd risen to the challenge and basically told him to bring it on.

Yes, his goal with the numerous night shifts was to ostracize her, but it wasn't working. He admired that. He didn't want to, but he did. She was right. It wouldn't work unless she was working by herself out in the middle of a desert somewhere. He was so impressed.

So she'll take whatever I give her.

It was time to throw her off.

"Tell you what. You're on days as of Saturday. Take tomorrow off and readjust your inner clock. I'll see you at zero nine hundred hours. Get some sleep. You obviously need it."

He didn't give her a chance to respond; he turned and walked away, trying not to let her see his limp, because his leg had been bothering him today, and maybe because of that he'd decided to be a bit soft on her.

No, that wasn't it. At least, that was what he told himself.

Just as she wouldn't back down, he wouldn't either.

Thorne would make sure she left the hospital and that it would be her idea. Even though he kept his distance he was always aware of what she was doing and when he was around her he felt his resolve soften because she impressed him so.

He was drawn to her.

No woman had affected him like this in a long time. Even then he wasn't sure any woman had had this kind of hold on him.

Don't think about her that way.

Only he couldn't help himself. He'd been thinking about her, seeing her face for years.

She haunted him.

Why did I bring her here?

Because he was a masochist. He was taunting himself with something, someone he couldn't have.

A twinge of pain racked through him. He needed to seek the solace of his office, so no one saw him suffer.

Erica had to go before things got out of hand.

He pushed the elevator button and when it opened he walked in. Thankfully it was empty at this time of night and he could lean against the wall and take some weight off his stump. Even if it was just a moment, he'd take it.

He waited until the doors were almost shut before relaxing, but just as the doors were about to close, they opened and Erica stepped onto the elevator.

Damn it.

He braced himself. "Can I help you, Commander?"

"Excuse me, Captain, but I don't understand why you've suddenly changed your mind about my shifts. Didn't you understand what I was saying to you?"

"I do understand English," he snapped.

Go away.

"Why did you suddenly change my shift? Especially so publically. Others will think you're being easy on me or that I'm a whiner."

"Weren't you whining?"

"No. I don't whine. You don't have to give me a day shift."

"I thought that's what you wanted."

Erica pushed the emergency stop and the elevator grinded to a halt. "I want you to treat me like any other surgeon, like any other officer. I'm not green behind the ears, or however that saying goes."

"It's *wet* behind the ears," Thorne corrected her.

"Well, I'm not that."

No. You're not.

Thorne resisted the urge to smile and he resisted the urge to pull her in his arms and kiss her. Her brown eyes were dark with what he was sure was barely controlled rage, her cheeks flushed red. She was ticked off and he loved the fire in her.

His desire for Erica was unwelcome. He couldn't have a romantic attachment.

I don't deserve it.

Emotions were weakness.

Compassion for his patients, he had that in plenty, but these kinds of feelings were unwelcome. Still, he couldn't stop them from coming, and as she stood in the elevator berating him he fought with every fiber of his being not to press her up against the elevator wall and show her exactly what he was thinking, that he'd fantasized about her for five years.

"Well?" she demanded and he realized he hadn't been listening to a word she'd been saying. He'd totally zoned out, which was unlike him. He rarely lost focus, because if you lost focus you were dead.

At least that was what he'd picked up in his years in the Navy SEALs Special Ops and on the numerous dive missions.

Tyler had lost focus and that was why the sniper would have finished him off, if Thorne hadn't thrown himself in the path. Just like the stupid mistake he'd made when Liam had thrown him out of the way and paid with his life. Thorne had only lost a leg saving Tyler's life.

Just thinking about that moment made his phantom limb send an electric jolt of pain up through his body and he winced.

"Are you all right?" Erica asked, and she reached out and touched his shoulder.

He brushed her hand away. "I'm fine." He took a deep breath.

"You look like you're in pain."

"I said I was fine!" He straightened up, putting all his weight on his prosthetic and working through the pain. "I won't give you an easy ride, but I also won't be so cruel. I realize that my actions are detrimental to your mental health."

The words "mental health" struck a chord with her. He could tell by the way the blood drained from her face. He knew they would hurt. In her file he'd read that her first commendation had been turned down due to her being unfit emotionally. Though he didn't have the details as to why, that was unimportant. His barb worked and he regretted it.

"My mental health is fine," she said quietly.

"Is it?"

She didn't glance at him as she slapped the emergency button, the elevator starting again. The elevator stopped on the next floor and the doors opened. She stepped out. The confidence, the strength which had been with her only a moment ago, had vanished.

And, though he should be pleased that he'd got to her, he wasn't. Thorne hated himself for doing that to her.

It's for the best. She's dangerous to you.

"Thank you for your time, Captain. I will see you on Saturday at zero nine hundred hours." The doors closed and she was gone and Thorne was left with a bitter taste in his mouth. His small victory wasn't so sweet.

CHAPTER THREE

"AHA!" ERICA PULLED out her sneakers from the box. "It's been a long time."

Great. You're talking to sneakers now.

Maybe she was overtired. As she glanced around the room at all the boxes she realized how disorganized her life had become.

It wasn't many boxes, but she didn't really like living in a state of chaos. She'd gone from the USNV *Hope* to San Diego and within forty-eight hours she'd been posted to Okinawa.

If she kept busy she didn't notice it so much, but now that she had some free time it irked her.

She'd rather be busy than not. Relaxation was all well and good, but she had a job to do. She stared at her bright-blue sneakers with the neon yellow laces. Although she loved running, it was not what she wanted to be doing today.

Erica would rather be in the hospital removing a gall bladder. She'd even take paperwork.

This was a new posting and she had a lot to prove.

Not only to herself, but to her comrades.

Damn Captain Wilder.

Questioning her mental health like that. How dared he?

Are you surprised?

He was probably just like Captain Seaton—threatened by her. She cursed Captain Seaton for being a major *puenez*, or "stinkbug", as her *mamère* often said about men who were scared of strong women. She was also mad at herself for being duped by Captain Seaton and letting him affect her career.

And then she chuckled to herself for condemning her superior who had given her the day off. Most people wouldn't be complaining about that and she found it humorous that she was condemning the man again.

Hadn't she done enough damage when she'd had to take his leg after it had got infected?

The guilt about ending his career as a SEAL ate at her, but not her decision to take his leg. There was no help for that. He would've died.

Perhaps he would've preferred death?

"Your father wanted to die and the Navy gave him the means to do so."

Erica shuddered, thinking about her mother's vitriol, because it made her think of that last moment she'd seen her father—the haunted look in his eyes as he'd shipped out.

"Be good, Erica. You're my girl."

He'd held her tight, but it hadn't been the same embrace she'd been used to. Three days later, he'd gone AWOL. Two weeks later, after a dishonorable discharge, he'd ended his life.

You did right by Thorne. Just like the surgeons saved your father's life the first time he was injured. You saved Thorne's life.

It was her job to save lives, not end them. His desire to die was not her concern any more. She'd saved his life and they'd taken him away. Captain Thorne Wilder was no longer her concern.

She'd done her duty by him and that was how she slept at night.

Erica sat down on her couch and slipped on her running shoes, lacing them up. There wasn't much she could do. She wasn't on duty today, unless there was an emergency, so she might as well make the best of it. Besides, running along a beach might be more challenging than running laps on a deck.

She stretched and headed out to a small tract of beach near her quarters. Though the sky was a bit dark, the sea wasn't rough, and the waves washing up on shore would make her feel like she was out on the open sea. Back on the *Hope*.

As she jogged out toward the beach she got to see more of the base. It was pretty active for being on such a small island far off the mainland of Japan.

The hospital was certainly more active than being on the *Hope*. Unless they were responding to a disaster, there were stretches at sea where they weren't utilizing their medical skills. Those stretches were filled with rigorous drills and simulations.

As she headed out onto the beach, she followed what appeared to be a well-worn path along the edge so she wouldn't have to run in the sand.

Erica opted to go off the path and headed out onto the sand. It slowed her down, but she didn't care. It would work her muscles more.

Besides, even though it was a bit overcast, it was still a beautiful day on the beach. The palm trees were swaying and the waves lapping against the shore made her smile.

As she rounded the bend to a small cove, she realized she wasn't the only one who was on the beach at this moment and it made her stop in her tracks.

Thorne.

He was about fifteen feet away from her, in casual clothes, his arms crossed and his gaze locked on the water. She followed where he was looking and could see swimmers not too far out in the protected cove.

I have to get out of here.

She turned to leave but, as if sensing someone was watching him, his gaze turned to her. Even from a distance she could feel his stare piercing through her protective walls. A stare which would make any lesser man or woman cringe from its hard edge, but not her.

Of course, now she couldn't turn and leave. He'd seen her, there was no denying that. He walked toward her fluidly as if there was no prosthesis there. So different from yesterday when he'd moved stiffly, his chiseled face awash with pain.

His face was expressionless, controlled and devoid of emotion.

So unlike the first time she'd met him, when he'd begged her not to take his leg and made her heart melt for him just a little bit.

"Commander, what a surprise to find you here," he said pleasantly, but she could detect the undertone of mistrust. He was questioning why and she had the distinct feeling her appearance was an unwelcome one.

"It's my day off and I thought a run along the beach would be nice."

It was nice until I ran into you.

"Never heard someone mention a run as nice." He raised an eyebrow.

Erica gritted her teeth. "I haven't seen much of the base since I first arrived. I'm usually sleeping when the sun is out."

Ha ha! Take that.

He nodded, but those blue eyes still held her, keeping her grounded to the spot as he assessed her. No wonder he'd been a Navy SEAL; apparently he could read people, make them uneasy and do it all with a cold, calculating calm. Even though it annoyed Erica greatly that it was directed at her at this moment, she couldn't help but admire that quality.

It was why it made the SEALs the best of the best.

Only, she wasn't some insurgent being interrogated or some new recruit. There was a reason she'd been one of the top students in her class at Annapolis.

She wasn't weak. She was tough and stalwart and could take whatever was dished out. She'd told him as much.

This she could handle. It didn't unnerve her. When he'd shown that moment of weakness, begging for his leg, that had shaken her resolve.

"No," he finally said, breaking the tension. "I suppose you haven't seen much of the base."

Erica nodded. "No, I haven't, but I'm not complaining."

A smile broke across his face, his expression softened. "I know you're not."

"What's going on out there?" she asked.

"SEAL training," he said and then shifted his weight, wincing.

"I didn't know this base was equipped for that."

"Yes. It's where I did my training." He cleared his throat. "I mean…"

"I knew you were a SEAL." She held her breath.

He feigned surprise. Captain Wilder might be good at interrogating and striking fear into subordinates, but he wasn't much of an actor. "How?"

Erica wanted to tell him it was because she'd been

the one who'd operated on him—that he'd been on her ship—only she didn't think that would go over too well. He was obviously hiding from her that he had a prosthesis, as if such a thing would make her think differently of him.

Did he think it was a sign of weakness? If he did, he was foolish, because Erica saw it as a sign of strength. A testament to his sacrifice for his country. Only she kept that thought to herself. She doubted he'd be overly receptive to it right now. The last thing she needed was to tick him off and have him state she was mentally unstable or something.

So instead she lied. "I looked up your record before I shipped out. I wanted to know who my commanding officer was in Okinawa."

His gaze narrowed; he didn't believe her. She could tell by the way he held himself, the way his brow furrowed. Only he wasn't going to admit it. "Is that so?"

"How else would I know?" she countered.

"Of course, that would be the only way you'd know." Thorne crossed his arms and turned back to look at the ocean. "Aren't you going to ask me why I'm not out there swimming with them?"

"No," Erica said.

He glanced over at her. "No?"

"With all due respect, Captain Wilder, that's not my business."

"Yet knowing I am a former SEAL was?"

"Any good officer worth their salt tries to find out who they're serving under. The reasons you left the SEALs or aren't active in missions any longer is not my concern. Some things are better left unsaid."

His cheeks flushed crimson and she wondered if she'd pushed it too far.

"You're right. Well, I may be retired from the SEALs, but I still oversee some of their training. Anything to keep involved."

Erica nodded. "A fine thing to be involved with."

Thorne smiled again, just briefly. "Well, I don't want to keep you from your run. If you continue on down the beach, there's another nice path which wraps around the hospital and forks, one path leading into the village and the other back to base. If you have the time, be sure to check out the village and in particular the temple."

"Thank you, Captain."

"When we're off duty, you can call me Thorne."

Now it was Erica's turn to blush. It came out of the blue; it caught her off guard.

Maybe it was supposed to.

"I'm not sure I'm comfortable with that."

"What harm is there in it?"

She didn't see any harm. When she went on shore leave with other shipmates or was off duty she didn't address them so formally. What was the difference here? The difference was she was never attracted to any of them, had never seen them so vulnerable and exposed.

"I'll think about it."

He cocked an eyebrow. "I have to say, I'm hurt. Am I so monstrous?"

"No." Erica grinned. "I only address my friends so informally."

"I'm not your friend?"

Now it was her turn to cock an eyebrow. "Really? You're asking me if we're friends?"

"I guess I am." He took a step closer to her and her pulse raced. She'd thought he was handsome when she'd first seen him, but that was when he'd been injured. Now he was healthy, towering over her and so close. She was highly attracted to him, she couldn't deny that. He stirred something deep inside her, something she hadn't felt in a long time.

Yearning.

There had been a couple other men since Captain Seaton, but not many, and none in the Navy. She didn't have time or interest.

Until she met Thorne.

Thorne was dangerous and, being her commanding officer, he was very taboo.

"We barely know each other, Captain. How can we be friends?"

"Easy. We can start by using our given names. I'm Thorne." And then he took her hand in his. It was strong and sent a shock of electricity through her.

Get a grip on yourself.

She needed to rein this in. This was how she'd fallen for Captain Seaton. He'd wooed her. She'd been blinded by hero worship, admiration, and she wouldn't let that happen again.

"We're not friends," Erica said quickly.

"We can be." His blue eyes twinkled mischievously. He was playing with her and she didn't like it. Thorne ran so hot and cold. He was trying to manipulate her.

"I don't think so, Captain." She suppressed a chuckle of derision and jogged past him, laughing to herself as she continued her run down the beach and perfectly aware that his eyes were on her.

Thorne watched her jog away and he couldn't help but admire her. Not many had stood up to him. He had the reputation of being somewhat of a jerk, to put it politely. He'd always been tough as nails. As Liam had always said. Yet Liam had gone straight into Special Ops and Thorne had become a medic. He wasn't without feelings.

He hadn't always been so closed off, but when you saw your identical twin brother lying broken on the ground after an insurgent attack, after he'd pushed you out of the way, then pieces of you died. Locking those parts of him away, the parts which still mourned his brother, was the only way to survive.

The only way to continue the fight, so that his brother's death wasn't in vain.

Thorne had hardened himself and, in doing so, had driven so many people away. They kept out of his way, they knew not to mess with him or challenge him. It was better that way. No one to care about. He didn't deserve it.

Erica was different.

You knew that when you approved her request to come to Okinawa.

His commanding officer still talked about the courage it had taken to stand up to him during that covert operation. How Erica had been adamant that Thorne was to remain on the USNV *Hope*. It had impressed Mick and that was hard to do.

Perhaps in Erica he'd met his match?

She's off-limits.

He needed that internal reminder that Erica was indeed off-limits. Thorne couldn't let another person in. There was no room for someone else in his life, so he had to get all these foolish notions out of his head.

Except, that was hard to do when he saw her, because those hazy, jangled memories from that time flooded his dreams—only now she wasn't just some ghost. The face was clear, tangible, and all he had to do was reach out and touch her to realize that his angel was indeed on Earth.

"Captain!" The shouts from the water caught his attention and he tore his gaze from Erica and out to sea.

The few men who had been doing their training were trying with futility to drag one of their comrades from the water, but the waves were making it difficult and the crimson streak following the injured man made Thorne's stomach knot.

Shark.

It was one of the dangers of training in the sea, though attacks were rare.

His first instinct was to run into the fray to help, but he couldn't step foot into water. His prosthesis had robotic components and it would totally fry his leg. He needed his prosthetic leg to continue his job.

He was useless.

So useless.

He pulled out his phone and called for an ambulance, then ran after Erica, who wasn't far away.

"Erica!" he shouted, each step causing pain to shoot up his thigh. He hadn't run in so long. "Commander."

Erica stopped and turned, her eyes wide and eyebrows arched with curiosity. Without having to ask questions, she looked past him to the blood in the water and men struggling to bring their friend safely ashore.

She ran straight to them, whipping off her tank top to use as a tourniquet, wading into the surf without hesitation to aid the victim, while all he could do was stand there and watch in envy.

Only for a moment, though, before he shook off that emotion.

He might not be able to help in the same way as Erica, but he'd do everything he could. As soon as they had the man out of the water and on the beach, Thorne dropped down on one knee to survey the damage to the man's calf.

"What happened?" Thorne asked, not taking his eyes off the wound as Erica tightened the tourniquet made out of her Navy-issue tank top.

"We were swimming back in and Corporal Ryder fell behind. It was then he cried out. We managed to scare the shark off," one of Corporal Ryder's comrades responded.

"My leg!" Corporal Ryder screamed. "My leg is gone."

Thorne's throat constricted and his phantom leg twinged with agony, which almost caused him to collapse in pain.

You're fine. Your leg is gone. There is no pain.

"Your leg is there, Corporal," Erica responded. "You hear me? Your leg is there."

Corporal Ryder howled in agony and then cursed before going into shock.

"Lie him down, he's going into shock." Thorne reached out and helped Erica get Corporal Ryder down.

Erica was helping the other recruits assess Corporal Ryder's ABCs, the water still lapping against them as they worked on the leg, and Thorne stood there useless because he couldn't get his prosthetic leg wet; the corporal was still half in the water.

"How bad?" Thorne directed his question to Erica.

"We can probably salvage the leg. We won't know until we get him into surgery."

The ambulance from the hospital pulled up in the parking lot. Two paramedics were hurrying down the hill to the beach with a stretcher.

"Well, Commander Griffin, it looks like we're both

scrubbing in. I don't know how many shark attacks you've seen…"

"Enough," she said, interrupting him, her expression soft. "Thank you for letting me assist you, Captain Wilder."

Thorne nodded and stood, getting out of the way as the paramedics arrived. "Commander, you go with the paramedics in the ambulance. I'll be there shortly."

There was no way he could keep up with the stretcher.

He'd get there in enough time.

Corporal Ryder needed all the help he could get.

Erica nodded and, as the ABCs of the corporal's condition were completed, he was on the gurney, headed toward the ambulance.

Thorne stayed behind with the other men, his stump throbbing, phantom pain racking him as his own body remembered the trauma he'd suffered.

He needed a moment to get it together.

To lock it all out, so he could be of some use to the corporal and help save that man's leg, where his own hadn't been.

CHAPTER FOUR

"MORE SUCTION."

Erica glanced up from the corporal's leg wound, but only briefly, as she carefully suctioned around the artery.

"Thank you, Commander," Thorne responded.

Their eyes locked across the surgical table. Even though she'd been here two weeks she had yet to operate with Thorne. When he had stitched his own leg, Erica had admired the work, given the condition and the crude tools he'd used. Now, watching him in action in a fully equipped and modern OR was something of beauty. She was so impressed with his surgical skill. There was a fluid grace with his hands, like a fine musician's, as he worked over the corporal's calf.

It was a simple wound to the leg, if you could call a shark bite simple. It didn't need or require two seasoned trauma surgeons, but Thorne had requested she be in there with him.

"You triaged him in the field. You have the right to be there too, Commander."

Even though she wasn't needed and it was her day off, Erica went into surgery with Captain Wilder against her better judgment. He'd been accommodating, but she still had a feeling that she was being scrutinized, manipulated, and that one wrong move and he'd send her packing. Well, maybe not personally send her packing, but she was sure he'd expedite it.

He probably wants to make sure you don't hack off Corporal Ryder's leg like you did to his.

Erica *tsked* under her breath, annoyed she'd let that thought in.

"Is something wrong, Commander?" Thorne asked.

"No, nothing. Why?"

"I thought you might have been annoyed about working on your day off. I know I've been pretty hard on you since you've arrived."

"No, I'm not complaining—far from it."

"You were huffing."

Erica glanced up again. Thorne's blue eyes twinkled slightly in what she could only assume was devilry.

What was that old saying her grandma had had? *Keep away from men who are* de pouille *or who are* possede. *They're just as bad as* rocachah.

Or, *keep away from men who are a mess or mischievous children. They're like beach burrs.* Erica had thought at the time her *mamère's* advice was a bit nuts, but Captain Seaton certainly had been a *peekon* in her side and Thorne had the look of a *possede* for sure.

Great. I'm now channeling Mamère.

"I wasn't huffing over the work. The work, I love."

"Yet something rankled you."

"Why are you being so *tête dure*?" Then she gasped, realizing some of her Cajun had slipped out.

"So what?" Thorne asked, amused.

"*Tête dure* is stubborn, persistent and hardheaded. I'm from Louisiana."

"Really? I wouldn't have guessed it."

Erica rolled her eyes. "Don't judge a bed by its blanket."

"You mean a book by its cover?"

"Whatever."

"So why are you huffing?"

"Why are you being persistent?" she asked.

"Why not? I am the commanding officer of Trauma. I want to make sure those under my command..." He trailed off and Erica's stomach twisted. Was he alluding to her past in Rhode Island again?

Not everyone is out to get you. Just because one commanding officer accused you based on what happened to Dad doesn't mean they all will. Captain Dayton hadn't.

Then why did he keeping hinting at it? Maybe it was some kind of psychological warfare. Not that Thorne was at war with her. Perhaps it was some kind of SEAL training? It probably was and she shouldn't take it personally.

Erica cleared her throat. "If you want to know the reason I'm *tsking*, which is totally different from huffing, the reason is the wound. He's pretty mangled."

Thorne sighed. "His dreams of being in the Special Ops are over."

"He's lucky it didn't sever his femoral artery or we would have lost him on the beach." Erica continued to work, her hands moving as fast as Thorne's, working to repair the damage. It was an automatic process, one she didn't have to think too hard about. "More people die being trampled by hippos than by shark attacks."

"Hippos, Commander?" There were a few bewildered looks in the OR.

"Twenty-nine-hundred people annually."

"You're joking. That can't be right."

"It is. Look it up."

"Hippos?"

Erica chuckled. "I know, right?"

"Do you think the leg is salvageable?" Thorne asked, changing the subject.

"Yes." Their gaze locked again for a brief instant. The intensity of that shared moment made her think he wanted to ask her why his, which hadn't been as mangled, hadn't been saved.

She'd wanted to save his leg, but the infection had been too virulent.

Still, she'd always thought about him. What had happened to him, that gorgeous, brave Navy SEAL who had begged her. Who had called her beautiful.

"Like an angel."

Erica tried not to let those memories back in, but it was a failure. Hot flames of blood rushed up into her cheeks and she was thankful for the surgical mask. She broke the connection, her pulse racing.

You can't have this. He'll turn on you like Seaton did.

"I think Corporal Ryder, barring any post-op infection, will keep his leg," she said.

"Infection. Yes." His words were icy. "Well, look at this."

Erica glanced up and in his forceps there was a milky-colored sharp object, which looked like a bone fragment.

"What is that? Did it come off his femur?"

"It's a shark's tooth." The corners of his eyes crinkled with a smile obscured by his mask. He placed the tooth in the basin. "That will be something the corporal will want to keep."

"Like a badge of honor," Erica chuckled.

Thorne laughed quietly. "That, or he'll be out hunting the shark that ended his career prematurely."

"You don't think so?"

Thorne nodded. "Corporal Ryder has it in him. He had a passion to be in Special Ops; he's going to be annoyed."

"His life was saved. The animal didn't do it on purpose."

"It doesn't matter," Thorne snapped. "You don't know what it's like to be in such an elite force, protecting your country. Nothing else matters. You endure endless hours of torment to train, to make your body ready for the most treacherous conditions, and you gladly do it. You'd gladly lay down your life for a chance to keep your country free."

"Very patriotic," Erica said, trying to control her annoyance. "I may not be part of that elite crew, but what I do serves my country as well. I feel the same way."

"It's not the same. He'll have a bone to pick with that shark. You mark my words."

"So, would you?"

"Would I what?" Thorne asked, not looking at her.

"Go after the person or animal that ruined your career."

Thorne cleared his throat. "I did."

There was something in his tone which made her shudder, like she was in danger, but probably not in the same kind of danger as the shark.

This was something different. This kind of danger made her heart beat a bit faster, made her skin hot and made her feel like she was already the cornered prey animal with its throat exposed, waiting for the predator to make its kill. She didn't think Thorne wanted to kill her, far from it—but what he wanted from her, she didn't know.

Get revenge on her? Bring her to her knees?

She had no idea.

It was the kind of danger which excited her and terrified her.

It was the kind of danger she didn't run from. It was the kind she stood up to and she was ready for whatever was to come.

* * *

Thorne watched Erica as she checked on Corporal Ryder's vitals. Ryder had developed a post-op fever and had been in the ICU since he'd come out of surgery. He hadn't even fully come out of the anesthetic.

"My leg. My leg. Oh, God. Please, no!"

That was what Ryder had been screaming as they'd pulled him from the water. He'd been screaming at the top of his lungs. Even though they'd all assured Ryder that his leg was still there, that it was attached and could be saved, it was like the young man had made up his mind that it wasn't going to happen.

Thorne had seen that before—when the spirit just wanted to give up and no amount of modern medicine would help that patient recover. It was like the soul was already trying to escape.

"Hold on, Liam. Just hold on."

"I can't, Thorne. Let me go."

"Why did you step in front of the IED for me?"

Thorne had read his own records, the ones which had been taken by his commanding officer from the USNV. He'd developed a post-op fever, no doubt from the virulent infection coursing through his body.

In his brief memories, when he could recall that moment, he remembered the feeling of slipping away, but something pulling him back.

An angel.

Erica.

Seeing her face hovering above him had grounded him.

Sometimes when the pain was bad, when it felt like the amputated leg was still there and he couldn't take it any longer, he hated Erica for saving his life.

Then again, after he'd been shot and they'd spent

those days holed up in the sewers, he hadn't thought he was going to get out of there. He'd thought he was going to die in the sewer, which would've been better.

One less body in a casket for his mother to weep over.

No, don't let those memories in.

He didn't want to think about his twin's funeral, because when he thought of Liam he inevitably thought about how he'd tried to save his life.

"You're crushing me, Thorne."

"I'm applying pressure. I'm the medic, you're the hero. Remember?"

Liam had smiled weakly. *"I'm past that point. Let me go."*

That moment of clarity, when you felt no pain and your body was just tired of struggling on. You weren't afraid of death any longer. Death meant rest.

Thorne glanced back at the ICU. He saw that look of resolution on Corporal Ryder's face and he hoped the young man would fight.

Ryder still had his leg.

Thorne didn't and if he hadn't been in the medical corps of the Navy, if he hadn't had so many commendations and something to fall back on, he would've been discharged.

Ryder has to live.

Thorne clenched his fists to ease the anger he was feeling, because if he marched in there now to do his own assessment of the situation, to ease the guilt and anguish he was feeling over Corporal Ryder, he was likely to take it out on Erica.

The surgeon who had taken his leg. Only, she'd tried to save it. He'd seen the reports. It was the infection from the dirty water he'd been forced to live in.

There was nothing to be done at that point. There had

been no one to blame but himself. He was the one who'd decided to step in front of that bullet to protect Tyler.

He didn't blame Erica—only, maybe, for saving his life.

He'd thought about her countless times, about kissing those lips, touching her face. Of course, those had been fantasies as he'd recovered. He thought those feelings of lust would disappear when he met her in person.

Thorne was positive that he'd built her up in his head. That it was the drugs which had obscured his memories.

No one could be that beautiful.

He was wrong. Even though his memory had been slightly fuzzy, his fantasies about her didn't do her justice.

When she'd rushed into the fray to give Corporal Ryder first aid on the beach, he knew why she was one of the top trauma surgeons in the medical corps.

The real woman was so much more than his fantasy one. Which was dangerous, because he felt something more than just attraction…

It was dangerous, because he did feel something more than just attraction toward her. He wanted to get to know her, open his heart to her, and that was something he couldn't do.

He wasn't going to let in any one else.

There was no room to love. He wouldn't risk his heart, and if something happened to him, well, he wasn't going to put any woman through that. He'd seen what had happened to his brother's wife and children when Liam had died. And, make no mistake, it was his fault Liam had died.

Thorne couldn't do that to anyone else.

So these emotions Erica was stirring in him scared him.

He'd been alone almost a decade and managed. What

he needed to do was get control of himself. Then he could work with her.

No problem.

Yeah. Right.

He headed into the ICU, sliding the isolation door shut behind him. Erica glanced up at him briefly as she continued to write in Ryder's chart.

"Captain," she said offhandedly, greeting him.

"Commander," Thorne acknowledged, moving to the far side of the bed to put a distance between them. "How's he doing?"

"Stable." She said the word in a way that made Thorne think being stable was sufficient and in some cases—especially this one, where it wasn't even as serious as other wounds—stable should've been enough.

"Any sign of infection?"

"No." Her cheeks flushed briefly.

"Well, that's good. If the wound becomes infected and he doesn't respond to antibiotics we'll have to amputate."

She looked at him. "You have an obsession with amputation."

"Can you blame me?" And even though he knew he shouldn't, and even though he knew she already knew his leg was gone, he bent over and rolled up his scrub leg. "Titanium."

Their gazes locked and his pulse was pounding in his ears. He waited to see if she would admit to it. On one hand, he hoped she would and on the other hand, he hoped she wouldn't, but how long could they keep up this facade?

"I know," she said quietly without batting an eyelash, before she turned to her chart.

Thorne was stunned she admitted to it. When they'd first met again here in Okinawa she'd acted like she didn't remember him, just as he'd pretended he didn't recall her.

He smoothed down the scrubs over his prosthetic leg and then straightened up. The tension in the room was palpable. Usually, tension never bothered him and he thrived in high-stress situations, but this was different.

Against his better judgment, and under the guise that he wanted to see Corporal Ryder's charts, he moved behind her. Which was a mistake. Her hair smelled faintly like coconuts. He was so close he could reach out and touch her, run his fingers through her short honey-colored hair. He resisted and instead took the chart from her, flipping through it.

"Just a fever, then?"

"Y-yes," she stuttered. "Yes, a fever. There shouldn't be a reason why his vitals are just stable, because they were just that. One small change..."

Thorne stepped away from her. "I understand. As long as there isn't infection."

He didn't look at her, but he got the sense she wanted to say more, and he wanted her to say more.

"You know," she whispered, her voice shaking a bit with frustration.

Good. He wanted her to hate him. It would be easier. *Hate me.*

"Yes." He handed her back the chart. Thorne knew she was annoyed. It was good that she was, maybe then she'd avoid him. If she hated him, then he'd be less tempted to want her. There would be little chance of them ever being together, which was for the best.

Yeah. Tell yourself another lie, why don't you?

"Looks good, Commander Griffin. Keep me updated on any changes in the corporal's status." He turned and left the ICU, trying to put a safe distance between the two of them.

The hiss of the isolation room's door behind him let him know she was following him. Why did he think she wouldn't follow him? From the little he knew of Commander Erica Griffin, he knew she wasn't the kind of officer to take anything lying down.

He was in for a fight.

She grabbed his arm to stop him. "I don't think we're done talking, Captain Wilder."

They were standing right in front of the busy nurses' station, where a few nurses stopped what they were doing. Even though they weren't looking their way, he could tell they were listening in earnest.

Not many officers stood up to him.

"Commander, I don't think this is the time or the place to bring it up."

"Oh, it's the time and place." She glared at some of the nurses and then grabbed him by his arm and dragged him into an on-call room, shutting the door behind her, locking it.

"Commander, what's the meaning of this?" he asked, trying to keep his voice firm. He didn't like the idea of being locked in a dark on-call room with her.

Especially when his blood was still thrumming with wanting her.

"I think you know exactly the meaning of this. Why did you pretend you didn't remember me?"

"You did the same."

Her eyes narrowed. "Only because I thought you didn't remember me for the last two weeks."

He cocked an eyebrow. "So that justifies lying to me?"

She snorted. "I never lied to you. However, you lied to me."

"Why didn't you say anything to me?" He took a step toward her, though he knew very well he should keep his distance.

"Why would I? If you weren't going to mention the traumatic experience, I wasn't about to bring it up again."

"Perhaps you felt guilty." He was baiting her, pushing her buttons.

Hate me. Loathe me.

She advanced toward him. "I don't feel guilty for saving your life. I did what had to be done. You would've died if I hadn't taken your leg. You're a doctor, and I'm sure you've had access to the chart which magically disappeared off the ship when you were taken, so you know I had no choice—I don't regret what I did. Given the choice again, if it meant saving a life and having someone hate me for the choice I made, I would cut off your leg to save your life."

Thorne took a step back, impressed with her, but also annoyed that he was even more drawn to her and her strength.

He didn't know how to reply to that.

Didn't know what to say.

Suddenly there was someone pounding on the door.

"Commander Griffin, it's Corporal Ryder... He's crashing."

Suddenly there was nothing left to say. Erica flung

open the door and both of them sped toward the ICU, the sound of a flatline becoming deafening, and everything else was forgotten.

CHAPTER FIVE

ERICA FLIPPED THE tooth over, like it was a poker chip, staring at it morosely as she sat at a bar, which reminded her of *Gilligan's Island*, complete with bamboo huts, tikis and coconut shells. It was like a throwback to something from the sixties.

Normally, she wouldn't occupy a bar or pub, but tonight she needed company.

She needed a drink and this was the closest place to her quarters.

Besides, she'd never had a whiskey and cola adorned with a pink umbrella and glittery streamers before. Her drink reminded her of her first bike, which had had the same streamers. At least her drink didn't have spokey-dokes. The Bar Painappurufeisu, which she believed translated to "Pineapple Face," served alcohol and that was all that mattered at the moment.

"Scooby, hit me again," she called to the barkeep.

Scooby nodded and smiled, probably not really understanding what she was saying, and said, "No problem," before heading down to the other end of the bar.

Erica giggled again.

She definitely needed to lay off the liquor. She rarely indulged and this was what she got for that. She was a lightweight and laughing at everything.

At least if she was laughing she wasn't thinking about what had happened to Corporal Ryder. Then she glanced down at the shark's tooth in her palm and slammed it against the counter.

"To hell with it, Scooby. I need another drink."

"No problem," Scooby answered from the end of the bar.

"Don't you think you've had enough?"

Erica glanced over and saw that Thorne had sat down beside her.

Just what she needed. Someone else whose life she'd ruined. She wasn't a surgeon—she was apparently no better than the grim reaper.

"Scooby will let me know when I've had enough."

A smile twitched on Thorne's face. "The only English Scooby knows is what kind of drink you want, monetary value and 'no problem'."

Scooby looked up and gave a thumbs-up. "No problem."

Erica moaned and rubbed her forehead. "Great. I've been rattling off to him about various things."

Thorne shrugged. "He's a good listener. It's his job. Although, he was a fisherman before the base sprung up."

"I thought most Okinawans knew English."

"Most do. Scooby doesn't; he only learned what he needed to know."

Erica narrowed her eyes. She didn't believe a word Thorne was saying, though that could be the liquor talking.

"You don't believe me?" he asked, his eyes twinkling.

"Why should I? Since I arrived you've questioned me, *lied* to me and generally have been a pain in my butt. No offense, Captain."

"None taken, Commander."

Erica turned back to her drink, playing with the many glittery decorations. Her body tensed, being so close to Thorne. It wasn't because he was her commanding officer; that didn't bother her in the least. It wasn't because she'd taken his leg; she knew she'd made the right medical decision. It was because she was drawn to him and she shouldn't be. Captain Wilder was off-limits and it annoyed her that she was allowing herself to feel this way. That he affected her so.

Especially today.

"What do you have there?" Thorne asked, though she had a feeling he already knew.

She set it down on the countertop anyway: the shark tooth, gleaming and polished under the tiki lighting.

"Why do you have that?" he asked.

"I didn't think it should go to medical waste. I know we were saving it for…" She couldn't even finish her sentence. She was a doctor, a surgeon and she was used to death. People did die, and had died on her, but usually only when they were too far gone.

Thorne had been worse, yet he was here, beside her. Alive.

Corporal Ryder's death shook her because his death shouldn't have happened. It boggled her mind. She cupped the shark tooth in her palm again, feeling its jagged edge against her skin.

Thorne reached over, opened her fingers, exposing her palm, and took the shark tooth from her.

His touch made her blood ignite. A spark of electricity zipped through her veins.

Pull your hand away.

Only, she liked the touch. She needed it at this moment.

"Let me see that," he said gently. Erica watched him,

watched his expression as he looked over the tooth carefully. "Can I keep it?"

"Why?" she asked.

"I knew him—he has a younger brother. Perhaps I'll send it to him if he wants it."

"Sure." She picked at the paper napkin under her drink. It was soaked with condensation and came apart easily. "Did you get a hold of Corporal Ryder's family?"

Thorne nodded slowly. "I did."

"I don't have any siblings." Erica wasn't sure why she was telling him that.

"That's too bad."

She nodded at the tooth again. "Do you think that's something his family would want? I mean…under the circumstances."

"I think so. Though, the flag at his state burial will mean more."

Erica sighed sadly. "There was no reason for him to die."

"He was attacked by a shark."

"It was a simple wound. It didn't even sever the artery."

"You know as well as I do that sometimes there are things beyond our control as physicians. If he gave up the will to live… I've seen it so many times. Even if you fight so hard to save a life, if that person has decided that they're going to die there's nothing you can do."

Erica nodded.

It was true. She knew it. She'd seen it herself so many times, but Ryder's death was so senseless. He would've made a full recovery. Sure, he wouldn't have been able to continue his training to become an elite member of the SEALs, but he also wouldn't have been discharged from the Navy.

Was that worth dying over? Was that what had driven Ryder just to give up?

Was that why Dad just gave up? How much pain had he been in?

She sighed, thinking about him. Her father had had a loving family; he'd often told Erica she was the light in his life. Yet it hadn't been enough.

She hadn't been enough.

"Did they say what caused his death?" she asked, hoping Thorne could give her a more tangible answer.

"No, but there will be a postmortem, and maybe then we can get an answer. I'm thinking that the drugs, the shock of the attack and surgery was just too much of a strain on him. It's rare, but it does happen."

Erica nodded. "Well, why don't you join me and drink to Corporal Ryder's memory."

"Is that what you're doing?" he asked.

She nodded. "Oh, yeah."

"Then I'd love to join you, but you made it clear we can't be friends."

Erica winced. "I overreacted. I'm sorry. We can be friends."

"Okay." He motioned to Scooby who brought him a stubby-looking bottle.

"What's that?" she asked, because she couldn't read the Japanese on the label.

"It's beer. I don't know what kind, but it's damn good."

"I didn't know the Japanese brewed beer."

"You should've done your research before you took a posting in Okinawa prefect, then."

Erica snorted. "I did my research, I just somehow missed that."

"Okay, what do you know?"

She looked at him strangely. "Are you testing me?"

Thorne shrugged. "Why not? You said you studied."

Erica shook her head and pinched the bridge of her nose. "What part of 'pain in my butt' didn't you get?"

"Haven't you ever heard of a pub quiz before?"

"Really?"

Thorne chuckled. "Okay, fine. Although the prize would've been totally worth it."

"Prize?" Erica asked. "Now I'm intrigued. What would be my prize?"

He grinned. "Play and find out."

Just walk away.

The prize was probably something not worth it. Or something totally inappropriate—not that she would mind being inappropriate with Thorne, if he hadn't been her commanding officer; if they didn't have a history as surgeon and patient. Yet here she was, falling into this sweet trap again.

He's not Seaton. They're not all Seaton.

Which was true, but after a couple of drinks she was willing to let her guard down. *It's the booze.*

And maybe it was completely innocuous. Perhaps he was just being kind and just trying to get her mind off the fact that they'd lost someone today. Someone who shouldn't have died.

Since when has Captain Wilder ever been nice to you?

That was the truth. He hadn't been overly friendly or warm since she'd arrived at the base. Even when he'd been her patient he'd called her names and told her not to take his leg.

He didn't have the sunniest disposition.

"Like an angel."

That blasted moment again, sneaking into her mind, making her thoughts all jumbled and confused. She should just walk away, but she was too intrigued not to find out what the prize was. Besides, when was the last time she'd backed away from a challenge? If it was something inappropriate she could tell him where to go; they were off duty.

Still, she wasn't here because of a lark.

"I don't think it's appropriate."

"Because of Corporal Ryder?" Thorne asked.

"Yeah. Maybe I should just call it a night." She got up to leave, but he reached out and grabbed her arm, stopping her from leaving.

"Don't go," he said.

Erica sat down. "Okay, but I have to say I'm not in much of a jovial mood. Prize or not."

Thorne chuckled. "Tell you what, you'll still get your prize."

"And what would that be?"

"A tour around Ginowan and the countryside. You could test your knowledge."

Erica couldn't help but smile. When Thorne wanted to be, he was charming. "I don't think that's wise."

"Why?"

She didn't know how to answer that truthfully.

Because I don't want to be alone with you. Because my career is more important.

Because I'm weak.

"I don't think that's wise. You're my commanding officer."

Thorne's face remained expressionless. "You're right. Of course you're right."

Even though he didn't show any sign of anger, there was tension in his voice and possibly a sense of rejection. She knew that tone well enough from other guys she'd turned down, because there just wasn't time for romance.

And because you're frightened.

Erica stood. "I should go. Good night, Captain Wilder."

Thorne nodded but didn't look at her. "I'll see you in the morning, Commander Griffin."

Thorne watched her leave the bar; even though he shouldn't, he did. It was good that she'd turned him down. He didn't know what had come over him.

Probably the beer.

"You're looking for trouble with that one," Scooby said.

Thorne snorted. "I'm not looking for trouble."

"Good, because that one is strong willed. Why did you tell her I can't speak English?"

Thorne chuckled. "I was playing with her."

"Ay-ay-ay. Perhaps I should warn her off of you, Captain Wilder. Perhaps you're nothing but trouble." Scooby smiled and set another bottle of beer down on the counter. "I'm sorry to hear about the corporal. He was a good man."

"He was."

"I would like to send something to his family." Scooby reached behind the bar and pulled out a picture. "This was from last month. Corporal Ryder led our bowling team to victory."

Thorne smiled at the picture of Scooby, Corporal Ryder and some other officers in horrific bright-orange bowling shirts holding up matching color marble balls.

"I'm sure they'd like that."

Scooby nodded and walked away. Thorne carefully placed the framed picture down and then set the shark tooth on top of it.

Damn you, Ryder.

"You hold on, Liam. Do you hear me?"

"I hear you."

"It's not as bad as you think. You can live."

Liam shook his head. *"No, little brother."*

"Stop calling me little. I'm three minutes younger than you."

Liam chuckled, his pupils dilating, his breathing shallow. *"You'll always be my little brother, Thorne. Remember that."*

Thorne cursed under his breath and finished off his beer. He didn't want to think about Liam right now.

When do you ever?

It was true. Since Liam had died in his arms, he didn't like to think about him.

But then, who would want to think about a loved one they couldn't save?

One who could've been saved.

One that would still have been alive if he hadn't made such a foolish mistake.

CHAPTER SIX

DAMN AND DOUBLE DAMN.

Erica turned on her heel and tried to walk away as fast as she could, even though the little voice inside her head told her that she couldn't avoid Captain Wilder for the rest of her life. She was his second in command.

Needless to say, she was damn well going to try.

"Commander Griffin—a word, if you will."

Erica grimaced and cursed under her breath.

Damn.

She turned around slowly as Thorne walked toward her. He wasn't wearing his usual scrubs; he was in uniform. Not the full dress and not the fatigues—the service khaki and it didn't look half bad on him.

The khaki brought out the brilliant blue color in his eyes.

Damn.

"Of course, Captain Wilder. How can I help you?"

He shook his head. "Not here. Let's go to my office."

Erica's stomach knotted. Oh, great. What was going to happen to her now? Last time she'd been involved with a commanding officer she'd been sent packing. That was why she didn't mix work and relationships.

They walked in silence to his office. He opened the door for her.

"Please have a seat."

"I prefer to stand, if you don't mind, Captain."

Thorne frowned. "Why are you standing at attention, Commander?"

"Aren't I being called up on the rug?"

"It's called 'out on the carpet'. I think that's what you mean."

Erica sighed. "Right."

"No, Commander. You're not being scolded. At ease."

She relaxed, but not completely. This time she wasn't going to be caught unawares. This time she'd be ready for whatever Captain Wilder had for her. Erica planned to keep this commission. She wasn't going to be run out of another one. Not this time. Since her Rhode Island posting, when her reputation had been left in tatters, she'd worked damned hard to get it back. It was her prize intangible possession. Her reputation was at stake and that was all she had left.

"You can sit, Commander."

"I still prefer to stand, Captain."

"I'd prefer it if you'd sit."

"Why?" she asked.

"I never sit in the presence of a lady who remains standing. It's how I was raised. So if you would sit, then I could sit—and I'd really like to sit because my leg has been bothering me something fierce today."

Erica could see the discomfort etched in his face, the barely controlled pain. His knuckles were white as he was gripping the back of his chair and there was a fine sheen of sweat across his brow. It wasn't about nicety; he was suffering.

"I'm sorry, Captain."

He shook his head. "Don't be sorry, please just have a seat."

She nodded and sat down on the other side of his desk. Even though he told her she wasn't being reprimanded, she was still ill at ease. She had no idea why Thorne wanted to see her.

Performance review?

One could only hope. She'd been at the job for a month now.

"Commander, I called you up here because I want to apologize."

What? "I'm sorry…what, Captain?"

"Apologize, Commander. It's not an easy thing for me to say, but that's why I called you up here."

"I'm not sure I quite understand."

"For making you feel uncomfortable at the bar two weeks ago and on the beach. I know the corporal's death affected you and it looked like you needed a friend. I'm sorry if my actions were out of line."

"Thank you, Captain." Erica was stunned. She'd never had a superior apologize to her before. It surprised her. There were many things she'd been expecting him to say, but an apology had not been one of them. "I'm sorry too."

Thorne cocked an eyebrow. "For what?"

"For avoiding you."

A smile broke out on his face, his eyes twinkling. "I knew you were."

"You did."

"You're not that aloof, Erica. May I call you Erica now?"

She nodded. "Yes. I think we've established that when we're alone that's acceptable."

"So, why have you been avoiding me?"

"I thought it was for the best. I'm here to prove myself. I'm not here to make friends."

"Everyone needs a friend."

"Not me." And she meant it.

"Really? I'm intrigued—you have no friends?"

Erica rolled her eyes. "I have friends, just not here. At home and not in the service." Well, except for Regina, but he didn't need to know that.

"I'm talking about friends here. You need a friend."

"And what about you?"

Thorne leaned back in his chair, tenting his fingers. "What about me?"

"Who are your friends, if you don't mind me asking? You work just as much as I do, if not more. I've been to Scooby's bar a couple of times and two weeks ago was the first time I saw you there."

"Scooby knows English, by the way."

"What?" she asked.

"I was pulling your leg, but he warned me that I should tell you the truth."

She rolled her eyes. "I don't know why I fell for that. I knew he knew English. He's been living around the base his whole life."

Thorne shrugged. "It's a bit of an initiation."

"I thought my crazy shifts at the beginning were that."

"Partly." He grinned. "It's true, I don't have many friends here, being the commanding officer of the trauma department and being involved in Special Ops training. Well, as much as I can be with my prosthetic. I can't do much in the way of water training."

"We can be friends." Erica was stunned when the words slipped out of her mouth and she could tell Thorne was just as surprised.

"Really? After that whole rigmarole you just gave me about being here to prove yourself and not make friends?"

She smiled. "Perhaps you're wearing me down. Perhaps I do need a friend."

Their gazes locked and she could feel the blood rushing to her cheeks; hear her pulse thunder in her ears.

You're weak. So weak.

"I'm glad," he said, finally breaking the tension which crackled between them. "Very glad. So I can assume my apology is accepted."

"Yes."

"Good. So were you really avoiding me because you didn't want to be friends or was it something else? You know, I used to interrogate people in the Special Ops. I know when someone is lying to me." He got up and moved toward her, sitting on the edge of his desk in front of her. Their bodies were so close, but not quite touching.

Get a grip on yourself.

"Fine. I was avoiding you because I thought perhaps you might've been coming on to me."

"And if I was?"

Flames licked through her body.

"Then it would be inappropriate," she said, meeting his gaze. "It would be unwelcome."

No. It wouldn't.

Thorne nodded and moved away. "Good, because I wasn't—and I wanted to make sure you weren't avoiding me because you thought I was being inappropriate with you, Commander."

She should be glad, but she wasn't. If Thorne wasn't her captain or her former patient…if she hadn't seen him at his most vulnerable… Well, there was no point in dwelling on the past. The past couldn't be changed and there was no possible hope or future with Thorne. None. He was off-limits.

"I'm glad to hear that." She stood. "May I get back to my duties? I was about to start rounds."

"Of course. But, look, my offer still stands about taking you around Ginowan. As friends. I think it would do you good to get off the base and see some sights. I know you're used to working on a ship where there weren't many escape options."

"Thank you. I would like that."

He nodded. "It'll do you good to get out there. We'll meet tomorrow at zero nine hundred hours. You're dismissed, Commander."

Erica saluted and left his office posthaste. Not because she was late for rounds, but because once again she found she had to put some distance between her and Thorne. Why did he have to be her commanding officer? Why was she even thinking about him in that way? She'd lost her prestigious posting in Rhode Island because she'd dated a commanding officer and when it had gone south she'd been thrown under the bus.

"Lieutenant Griffin is mentally unfit to become a commander. Look what happened to her father."

Men couldn't be trusted.

She didn't need this, yet he was right. Erica was lonely and, even though she tried to tell herself otherwise, she wanted the companionship Thorne was offering.

She wanted the friendship and maybe something more.

And that thought scared her.

Thorne pulled up in front of Erica's quarters in his tiny Japanese-made turbo. She had to suppress a giggle when she saw him because the car was so small and he was so tall.

He rolled down the window. "I'd open the door for you, but once I get behind the wheel it's a bit of a pain to get out and back in with my leg."

"No worries." She checked to make sure her door was locked and then headed for the car. She climbed into the passenger seat. She was five-ten and it was a squeeze for her too. So she could only imagine that Thorne might've needed a shoehorn to get his big Nordic frame into this little hatchback.

"I thought you would've driven an SUV or something," she said.

"Not in Okinawa. Some of the roads are narrow. I do have a nice, big gas-guzzling truck on my mom's farm back in Minnesota."

"Minnesota. That doesn't surprise me, given your Viking name."

He grinned. "Yes, my family is from Norway. Your name, though: it's hard to figure where you're from."

"I was a Navy brat, but my *mamère*—my grandmother—lived in the bayous of Louisiana and I was born there."

"A Southern girl."

"Yes, sir. Though don't ask me to do a Creole accent or drawl or whatever. I don't have one. I was born in New Orleans, but I didn't live there very long. I was raised on the East and West Coasts. Except for a three-year stint in Arizona."

"Yet you blurt out some Cajun every once in a while."

"A bit. I spent a lot of summers with Mamère."

"You've been all over."

"Yes and working on a medical ship helped with that."

"I bet." He put the car into drive. "You haven't seen Okinawa yet."

"No. I haven't."

"You're in for a real treat, then."

He signaled and pulled away, down the road to the base's entrance. They signed out with the Master of Arms on duty. Once the gate lifted they were off down the road toward the city of Ginowan. The wind blew in her hair and she could smell the sea. She took a deep breath and relaxed. It was the first time in a long time she'd actually sat back and relaxed.

"Where are we headed?" she asked, not that she really cared where they were going. She was just happy to be off the base and seeing the sights.

"There's a temple in Ginowan that's pretty. Thought we'd stop there first. Maybe we can spot some Shisa dogs."

"What are Shisa dogs?"

"They guard the island. There are stone carvings of lion dogs hidden everywhere."

"Neat."

Thorne nodded. "Not much of the original architecture remains. Most was destroyed in 1945 during the Battle of Okinawa in World War II."

"I did know that. My grandfather fought during that battle, actually."

"With the Navy?"

"No, the Marines."

"Did he survive?"

Erica chuckled. "Of course, or I wouldn't be here talking to you today. My father was the youngest of seven children and he wasn't born until 1956."

Thorne laughed. "Good point."

"Did any of your family serve?"

Thorne's easy demeanor vanished and he visibly tensed. His smile faded and that dour, serious face she was used to seeing around the halls of the base hospital glanced at her.

"Yes. My brother."

"Navy?"

"Yes." It was a clipped answer, like he didn't want to say anything further, and she wasn't going to press him, but she couldn't help but wonder where his brother was. Did he still serve? Was Thorne's brother in the SEALs? Maybe that was why it was a bit of a sore spot for him.

Either way, it wasn't her business.

Just like her past wasn't his business.

"So, tell me about these dogs."

Thorne's expression softened. "I'm no expert on Okinawan history. Your best bet is to ask Scooby."

"Oh, yes? The man who supposedly doesn't know English? 'That'll be no problem'," she air-quoted.

Thorne laughed with her. "Again, sorry about that."

"I know, I know. It was all a part of my initiation. I've had several now; I should be used to them."

"Scooby wants to warn you off of me and vice versa."

"Vice versa?" she asked. "Why? What have I ever done to him?"

"He thinks we're both too pigheaded and stubborn to get along well."

Erica chuckled. "He could be right. I am stubborn, but not without just cause."

"So I've heard."

Now she was intrigued and a bit worried. "From who?"

"My commanding officer. He said you were quite adamant that I not be removed from the ship, even if the orders came direct from the White House."

She laughed. "That's true. When it comes to my patients. Some find it annoying."

"Not me," Thorne said and he glanced over at her

quickly. "It's the mark of a damn fine surgeon. Which you are."

Heat flamed in her cheeks. "Thank you."

"There's no need to thank me. I'm speaking the truth. I don't lie."

"That's funny," she said.

"What?"

"That you don't lie, when you *clearly* did." She regretted the words the moment she said them.

Good job. You are finally starting to make friends and you insult that one and only friend.

Instead of giving her the silent treatment he snorted. "I didn't really lie per se."

"How do you figure that?"

"I just withheld the truth."

Erica raised an eyebrow. "Right. And the definition of lying is…?"

Thorne just winked at her. "Here we are. I hope you wore socks. No shoes in the temple." He parked the car on the street and they climbed out. It was good to stretch her legs. The little temple was built into the side of a hill surrounded by an older part of town, which was bustling. The temple was overgrown with foliage and the stairs up to it were crumbling.

"It's beautiful." And it was. Erica had traveled around the world, and had seen many places of worship, but there was something about this temple which struck her as different and captivating. Something she couldn't quite put her finger on.

"Shall we go in?"

"Are we allowed to?" she asked.

"Sure." And then without asking her permission Thorne reached out and took her hand, sending a shock of electricity up her spine at his touch. He didn't seem to notice the way her breath caught in her throat when she gasped.

Instead he squeezed her hand gently and led her through the packed streets toward the temple. What was even weirder was that she didn't pull away.

She let him.

She liked the feeling of her hand in his. It was comforting, and in the few past relationships she'd had, she could never recall sharing such a moment of intimacy. There had been lust, sex, but hand-holding? Never. Such a simple act gave her a thrill.

Don't think like that. It means nothing. You're just friends.

Right. She had to keep reminding herself of that.

They were just friends.

That was all there was between them and that was all there could ever be.

CHAPTER SEVEN

THORNE DIDN'T KNOW why he reached out and took her hand to lead her across the busy Ginowan street. It was instinctive and a gentlemanly thing to do. They were halfway across the street when he realized that he was holding Erica's hand, that he was guiding her through the maze of people, whizzing motorbikes and cars toward the temple.

She didn't pull away either like she had before.

Erica let him lead her to safety. It was an act of trust and Thorne had a feeling that trust didn't come too easily to her.

Not that he blamed her. People couldn't always be trusted. He'd learned that well enough both in his service as a SEAL and a surgeon.

"Yes, Dr. Wilder. I quit smoking."

"No. I know nothing about threats to your country."

Thorne could usually read people like a book. It had been one of his strong suits when he was in the Special Ops. Erica was hard to read though and maybe that was another reason why he was *so* drawn to her.

He did like a challenge.

You shouldn't be thinking this way. She's your second in command. She made her feelings quite clear to you the other day.

She was a puzzle. One he wanted to figure out. He was a sucker for puzzles. Thorne cursed himself. He couldn't be involved with her or any other woman.

He couldn't emotionally commit to someone.

Not in his line of work.

Not after seeing what it had done to his brother's widow, to his mother.

When he'd lost his leg and woken up in that hospital in San Diego, unaware of where he was and how he'd got there, his first memory besides Erica's face haunting him had been seeing his mom curled up on an uncomfortable cot, a few more gray strands in her black hair, dark circles under her eyes.

It had almost killed his mother when Liam had died.

No. He couldn't do that to someone else and he couldn't ever have kids either. He didn't want to leave his children without a father should something happen to him.

You're not in Special Ops anymore. What harm could happen here?

A shudder ran down his spine. What harm indeed? Corporal Ryder probably hadn't thought his life would end during a simple training exercise. That it would end because of a shark bite.

Take the risk.

It was a different voice in his head this time, one that he thought he'd long buried, and it wasn't welcome here now.

No. She's off-limits.

"I think it's going to rain," Erica said, glancing up at the sky.

"What?" Thorne asked. "Sorry, I didn't hear you."

"Rain. It became overcast quite quickly."

Thorne didn't look at the sky; he glanced at the delicate

but strong hand in his. It felt good there, but it didn't belong. He let it go and jammed his hands into his pockets.

Her cheeks bloomed with pink and she awkwardly rubbed her hand, as if wiping away the memory of his.

"Maybe we should go inside," Thorne offered, breaking the tension between them.

"Sure," she agreed, but she wouldn't look at him. "Lead the way."

He nodded and led her up the walkway toward the temple entrance. This had to stop. She was affecting him so much. Usually he was so focused on his work. Now he was distracted and he knew he had to get control of this situation before it escalated any further. She'd agreed to be friends. They could be friends.

Who are you kidding?

He watched her as she made her way to the small, almost abandoned Ryukyuan temple. It was made of wood and stone and embedded in the side of a hill. It was more a tourist attraction than it was a functional temple, as most Okinawans practiced at home in honoring their ancestors.

She paused and touched the stone at the gate, glancing up, and her mouth slightly opened as she marveled at the architecture. It was old, mixed with new, as parts of the small temple had been destroyed during the battle of Okinawa.

"Beautiful." She smiled at him, her eyes twinkling and her honey-blond hair blowing softly in the breeze. She was weaving some sort of spell around him. He just wanted to take her in his arms and kiss her. The thought startled him because, even though it wasn't new, he'd been trying to ignore the desire, the lust which coursed through him. He didn't recall ever having this urgency before with women he dated in the past.

This need.

This want.

"I thought you wanted to get out of the rain?" Thorne asked.

"Right." She blushed and stopped at the door to take off her shoes and Thorne followed her, glad he was wearing slip-ons so he wouldn't have to struggle with laces and his leg.

"Welcome. You're welcome to look around; we just ask that there be no photography," the guide said from behind the desk as they entered the temple.

"Thank you." Thorne paid a donation to allow them in and explore the history of the temple. Erica was wandering around and looking at the carvings and the paintings on the wall.

"Are these the lion dogs you were talking about, Thorne?"

"Ah, yes," the guide said, standing. "The Shisa is a protective ward to keep out evil spirits. They're often found in pairs."

Thorne nodded and then moved behind Erica, placing his hand on the small of her back to escort her further into the temple, where a few other tourists were milling about, reading about the history and photographs on the walls.

Erica leaned over and whispered, her breath fanning his neck. "I really know nothing about Okinawa history."

"I know a bit."

"What religion do Okinawans practice?"

"There are several forms, but it all falls under the Ryukyuan religion. A lot of the worship has to do with nature."

Erica smiled. "Pretty awesome."

"I have some books for you to read, if you're interested."

"I don't have time to read." Then she moved away from him to look at some old pictures after the battle of Okinawa. "Crazy. They say it was the bloodiest battle of the Pacific War."

"It was and 149,193 of those lost were Okinawan civilians."

"Such a loss of life."

"It is," he said. "It's a hard line we walk as surgeons who serve. We don't like to see death, but yet we serve something bigger and greater. Something that helps innocents remain free."

Gooseflesh broke out over her at his eloquent words. She often felt at war with herself and her beliefs. Even though she was in the Navy she wasn't one who went out to fight. Though she'd learned about armed combat as part of her training during Annapolis, she hoped she'd never have to be in a situation to use it.

Thorne was different.

He'd actually served in combat situations.

He carried a gun and as a SEAL had undertaken covert operations that she couldn't even begin to imagine. She wanted to ask him if he'd ever killed someone before, but she could tell by the pain in his eyes when he read the names on the list, the names of those who had fallen during the Battle of Okinawa, that he had.

And it pained him.

Besides it wasn't her business to ask him that and she was enjoying his company; the last thing she wanted to do was drive him away by prying.

The moment he'd mentioned his brother he'd put a wall up.

"It is a hard line to walk," she said. She moved away from him into a hallway, which was carved. They were heading under the hillside and she could hear water running. When they got down at the end of the hallway there was a hole in the ceiling letting the light filter through and in the center was a pond where pots of incense were burning.

Misty rain fell through the opening, causing smoke to rise from the incense. It was beautiful, and the smell was spicy but welcoming.

"What's this?" Erica asked as she moved closer.

"It's called a Kaa, I believe. Water is holy, hence the incense."

"It's beautiful."

Thorne nodded. "It is."

They stood in companionable silence for a while around the Kaa. There was no one else in the room with them and suddenly she was very aware of his presence.

It was like there was some sort of spell being weaved here in this moment, next to the water and with the incense thick in the air, and for a moment she thought about kissing him.

It had been a long time since she'd kissed a man and the thought of kissing him here made her pulse race and her body ache with anticipation.

"It's pretty damp in here. Why don't we go find somewhere to have a cup of tea and maybe lunch?" He didn't wait for his answer, but turned and walked down the hall back to the entrance.

Erica followed him.

The spell was broken, for now.

After the temple and that moment in the Kaa, they drove back toward the base. The drizzle was making it impossible really to enjoy anything. Thorne did suggest heading over to the American village, but Erica didn't really feel like shopping.

Half the stuff she could or would buy, she couldn't even wear on a day-to-day basis anyway. She was either in scrubs working in the hospital, in fatigues or in dress uniform when she was on duty and that was what she was most comfortable in. It was no big loss.

Shopping had always been a luxury in her youth.

With her mother on a widow's pension, there hadn't been much money to go around.

After high school she'd gone straight to college and then Annapolis to help pay for her medical career.

Regina, her one close friend on the *Hope,* had always teased her about being tight with her money. When they would go on shore leave she would be the only one who didn't buy a lot of things.

Things were hard to transport.

Things took up space. Erica was a bit minimalist.

So they headed back to the base and found themselves at the Painappurufeisu.

"Isn't it a little early to drink?" Erica teased, though she was really ready for a drink. The ride back to the base had been silent and awkward.

"Scooby runs a full-service pub. He's got the best pizza near the base."

"Really?" Now she was intrigued.

"Do you like pizza?"

Erica shrugged. "It's okay, but then I really don't have a lot of experience with pizza besides the offerings of chain restaurants. The *Hope* didn't sail in the Mediterranean, so I didn't even get to experience any real Italian pizza. I'm not sure that pizza is my thing."

Great. You're rambling about pizza.

Thorne looked at her like she was crazy and she didn't blame him. She was saying the word "pizza" a lot. Instead he surprised her by asking, "How can pizza not be your thing?"

She chuckled. "I don't know?"

"Pizza has to be everyone's thing. Well, in moderation."

She rolled her eyes, but couldn't help but laugh. "I take it pizza is your thing?"

"And beer."

"Right. You have a taste for the local brews."

"They're good. You'd be surprised. They can have more of a kick than some American beers."

"I can give you a kick if you'd like."

He laughed. "No thanks. I'll take my chances with the local brew. So, are you up for trying some of Scooby's pizza?"

"Sure, but I have to tell you that sounds inherently weird and kind of sacrilegious to my childhood."

Thorne laughed. "His real name is Sachiho, but he actually prefers Scooby. Back before we were ever serving in the Navy, a drunk airman couldn't say his name and called him Scooby instead and it stuck."

"Sachiho...what does that mean?"

Thorne shrugged. "No idea. You could ask him. He would be impressed that you knew it."

"Or he'll just answer me, 'no problem'."

Thorne shook his head. "Again. I'm sorry for that little farce."

"Sure you are."

He pulled in front of the Painappurufeisu. Rock music was filtering through the open windows. The neon sign was flashing, letting everyone know the bar was open for business.

"You know, I was hoping you would take me to eat at a local place. Somewhere authentic."

Thorne held open the door to Scooby's. "Trust me, the pizza here is authentic."

"I don't know whether I should be eager or worried about that."

"You'll have to wait and find out."

As soon as they entered the bar Scooby waved at them. "Hey, Captain Wilder and Commander Griffin, it's a pleasure to see you again."

Thorne waved and then led them to one of the bamboo booths, which was upholstered with a jungle theme material. It was then Erica noticed the wall beside their booth was lined with a green shag carpet.

"I think I've fallen into a time warp." She reached out and touched it to make sure that it was really green shag.

"Why's that?"

"This reminds me of Elvis's jungle room at Graceland."

"Have you been to Graceland?"

"Yes. A couple of times. My *mamère* was an Elvis fan." It was only about four hours from her home in Louisiana to Graceland.

"Ah, I like Elvis too," Scooby said, interrupting. "The King of Rock and Roll. I've been to Graceland too. It's where I got the idea for my jungle-themed dining room."

"Well, Elvis lined the ceiling of his jungle room. Why did you line the walls?"

Scooby shrugged. "I wanted to go all out."

"That you did."

"I told Erica that your pizza was the best around these parts," Thorne said.

Scooby beamed with pride. "This is true. Would you like a pizza?"

"Your house special."

Erica's eyes widened in trepidation. She hoped the special didn't have some kind of delicacy she'd never heard of or something like eel or other sea creature that she had no stomach for.

"No problem—and two beers?" Scooby asked.

"Please." Thorne grinned.

Scooby glanced at her. "You look concerned, Commander."

"I'm not a big fan of pizza."

"No problem, Commander. You will be." Scooby nodded and left.

"He's a man of many layers," she remarked. "Elvis, Graceland and pizza?"

Thorne nodded. "Don't forget bowling. He loves bowling. He loves all things American."

"I can see that, but why didn't he move there?"

Thorne leaned across the table, his eyes twinkling. "His wife wouldn't let him."

Erica rolled her eyes, but she couldn't help but laugh, and she couldn't remember the last time she'd let loose like this. This was better than the tense silence, which had fallen between them at the old temple in Ginowan.

"You know, I would really like to go see the Cornerstone of Peace in Itoman one day," she said, but then realized she was somewhat angling for another date when that was the furthest thing from the truth.

Was it?

Even though the drive to Scooby's had been a little tense, when Thorne had put up his walls again, she was enjoying herself.

Besides, maybe she wasn't *exactly* angling for another date, but another outing with her friend, because that was what they were.

That was all they could be.

"It's impressive. I think everyone should see it once in their life."

"Have you been, Thorne?"

"I have. It lists everyone who died during the battle. Civilian, allied forces and axis powers."

"I'd like to see it."

"We can go after lunch if you want."

"S-sure." And their eyes locked across the table. His was face unreadable as they sat there, that tension falling between them again.

"Here we go. Two beers," Scooby said cheerfully, breaking the silence between them as he set down two dark bottles of beer.

"These have Shisa on them." Erica winked at Thorne.

"Ah, you learned about Shisa today, Commander Griffin?" Scooby asked.

"I did. I also learned your name isn't really Scooby but Sachiho."

Scooby grinned. "Aye."

"What does it mean in Ryukyuan?"

"It's not native to Okinawa. It's more common in Japan. My mother was from Japan. But, in answer to your question, it means 'a charitable man'."

"You're very charitable, Scooby," Thorne teased.

Scooby's eyes narrowed. "You're not getting a free lunch out of me again, Captain."

They all laughed.

"I'll go grab the pizza." Scooby hurried away.

"Did this drunk soldier try to get out of a tab and felt that Sachiho maybe didn't suit Scooby at the time?" Erica asked.

"I never thought of that, but I'm not going to ask him."

Scooby returned and set the pizza down in front of them. "Specialty of the house."

Erica breathed a sigh of relief. "The specialty of the house is pineapple?"

Scooby looked confused. "Painappurufeisu means 'pineapple face'. What did you think my specialty would be?"

Erica laughed. "I have no idea, but I have to learn not to trust Captain Wilder."

Thorne took a swig of his beer, amusement in his eyes.

Scooby *tsked*. "Captain Wilder, you should be nicer to your second in command. Don't listen to a word he says, Commander."

"I'll take that to heart, Sachiho. Thank you."

Scooby grinned and left them to eat.

"Is this why this posting was vacant with hardly any applicants? Do you drive your commanding officers away, Captain?"

He smiled. "Possibly."

"Well, I think I'll take Sachiho's advice and not trust you. Unless we're working in the OR."

"Probably best."

"I've never had pineapple on a pizza before," she remarked.

"Well, then, I wasn't totally off base. It is a delicacy and something you've never had before."

They dug into the pizza and Erica really enjoyed it. While they ate they chatted about life on base and about some of the more colorful characters.

When they were done, she leaned against the back of the booth, staring at the green shag carpeting, chuckling to herself.

"What's so funny?" Thorne asked.

"My *mamère* would really like this place. Hawaii was her favorite vacation spot, the second place being Graceland."

"How many times have you been to…where is Graceland, exactly?"

"Memphis, Tennessee."

"Really?" Thorne asked. "I thought that's where Beale Street was—you know, the birthplace of rock 'n' roll, home of the million-dollar quartet, where Cash got his big break."

Erica cocked an eyebrow. "And who do you think was part of that million-dollar quartet? It was Cash, Perkins, Lewis and Presley."

"I only know about Cash," Thorne said. "Cash was awesome."

"Well, Memphis is home to Beale Street and Graceland. Who do you think invented rock 'n' roll?"

Thorne grinned. "You have me there. That would be interesting to see one day, but don't let Scooby know I have any interest in going to Graceland."

"Why?"

"He'll start the slide show."

Erica laughed and then her phone began to vibrate. She glanced down and saw it was from the hospital. When she looked up she could see that Thorne was looking at his phone as well. "Incoming trauma."

"I know," he said. "Accident on trawler."

"We better go."

Thorne nodded. "Agreed."

They slipped out of the booth and he paid Scooby. As they headed outside Erica could hear the choppers bringing the wounded from the trawler out at sea. The chopper was headed straight for the helipad at the hospital. Several vehicles whizzed by as on-call staff raced toward the hospital.

As she opened the door to Thorne's car a large chopper zoomed overhead. It was loud and nearly ripped the door from her hand, it was flying so low and so fast toward the hospital. It reminded her of the chopper which had brought Thorne aboard the *Hope*.

Only this time it wasn't night, they weren't on a ship in the middle of the ocean, which had gone into silent running and it wasn't a covert operation. This was what she was used to, though she couldn't even begin to fathom the kind of emergency, which would've happened on a trawler off the west coast of Okinawa.

"Let's go, Commander."

Erica nodded and climbed in the passenger seat.

"You know," Thorne said as he started the ignition. "I had every intention of taking you to the Cornerstone of Peace today."

"You did?"

He nodded. "I did."

"Well, maybe another day, then."

Thorne nodded. "Another day."

CHAPTER EIGHT

"WHAT HAPPENED?" THORNE asked the nearest nurse as he came out of the locker rooms, his casual attire abandoned for scrubs. Once they'd pulled up to the hospital Erica had left, running ahead into the fray. Thorne couldn't keep up with her and when an emergency like this was called it was all hands on deck.

He grabbed a trauma gown, slipped it over his scrubs and then grabbed gloves.

"There was an explosion on a trawler. It burned a lot of men and then the trawler started to go down. We have some men with hypothermia and water in their lungs."

"Okinawan?"

"Some. Most of the men are Indonesian, but the trawler was registered to several different countries off the east coast of Africa."

Thorne frowned. "They're fishing far from home."

"You said it, not me."

Thorne nodded at the nurse. Maybe the trawler hadn't been fishing exactly and maybe the men had been up to something else. Either way it didn't matter and it was out of his jurisdiction. Right now he had lives to save. He headed out to meet the gurneys as they came in.

It wasn't long before the doors opened and the rescue team wheeled in a burn victim, who was screaming.

"Male, looks to be about twenty. Indonesian, doesn't speak a word of English."

Great. It was going to be tricky to get any kind of history.

"Get me a translator that knows Indonesian here, stat!" Thorne demanded.

"Yes, Captain!" someone in the fray shouted. He didn't know who, but it didn't matter, as long as his order was taken care of. He needed to know if this boy was allergic to anything and he needed to know what had caused his burn.

Was it fire? Was it chemical? These were the questions he needed answered before he could help his patient. He wanted to make sure if it was a chemical burn that any trace of the chemical was washed from his skin.

"I've got it." Thorne grabbed the gurney and wheeled it to an open triage area. "Don't worry, I'm a doctor, and you're in good hands."

The young man just whimpered, his brown eyes wide with fear and pain. It was obvious that the boy was in shock by his pale complexion, his shaking and his shallow breathing. Thorne slipped nose cannula into his nose.

The boy started to freak out, but Thorne tried to calm him down.

"Breathe, just breathe. It's oxygen."

The boy began to shake, but his breathing regulated as he inhaled the oxygen.

"We need to start a central line." A nurse handed Thorne a tray and he moved into action. The boy reached out and gripped his arm. His eyes were wild as he watched Thorne in trepidation. "I'm sorry, this will hurt—but only for a moment and then it will help."

The boy shook his head, not understanding. He took one look at the needle and started to cry out in fear.

"I need that translator now!" Thorne barked.

"I'm here. I can help." Erica stood in the doorway.

"You know Indonesian?"

"I know a few languages and we helped out in Indonesia quite a lot when I was on the *Hope*."

"Good. Could you tell him that this will help with the pain?"

Erica nodded and leaned over the patient. *"Hal ini akan membantu."*

"Ask him what kind of burn he has."

Erica asked the boy how he'd got his burns.

"Api."

"Fire, Captain."

"Okay. Then we know how we can proceed. Tell him we'll help him, that this will ease his pain and we'll take care of him."

Erica gently spoke to him. The boy nodded and calmed down. Erica continued to hold his hand.

Thorne inserted the central line as Erica continued to murmur words of encouragement to the frightened boy. Soon he was able to feed the boy medication to manage the pain and the grip on Erica's hand lessened until she was able to let it go.

"You should go back out and lend a hand."

Erica nodded but, the moment she tried to leave, the boy reached out and grabbed her.

"Silakan tinggal."

"What's he saying?" Thorne asked.

"He wants me to stay with him."

"We have other trauma."

"And other surgeons. I can stay for a while. At least until he passes out. He's scared."

Thorne frowned. "I understand your compassion, but this boy's burn will require hours of debridement. Your presence as my second in command is required on the floor."

"I'm sorry, Captain. I have to stay here."

"Are you disobeying me, Commander?"

Erica's eyes narrowed and he could tell she was angry. Heck, he was too. He wished he had the luxury of keeping her in the same room as him as he did his work, but he needed her out there helping, not catering to this boy.

Bunny poked her head into the triage room. "The translator showed up."

"Thanks, Bunny." Thorne turned to Erica. "The translator is here. Go back to the floor, Commander."

Erica bent over and whispered some words to the boy, who nodded and let go of his hold on her. Once he did that Erica moved out of the triage room without so much as a backward glance at him.

Thorne didn't want to annoy her, far from it, but she was a valuable asset to the trauma floor. He couldn't have her playing translator to a scared young man.

"Captain Wilder?"

Thorne glanced up to see a young lieutenant standing in the doorway. "You the translator?"

"Aye, Captain."

"Good. I need to explain what I'm doing to this young man and reassure him that this will help. Nurse, will you gown our translator?"

"Of course, Captain."

Thorne turned back to his instruments while the nurse put a gown and mask on the translator. He glanced out into the trauma floor and saw Erica assessing another patient who had just been brought in. The paramedics had been working on him, giving him CPR as they wheeled him through the hospital doors.

Only now Erica had taken over, shouting orders as she climbed on the gurney to administer CPR, nurses and intern surgeons racing to wheel her away from the oncoming traffic and to a triage room.

Thorne knew he'd made the right decision booting her out of the room. She was a surgeon and a damn fine one.

One that he was proud to have on his team.

Erica stretched. It felt like her back was going to shatter into a million pieces and her feet were no longer useful appendages that she sometimes liked to apply the occasional coat of red nail polish to. No, they now were two lumps of ache and sweat.

"How long was that surgery?" she muttered under her breath as she scrubbed out because she'd lost track of time in there.

"Eight hours," a scrub nurse said through a yawn. "Good work in there, Commander." The nurse left the scrub room and Erica stretched again.

Yeah, she'd believe eight hours for sure, though it felt like maybe that surgery had lasted days. There were a few times she hadn't been sure if her patient was going to make it. She placed her scrub cap in the laundry bin and headed to her locker.

"I heard you had a piece of the trawler's engine embedded in your patient's abdomen?"

Erica groaned, recognizing Thorne's voice behind her. She'd been angry with him for forcing her away, for not letting her comfort that young man, but Thorne had been right.

She needed to be out on the trauma floor, practicing medicine and not translating. If she'd disobeyed orders she wouldn't have been able to operate on her patient and save his life. Her back might've liked that, and definitely her feet, but she was glad she was in the OR doing what she loved.

Saving a life.

Damn. He was right and he probably wasn't going to let her live it down.

"Yes. Part of the engine decided my patient was a good resting place."

Thorne winced. "The prognosis?"

"So far so good. He's in the ICU. How's your patient?"

"Resting comfortably in the burn unit. From what he was telling the translator, that trawler was not fishing off the coast of Okinawa."

"I thought as much."

Thorne crossed his arms. "What made you think that?"

"There were traces of methamphetamine in my patient's blood stream. We had a few close calls on the OR table. A few codes."

Thorne nodded. "The proper authorities have been called. Since they weren't in international waters, we've called the Japanese officials. I'm sure several patients will be interrogated."

"I wouldn't doubt it."

Thorne hesitated, as if he wanted to say more, but couldn't.

Or wouldn't.

Though she barely knew him, Erica recognized a stubborn soul. Sometimes it was like looking in a mirror, because she was stubborn too. Stubborn to the point it had almost cost her her commission a few times.

"You did good in there, Commander."

Erica nodded. "Thank you, Captain."

"Go rest." Thorne turned to leave, but then stopped. "I heard the *Hope* will be in port in a week."

"Really?" she asked.

"Does that make you happy?" he asked.

"It does bring some cheer. Yes. It'll be good to catch up with some old friends."

A strange look passed over his face. "I thought you didn't make friends. I thought you were something of a lone wolf. Like me."

"I had a select few on the *Hope*. It's hard to be confined in close quarters and not make friends, Captain."

"You're right." Then he turned to leave.

"What about our rain check?" she asked, not really believing that she'd asked that. "The Cornerstone of Peace?"

He glanced over his shoulder briefly. "Maybe some other time."

And with that he walked away. He never once brought up her insubordination to her. How she'd almost disobeyed his orders in that triage room. Nor did he apologize for ordering her out. Not that he had to. Captains rarely apologized.

Especially when they were right, and he'd been right.

She'd been the fool. The one in the wrong. And it had probably cost her the friendship.

And more.

Erica closed her eyes and took a deep, steadying breath before turning and heading back toward the locker room. Really, she should be glad that it was such a quick break. That nothing awkward had come between them, which would make it impossible to work with him and would result in her eventual transfer.

This was better.

A working relationship. That was all she wanted from him. He was her commanding officer and she'd do her duty right by him, this hospital and her country.

Still, it stung when he walked away from her and she hated herself a bit for that because, despite every lie she told herself, she really enjoyed their day together.

She liked being around him.

For that one brief moment, it was nice to have a friend.

It was nice to go on a date.

CHAPTER NINE

SHE DIDN'T KNOW he was watching her and Thorne didn't really know why he was watching her. From the research room, he could see out onto the trauma floor. After the trawler accident he'd put her back on some night shifts just so he could get some space from her.

With the *Hope* coming into port, well, it reminded him of when she'd taken his leg. It reminded him of his pain, of his vulnerability, and that she had seen him so exposed.

It was an easy way out, but he hadn't seen her in a week.

Erica had the next two days off while the *Hope* was docked in port.

Still, he didn't know why he remained after hours to do research.

So you could see her. Who are you kidding? He liked to torture himself, apparently.

The research room had a one-way window. You could see out, but not in. He'd really intended to catch up on some work, but the trauma floor was quiet tonight and she was spending a lot of time working on charts at the nurses' station. Again he acted irrationally and avoided her. It was easier than dealing with the emotion she was stirring inside him.

He knew that she was breaking down his walls, ones he'd had up for ten years since Liam had died. He didn't deserve to be happy again. He'd been the foolish one who'd cost his brother his life.

So he hated himself for wanting Erica, for enjoying the time they spent together. He hadn't realized he was so lonely.

Focus.

Thorne tore his gaze from her and returned to his work. There was a knock at the door.

"Come."

The door opened and Captain Dayton of the USNV *Hope* opened the door.

Thorne stood, saluting the other captain. "Captain Dayton, I wasn't expecting you until tomorrow."

"We got in a bit early and I wanted to check in at the hospital and visit with an old colleague of mine."

"Commander Griffin?" Thorne asked.

Captain Dayton smiled. "Yes. She was a formidable surgeon. I took her under my wing, thought of her like a daughter."

Thorne nodded toward the trauma floor. "She's out there charting if you want to speak with her. I'm sure she'll be pleased to see you."

Captain Dayton smiled. "I will. Thank you. And thank you for accommodating some of my nurses and surgeons. It's very important we have this simulation training to keep us up to date. After this we head back to San Diego to get some retrofits and some much-needed shore leave."

"No problem, Captain Dayton. Your staff has free run of facilities here."

"My thanks, Captain Wilder."

"I hope your staff can have a bit of off-time here in Okinawa. There is a lot to offer."

Captain Dayton cocked an eyebrow. "Is that so?"

"Yes. In fact, I know Admiral Greer was planning on throwing a bit of a social while the *Hope* is in port. Though that's supposed to be a secret."

Captain Dayton laughed. "I'll keep that secret safe. That sounds like fun. Well, after my crew completes their simulation training, I think they'll have earned the right for a bit of rest and relaxation before heading to San Diego. I'm very much looking forward to your simulation course, Captain Wilder."

Captain Dayton extended his hand and Thorne shook it.

"I look forward to presenting it."

"I think I'll go visit with my former prized officer."

Thorne sat back down as Captain Dayton left the research lab and headed over to Erica. He tried to look away, to give them their privacy, but he couldn't. Something compelled him to watch.

When Erica saw Captain Dayton her face lit up as she saluted him and then embraced him, kissing his cheek. A surge of jealousy flared deep inside him as he watched Erica being so intimate with another man. His jealousy was misplaced. He had no right to feel this way.

He had no claim.

Erica wasn't his.

She could be.

He cursed under his breath and turned back to the computer, but his curiosity got the better of him. Even though he knew he should keep away from Erica, he couldn't help himself.

Despite the warnings he watched the interplay between

the two. Captain Dayton was old enough to be Erica's father, but what did that matter? Age was meaningless.

As she talked to her former commanding officer Thorne saw her eyes twinkle. Her smile was genuine and as they talked she reached out and touched him.

When Thorne and Erica talked there was no touching. When they were together it often felt tense at best because Thorne was too busy trying to keep Erica out.

Thorne sighed. His leg was aching. It was time to get back home, have something to eat, a shower and then bed.

He didn't have time to worry about Commander Griffin. There wasn't enough emotion in him to invest in her.

At least, that was what he kept trying to tell himself.

He went to log off when the door to the research lab opened again.

"Captain! I'm sorry I didn't know you were in here." Erica's face flushed pink, but only for a moment.

"I was just leaving for the night, Commander."

She nodded and stepped into the room, shutting the door behind her. "Are you prepping your simulation for the crew of the *Hope*?"

"I am. It's how to deal with some common medical issues and emergencies Special Ops have to face. Wounds…infections."

Erica sat down at the computer next to him. "Infections like yours?"

"And more. Communicable diseases as well."

"Sounds like a potpourri of fun that you have planned."

He chuckled. "I try my best. I see Captain Dayton found you."

"Yes," she said quickly. "He was a good commanding officer, but a bit suffocating."

Now he was intrigued. "Suffocating? You looked pleased to see him."

"Were you watching me?"

"For a moment."

"For someone who has been ignoring me the last week and giving me endless night shifts again, you're very observant about who I associate with."

"Is this how you usually talk to your commanding officer?"

"No." She grinned. "Just you."

He rolled his eyes. "Thanks. I do appreciate that, Commander Griffin."

"So, you wanted to know how he suffocated me— well, he wouldn't let me do anything without clearing it with him first. At least, for the first year I served under him."

"Everything?"

"Everything. I have to say it's a nice change being under your command, Captain."

"Why's that?" he asked, secretly pleased to hear it.

"You let me do my work."

"I expect nothing less from members of my surgical trauma team. I pick the best of the best."

She blushed. "And I'm the best?"

"One of." He had to get out of here. When he'd moved Erica to some night shifts it was to get some distance between the two of them. This was not distancing himself from her, but Erica had this way of drawing him in.

He both loved and hated that.

"I better go. My shift ended hours ago." He stood. "Have a good night, Commander."

"Thank you, Captain."

Erica had seen many men turn tail and run from an uncomfortable social situation. Usually she thought it looked a bit ridiculous. So much so that it amused her. But this actually made her feel a bit of hope again.

Hope that maybe Thorne hadn't completely washed his hands of her. That maybe, just maybe, he would tear down his walls to let her in.

You're not tearing down any walls.

Which was true.

She wasn't exactly an open book either.

Scooby had called them both stubborn and thought that Thorne and her together would be volatile. She thought maybe Scooby was right in this instance.

Still, she was drawn to him.

She was attracted to him.

She wanted him.

Get a grip on yourself.

She couldn't want him. She couldn't have him.

Keep lying to yourself.

Erica didn't know he was still in the hospital. She'd come in early to see if she could catch a glimpse of him, but he'd stayed holed up in his office for the entire week. She had heard from some of the nurses that he was dealing with the aftermath of the trawler explosion with the authorities as well as protecting those who were on board the ship and were innocent.

Like the burn victim, Drajat.

He was only eighteen and had had no idea that his uncle, the patient Erica had saved who'd had part of the engine in his abdomen, was drug running.

Drajat had told the authorities that he thought they were actually on a fishing trip. He thought he was earning money so he could attend school; the trace amount of methamphetamines in his system was equal to that of an innocent bystander being around the drugs, but not using them.

Meth was easily absorbed into the skin.

As soon as Drajat was stable enough he would be flown back to Jakarta.

As for Drajat's uncle… He was progressing well, but was still in ICU. Once he was able to be interrogated, well, Erica wasn't sure what the Okinawan police would do with him. This was an international issue as the trawler had crossed into Japanese waters.

"Commander?"

Erica turned in the swivel chair to see that Thorne had returned.

"Yes, Captain? Is there something I can help you with?"

He opened his mouth but then shook his head. "No. It's nothing."

"It's obviously something. I thought you were leaving for the night."

Thorne scrubbed his hand over his face. He looked tired and she didn't blame him in the least. There was also pain behind those eyes. His whole body was clenched tight, taut like a bowstring. It was the leg again.

"I'm sorry for bothering you, Commander. It's nothing." He turned to leave, but hissed through his teeth and reached down.

The last time she'd seen him suffering like this had been when she'd first arrived at the base. When she'd tried to help him he'd bit back at her, lashing out in anger and humiliation.

"You're in pain."

"I've been here too long. It's nothing."

"It's not nothing." She stood and went to the research lab door. Locked it.

"What're you doing?" he asked.

"You're going to sit down and I'm going to massage your leg."

"I don't think so," Thorne snapped. "That's highly inappropriate."

"Do you have a massage therapist who does it for you? Or how about physical therapy?"

Thorne glared at her. "I don't need either. I've been managing well with this prosthesis for some time now."

Erica rolled her eyes. "Sit down, Captain, and that's an order."

"You're ordering me now?"

She crossed her arms. "I am. You should have weekly massage therapy or physio appointments for your leg. It might have been five years since you lost it, but a prosthetic leg can be hard on the muscle. It's painful."

"I know it is," he growled.

"Thorne, I can help relieve some of your pain. You can barely move, so I can't even begin to imagine how you'll get back home."

She stared him down.

With a grunt of resignation he sat down in an office chair. "So how are you going to help me? Are you going to give me a shot of morphine or some other analgesics?"

"No, I'm going to massage you myself." She slipped off her lab coat and set her phone down on the counter with her stethoscope.

"You're...what?"

"I'm going to massage you. Drop your pants, Captain Wilder."

CHAPTER TEN

THERE HAD BEEN many times since he'd first met Erica when he'd pictured her telling him to drop his pants and in all those scenarios it involved her in a bed, underneath him.

Not once had he ever fantasized about being locked in the research lab, in pain and having her ordering him to take his pants off so she could rub his stump. This was not perfection at all. This was far from it. He didn't want her seeing him like this.

In pain.

Exposed.

"I don't think I heard you correctly, Commander Griffin. You want me to take off my pants?"

She nodded. "Yes. You're wearing suit trousers; it'll be impossible to roll up the leg of said trousers over your prosthetic. Besides, you need to remove your prosthetic so I can massage where it hurts."

"I don't think that's appropriate." He tried to move away, but she blocked him.

"With all due respect, Captain Wilder, I've seen that leg before. I know that leg. I know what was done to it and I know how to relieve your pain."

Though he didn't want to, Thorne took a deep breath and then stood, unbuckling his pants and slipping them off. He tried not to let it bug him that she was seeing him like this: vulnerable. He didn't let any woman see him with his pants off. He didn't let any woman see him with just his prosthetic, let alone the remains of his leg.

Erica did have a point, though. She was the one who'd performed the surgery. She was the one who'd removed his leg, fashioned the stump which had left minimal scarring and a good socket to work a prosthetic in.

The surgeon side of him knew it was a damn good amputation.

The other side of him saw it was a fault. An imperfection. The absence of his leg reminded him that a piece of him was missing and how was that desirable to any woman?

What does it matter? She's off-limits.

And that was why he did as she asked.

He sat down and unhooked the prosthetic, embarrassed that she was there. Their eyes met as she knelt down in front of him, helping him remove the prosthetic and the wrappings underneath, which helped prevent the chaffing.

Her touch was gentle as she ran her hand over his thigh. The simple touch made him grit his teeth as he held back the intense pleasure he was feeling. Her hands on him made his blood burn with need.

It had been so long since he'd been with a woman, but this was not how he'd pictured it. Not even close. The way he fantasized about Erica had nothing to do with his stump, of massaging the knots out of his muscles.

"It healed nicely," she remarked, which kind of shattered the illusion.

"What?" he asked.

"The wound healed really nice. Barely any visible scarring."

"It did. It was a good job."

"I didn't know. You were taken out of my care hours after surgery and then I never knew what became of you. You had no name, no record."

Thorne shrugged. "Special Ops."

"I know." Her brow furrowed. "Do you have a lot of chaffing?"

"Only when I work long hours. Lanolin helps."

She nodded. "Good. I'm glad to hear it. Let me know if I hurt you."

"It'll hurt no matter what you do, but I'm sure it will feel good after a while. It always does."

"I thought you didn't get a regular massage?"

"I don't—well, not by someone else. I usually handle it on my own."

Erica glanced up. "You should have someone else do it."

"Don't have time for that." He winced as she touched him.

"Am I hurting you?"

Far from it. He loved her touching him.

"Get on with it," he snapped.

"Just try and relax." She began to rub the muscle in his thigh, which was hard as a rock and tense from the pain.

He let out a string of curses.

"Do you want me to stop?" she asked.

"No. It does feel good."

"Your muscles are so knotted."

He nodded and tried not to think about the fact that Erica was kneeling on the floor between his legs, touching him. If he thought about that, then he wouldn't be able to hide anything from her.

So he focused on the pain, but that made it worse.

"Thorne, are you okay?"

"Fine," he lied.

She deepened the massage and beads of sweat broke across his brow. His mind began to wander to that moment when Tyler had been lying in a pool of dirty water. The bullet had grazed him, but Thorne's leg was on fire.

Still, he was the unit's doctor first and foremost. He'd done his duty to make sure Tyler survived.

"You're bleeding, man," Tyler had said as he'd knelt down to tie a tourniquet around his leg.

"I'm fine," Thorne had said. "It didn't nick the artery. Just a bit of bleeding. It'll be fine."

"It's an open wound in the sewer, Wilder."

"I have antibiotics." Thorne had dug through his first aid kit and pulled out a syringe of morphine and a needle and thread.

"What the heck are you doing, Wilder?" Tyler had asked in trepidation.

"Stitching. We still have to swim out to the sub waiting for us. It's shark-infested water. I'm closing up the open wound now."

"It'll get infected that way."

"It doesn't matter. We'll get back to the submarine and it'll be fine. You'll see, Tyler."

Thorne had injected the painkiller and then threaded the needle…

He relaxed, as the pain from his stump seemed to be dissipating. He looked down at Erica working the muscle in his thigh and rubbing around his socket. It was a firm touch, but soft. Her hands were incredibly soft.

Don't think about that.

"Tell me about the surgery," he demanded.

"What surgery?"

"Mine," he said. "Tell me about it. How bad was the leg?"

"Didn't you read your report?"

"There wasn't a lot of information. So tell me. How bad was it?"

"Bad. I won't lie. Your leg was highly infected."

Thorne nodded. "It went down to the bone?"

"Into the tissue," she said. "You did a good repair job on yourself, but…"

"You don't have to say it. I was trapped in an old sewer system for days. If we had been able to get out of there faster and get back to the sub I wouldn't have lost it. I would've been able to stop the spread of the infection."

"Yes. Most likely you could've."

Silence fell between them. It all came back to that moment. She was the one who'd taken his leg and he'd lost it.

"I don't blame you."

She snorted. "Really?"

"I did maybe at first, just a bit."

"You had some pretty choice words for me when you heard me talking about taking it."

"I was a bit fevered by then. My apologies."

"I'm glad to hear you don't blame me. I was worried you did," she admitted, not looking at him, but he could see the pink rise in her cheeks.

"No. If the roles were reversed, and I was given no choice but to amputate or let you die, I would've done the same."

"Does that help?" she asked gently as her ministrations softened.

"It does."

She smiled. "I can tell. Your muscle isn't so knotted. It's relaxing."

"You're good with your hands," he murmured and then gasped when he realized what he'd said. "Erica… I didn't mean…"

Erica was stifling back a giggle and then he couldn't help but laugh as well. It broke the tension that had fallen between them.

Smooth move.

"Well, I suppose I was due for something like that. I did order you to take off your pants." She wiped a tear from her eyes and then stood. "I would hate for someone with a key to open that door and see me kneeling between your thighs without your pants on."

"Good point." He reached over and began to put on his prosthetic.

"No, let it breathe for a moment. Wearing your prosthetic for so long without a break is why your muscles were so tense."

"So you want me to sit here in the research lab without pants."

Erica grinned, her eyes twinkling. "For another ten minutes and then you can make yourself respectable and head for home. You need rest."

"You do too."

Her smile wobbled and she ran her fingers through her hair. "I have another eight hours on this shift and somehow during my day off I have to study for your intensive simulation."

"You're attending my simulation? I gave you two days off."

"I'm not missing a chance to train with a former Special Ops Navy SEAL. Especially one who performed first aid on himself in the field."

"That was nothing. That was survival."

"I know."

They smiled at each other. It was nice. He'd forgotten how much he missed being around her. His stupid avoiding tactic had cost him.

"Why don't you find a nice on-call room and crash?"

"I think I'll do that. I'll leave you to put your pants on by yourself."

"One leg at a time… Right—I only have one." He winked at her.

"That's a terrible joke."

"I have more." He grabbed his prosthetic. "Go. Rest. You have to rest while you can when you're doing these long shifts."

"I will, but promise me you'll head for home and do the same. I am your second in command here; I can relieve you of your duty."

"Would you get out of here?"

She smiled, grabbed her things and left. Thorne leaned back in the chair, closing his eyes.

He was relaxed for the first time in a long time. When he'd been at the San Diego hospital recovering in a private ward until he'd been able to be debriefed he'd balked at the idea of physiotherapy and massage therapy.

He was made of tougher mettle than that. He only did what was necessary to survive and any physiotherapist who got in his way didn't last long. When he'd lost his leg, he hadn't wanted anyone touching it. The pain was penance.

Erica was right. He needed more help. He needed someone who knew how to massage an amputee. He needed pain relief that wasn't in the form of a pill.

He needed to learn how to manage his pain.

He wrapped his stump, put on his prosthetic, then

pulled on his pants, making sure everything was presentable. When he put weight down on his legs, they ached, but they weren't as bad.

A nice, hot shower and bed would help.

He left the research lab and, as he passed an on-call room, he saw Erica was passed out on a cot. She was lying on her side, with her hands curled up under her head. She looked like an angel.

Heck, she was an angel, and he was the very devil himself, because he wanted to join her. He wanted to curl up beside her, wrap his arms around her and lose himself. Only he didn't deserve happiness. One wrong move had cost him his brother. Since he'd cost his brother a life of happiness, he couldn't have what he'd taken from him.

He was unworthy.

You deserve it. It wasn't your fault.

He ignored that voice.

He shut the door to the on-call room and headed out to his car, trying not to think about her between his legs, her hands on a part of him no one had seen in a very long time. He tried not to think about *her*.

Only, that was foolish.

He was a doomed man.

After her shift Erica showered, changed into some casual, comfortable clothes and headed down to the docks. The white hospital ship could be seen blocks away and she couldn't help but grin when she saw it.

She'd served on the USNV *Hope* for so long it was home to her. It felt like she was going home and as she approached the docks, crew members and staff were filtering down the steps off the ship for a brief shore leave before the simulations started tomorrow.

Erica waited on the other side of the barricade, anxiously scanning the crowd for Regina. Of course, her people-watching was constantly interrupted by other colleagues and former crew members who were happy to see her.

When she'd served her time on the *Hope* she'd flown out of Sydney, Australia. *Hope* had been returning out to sea to start a three-month voyage of the South Seas and aid a tsunami disaster.

She hadn't gotten a chance to give a lot of people a proper goodbye. Including Regina, who was very angry that Erica had left in such a rush, but when you were called by the Home Office there was little chance to say proper farewells. There were no gold watch ceremonies in the Navy. One day you were here, the next you could be reassigned and off somewhere else.

Regina was a nurse, but she wasn't part of the Navy, and didn't quite get all the nuances or strict rules which Erica was bound by.

"Erica!"

Erica turned and saw a short, ebony-haired girl pushing her way through the throng of people toward the barricade.

Erica waved at her friend and waited while the Master of Arms cleared Regina for entrance. It only took a few minutes and then that ball of energy was running toward her and throwing her arms around her.

"Oh, my goodness. I've missed you, you crazy lady," Regina said, shaking Erica slightly. "Why the heck did you have to go and get reassigned, and to Okinawa of all places?"

Erica chuckled. "It's good to see you too, Regina. And for your information I quite like Okinawa Prefecture. It's very laid-back here."

"A Naval base laid-back?" Regina asked in disbelief. "I find that laughable."

"Okay, the base may not be laid-back, but the feeling around the island certainly is. Wait until you meet Scooby. He runs the Pineapple Face."

Regina wrinkled her nose. "Please tell me that's a bar?"

"Yes. It's awesome. It's like something out of old sixties sitcom reruns, and the proprietor Scooby is a huge Elvis fan. Huge."

"Oh, I like him already!" Regina slipped an arm through hers and they walked away from the docks. "So I'm being put up in your quarters, eh?"

"Yes. I hope you don't mind that I made those arrangements."

"Are you kidding me? Of course I don't. My new bunk mate on the *Hope* is a bit loony and she snores. Loudly."

"Sorry to hear that, but I talk in my sleep. You used to complain about that."

"I'd rather hear you spout off about elves, turkeys and whatever other nonsense you're dreaming about than Matilda's snore conversations with herself. It's horrible. I suggested she hit the hospital and the sleep apnea clinic. Seriously, there were a few times I thought she was going to inhale her pillow."

Erica laughed until her sides hurt. "So what else is happening on the ship?"

"Same old same old. There's nothing new to report other than Captain Dayton has a new protégé. His name is Lieutenant Clancy and he's really good-looking."

"How good-looking?" Erica asked, having an inkling where this was going. Regina was married to an officer who worked in San Diego, but just because Regina was married it didn't seem to stop her from scoping out gorgeous guys and potential husbands for Erica.

"It's my hobby," Regina had remarked once.

Regina scanned the crowd and then subtly pointed ahead of them. "There. That's how good-looking he is."

Erica glanced over, trying to be nonchalant. Regina was right; he was handsome. Tall and broad-shouldered from the rigorous training. His officer ranking meant he was probably fresh out of Annapolis: Captain Dayton only picked protégés who came from his alma mater. It also meant that he was most likely a trauma surgeon, as was Captain Dayton.

As she was looking at him, he glanced their way and smiled at her. One of those smiles that made Regina swoon and Erica want to put up her defenses.

"He's coming this way," Regina hissed in Erica's ear, barely containing her excitement.

"Hi, there," he said.

"Lieutenant Clancy, this is my friend, Commander Erica Griffin." Regina could barely contain her excitement.

Lieutenant Clancy came at attention and saluted. "I'm sorry, Commander. I didn't realize who you were."

"At ease. It's okay, Lieutenant. I'm not wearing my uniform. How would you know?"

Clancy smiled. "Are you assigned to this base, Commander?"

"I am. My previous assignment was the *Hope*."

"Really? So you're the surgeon who Captain Dayton has been gushing over since I arrived on board."

She chuckled. "One and the same."

"He didn't mention how beautiful you were, Commander."

Erica tried not to roll her eyes. She really didn't have time for this kind of come-on. And, no matter how cute the lieutenant was, he was Navy and off-limits. All Naval men were.

Except one.

If Thorne had come up to her and given her that cheesy pickup line she might've fallen for it, but then Thorne would never do anything like that. He had pride—an alpha male through and through.

A hero.

"Well, it was a pleasure to meet you, Lieutenant, but Regina and me have some catching up to do and it's my day off." Erica gripped Regina by the arm and forcibly marched her away from the docks at a quick pace.

"Are you crazy? He's really into you."

"Regina, we've been together for what…five minutes?…and you're already up to your old antics."

Regina laughed and squeezed Erica's arm. "And you love it. Come on, admit it, you've missed me."

Erica chuckled. "I've missed you and possibly your tomfoolery."

"Tomfoolery? Easy there, Shakespeare, or I may start up with my buffoonery or clownery."

They laughed together.

"I have missed you," Erica admitted.

"What's it like on the base?"

"Good. It feels odd to not be at sea. When I was back in San Diego before this assignment it was hard to get my land legs back."

Regina grunted. "I know. Every time I have leave and I'm in San Diego with Rick, for two days I swear I'm walking around like I'm drunk."

"You don't have the best land legs."

"Don't even get me started." Regina glanced around.

"It's pretty here, though. How far are we away from mainland Japan?"

"Well, you have to take a twenty-four-hour ferry to get to Kagoshima."

"Wow. That's far. I guess living it up in Tokyo is out of the question."

"Yes. You seriously suck at geography."

Regina stuck out her tongue. "So, what else is interesting about this base? You're holding something back. Something you're not telling me."

"What're you talking about?"

"I know when you're hiding something from me."

"I'm not hiding anything from you." Erica let go of Regina's arm. Damn, she hated that Regina was so intuitive. It was what made her a good nurse; she could always glean that little nugget of information out of a patient. "Are you hungry? I'll take you to that pub I was talking about."

"What are you hiding from me?"

"Nothing! I'm just trying to feed you." Then Erica spied exactly what she was trying to hide. Thorne was walking their way.

Regina had been there, working with Erica when Thorne had come in. She'd been his nurse for the few brief hours he'd been on board. Of course, he hadn't pleaded with her about his leg; he hadn't reached up and kissed her and called her beautiful.

"Angel."

"Oh, my God!" Regina froze. "Look who it is."

Erica grabbed her and pulled her behind a shrub. "Get down!"

"What?" Regina smiled then. "That's what you're hiding."

"Shut up!"

They crouched behind the bush until Thorne walked past and was out of sight. Erica let out a sigh of relief.

"That's that SEAL from…what…five years ago? The one who you were fighting so hard to keep on the ship. I thought for sure he would've died."

"I thought he did too."

Regina crossed her arms. "So why are we hiding from him, then?"

"We're not."

"Please. What was with the 'get down!' then?"

"I thought I saw a bug." Erica was not the best liar in the world, especially when she tried to lie to Regina; she didn't even know why she bothered with it.

"Please. Since when have you been afraid of bugs? Remember when we stopped in Hong Kong? You were the only one who tried those fried bugs. Which, by the way, still freaks me out to this day."

"There's nothing to tell."

"Who is he?"

"Captain Wilder is my commanding officer," Erica responded. There was no point in hiding that aspect. Regina would find out.

"Does he know?"

Erica shook her head. "I'm not talking about this. I'm going to get something to eat."

"Well, first can I drop my duffel bag off at your quarters?"

"Okay. Then eat."

"Yes. Then eat." Regina rolled her eyes. "In time you'll tell me. You always do."

Not this time, Erica thought to herself. She wasn't saying anything more, because there was nothing to tell. Absolutely nothing.

Except undeniable chemistry.

She cursed silently to herself. It was happening again and she didn't want it to.

Yes, you do.

No. There was nothing secretive or gossip-worthy in nature about her and Thorne. All Regina needed to know was that Thorne was her commanding officer and that he would be running the simulation tomorrow. That was it. End of discussion.

CHAPTER ELEVEN

WHY IS HE TOUCHING HER?

It was ticking him off because he should be focusing on the simulation lab, which was about to start. He'd been collected and ready to start at zero nine hundred hours, until some young lieutenant had come in and sat down next to Erica.

She was smiling at him as they spoke quietly to each other and then the lieutenant put his arm on the back of her chair. He wasn't totally touching her, but it was close enough.

Why should you care?

He shouldn't. He had no prior claim to Erica. She was off-limits. She wasn't his. Though he wanted her. He desired her. There was no use denying it anymore, to himself, at least. That was where those feelings were going to stay, buried deep inside.

Thorne cleared his throat and shuffled his papers, trying to ignore Erica and the lieutenant, but he couldn't.

Just like he hadn't been able to keep his eyes off of her last night at the pub. She'd been laughing and having a good time with a friend from the *Hope*. The lieutenant had been there, joking and smiling with them.

Thorne's only company had been Scooby.

"She doesn't laugh like that with you."

"Thanks for pointing that out, Scooby. I appreciate it."

Scooby had shaken his head. "That's not what I mean. It's all fake."

"I find that hard to believe, Scooby."

"It's fake. When she looks at you, that's something more. It's better."

Though Scooby hadn't been able to elaborate on how it was better.

Thorne found that hard to believe. She didn't look at him *different*. Not that he could tell. Then he uttered a few oaths under his breath, mad at himself for thinking about Erica and thinking about looks and lieutenants.

He glanced at the clock on the wall. It was nine. Time to start.

"Welcome everyone to my simulation lecture today." He moved around the other side of the podium. "Today we're going to be using robotic simulators and your tools would be the general tools that could be used in battle or emergency situations. There will be very basic tools, because in extreme circumstances you have to think with your head and improvise. I will be breaking you off into teams and each team will be given a different scenario."

"How long do we have, Captain?" a young ensign asked.

"I will start the timer. The first team to finish successfully, well, I don't have a prize." He grinned. "But perhaps I can be persuaded."

There was a bit of laughter and his gaze fell on Erica. She was smiling at him warmly. The same way she'd looked at him when they'd had pizza together at Scooby's place and, though he should just ignore it, he couldn't help but return her smile.

Concentrate.

"Okay. Organize yourself into teams. I want a mixture of levels of command. Not all surgeons with each other. I want to see a true team of medical professionals."

As they organized themselves into teams, he got his cards ready and Erica came up beside him.

"I think your prize should be one of Scooby's house pizzas."

"That might appeal to some, but really, what's so special about a pineapple pizza?"

"That it's one of Scooby's," she said matter-of-factly.

He chuckled. "Well, if I'm offering that, I don't think it's very fair that you're participating in this simulation. You've already had a taste of the prize. It might drive you to cheat."

"Are you calling me a cheater, Captain Wilder?"

"If the shoe fits."

"I'll have you know…" She trailed off and then the joviality disappeared. "Well, I better get to my team."

He watched her walk away, and then turned back to see that friend of hers watching them with a strange look on her face, like she'd caught them doing something naughty. What the heck was happening to his hospital?

Since when had he reverted back to high school? Because that was what it felt like and he was not happy about that.

"Can I help you…?"

"I'm a nurse, Captain." She stepped forward. "My name is Regina Kettle. I'm a nurse on the *Hope*."

Thorne nodded. "And is there something I can help you with? Do you have a question about the simulation?"

"No, not at all. My apologies for staring, but I think I know you."

So that's why she was staring and why Erica was acting weird. Did this nurse remember him as a patient? Had this nurse seen him when he'd been so vulnerable? That thought made him nervous.

"I don't think so."

She narrowed her eyes. "Well, maybe not, then."

"We're about to get started."

"Sure thing, Captain." She moved past him and returned to her team.

Don't let her shake you.

It didn't matter if she remembered him. It didn't matter if she'd been there when he'd lost his leg. It didn't make him less of a soldier or a surgeon.

Something it had taken him a couple of years to deal with himself when he could no longer be a part of the Special Ops.

So why is it bothering you so much?

He silenced the niggling voice in his head. When he looked over at Erica she was on the lieutenant's team and he was leaning over her, whispering in her ear while they went over what supplies they had.

"Lieutenant!" he snapped.

The lieutenant in question looked up, his cheeks flushing with color. "Yes, Captain Wilder?"

"What's your name, seaman?"

"Lieutenant Jordan Clancy." He saluted.

"Tell you what, I'd like you to switch places with the Ensign Fitz over here. I think the ensign would benefit more from working with Commander Griffin."

The blush remained. "Of course, Captain."

Lieutenant Clancy and Ensign Fitz switched places.

Thorne felt a little inkling of satisfaction and then he noticed the nurse was smiling smugly to herself, as if she'd uncovered some kind of secret.

He was not handling this well.

Pathetic.

And he was angry with himself for being so petty. This was what Erica did to him. She made him think and act irrationally. Before she arrived he'd led a relatively quiet existence. He didn't wrestle with his guilt every day.

What existence?

"All right, I'll be handing out your scenarios. Do not look at them until I start the clock." He passed cards to all the teams and then pulled out his timer. "Okay, go!"

The teams began to move quickly, moving through the scenarios and working together with the minimum equipment they had.

There were some promising officers, surgeons and medical personnel training in the simulation today. Erica handled her team efficiently as they dealt with the trauma to the chest wall. She immediately reached for the plastic bag and tape to stop the wound and the patient from bleeding out so they could properly assess them.

It gave him a sense of pride to watch her.

She was incredibly talented, beautiful, poised and a commendable second in command and officer.

And totally off-limits.

At least that was what he kept trying to tell himself, but he wasn't sure if he wholly believed it anymore.

"Are you sad your team lost?"

Erica was startled to see Thorne taking the seat next to her at the bar.

"No, not at all." She took a sip of her drink. "We would've won except for Ensign Fitz's blundering mistake."

"You mean when he killed your patient?" Thorne asked.

She laughed. "Yes. That does put a damper on the contest."

"He needed to learn."

"I could've won had you not taken Lieutenant Clancy from me."

His expression changed just slightly and he shifted in his seat. "Were you mad at my decision?"

"No, other than I lost." She leaned over. "I hate to lose, by the way. Just for future reference."

He smiled and nodded. "Noted."

"So why did you pull the lieutenant from my team?"

"I thought you said you weren't mad," he replied.

"Not mad. Just curious. I want to know what drove you to your decision."

"Ensign Fitz has a lot to learn and you're a damn fine surgeon."

Somehow she didn't believe him. Regina had suggested that Thorne had moved Lieutenant Clancy because he was jealous and possessive at the time. Regina had said she saw the way Thorne looked at her and, the moment Jordan had begun to whisper sweet nothings in her ear, Thorne moved him.

Erica thought the whole thing was preposterous.

Although the "sweet nothings" wasn't totally off; Lieutenant Clancy had been flirting with her, telling her how good she looked and asking her out for a drink later—which Erica had promptly turned down, much to Regina's chagrin.

"It's Captain Wilder, isn't it? You have the hots for him."

"I don't have the hots for him, Regina. I just have no interest in dating a superior or any officer."

Regina had rolled her eyes. "Then who are you going to date?

"No one."

"You're hopeless."

This was why Erica didn't date. Maybe she was hopeless, but there was good reason. Her career was too important.

She would never risk that for anything. Even a stolen moment with Thorne.

"Thank you, Captain. I appreciate the compliment."

"Thorne, remember? We're off duty."

"Right." She began to peel at the label on her domestic beer. The happy-looking squid was starting to lose tentacles as Erica nervously shredded the label, which was soft as the water was condensing on the outside of the bottle.

Don't think of him that way.

"So what did you think of the simulation today?" he asked.

"I thought it was good. Better than some other simulations I'd been involved in. Some are just endless lectures."

"I don't lecture."

She laughed. "I saw you tear down Ensign Fitz when he killed our robotic patient."

"That's a stripping down. It's not a lecture."

"It sounded like one of my father's." She took another swig of beer.

"Your father served, didn't he?"

"He did. He was a good officer, but I'm not like him." She didn't want to talk about her father. Not because she wasn't proud, but because people's condemnation and their scrutiny of her father cut her to the quick.

"How do you mean?"

She shook her head. "I'm not as strong as he was."

"You're just as strong. I see it."

"He wasn't called mentally unstable while he served."

It was only after.

She sighed. "Sorry."

"No, it's okay. I apologize for that. It was uncalled for."

"I'm used to it. It seems wherever I go I'm judged on that. Judged for making one mistake. I've had so many psychiatric evaluations and understanding conversations…"

Thorne held up his hands. "Erica, I was just making conversation. I don't think that at all."

Had she just heard him right?

"You don't?" she asked in disbelief.

"Why would I? Why I would judge you on the mistakes another made? You're a totally different person—I think, perhaps, stronger with all you've had to deal with. Was your father a medical officer?"

"No."

"Well, then, I don't know how you can be held to the same standard as him and vice versa. Serving as a medical officer is totally different than a plain officer."

"And being a Special Ops SEAL is so much more." She reached out and squeezed his hand. "Did you deal with PTSD when you returned home?"

"That's classified." He winked.

"I can always request your medical record as your surgeon."

He leaned over and she felt his hot breath as he murmured in her ear. "You can't. You're not on my record. It was wiped. I have never been on board the *Hope*."

"That's terrible! So who did they say did the surgery, then?"

He shot her a wicked grin. "Me."

"You?"

"Me. I was the medical officer with the unit."

"So you amputated your own leg, in the field in a very neat and dare I say brilliant way?"

His blue eyes twinkled. "You got it."

"You're not serious, are you?"

"Would I lie to you?"

Erica laughed. "Really, we're going to head back into *that* territory, are we?"

Thorne shrugged. "I'm absolutely dead serious. According to my official medical file out of San Diego where I recuperated, I was the chief medical officer in my unit, and I alone amputated my own leg."

Erica muttered a few choice curses that were quickly drowned out by an inebriated seaman shouting for music.

"No problem!" Scooby got up and selected music on his tiny digital jukebox, blasting a song at an obnoxious level as people crowded the dance floor.

Thorne laughed. "Do you want to dance?"

"Are you insane?"

"No, I'm serious. Come on; this is a fun song."

Erica shook her head in disbelief as a weird, drunken crowd formed on the small dance floor in front of them.

"I can't believe what I'm seeing."

"What, the dance or the crowd?" Thorne teased.

"Both." Erica took a swig of her drink. "I'm surprised that no one is filming this. This is going to end up on the internet."

"Good idea." Scooby scurried away.

Erica gave Thorne a sidelong glance. "You don't think he's going to get a camera, do you?"

"Don't put it past him. He might actually still have a camcorder back there."

Scooby returned and held up his phone. "Come on, Captain Wilder and Commander Griffin. Get out there and dance."

"She said no, Scooby."

Scooby frowned. "Why?"

"I don't dance in such an organized fashion." She winked at Thorne, who was laughing.

"Bah, you're no fun. I'll film you anyway."

"I have to get out of here," Erica shouted over the din. She set the money down on the counter. "Do you want to get out of here, Thorne?"

"What?" he asked, wincing.

"Let's go!" she shouted and took his hand, pulling him out of the bar. They managed to avoid Scooby's camera by disappearing in the throng of people that was now gathering around the edge of the dance floor.

She hated really thick crowds in small spaces. So it wasn't that she was afraid of dancing, or being caught on Scooby's video and ending up online, she just knew it would be a sudden crush of people and she didn't want to have a panic attack in front of Thorne.

When they were outside Erica took a breath of fresh air and began to laugh. "That was crazy. I didn't think Scooby had that repertoire of music."

"He has all kinds."

"I thought he only liked Elvis?" she asked.

"He's a man of many layers. Like an onion."

They began to walk along the sidewalk. The stars were out and a large full moon was casting an almost near-perfect reflection on the water of the bay. The *Hope* loomed up out of the darkness. The white color of the ship caught the light from the moon and the bridge was lit. She knew Captain Dayton was up on his bridge over-seeing some of the minor works before they set back out on the ocean again the day after tomorrow. The major retrofit would happen when they docked in San Diego.

"Do you miss serving on the ship?" he asked, break-ing the silence.

"Sometimes," Erica said. "I wanted a change. I like the different opportunities. I'm pretty blessed to do what I love to do."

"I get it."

"Do you miss being a part of Special Ops?" she asked.

He cocked his eyebrows.

"Yeah, I know, a dumb question. Of course you do." She sighed. "It's a beautiful night; do you want to walk down to the beach?"

"No, my leg isn't so good on the sand at the best of times. I don't want to be stumbling at the moment."

She didn't know what he meant by that, but they kept on the main path toward the officers' quarters.

"What do you remember of that day?"

"What day?" she asked.

"I guess I should say *night*, but I'm not really sure if it was night when you took my leg."

"I didn't take your leg, Thorne."

"I know—when you operated," he said, correcting himself.

"I remember everything."

"You do?" he asked, surprised.

"I do. I wondered what happened to you for so long."

"So it was just curiosity about my well-being?"

"No, there was more to it." They stopped in a small green, which was between the hospital, the docks and the officer quarters. Suddenly she was shaking and she didn't know why; she was falling fast and she was so scared about taking the step.

What if I get burned again?

"What else?" He took a step toward her, his hands in his pockets, like he was trying to stop himself from something.

"Your eyes." Then she reached out and lightly touched his face. "You were scared, but I don't think it was fear. It was something else. Your eyes haunted me."

"So my eyes haunted you?"

"You mentioned someone: Liam. Who was he?"

Thorne stiffened at the name. "Someone I knew a while ago."

It was apparent that the topic of Liam was off-limits.

"You said I was as beautiful as an angel." Her cheeks burned with heat; she couldn't look up at him and when she did he ran his thumb over her cheek.

"You are," he whispered. His eyes sparkled in the dark; her pulse was thundering between her ears and her mouth went dry. Thorne's hand slipped around her waist, his hand resting in the small of her back. He was so close, they were so close, and all she wanted him to do was kiss her again.

You're so weak.

She couldn't let this happen again but she wanted it too. She was so lonely.

"Thorne, I don't know… This isn't right."

He took a step back. "You're right. I'm sorry."

"No, don't be sorry. I want to, trust me, but…I can't. I don't have room for anyone in my life but me."

"Neither do I, Erica. I can't promise you anything."

"I don't need promises. I've had promises made before and they were always broken. I don't rely on them." This time she was the one who closed the distance between them. "I don't expect any promises."

"Then what do you want?" he asked as he ran his knuckles down her cheek.

She wasn't sure what she wanted. She wanted to be with Thorne in this moment, but what would it do to her reputation? Could she just have one night with him?

That was what she wanted.

Just one night of passion.

Perhaps, if she fed the craving she had for him, then it would burn him from her system and she could move on. It would clear the air.

You're weak.

"What do you want, Erica?" His voice was husky as he whispered the words into her ear.

"I want you to kiss me." She reached out and gripped his shirt.

He leaned forward and she closed her eyes as he kissed her. And then it deepened and she was lost.

CHAPTER TWELVE

ERICA WASN'T SURE how they got to Thorne's door. All she knew at that moment was she had him pressed against the door, was melting into him. His kiss made her weak in the knees, senseless, and she didn't want it to end.

He gently pushed her away and she moaned.

"What?" she asked.

"I have to open the door," Thorne answered, his voice husky with promise.

"Good; I thought you'd changed your mind."

"No, never." And then he pulled her into another kiss, which seared her blood and made her swoon against him.

"Open the door." Erica let him go for just a moment as he unlocked the door. Once it was open he scooped her up, causing her to shriek.

"What're you doing?"

He shut the door behind him with a kick from his right leg. "Carrying you to my bedroom."

"You can't."

Thorne kissed her. "Watch me."

And he did carry her to his bedroom, then set her down on her feet. She slowly slid down the length of his body, feeling the heat of him through seemingly many layers of his clothes. Clothes she wanted gone as soon as possible.

"You look good enough to eat," he whispered against her neck.

Her pulse quickened. "Pardon?"

"You heard me. I've been fighting it all evening. Seeing you in the bar by yourself… I've been fighting the urge to take you in my arms from the moment you landed in Okinawa."

"Tell me more."

Thorne moaned and held her tighter. Her body was flush with his and Erica wanted the layers separating them to be gone. She wanted them to be naked, skin to skin.

"Do you want me to tell you or do you want me to show you?"

Erica didn't respond to that, instead she used her mouth to show him exactly how much she wanted from him. She was tired of being alone and for once she wanted to feel passion again, even if it was only fleeting. Thorne was worth it.

The room was dark except for a thin beam of light through the curtains and she was aware how close they were to Thorne's bed. She was suddenly very nervous. It had been so long since she'd been with a man. It felt like the first time again.

"What's wrong?" Thorne asked, brushing her hair from her face. "Are you having second thoughts?"

"No. No, I'm not having second thoughts. It's just been a long time since I've been with a man."

"It's been a long time for me too."

"I want you, Thorne. All of you." And she wanted it. She wanted him to possess her. For once she didn't want to be the woman men were afraid of because of her rank and her training. Tonight she was just Erica. She was just a woman and he was a man.

He kissed her again, a featherlight one, then buried his face against her neck. His breath caressed her skin, making goose pimples break out. A tingle raced down her spine and she sighed. She couldn't help herself.

"Take off my clothes," he whispered.

Erica did just that. Unbuttoning his shirt and running her hands over his chest, it was mostly bare except for a bit of hair, which disappeared under the waist of his pants. Next she undid his belt, pulling it out and snapping it. He slid his hands down her back and cupped her butt, giving her cheeks a squeeze.

"Don't be naughty," he teased.

"I swear I won't." And then she undid his pants, crouching to pull them down. He kicked them off and then moved to the bed, sitting down to remove his prosthetic leg. "Let me."

His body stiffened as she ran her hands over his thigh again and undid his prosthesis, setting it against the nightstand. She started to massage his thigh; he moaned.

"That feels good, but I don't want you to massage me," he said.

"Oh, no."

"No." He pulled her close, kissing her. "Now it's your turn. Undress."

Erica stood and began to take off her clothes. His eyes on her excited her, making her heart race. She'd never done anything like this before. It was usually lights-out, under the covers. She'd never stripped for a man before.

"You're so beautiful. Like an angel," he murmured. He reached out and pulled her down to him. "So beautiful."

"Thorne…" She trailed off because she didn't know what else to say to him. His hands slipped down her back, the heat from his skin searing her flesh and making her body ache with need. She was so exposed to him; it thrilled her. She'd never felt like this before. He cupped her breasts, kneading them, and she moaned at the sensation of his hands on her sensitized skin.

He pinned her against the mattress, his lips on hers, their bodies free of clothing and skin to skin.

She was so ready for him. Each time his fingers skimmed her flesh her body ignited. He pressed his lips against her breast, laving her nipple with his hot tongue. She arched her back. She wanted more from him. So much more.

Erica wanted Thorne to make her burn. To make her forget everyone else. His hand moved down her body, between her legs. He began to stroke her, making her wet with need.

"I want you so bad."

Erica moaned as he moved away and pulled a condom out of his nightstand drawer.

Thorne moved back to her. "Now, where were we?"

He pressed her against the pillows and settled between her thighs. He shifted position so he was comfortable. The tip of his sex pressed against her. She wanted him to take her, to be his.

Even though she couldn't be.

Thorne thrust quickly, filling her completely. She clawed at his shoulders, dragging her nails down his skin as he stretched her. He remained still, but she urged him by rocking her hips. She wanted him to move. To take her.

"You feel so good." Thorne surged forward and she met every one of his thrusts.

She cried out as he moved harder, faster, and a coil of heat unfurled deep within her. Then it came, pleasure like she'd never experienced before. It flooded through her and overwhelmed her senses, her muscles tightening around him as she came. Thorne's thrusts became shallow and he soon joined her in his climax.

His lips brushed her neck as she held him against her and then he rolled onto his back, pulling her with him, so she could hear his heart beating. She lightly ran her fingers across his skin while his own fingers stroked her back.

"I'm sorry that was so fast. I needed you so bad, I couldn't hold back."

"It was amazing," she whispered. "No apology necessary."

Erica settled against him, the only sound was that of the ocean outside and his breathing and then she tensed as she realized what she'd done. She'd fallen in with another commanding officer, something she'd sworn she'd never do again. As the euphoria melted away, she was angry at herself for being so weak.

How could she have let this happen again?

Thorne isn't like Captain Seaton. You didn't make any promises.

Captain Seaton had been angry that she'd been the one to reject him ultimately and that was why he tried to ruin her career.

She didn't think Thorne was like that. He seemed to have a good head on his shoulders. He was rational, but a bit of niggling self-doubt ate away at her. Trust was a big issue for her. She wasn't sure if she could trust Thorne.

She wasn't sure if she would honestly trust another man again.

Thorne watched her. He wasn't sure if she was sleeping. Her eyes were closed, but her breathing wasn't deep, as if she was in sleep. He knew he'd promised her that nothing had to happen out of this, that was the way she wanted it and that was what he wanted. Wasn't it?

Of course that was what he wanted.

They'd made no promises; if promises had been exchanged he wouldn't have gone through with it, because he was never going to have a relationship. He'd been weak and forgotten that he couldn't have her.

He rolled over onto his back and scrubbed his hands over his face, staring up at the fan slowly rotating on his ceiling. What had he done? The guilt ate at him.

"What's wrong?" Erica murmured.

"Nothing." He turned to his side again. "Just watching you sleep."

"Why are you watching me?" she asked, moving onto her side and tucking her hands under her head.

"I couldn't help it. It was relaxing."

"That groan you gave out didn't sound like you were at ease."

"Perhaps not."

She smiled and then frowned. "So, what happens now?"

"What do you mean?"

"I mean when we're back on duty." Erica leaned on an elbow. "I don't want any awkwardness. I'd like to act like nothing happened between us."

"We'll just go on as normal. Nothing has to change; I think we both made our intentions clear."

"We did." Then she got up, holding the sheet against her.

"Where are you going?"

"Back to my quarters." She bent over, picking up the pieces of her clothing scattered all around the room.

"I'm not kicking you out, Erica. You don't have to leave."

"I do." She sat down on the edge of the bed and began to dress. "If I stay, then it might mean more."

"I won't think that. Come back to bed."

Erica chuckled. "Is that your best 'come hither' look?"

"I wasn't aware I was doing one." He leaned across and pulled her back down against the mattress to place a kiss on her lips upside down. "Stay."

"I can't. Remember, I have Regina staying with me. If I don't come back to bed, she's going to wonder and then start poking around. She might even get a transfer until she figures it all out."

Thorne shuddered. "Okay, you better go, but know this—it's against doctor's orders."

She rolled her eyes, got up and finished dressing. Then she came around to his side of the bed and kissed him.

"Thanks for tonight."

"Anytime." He wanted to say more things. He wanted to tie her down in his bed and never let her go, but she was right. If she came out of his quarters the next morning and someone saw her, there would be gossip. She didn't want any more gossip about her, which was fair.

He didn't want the gossip either. Thorne didn't want to get her in trouble or transferred. Losing her would be detrimental to the welfare of the base hospital.

And you too.

Yeah, he'd miss the comraderie. She was the only second in command he'd ever met who'd stood up to their commanding officer. Who worked alongside him as a team. They were equals.

She was strong.

Thorne had thought being with her once would flush her from his system, instead he found himself wanting more.

So much more.

* * *

Erica tried to sneak back into her quarters. The television had been flickering in the window when she approached and she was worried that as soon as she walked through the door she'd be bombarded with questions, but when she peered through the window she could see that Regina was passed out in front of the TV.

Maybe dancing at Scooby's had exhausted her.

One could only hope.

Erica shut the door behind her as quietly as she could, locked it and then slid off her shoes to creep along the tiled hallway to her bedroom.

She was almost home free.

"Where were you tonight?"

Darn.

Erica turned to see Regina sitting upright, no sign of being asleep or having been asleep. "You were awake when I came home, weren't you?"

"I was. I saw you peek through the window."

"You're a pain." Erica tried to escape again, but she was up against a pro.

"Where were you?"

"I'm an adult. You're not my mother."

Regina crossed her arms. "I was worried when you disappeared from the bar. It would've been nice if you had told me where you were going."

"You're so good at guilt."

A small smile played around Regina's lips. "I'm sorry, but it's true. I was worried."

"You were worried? You were too busy dancing." Erica mimicked Regina's terrible but endearing moves.

Regina rolled her eyes. "Come on. I don't get out much."

"It's apparent."

"I still don't know how that song started."

"Some poor seamen who had had too much to drink." Erica set her purse down on the counter in her kitchen and went to get a glass of water. Regina laughed. "And why didn't you jump in?"

"Oh, I was in the middle of talking to Thorne." And then she cursed under her breath, realizing she'd said "Thorne" to Regina instead of calling him Captain Wilder. Dang.

"Who?"

"Captain Wilder."

"So we're on a first-name basis with Captain Wilder, now, eh?"

"Shut up." Erica took a big swig of water, trying to ignore Regina who was smugly dancing around the kitchen.

"I knew it. I knew something was up. You were with him, right?"

"Yes."

"You are such a bad liar!" Regina exclaimed. "I so *knew* you two had chemistry floating around. Why else would you dive behind a bush to avoid someone? You've never hid from anyone or anything before. Tell me everything!"

"There's nothing to tell."

Liar.

There was a lot to tell, but it was stuff she wasn't sure she wanted to share at this moment because she wasn't exactly sure of how she was feeling herself. When she'd come here and seen that her commanding officer was Thorne, she'd been worried that she would be too weak to resist him. She didn't want another relationship. That was what she kept telling herself. It became a broken record in her head.

And, just like any song you heard over and over, the broken record had become nothing more than background noise when Thorne took her in his arms and kissed her. Now she didn't know what to do with all these emotions swirling around inside.

She was torn and frightened.

"Come on, there has to be something going on. You're sneaking into the house in the middle of the night." Regina looked her up and down. "You reek of guilt."

Erica rolled her eyes. "How can I reek of guilt?"

Regina leaned forward and sniffed. "Okay, not guilt, but cologne or something very manly. Unless you've taken to wearing men's deodorant."

"You know what? I have." Erica set the glass in the sink. "I'm kind of tired. I think I'm going to hit the hay. I have a long duty-shift tomorrow."

"Erica, it's okay to admit you like this guy."

"No, it's not. You know my story. You know what happened to me before. I was in a relationship with my commanding officer before the *Hope,* and I thought he loved me, but he didn't. Not the way I loved him and so I broke it off. I was the one that was isolated. I was the one who was getting the crummy shifts. I was the one passed up for commendation and promotions. I was the one he reported as mentally unstable. It's why I left."

"I thought you didn't want a relationship because of your mom losing your dad."

Erica sighed and leaned against the counter. "That's part of it, but not really. I saw what my father's service did to his marriage and his family, but that didn't stop me from serving. That didn't stop me from proving to everyone that I was a good officer too. I stepped out of my father's shadow long before my relationship with Captain Seaton."

Regina nodded. "Okay, so your holdup is not your parents' marriage, but being burned by a lover?"

"I guess so. See, before I was hurt I thought my perfect match would be someone who served in the same capacity as me. My mother was not in the Armed Forces."

"Erica, you had one bad relationship. Who doesn't?"

"Has a former lover almost ruined your reputation and career by calling you mentally unstable?"

Regina bit her lip. "Well, no."

"Then you're not an authority."

"Look, we've all been hurt by love before we found that perfect someone. I think that Thorne is your perfect someone."

"And how would you know that? You've met him once."

Regina shrugged her shoulders. "I just know. I'm quite intuitive and you've said that countless times. I have it on record."

Erica chuckled. "Intuitive in your job."

"Well, it counts for knowing good relationships too."

"There's no relationship. He doesn't want one either."

"How do you know?"

"He told me."

Regina frowned and pursed her lips together. "I don't buy that. I think you should talk to him about your feelings."

"What feelings?" She would have got away with that except she blushed. There were feelings there; she just wasn't sure she was ready to admit those feelings. Not yet.

When?

And that was the conundrum she was in. She was being a coward and she hated that. Erica wasn't a coward.

"I don't know why you're trying to deny them." Regina sighed. "Whatever you do, you have to tell him."

"I'm telling you, he doesn't want anything more than what we had tonight, Regina."

"Do you know that with one-hundred-percent certainty?"

No, she couldn't. She really didn't know how Thorne was feeling. Maybe he'd just been saying those things to get her between the sheets, maybe not. Damn it, she didn't have time for this. A relationship was not on the cards for her.

She wasn't going to put her heart on the line again.

Career was all that mattered. She just wanted to keep advancing until she commanded a posting of her own.

Relationships, love, family: they just tied you down.

You're lonely.

Lonely or not, it wasn't an excuse to go out and just marry the first guy you came across so you could get those two kids you'd secretly been longing for, which would put a strain on the marriage, which would eventually result in divorce because that significant other didn't get your passion, your drive.

Her head began to pound.

"I'm going to bed. Good night, Regina." Erica turned to leave, but Regina stopped her. "Regina, I'm really tired."

"I know. Look, I'm sorry." Regina gave her a hug. "I just want you to be happy. I saw the way you two looked at each other, and I think it's mutual, but until one of you opens up nothing is going to happen. I know you don't want to hear it, but I think you two are perfect for each other."

I think so too.

"I can't open up, Regina. I just can't." She gave her friend another hug. "I'm going to get some sleep. Should I wake you to say goodbye before I go to work?"

"Yes," Regina said. "Or I'll kick your butt."

Erica grinned. "Just think, in a few days you'll be on a leave with Rick in San Diego."

"Not just a leave."

"Oh?"

"I'm going to take a job at a private clinic in San Diego. Rick and I are trying."

"For a baby?" Erica asked surprised.

"Yep."

"So you won't be going back on the *Hope*?"

Regina shook her head. "Nope. This was my last run."

"So that's why you're trying to fix me up. You're trying to make sure I'm taken care of before you head for the public sector."

"You got it. I will succeed."

"Keep thinking that."

"I'm glad I got to see you. Perhaps Rick will get stationed in Okinawa. If not, I'll come visit."

"You better."

Regina smiled. "Go sleep. I'll see you tomorrow."

Erica nodded and took herself off to bed, but she doubted she'd get any sleep, and she was right. As soon as her head hit the pillow, she rolled over on her right and stared at the empty spot beside her.

The emptiness had never bothered her before, but

now it did. She was very aware how empty her bed was and she was mad at herself for caring.

She was mad at herself for wanting something she knew she couldn't have.

CHAPTER THIRTEEN

"GOOD MORNING," THORNE WHISPERED, his breath fanning against her neck. She didn't even hear him come up behind her. She was busy charting after an early-morning shift in the ER. Even though they were alone, she felt uncomfortable that he was so close, making the butterflies in her stomach flutter.

She cleared her throat and rubbed her neck, shifting away slightly. "Good morning, Captain."

"Formalities?"

"Yes." Her cheeks flamed with heat. "We are on duty, after all."

"Good point. My apologies, Commander. What happened while I was off duty?"

"There was a motor vehicle collision. Minor. One went to surgery with Lieutenant Drew." She handed the chart to Thorne.

"Why?" he asked, flipping through the pages.

"Spleen was bleeding too much. Lieutenant Drew is performing a splenectomy as we speak." She glanced at his watch. "Barring complications, he should be finished soon."

Thorne nodded. "Anything else?"

"Seven people with a cold, and a couple crewmen of the *Hope* stumbled in for help easing their hangovers before they boarded." She shook her head. "It was like a flash mob last night at Scooby's, a really inappropriate flash mob."

Thorne pulled out his phone and pulled up the web. "It was, in fact."

Erica leaned over to see the video from Scooby's, the choreographed movements to the song. "Pretty impressive for a bunch of drunkards."

"I know. Scooby was quite happy he got to film it." Thorne's eyes twinkled.

Erica laughed. "I bet he was. That man is obsessed with pop culture."

"Who?" Bunny asked, appearing behind the charge desk.

Erica jumped back from Thorne and cleared her throat again as she stared at the chart. "Sachiho."

Bunny cocked an eyebrow. "Who?"

"Scooby," Thorne interjected. "There was a bit of a scene of the weird kind last night at Scooby's bar."

Bunny chuckled. "When isn't there?"

"Is there something I can help you with, Bunny?" Erica asked, hoping that she could throw herself into busywork.

"Nope. I'm just about to head out. My shift is over." Bunny put the last of her charts away. "Have a good day, Commander and Captain."

Bunny left the two of them standing there at the charge desk alone.

"Why did that feel awkward?" Thorne asked.

"I have no idea."

Only she did. Well, at least she knew why she was feeling awkward, because she didn't want to be alone with Thorne again. Only, that was ridiculous. She was going to be alone with him again. Sex had changed it.

Your feelings for him, too.

"I thought you were going to watch some SEALs train down at the aquatic center?" she asked, trying to sound nonchalant and failing.

"I might yet."

"What test is it?"

"Drown proofing. The next week there will be several rounds of it."

"Oh, that test looks brutal. I've seen it."

"It's hard-core. Though, I can't really demonstrate it anymore. I was pretty darn good at it, though." He smiled to himself.

"I'm sure you were. You swam in open water with an infected leg wound."

The smile disappeared. "Yes."

"I'm sorry. I didn't mean to bring it up. You don't like talking about it, do you?"

He shrugged. "I don't like to dwell on the past. I can't change it. Just got to keep one foot in front of the other and move forward; the future hasn't been written."

"So you don't believe things are predestined?"

He shook his head. "Nope and, if they were, I'd have to have some words with someone about the rough end of the stick I got a few times—and I'm not just talking about my leg."

Erica smiled. "I understand."

"Well, I better check on the lieutenant's surgery. Make sure the splenectomy is going smoothly and we don't lose the patient."

"I'll see you later."

"I hope so." He turned and left her standing there with her charts. She watched him walk away. There was just a slight limp to his gait, but he was still that strong,

Navy SEAL Special Ops officer who had begged her not to take his leg.

There were so many admirable things about him. Also there were many annoying things about him. Maybe Scooby was right. They were too volatile together. That was what Scooby had told Thorne and Thorne had told her.

What does Scooby know? He has green shag carpet on his ceilings and walls.

"I saw the way he looked at you and the way you looked at him."

Erica shook Regina's words from her head. They were the last words Regina had said to Erica before she'd walked back up the gang plank to board the *Hope*. Erica had had a break and had gone outside to watch as the *Hope* sailed east towards the States. She'd wished for a moment she was back on the ship headed for San Diego.

Not that she knew any one besides Regina and Rick in San Diego, but it was the gateway to a new port of call. Headquarters. It was one thing she'd loved about serving on the *Hope*. Every day was something new and exciting, but she'd only been able to go so far on the ship.

Here in Okinawa or another similar base she could rise above her current rank. That was, if she didn't mess it up by sleeping with her commanding officer.

Oh, wait: she had done that.

Erica pinched the bridge of her nose and shook her head. No, she couldn't let this escalate any further.

They'd shared one night of passion and that was all it could be.

Keep telling yourself that.

Her phone pinged with an email. She glanced down and saw it was from Admiral Greer. Confused as to why the admiral would be emailing, she opened it, reading it quickly. She almost dropped her phone and had to read the email again, her hands were shaking so bad.

All her hard work was about to pay off as her dream post was offered to her.

All she had to do now was tell Thorne she was leaving.

You're here to see SEAL training. That's it.

It was the end of the week of SEAL training and she was coming to watch that and not tell Thorne that she'd accepted a new posting at Annapolis in Maryland.

The email from Admiral Greer had been to promote her from commander to captain and offer her a position at the prestigious school. Her dream position. She'd said yes without a second thought. Now she had to tell Thorne and she was positive he'd understand.

At least that was what she kept trying to tell herself, but she wasn't a good liar. Even she didn't believe herself.

She'd always wanted to go and work at the United States Naval Academy. She'd be training medical corp recruits. It was something she'd always dreamed of, but the opportunity had never presented itself. After that fiasco in Rhode Island she'd never thought it would, to be honest.

Now it had, she had to jump at the chance. Even if it meant leaving Thorne behind.

He didn't make any promises. Neither did you.

This was her career. Love had screwed it up before and she couldn't let that happen again. No matter how much she wanted to stay with him.

The last time she'd chosen love over career it had burned her. Seriously burned her. And that hadn't even been love. That had just been lust.

With Thorne it was different. They connected.

And now she was leaving.

He'll understand.

If the situation was reversed, he would jump at the opportunity.

She snuck into the aquatic center and took a seat in the bleachers. The trainees were in the water doing their drown proofing, which consisted of bottom bouncing, floating and various retrievals. The test usually exhausted the swimmer, but also prepared them for rigorous missions.

Thorne was walking along the edge of the pool with another instructor. She could tell by the way he paced on the deck that he wanted to be in there with them, but couldn't.

He turned away from the testers and looked up at her.

Damn it.

She wasn't ready for this. Blood rushed to her cheeks as he headed in her direction, up the few stairs to where she was sitting.

"Erica, what're you doing here?"

"I've never witnessed this particular test. I thought it might be interesting to watch."

He smiled and then sat down on the bench next to her. "You just came off an extremely long shift. I know because I scheduled it. You should be at home sleeping."

"I'm a bit tired, but I had to come see this." She looked closer. "I thought their hands are tied?"

"They will be; the instructor is just acclimatizing them, getting them ready for the test. These guys are pretty green. Besides, the instructor will pull them out of the water, freeze them out a bit."

"I bet they'll freeze."

"Get them used to hypothermia, but not really. This

is a controlled environment and they won't be out of the water that long." And just as he said the words a whistle echoed and the trainees clambered out of the water as fast as they could. When they were standing to attention, that was when the instructors begin to tie the trainees' hands together.

"I thought my training at Annapolis was difficult," she muttered under her breath.

"You have to be tough to go on the kind of missions these men could go on."

"I don't doubt that. It's why I never even contemplated becoming a SEAL. I just wanted to be in the Medical Corp. Going the officer route helped pay for that training."

"That's how I originally started," Thorne said a bit wistfully as he stared down at the group of ten seamen, dripping and trying not to shiver on the pool deck.

"What made you go into the SEALs?"

"The death of my twin brother." There was a sadness to his voice. One she was familiar with. One she had used herself when talking about her father. It was pain.

"I knew you had a brother, but I didn't know he was your twin. I'm sorry," she said and she placed a hand on his knee, at a loss for words. "How did you...? How did he...?"

"Die?" he asked.

"You don't have to tell me. I didn't mean to pry."

"It's okay."

Thorne ran his hand through his hair. "He died in service. He showed up at the field hospital I was stationed at. I was called off my ship to assist. In the field hospital there was an IED. There was an explosion and Liam died in my arms."

She took his hand in hers and squeezed it. "I'm sorry. So sorry."

"I appreciate the sentiment, but it was my fault."

"How?" she asked, confused.

"I don't want to get into it."

"I get it."

He glanced up at her. "Do you?"

"I do. I don't like talking about my father to many people."

Thorne nodded. "Did he die in service?"

Erica's stomach knotted. "No. He didn't."

She didn't talk about her father, not to anyone.

She sighed again. "He died as a result of service. He was wounded on a mission, came back home and the doctors cleared him—but I think the wound and losing most of his unit caused PTSD. He went back when he healed and was on a covert operation when he went AWOL, blowing the mission, and he was dishonorably discharged. It was then he killed himself."

"I'm sorry to hear that."

"He was my hero. If he could've got the help he needed…"

"I understand." He stared down at her hand, tracing the back with his thumb, which made her blood heat as she thought of his hands stroking her body.

"I better go." She took her hand back, feeling uncomfortable, and stood. She'd opened up to Thorne too much. It was dangerous letting him know that about her.

He opened up to you.

And that was a problem. She was scared.

"I'll walk you back to your quarters."

"It's broad daylight, Thorne. I think I can manage."

"I don't mind." The tone of his voice implied that he wouldn't take no for an answer. He was going to walk her back whether she liked it or not. She didn't mind it, except the fact that she might not be able to resist asking him inside.

Remember how Captain Seaton hurt you. Don't do this to yourself.

Only Thorne wasn't Captain Seaton. Thorne was different. He wouldn't report her as mentally unstable because she was taking a new position and leaving him.

At least that was what she kept trying to tell herself, but it was so hard to open up and trust again. She'd resigned herself a while ago to the fact that love was not to be a part of her life and then she'd met Thorne.

He limped slightly as they walked to her quarters.

"Why don't you go back?" Erica asked. "You don't have to do this. I am a big girl."

"It's not a bother. I needed to stretch my leg. The moisture actually bothers me sometimes. Phantom leg pain."

"I'm sorry you have to go through that."

"Most people do. With the trauma inflicted, the brain can't really understand why the nerves aren't there any longer. Besides, I was hoping you can give me another massage sometime."

She laughed. "Oh, really? So that was your master plan—take me home and, instead of letting me sleep, I'm supposed to massage you?"

"Well, we could do something else."

Heat bloomed in her cheeks. "Thorne, I don't think it's wise. Do you?"

Then he pulled her close to him. "No, it's not wise, but I can't resist you. Believe me, I've tried. I want to resist you."

Her pulse thundered in her ears. She was pressed against his chest and very aware of how close they were.

"Thorne," she whispered, closing her eyes so she

wouldn't be drawn into his eyes, which always seemed to melt her. "I can't. I just… I can't."

"Why?"

"I thought we were going to be friends?"

Thorne let go of her. "I'm sorry, Erica. I wanted to respect your wishes. I did, but when I'm around you I can't help myself. I didn't… I don't want a relationship. I can't give you a relationship."

"And I can't give you one either." She reached up and touched his cheek. "I can't be with another commanding officer. The last time I got involved with someone I work for it almost cost me my career. Unless you can promise me a lifetime, unless you can promise me that our relationship won't affect my career, then I just can't. I can't."

Because I'm leaving.

Only she couldn't verbalize those words.

Chicken.

She tried to turn and leave, because she was embarrassed she'd admitted it to him. Embarrassed that he knew she'd been foolish enough once to believe in forever with someone who wasn't worthy. She made it to her quarters and opened the door. Just as Thorne came up behind her.

"Erica, I would never jeopardize your career. I hope you know that."

"I know. I just wanted you to know why… I couldn't really hide it any longer. I thought for sure you knew. I was pretty sure it was on my service record."

"No, why would it be? If you were passed up for commendation or a promotion in rank, do you really think those responsible for denying that would record it on your service record?"

She was a bit stunned.

"You look surprised," he commented.

"Captain Dayton knew why I was passed up for promotion. I don't even know why he actually picked me to come aboard the *Hope*."

"Captain Dayton is a smart man. He saw talent. Just like I did." Thorne rubbed the back of his neck, frowning, as if he was struggling to tell her something and she was expecting him to tell her why he couldn't be with someone.

What was holding him back?

What's holding you back?

Still she waited. She waited for him to open up to her, waited pathetically for a sign that maybe it would be worth a second thought. Only he said nothing to her and she was angry at herself for even thinking for one moment that she'd give up on her dreams for a man. When had she become so weak?

Her career mattered. Her life mattered.

"Thorne, I have something to tell you."

"Erica, don't say something we'll regret."

"I'm transferring to Annapolis."

The blood drained from his face and his brow furrowed. "Pardon?"

"I'm transferring to Annapolis, Maryland. I was offered a position as Captain and I would be working with medical corps recruits. It's a chance of a lifetime and I couldn't turn it down."

"No, of course not." He smiled, but it was forced. "Who gave you the commendation?"

"Captain Dayton actually recommended me."

He chuckled, but it was one of derision, not mirth. "Is that a fact? When do you leave?"

"In a week."

Thorne nodded slowly. "Well, of course you have to go."

"I do." Only part of her was screaming not to go—the part of her that wanted to stay with Thorne, marry him and settle down. But he couldn't give her any promises and neither could she. If he didn't want her, she didn't want to settle down with a man who would resent her down the road or, worse, she would resent him for making her give up on her career.

No, she had to go.

"I'm sorry I'm leaving you without a second in command."

"I'll make do until a replacement can be sent." He wasn't looking at her as he backed away from her door. "I better put in a request now."

"Do you still need me to look at your leg?"

"No," he snapped. "It's fine. I'll see you tomorrow, Commander Griffin."

Her heart ached as she watched him walk away quickly and she tried to tell herself it was all for the best.

This way she wouldn't get hurt.

It was her last day. She was shipping out tonight, but this was her last day working at the base hospital. Her last day working with Thorne.

Things had been awkward since she'd told him that she was accepting a post in Annapolis. They spoke, but barely, and it was about work. She waited for the other shoe to drop. She waited for him to report her as unfit or something.

And when the conversation drifted from work or the duty roster it became tense. It was like he was mad that she was leaving. But it was part of life in the Navy. Officers took postings, left postings.

Her promotion to captain was something she couldn't give up but, anytime she went to talk to him about it, he turned and walked away from her, making it blatantly obvious that he was avoiding her.

She'd even gone to Scooby's a few times, trying to catch him. Only he hadn't been there and Scooby was even concerned he hadn't seen Thorne in a while.

"He shouldn't be alone, Commander. He thinks he can handle it. He can't. I know he's not the only one around here."

Erica was sure that last part was a jab at her. Scooby didn't understand her circumstances. He didn't get why she couldn't be with someone again. She couldn't tether herself to another person and Annapolis was the dream.

It had been since she'd graduated there.

Only, being around Thorne had made her think for a moment that maybe it might be good to be with someone. She wanted it to be him, but he didn't seem to have an interest in letting her past his barriers.

"Commander!" Bunny shouted from the charge desk, a phone in her hand. "Commander Griffin."

Erica rushed over. "What's wrong?"

"It's a code black," Bunny whispered. "You're to go out to the helipad. The west part of the trauma floor is being cleared. Need to know only."

"Tell them I'm on my way." Erica started running toward the helipad. The wing in question was being cleared quickly and Masters of Arms were beginning to block off the entrances and barricade people from that section of the trauma floor.

A shudder traveled down her spine as she thought of that moment five years ago: silent running on the ship. Pitch-black, and the flare from the submarine illuminating the sky to direct the helicopter.

Another covert operation.

When she got to the helipad Thorne was there waiting, the helipad surrounded by armed military police.

"It's about time," Thorne snapped.

"Who's coming in? The president or something?"

"They didn't say. Just that it was covert. Most likely
Special Ops."

The roar of the helicopter sounded in the distance
and they braced themselves for the wind being stirred
up as the helicopter landed. Once they had the all clear
they ran forward with the gurney and loaded the patient,
who was screaming in agony.

The patient's commanding officer leaped down beside the gurney and helped them wheel the man toward
the hospital.

"Prepare for more incoming," the commanding officer said. "We had a few casualties, but he was by far
the worst."

"Do we get any specifics?" Erica snapped. "Or do
we refer to him as John Doe?"

"Commander Griffin!" Thorne warned.

"John Doe, Commander," the unit's commanding
officer responded. "It's all classified."

"Understood," Thorne said. "We'll take care of your
man. What happened to him?"

"Explosion. Shredded his arm. We packed it the best
we could, but I think it's infected."

"Are you medical?" Erica asked sharply as they wheeled
the John Doe into a triage room and began to undress him
to get to the damage.

"I am."

"Maybe you can scrub in," Thorne suggested.

"I can't. As soon as the men are stable we have to ship
to our meeting place."

Erica snorted and Thorne sent her a look to silence her.

The moment Erica came close to the man's left arm, he screamed in pain, and as soon as she got close to him she could see the infection. It was worse than Thorne's had been. She didn't know how long these men had been in the field, but this John Doe was lucky to be alive.

"He needs surgery," Erica said, turning quickly to start a central line to get antibiotics into the John Doe and sedate him.

"Agreed," Thorne said. "Don't worry, seaman, we'll take care of you."

Erica had the central line in as fast as she could and was pumping the medicine the John Doe needed. He was also severely dehydrated, by the way his lips were cracked, and she couldn't help but wonder how much blood loss he was suffering from.

Thorne sedated him and then was inserting tubes down the man's throat so that he could breathe.

After a few orders, the nurses who were in the know had the OR ready to go and they were wheeling their John Doe off to surgery.

Erica scrubbed alongside Thorne as the nurses prepped and draped the patient.

"Pretty basic, I think," she said.

"What's basic?" Thorne asked.

"Amputation of the arm."

Thorne stopped scrubbing for a moment. "If it's deemed necessary."

"I think it's necessary. Don't you?"

Thorne ignored her and walked into the OR where a nurse gowned him and put gloves on him.

Erica cursed under her breath and followed him, jamming her arms angrily down into the gown that was held out for her.

As she approached the table she could see the damage the IED had caused and this time she did curse out loud.

Thorne glanced at her quickly. "I know."

"He's lucky to have lived this long. Do you think it can still be saved, Captain?" The tone was sarcastic. It was meant to be, but then the scrub nurse beside Thorne gasped, and few others looked at her like she'd lost her mind.

She was being insubordinate to her commanding officer in his OR.

"Get out," Thorne said.

"What?" Erica asked.

"I said, get out."

"Why? He obviously needs an amputation. Are you telling me that you're going to work on his arm when it's clearly not salvageable?"

"That will be my decision as head surgeon. Now, Commander Griffin, if you'd kindly leave my OR and send in Ensign Benjamin. He's been cleared for this level of security and he can assist me in saving John Doe's life."

"With all due respect, Captain. I'm scrubbed in and ready to go. I've dealt with infections of this caliber before. I think I should be the one assisting."

"Do you?"

"I do." Erica held her ground. She had nothing to lose anyway, as she was heading to Annapolis.

"I don't think so, Commander. You wrote off his arm before you had X-rays done or even thoroughly examined the wound. Is that how you made your decision when you took my leg and ruined my career?"

The room was silent—at least, she assumed it was,

since her head was filled with the thundering of her blood as it boiled.

She thought he'd forgiven her or didn't blame her for the decision she'd made five years ago, which had taken his leg, but apparently that wasn't true. He still resented her. Enough to bring up her competence in front of other staff members; he'd humiliated and embarrassed her.

Erica took a calming breath and stared at him across the OR.

"I saved your life."

"And I will save his. Now, get out of my OR, Commander. That's an order."

Erica didn't say anything but obeyed her commanding officer. She ripped off the gloves and gown and jammed them in the soiled bin and then scrubbed out as quickly as she could. When she was in the hall, she ripped off her surgical cap and tossed it against the wall.

She'd been so foolish to fall in love with her commanding officer, a former patient, even. She was stupid to think about trying to make it work, to think of having it all and settling down. She was weak for letting herself be momentarily ruled by her heart.

Well, it wouldn't happen again. She would never open her heart again.

She was tired of it being broken.

Thorne couldn't save the John Doe's arm. Erica had been right. He'd known from the moment he'd seen it briefly in the triage room, but instead of listening to her he'd been ruled by his emotions, by the feelings of betrayal he'd felt ever since she'd told him that she was leaving Okinawa to take a prestigious posting at Annapolis.

If it had been anyone else he would've been happier

for them. He was happy for Erica, but the fact was she was leaving him, and he was acting like a fool.

She was leaving and he didn't want to let her go.

This is what you wanted, wasn't it?

He deserved this. He didn't deserve to be happy. It was fitting she was leaving.

He wanted her to leave Okinawa so he wouldn't be tempted, the only problem being he'd been tempted long before she'd decided to leave and now he didn't want her to go. He wanted her to stay with him. Only, she couldn't.

Thorne had to let her go.

It was for the best.

She would move on.

Erica wanted to advance her career: it was evident from the postings she'd chosen, by how far she'd come and what she'd endured to get to her position.

He couldn't be selfish, because he couldn't promise her anything.

Why not?

So he had to let her go. But first it was up to him to explain to the John Doe how his career was over and up to him to see the Special Ops team off to wherever they were going. Most likely San Diego.

As he headed out into the private room where the team was waiting, he caught sight of Erica in her uniform, her rucksack over her bag. She'd obviously cleared out her locker.

Let her go. She's mad at you and doesn't want to speak with you.

"Commander Griffin."

She turned and faced him. Her expression was unreadable as she dropped her bag and saluted him, holding herself at attention.

"Erica," he said.

"Captain." She would not look him in the eye.

"You're being ridiculous."

Her eyes narrowed and she looked at him, but wouldn't speak to him.

"You're at ease, Commander."

Erica relaxed her posture. "Can I help you, Captain?"

"I need to speak with you. Privately."

"I don't think that's wise, Captain. I think everything has been said."

"Please."

Erica sighed and picked up her rucksack, following Thorne into a small exam room. She shut the door behind her.

"What do you need to talk to me about? Whatever it is, make it quick. I'm catching the next transport back to the US."

"I know. I wanted to apologize."

"Apologize."

"I was out of line. You're right; the John Doe lost his arm. There was no way to salvage it."

Erica frowned. "I'm sorry that it couldn't be saved. I am."

Thorne nodded and then reached into his lab coat pocket for the small package he'd been carrying around since before she'd been leaving. Maybe because on some certain level he always knew she'd leave. "There was no excuse for my behavior. I wanted to clear the air before you left and give you this."

Erica glanced at the box with trepidation. "What is it?"

"Open it."

She shook her head and handed it back to him. "I can't accept this."

"You can. It's just a token, a reminder of your month here in Okinawa Prefecture."

Erica opened the box and pulled out the tiny bottle full of sand. "Sand?"

"It's from Iriomote Island, a bit of a distance from here, but it's *hoshizuna*—also known as star sand."

A brief smile passed on her face. "Thank you."

"Good luck."

She paused and then nodded. "Thank you, Captain."

Say something.

Only Thorne couldn't express what he wanted to say to her. He couldn't tell her how he felt; he just stood there frozen, numb, as she picked up her rucksack and turned to open the door. He moved quickly and held his hand against the door.

"Thorne, what're you doing?" she demanded. "I'll miss my transport."

"Stay," he said. "I'm sorry for kicking you out of my OR. That won't happen again. Just stay."

"Why should I?" she asked.

"You're my second in command. The best I've had since I took this posting."

"That's the only reason? Because I'm a good commander?"

No. That's not the only reason.

"Yes."

She shook her head. "I can't stay, Thorne. I'm being promoted to captain and to a position I've dreamed about holding for a long time. I'm sorry, but I have to go."

"What more do you want from me?" he snapped. "I can't give you any more than that. If you were expecting something more after our night together, I made it very clear."

"As did I," she said. "I should've known better than get involved with a commanding officer again."

"I'm not that man."

"You basically questioned my judgment in that OR."

"I apologized for that!" Thorne shouted. "What more do you want from me, Erica?"

"Nothing. There's nothing I want or need from you. Let me go, and please don't damage my professional reputation."

He clenched his fists. "Do you think I would damage your career out of spite?"

"You're not the first. It took me a long time to earn back what shred of respect I have and now I'm finally getting the promotion I deserve. I won't let anyone take that away from me."

"You obviously don't know me."

"I thought I did."

"You don't because you must think so little of me to think that I would stoop to Captain Seaton's level."

The blood drained from her face. "I never mentioned his name before."

"The name of your former commanding officer is on your record and, since I know you didn't have an affair with Dayton, I put two and two together. You really get around with your commanding officers, don't you?"

The sting of her slap rocked him. He deserved it. What he'd said was out of line and totally inappropriate.

"Goodbye, Captain Wilder."

And this time he didn't stop her from leaving.

He'd severed the tie and let her go.

CHAPTER FOURTEEN

IT WAS BEST to let her go.

Was it?

No, it wasn't. Erica had been gone a week and he missed her. The guilt ate at him for the things he'd said to her. It made him angry when he thought about it. If Liam had heard him speak that way he would've beat his butt. Day to day he just moved through the motions; sometimes he wasn't aware of the passing of the day. Another mistake he'd made, and he had to live with it, but it was difficult.

Things she'd brought alive were dull and gray in comparison now. He went to Scooby's every night and all he could hear was her laughter above the noise. When he glanced at the green shag carpet in the Jungle Room, and saw the booth they'd shared, his stomach would knot up.

And the pineapple pizza… He couldn't stomach it.

"You miss her."

Scooby had said that numerous times, but Thorne had never deigned to respond to him. He was trying to ignore the obvious, because if he ignored it, if he pretended it hadn't happened, then it wouldn't hurt so much.

The pain would go away.

Yeah, right.

Her quarters were still empty, waiting on the next

commanding officer to take over. He walked by them daily, thinking about how she'd opened up to him about why she couldn't be in a relationship and he'd said nothing at all.

Just kept her out, because he'd thought it would be for the best.

A quick break.

Only, no matter how he tried to purge her from his system, he couldn't. She'd haunted him for five years before she'd come to the base. Now that he knew her, now that he'd touched, kissed and caressed the woman of his fantasies, he couldn't expel her to the dark corners of his mind.

She wasn't just a memory to look back on fondly. She was everywhere, even in his flesh. There was no way he could purge her from his system and he didn't want to.

Erica was so much more and he was too obtuse to see that.

"You look deep in thought," Scooby remarked, setting down a beer.

"What?" Thorne glanced around and didn't even realize that his walk had led him to Scooby's place or that he'd sat down at the bar. He rubbed his face and groaned.

"I said you look deep in thought, but not anymore. Sorry for interrupting your thoughts, Captain, but you looked a bit like a zombie."

"As long as I wasn't moaning." Thorne took a quick swig of beer, but it was flat in his mouth.

"How can I help you, Captain? I hate seeing you walking around here like some *deretto* fool."

"Deretto?"

"Love-struck."

Thorne snorted. "Who said I was love-struck?"

"The expression on your face speaks volumes. I may

be old, Captain Wilder, but I'm not blind. You were in love with her."

"No. I'm not." Only he was, but he didn't deserve her. Because someone who was in love with someone didn't hurt them the way he'd hurt her. They didn't deserve to have a happy ending. He didn't deserve love.

"You're pulling my leg, Captain. You love Commander Griffin and she loves you."

Thorne chuckled. "She doesn't love me. Well, she may have, but not anymore. Not after the way I hurt her."

"Hurt her? What did you do to her?"

"I said some things I regret and she left." He touched the side of his face where she'd slapped him a week ago. It still hurt.

After he'd talked to the Navy SEALs about the John Doe, he'd gone out to arrange their transport and had seen Erica heading across the tarmac. Without thinking, he'd run after her, calling her name. She'd turned and looked, but ignored him as she boarded the plane.

He deserved it.

He didn't deserve her.

"You said things to her? What kind of things?"

"It doesn't matter. She's gone."

Scooby reached across the bar and gave him a quick smack upside the head. *"Baka!"*

"What? Why did you do that?"

"Idiot. You're an idiot, Captain Wilder." Scooby shook his head and uttered a few more choice swear words in Japanese. Probably all of which meant Thorne was an idiot or worse.

"What the heck have I done to you lately, Scooby?"

"Fuzakeru na! Stop being stupid, Captain Wilder. Go after her."

"Who?"

That earned him another cuff around the head and another oath in his direction. "Commander Griffin. You need to go to Minneapolis and get her back."

"You mean Annapolis."

"Isn't it the same?"

"No."

Scooby shrugged. "I've heard of Minneapolis. I've been to Minneapolis. Where is Annapolis?"

"Maryland."

"And that's not near Minneapolis?"

Thorne shook his head. "No."

"Then you need to go there. Tell her how you feel and apologize for your obtuseness. Apologize for driving her away, like you've always driven away people who try to become close to you."

"It's not that simple."

"*Fuzakeru na!* Of course it's simple. You love her, don't you?"

Yes. Still, he couldn't say it out loud.

He'd been hiding it from himself for so long, trying to suppress it, but, yes, he loved her. He was in love with Erica and he was an idiot for letting her go.

For so long he'd fought love, but maybe it was worth the risk. It was better than living a numbed existence. Still, he didn't deserve it. Not after what he'd done to Liam.

Liam never blamed you. Liam would want you to be happy. Stop blaming yourself.

But it was hard to let go of years of blame.

Tyler.

It went off like a lightbulb. Tyler had come to him a couple of years ago to apologize for his mistake which had cost Thorne his leg.

It had torn Tyler up inside to know he was responsible.

Thorne had sat him down and told Tyler that it wasn't his fault and that he didn't blame Tyler for the loss of his leg. It was part of serving. Thorne had told Tyler to let go of his guilt and get on with his life.

Yet, he hadn't done that.

He was a hypocrite.

The John Doe had been disappointed that he'd lost an arm and could no longer serve, but he'd put a positive spin on it.

"At least my wife will be glad that I'll be home permanently."

Even the John Doe had someone waiting for him. Liam had had a wife and two beautiful kids. Neither of them had been afraid of serving their country and coming home to their families. Why was he so scared?

"I can't just leave my command. I have to arrange for a leave."

"Bah, you're making excuses."

"I'm not making excuses." He closed his eyes. "Maybe I am, Scooby. I don't know why I'm so…"

"Afraid?" Scooby shook his head. "Love, it sucks. It's hard and painful, but it's worth it."

"I've always said you're a man of many layers, Scooby."

He nodded. "Well, when you own a bar where a lot of different armed forces personnel move through, you pick up the odd thing. You all think the same thing: you're not afraid to lay down your life for your country, but when it comes to matters of the heart a lot of you are a bit more hesitant. Love is a powerful thing."

"Is it only the men?" Thorne asked.

"No, it's not. Commander Griffin is scared. I know she is. You two are the same and I believe I told you that when she first arrived here. You two are so volatile."

"I don't think you quite know what volatile means."

Scooby cursed under his breath. "Bah, you know what I mean. You two are both hotheaded, stubborn officers. You'll rub each other the wrong way, but you're meant to be together. Nobody else can put up with you."

"I'll arrange for a replacement and a transport."

"Good! You do that, Captain. Make the arrangements and go."

"And if she still doesn't want me?"

Scooby shrugged. "Then it's her loss, but at least you'll have closure."

"Thanks, Scooby. I think." Thorne set money down on the counter. "Though, you do know 'volatile' means something explosive?"

"Exactly my point, Captain. Now, get out of here."

Thorne chuckled. "Thanks."

"No problem." Scooby moved down the bar, muttering under his breath.

Even though he didn't deserve Erica, even though he'd messed it all up, he was going to try. He was brave enough to find out the answer—and if it was yes. If she loved him, he'd make it up to her even if it took him the rest of his life.

One month later, Annapolis, Maryland.

Erica had been paged by the recruitment office, something about a new plebe for the medical corps that they were eager to have at Annapolis.

She wasn't sure why they needed her there, but since it came from Admiral Greer she wasn't going to question anything, even though she was just about to head into class. Thankfully her second in command could take over the class while she dealt with this special request.

As she moved across the grounds, the trees were just

starting to bloom with the first sign of spring and the red tulips in the center green were waving slightly in the warm breeze. It was familiar and, even though she was by the sea, she kind of missed being in Japan.

She absolutely loved her new position at Annapolis, but often there were times her mind drifted back to Okinawa.

There'd been a difference in the air there and it had been nice to see palm trees and white beaches. Not that Maryland wasn't beautiful, with the colonial charm and tall sails filling Chesapeake Bay; it was the company she missed.

Thorne.

She missed him and she didn't realize how much. Her day-to-day operations at Annapolis were just an existence.

Maybe it was because she was now a teacher at the most prestigious academy in the United States, but there was none of the familiarity or comraderie that she'd had when she'd been in Okinawa or serving on board the *Hope*.

Her commanding officer wasn't close to her age. He was older and didn't seem to have much of a sense of humor. Admiral Greer seemed to live on pomp, circumstance and regulations. So when she wasn't doing a shift at the base hospital where she could be in scrubs, the rest of the time she had to stay in her everyday dress uniform and heels.

She hated heels.

So, yeah, there was a lot to miss about Okinawa, but for the most part it was Thorne. When she'd left Ginowan she didn't realize how lonely she was until her companionship was gone.

It tore her heart out to leave him, but it was obvious

that he didn't feel the same way as she did. Not after that fiasco in the OR when he'd made it quite clear that he still blamed her for the loss of his leg. When he'd thrown her out of his ER she'd tried to get him out of her mind—then he'd apologized and for a brief moment she'd thought he was going to open up to her. Instead he'd hurt her.

He'd expected her to give up on her dream so that she could stay with him. That was something she couldn't do.

Even though she was in love with him. Because there was no point in denying it: she loved Thorne. But she couldn't give up the life she'd mapped out for herself. Just like she didn't expect him to give up his life and his command posting in Okinawa.

It was cruel how love worked out that way sometimes. They were not meant to be together and she had to try and forget him.

Which was not easy.

She'd tried to do just that, but to no avail because, instead of the mysterious stranger with the intense blue eyes who had called her an angel, the Thorne she'd fallen for invaded her dreams. Every time she closed her eyes he was there.

So real and intense. She could recall his kisses, his touch. He was everywhere, his memory haunting her like a ghost. In the naval base hospital when she saw wounded warriors coming through, trying to heal themselves and continue to serve, she saw Thorne's determination to continue on.

Or, when watching a batch of plebes training to become Navy SEALs by drown proofing in the pool, all she had to do was close her eyes and picture him watching them, his arms crossed, assessing them.

Or when she went out and had a slice of pineapple pizza, which didn't hold a candle to Scooby's house specialty.

It pained her physically not be with him.

She'd grown numb.

Don't let him in now.

Right now she had a job to do. There was no room for Thorne in her mind. She didn't know why she was thinking of him constantly.

You miss him.

Erica took a deep breath and stopped to glance up at the blue spring sky. Yeah, she did miss him.

When she had started to unpack she'd found the star-shaped bottle with the sand. The one he'd given to her. She'd almost thrown it out, trying to sever the tie, but she couldn't bring herself to do it. Because, even though he'd made it clear he didn't want her and didn't care for her, she loved him. She wished things between them had been different, but it was the way it was.

Besides, he didn't want her. He'd let her go.

He'd severed the ties long before she'd left Okinawa.

With a deep breath to ground herself, she headed up the white steps of the building she'd been asked to report to.

Before she headed into the recruitment office, she tidied her hair in a mirror and straightened her dress uniform jacket.

"Captain Griffin, the new recruit is waiting in room 407," Lieutenant Knox said, rising from his seat from behind his desk. He handed her the file.

"Thank you, Lieutenant." She flipped open the file. "A Navy SEAL?"

"Yes, Captain."

"His name is John Doe?" Erica asked, annoyed.

"Yes. I wasn't given specifics about why he stated his name was John Doe. He was quite unbending."

"He has to have a name. Why wouldn't he give you specifics?"

Lieutenant Knox shrugged. "Perhaps he's Special Ops. I don't know. I didn't see him. He was ushered in under a covert detail."

Erica was confused. "A covert detail? This doesn't make any sense."

"I'm sorry, Captain. That's all the intel I have."

Erica nodded and then headed to room 407. She didn't know what was going on here, but she was tired of covert operations and Navy SEALS. She'd taken this position at Annapolis to escape all that. There was only so much she could take in one lifetime of Special Ops, Navy SEALS and secrecy.

And she was tired of reminders of Thorne.

She knocked once and headed into the room. "Seaman, I understand you want to join the Med…"

She gasped and almost dropped the file in her hands, because they were shaking so bad. Standing in front of her in his dress whites was Thorne. He took off his white cap quickly and tucked it under his arm.

"Captain Griffin." He saluted her.

"C-Captain Wilder?"

He smiled. "Yes."

"What're you doing here? You're already a member of the Medical Corp."

"I know."

"Then why are you at the recruitment office?"

"I called in a favor from the admiral." Thorne set his cap down on the desk and took a step toward her.

"What kind of favor?" Her pulse began to race; he looked so good in his dress uniform. She'd never seen him in it. It suited him and made her weak in the knees.

Jerk. Remember what he did to you. How much it hurt.

"I told the admiral that I made a foolish error letting my second in command come to Annapolis."

"This is about getting me transferred back to Okinawa?" Rage boiled inside her. She threw the file at him, which he dodged. "Get out!"

"That's not why I'm here."

Only she wasn't going to listen to him. "How dare you? I'm not going to return to Okinawa as your commander. I can't believe you traveled halfway around the world to start up this old fight. You...you...."

"Erica, would you just calm down a minute and listen to me?" He tried to pull her to him, but she brushed off his embrace.

"Don't touch me—and it's Captain Griffin!"

"Erica," he said sternly. "I'm not here to take you back to Okinawa."

"You're not?"

"No, I'm not. Besides, that's not my posting any longer."

"What?" she asked in disbelief.

"I took an open position here at Annapolis."

"You what?" She took a step back and then leaned against the wall to collect herself. "You transferred here, but why?"

He smiled at her, those blue eyes twinkling. "Isn't it obvious?"

"No. It's not." Her voice shook as she braced herself. It was obvious, but she was in disbelief about it.

"I love you."

Erica's knees wobbled as the words sank in. "You love me?"

Thorne nodded. "I tried to resist you. I tried to wipe you from my mind, I tried not let you in. I told myself after my brother died in my arms and I saw the pain on his widow's face, the hole left in his children's hearts, that I wouldn't ever allow someone to mourn me. I joined the SEALs to fulfill my brother's dream and I blamed myself for Liam's death, and for that I felt I didn't deserve any kind of happiness."

"I don't understand what you're trying to tell me."

He ran his hands through his hair. "I was happy as a SEAL and then on a covert operation I was injured saving another man's life and I met you. You entranced me. My foggy memories had one bright spot and it was you. Of course, then I actually did meet you, and you weren't exactly as angelic as I thought you were in my fantasies."

Erica chuckled at that. "I'm not gentle. Must be the Cajun in me."

"I'm sorry for trying to shut you out, for embarrassing you that day when the John Doe came in. You were right. He lost his arm. It was too far gone and, what I said? I was out of line."

Erica nodded. "I know. I saw his medical chart when he returned to San Diego. You did a good job with his amputation. As for the other things, well, I wasn't exactly easy on you."

"Thank you." Thorne closed the distance between them again. "Look, I just couldn't tell you how I felt about you, because I didn't think I deserved it. How could I be happy when I'm the reason Liam lost his life?"

"You deserve to be happy."

Thorne took a step closer. "So do you."

"Perhaps."

"I don't know what the future holds for me or you, but I know one thing: I love you and I can't live without you. It's worth the risk to be with you. I need to be with you, Erica."

She couldn't believe he was saying the words that she herself hadn't known she was longing to hear, but now that he was saying them she knew that she could have both her career and him. Something she never thought before. Most men had been intimidated by her rank, her career, except Thorne.

He was her match in every way.

Thorne ran his knuckles down her cheek. "I love you, Erica. I'm sorry for being such a…"

She suggested a word in Cajun and laughed at her secret joke.

"Sure, but I'm not sure I should admit to anything you say in Cajun."

"Then how about 'I forgive you'?"

Thorne smiled. "That I can live with."

He leaned forward and kissed her. His lips were gentle, urging, and she melted in his arms, totally forgetting that she was angry at him, that he'd hurt her, because he was sorry for what he'd done. He hadn't meant it. Thorne had tried to push her away just as much as she'd tried to push him away, but as Scooby had said they were "volatile" together.

Explosive. And, even though they were a combustible match, they were made for each other. They both had just been too stubborn to see it.

"What're you smiling about?" he asked.

"Something my *mamère* said."

"You better keep it to yourself."

"Why?" she asked.

"I don't want to be left in the dark with all the Cajun words."

Erica kissed him. "I promise to fill you in on Cajun when I can, but then again maybe not, as I have an advantage over you when you tick me off."

Thorne rolled his eyes, but laughed. "Well, I have to get used to living stateside again."

"Are you sorry you left Okinawa?" she asked.

"I'll miss it, I won't lie, but you're more important to me. I can get used to having soft-shell crab instead of pineapple pizza."

"Have you ever had soft-shell crab?"

"No."

She grinned. "Well, I hope you'll let me take you for your first time."

"Deal."

"I'm sorry too, for what it's worth."

"For what?" he asked.

"For walking away. For being insubordinate to my commanding officer on numerous occasions and for not telling you that I love you too."

He grinned. "Well, there are ways you can make it up to me."

"Is that so? Well, I can start off by giving you a massage."

"Oh, yes." He cupped her face and stroked her cheek. "That's a good start But first I have to check in officially."

"I'll take you there."

Hand in hand, they walked out of the recruitment office.

EPILOGUE

One year later, Annapolis, Maryland.

ERICA'S HEART RACED and she was shaking as she stood in a small anteroom off the side of the chapel on the naval base, a historic building. She thought if she was ever going to take the plunge and get married she was going to have her ceremony at the Naval Academy Chapel.

There were so many things architecturally about this chapel she loved. So much represented her core beliefs about being in the Navy. Like the stained glass window of Sir Galahad and his ideals which every Naval officer tried to live up to; and the domed ceiling, which reminded her of a cathedral in Florence, Italy, and was beautiful to look at.

Of course, when she'd originally had that thought when she was going for training here, she hadn't thought it would actually come to pass because she hadn't thought that she'd actually get married.

It hadn't mattered if she ever got married, until she'd met Thorne. Even if he'd never asked her, she'd have been happy with the life they were living in Annapolis. Both of them had been furthering their careers in the Navy, saving lives and training recruits when the proposal had happened. She hadn't been expecting it. They'd been walking along the shore a month ago, watching the sailboats with the colorful sails moving across the blue water, when he'd cried out in pain, dropping to his knee.

When she'd tried to see if he was okay, worried it was his phantom leg pain, he'd opened a small velvet box and proposed.

It was like something out of a dream; she still felt a bit dazed by it all.

And now she was standing in the antechamber, her knees knocking under the white silk of a very simple wedding dress.

"You could've worn your Navy uniform," Commander Rick Kettle, Regina's husband, whispered in her ear. "You are a captain."

"No, she's not!" Regina screeched and Erica chuckled.

"She's a captain, Regina. She has every right to wear her dress uniform."

Regina shot her husband the stink eye. "She looks beautiful and she's going to get married like a proper bride. This is a momentous occasion."

Rick shook his head and Erica glared at Regina, who was rocking back and forth, holding her newborn daughter named after Erica.

"If you weren't holding my goddaughter you would be in serious trouble, my friend."

Regina winked. "Well, at least it got your mind off your nerves, now, didn't it?"

Erica was going to say more when there was a knock at the door and Erica's mother stuck her head into the room. Erica had resolved things with her mother and, even though her mother didn't totally agree with Erica's career choice, she'd absolutely been won over by Thorne.

The rift between her and her mom was healing and she was very excited to be a part of the wedding.

"It's time."

Regina came over and squeezed Erica's arm. "You can do this!"

Erica nodded, but she was still shaking.

Regina and her mother left the anteroom. Erica didn't have any bridesmaids because the only man Thorne had wanted to stand up with him was his brother and he couldn't have that. So they'd both opted to keep the wedding small.

The only people attending were close friends and family.

Erica would've liked Captain Dayton to walk her down the aisle, but he was out at sea on the *Hope,* so Regina's husband was stepping in, and he did look quite dashing in his white dress uniform.

"You ready to go?"

"Yes; if I linger too much longer I might bolt from sheer terror."

"As long as it's not Captain Wilder making you bolt."

"No," Erica said and then smiled. "No, not him."

Rick smiled and took her arm. "Left and then right, Captain Griffin. Just one foot in front of the other."

Erica nodded and he walked her out of the antechamber to the main chapel. The large pipe organ began to play the bridal song, but she couldn't hear it over the sound of her pulse thundering in her ears.

As she started walking up the aisle there was a call out and a salute, which caused her to gasp, as a group of Navy SEALs decked out in their dress uniforms stood at attention for her, their sabers hanging at their sides.

They were Thorne's old unit. She recognized Mick the commanding officer she'd stood up to all those years ago on the *Hope*—and then she got a glimpse of Thorne standing there in his dress uniform and suddenly she wasn't so nervous any longer.

She walked up the aisle and glanced at all their friends and family; she welled up when she saw Bunny and Scooby in the aisle, smiling at her. Scooby bowed quickly, beaming at her. She stopped Rick, breaking rank, so she could hug them briefly, trying not to cry.

When she got to the front Thorne took her hand. She didn't even remember the ceremony, because all she could see was Thorne—the man who'd had no name when she'd first met him but was full of fight, spirit and a passion to serve his country.

He enchanted her and enraged her at times. They were volatile together, so explosive, and Erica loved every minute of it.

Before she knew it, she was kissing her husband to an audience that was cheering and clapping.

"Are you okay?" Thorne whispered in her ear.

"I'm fine, why?"

"You look a bit shocked."

"A deer trapped in barbed wire?"

Thorne chuckled. "Headlights. I'm buying a book of old sayings for our first anniversary."

Erica pinched him as they headed down the aisle. "If we survive that long."

"We will."

"How do you know?" she teased. They paused at the entrance of the chapel as his old unit raised their sabers in a salute. Erica and Thorne passed under them, kissing at the end.

"Because I love you and I'm never letting you go."

* * * * *

15_ST15

MILLS & BOON®

MEDICAL
ROMANCE™

THE ULTIMATE IN ROMANTIC MEDICAL DRAMA

0715/03